# A Pattern of Shadows

## Small Things Vol. 3

by

# Joe DeRouen

## Small Things Press

*For my wife Andee and our son Fletcher; without their love and support, this book definitely wouldn't exist*

Novels by Joe DeRouen

The Small Things Trilogy:
Small Things
Threads
A Pattern of Shadows

Memories of a Ghost
Splinter the Ghost*

Leap Year

Short Story Collections by Joe DeRouen

Odds and Endings: Fiction Short and Otherwise
Untitled Patreon Stories*

Anthology Appearances

Klarissa Dreams Redux: An Illuminated Anthology
May the Fourth: A Collection of Stories Across Time and Space
The Cat, the Crow, and the Cauldron: A Halloween Anthology
Mistletoe Magic: A Christmas Anthology

* Not yet published

## Acknowledgements

I'd like to thank everyone who contributed to helping make this novel happen, including my wife (and alpha reader) Andee DeRouen, my son Fletcher DeRouen, Bruce Diamond, Melodie Maynard, Susan Jarrett, Tina Hammond, Eric and Chris Greenberg, Meleah Whitehead, Celia Burkheimer, Mia Kleve, Michael Neill, Desiree Sprague, Faye Smith, Joe Deaver, and Robin Raven.

Special thanks also go to Lisa Lauenberg, Tasha Derouen, my original cover artist Renée Barratt, my new cover artist Mallory Rock, Ryan Hupfer for the wedding vows, and Maritza García Boak (may she rest in peace) for her tremendous help translating English to Spanish.

Big thanks to my beta readers Chris Greenberg and Sara Kinsella. Without them, this book wouldn't be nearly as good.

Big thanks also to Angela Barnes, Cassie Cook, Bruce Diamond, David and Paulette Green, Chris Greenberg, Rebecca Jones, Sally Kuehne, Elizabeth Liberman, Sarah Liberman, David Pollard, Hannah Roberts, Tamara Sipes, Sinead Smee, Annie Sturdivant, and Meredith Wells for supporting my Patreon at Patreon.com/JoeDeRouen

# A Pattern of Shadows

## Small Things Vol. 3

# Preface

You hold in your hands the final book in the *Small Things* trilogy. I began this journey in November of 2004, when my good friend Bruce Diamond challenged me to participate in NaNoWriMo. (National November Writing Month, in which people attempt to write the first 50,000 words of a novel within 30 days.) I successfully completed the challenge, never dreaming at the time I'd write a sequel, let alone a third book and three other books besides. Thanks, Bruce.

I also never dreamed it would take me eight years to finish the trilogy. (*Small Things* was published in 2012, *Threads* in 2013.) My only excuse is that I got sidetracked with other books and projects, but I never forgot Shawn, Jenny, Fred, Tanner, Katy, Ben, Emily, or any of the other characters from the *Small Things* universe. In fact, you might just find their footprints in some of my other books…

*A Pattern of Shadows* contains characters from my standalone novels *Memories of a Ghost* and *Leap Year* as well as the first two *Small Things* books. Having read these books isn't necessary to understand and enjoy this one, but it does answer questions you might have regarding Claire Locke, Mr. Kingfisher, Mr. Quarry, Miss Pahari, and Gavin Young.

Having read *Small Things* and *Threads* also isn't strictly necessary, but you'll probably enjoy this book much more if you've read the first two volumes in the trilogy. Go on, you know you want to!

Rogers, Arkansas, August 31<sup>st</sup>, 2021

# Chapter 1

Shawn Spencer shivered, pulling his parka tighter to shield his skin from the harsh wind and the falling snow. It was -15° Fahrenheit out here, and he was freezing his ass off. They'd been hiking for two miles, not wanting to alert anyone who might be guarding the compound, and he could no longer feel his toes. He looked behind him and realized their trail had been completely obscured by ice and snow. They could die out here, and it might be months or even years before anyone found them.

It had been a little over five years since the demon Azazel took possession of his son's body and disappeared with the fused nickel, the magical talisman that had been combined with an alternate universe version of itself to be made exponentially more powerful, and they had done nothing but search for him since. If Claire Locke's intelligence were correct, their search might, at long last, be at an end. They might finally bring Ben home today.

Claire, who was leading their little troupe of would-be rescuers, made a sharp downward gesture with her hand, bringing Shawn out of his reverie. He stopped in his tracks, as did his daughter. He hated bringing Emily on this trip, but without her particular talent they would probably fail. Even with her along, the odds were against them.

"The compound should be just past this hill," Claire said, gesturing to a hill in front of her.

"All I see is more snow," Emily complained, "the same thing we've seen for the last two miles."

That sounded like something Fred Ruskin would have said, and Shawn once again second-guessed not bringing the former sheriff along. If their plan were to work, however, they needed Ruskin right where he was, back in Carthage.

Ruskin would celebrate his 92$^{nd}$ birthday later this year, but still looked and moved like a man in his early fifties. Both Shawn and Jenny were in their late fifties but appeared to be in their mid-to-late twenties at most.

Years ago, Shawn had used the magic of the five talismans bound together to heal all three of them of their wounds after their battle with an immortal Mayan priest, and as a byproduct had greatly lengthened their lives. He still didn't understand what had happened, or how long they might live, but had long ago learned never to look a gift horse in the mouth.

Shawn glanced over his shoulder at Emily, who was gamely trudging along through the snow. Like all of them, she was dressed in a white parka. An errant wisp of red hair stuck out from her hood, the wind and snow having frozen it to her goggles. She was almost nineteen, and he couldn't get over how much she resembled Jenny at that age, red hair, freckles, and all.

Mr. Kingfisher and Mr. Quarry brought up the rear. Shawn had dealt with them briefly when he was sixteen, and had been surprised that Claire knew the duo, and even more so when she suggested bringing them into the mission. Much like Shawn, they didn't seem to have grown a day older since he first met them in 1976.

To say that they weren't nice men would be a gross understatement. They were, however, very effective, and had more than made up for the fee they'd charged. They seemed to have a history with Claire as well, and not a good one, but a temporary truce had been called for this mission.

Kingfisher and Quarry had a different partner than they did when he first met them all those years ago, a girl a little younger than Emily named

Nadine Pahari, who currently walked along between them. She didn't speak much. Shawn wondered what her story was but was almost afraid to ask. She and Emily had a brief conversation on the plane ride to the Yukon, the barren tundra they presently found themselves in, but that was it.

"Okay, I'm going to approach," whispered Claire, producing a pair of binoculars from the folds of her parka. "If I'm not back in five minutes, get the hell out of here, Emily-style."

Shawn watched helplessly as Claire scaled the hill, dropping to her stomach and crawling the rest of the way once she was high enough to potentially be seen from the other side.

Claire Locke was the sister of Katy Ruskin's former roommate Melissa Fleming. Shawn had met her by chance when the two were in town visiting Katy and his granddaughter almost two years ago. Was it a coincidence that they'd been brought together? Once upon a time Shawn would have said yes, but he no longer believed in coincidences.

Claire had satellite images of the entire area, but the lodge had apparently been painted white to blend into the snowy Canadian terrain. The only reason she'd spotted it, she said, was because an assistant to one of the contractors who'd been hired to make some alterations to the lodge told her where it should be. Shawn didn't even want to imagine how she'd gathered that intelligence.

He reached into his pocket to withdraw the jaguar's tooth he'd borrowed from Katy. He was only 15 the first time he'd held the tooth, one of the five great talismans of power that had existed on Earth since before the dawn of man. It had all come full circle, in a way. He didn't want to have to use its magic any more than necessary—it always seemed to draw the wrong kind of attention—but having the tooth might be the difference between success and failure on this mission to rescue his son.

Less than two minutes after Claire vanished into the snowy terrain, she appeared atop the hill again, skidding down to stand before them. She was smiling.

"What did you see?" asked Shawn.

"Found it," she said. "It was exactly where my contact said it would be. A roughly 4,000 square foot, one-story converted hunting lodge with a wraparound porch, less than a mile from here. Two bored-looking guards with AK-47s on the front entrance, probably more in the back and who knows how many more inside. Unfortunately, it's all flat terrain once we're over that hill. We'll be easily spotted, even with the white parkas. And that's where Mr. Quarry comes in."

"Indeed," said Quarry, pulling a package wrapped in brown paper from a satchel he'd been carrying.

He unwrapped the package to reveal six small, round mirrors, each one identical, with an attached leather cord that fashioned the mirrors into necklaces. He passed these out to the members of their party and instructed everyone to slip one over their heads.

"What does it do, exactly?" asked Shawn, looping the mirror over his neck. He immediately felt dizzy and had to lean against Quarry for support.

"It grants invisibility to all but the most persistent eyes," answered Kingfisher for his diminutive partner. "Unfortunately, the side effects are a bit disorientating for the wearer. Just give it a moment, Mr. Spencer, and you'll get used to it. As long as we don't make much noise, we should be fine approaching the guards within about ten feet."

"Which still gives them enough time to kill us."

"As long as I'm in front of you, Mr. Spencer, you won't have a thing to worry about," Kingfisher responded, moving to stand beside Claire.

"Once the guards are down, we're still not safe," said Claire. "The building has security cameras, and the door has a keypad. Neither piece of information was in the intelligence, but that's okay. Mr. Quarry's mirrors will help with the cameras, but only up to a point. By the time we take out the guards, they'll know we're coming, so using a code scanner on the door is not an option. I'm going to blow it. Once that's done, again, Mr. Kingfisher will take point. Got it?"

Everyone nodded.

Claire started up the hill, followed in single file order by Kingfisher, Shawn, Emily, Nadine Pahari, and Quarry. The terrain was mostly flat, and their snowshoes served them well. Less than 30 minutes later, they found themselves approaching the hunting lodge. Claire and Kingfisher exchanged positions, and Kingfisher led the rest of the way.

Just as the giant had promised, the guards—two huge men carrying rifles—didn't seem to notice Shawn and the others until they were about ten feet away. The first guard's eyes went wide as they approached, the second following his lead as he shouldered his weapon and aimed it at Kingfisher.

"Holy shit, where'd you come from?" asked the guard, finger on the trigger of the AK-47.

Kingfisher said nothing, but continued walking. The guard pulled the trigger again and again, but his rifle wouldn't fire. The second guard tried to fire his weapon as well, with the same result. The giant was upon them in seconds, grabbing both by their necks and slamming their heads together. The guards crumpled to the ground, unmoving.

Claire knelt beside each in turn, checking their pulses. Satisfied, she removed two pairs of zip tie handcuffs and cuffed their hands behind their backs before wrapping a length of duct tape across each guard's mouth.

"It would be more expeditious were I allowed to kill them, Ms. Locke," said Kingfisher, shaking his head, "but so be it."

"You knew the rules coming into this," she snapped, pulling something from her parka and running for the door. "No deaths unless absolutely necessary."

Shawn had insisted on that part. Enough lives had been lost dealing with the supernatural over the years. He tensed. Subduing the guards had been easy compared to what would come next. He reached behind his back and Emily's fingers grasped his hand. It was now or never.

Everyone else held back as Claire raced up the steps, pressed some-thing against the keypad, and took up position on the far side of the porch. She pulled a remote from her pocket, flipped a switch, and the door exploded inward in a cacophony of metal and wood.

Smoke clouded the entrance, but Kingfisher was already moving, his massive legs taking him to the door in three steps. Shawn heard fighting but couldn't see anything. And then they were moving as well, following Kingfisher and Claire inside as they cleared the way.

The entryway was huge, and filled not only with massive, floor-to-ceiling bookshelves crammed with books, but also with all sorts of fa-mous artwork: there was da Vinci's *Mona Lisa*, Munch's *The Scream*, and at least three works by Monet, as well as a few other pieces Shawn didn't recognize. He took all of this in during his first few seconds inside the hunting lodge, as Claire and Kingfisher disposed of more guards.

The two guards who had been stationed in this room were already down, but more poured through doors to the north, west, and east. Claire took down one of the two from the east while Kingfisher plowed through the pair from the north, and so Shawn used the magic from the jaguar's tooth to put one of the remaining two guards to sleep. He wasn't nearly as attuned to the tooth as he had been to the nickel, but he was learning.

A bullet whizzed by Shawn's head, hitting Emily in the shoulder. The girl cried out and stumbled back into Mr. Quarry, who gently lowered her to the ground. Kingfisher was on the shooter in an instant, wrench-ing the rifle from his hands and hitting him across the face with the butt. He went down instantly, and then Claire was kneeling beside Emily, a brief look of concentration passing over her features.

"Straight through, that's good," she said, laying a hand on Emily's wound. A few seconds later the hole in Emily's parka was still there, but her skin had knitted itself together. Not even a scar remained. "Sorry about that."

"That's…okay," said Emily, staring up at Claire. "It doesn't even hurt now. Thank you."

Claire was already up and moving again, throwing herself back into the fray. A spinning back kick doubled over the last guard, and an elbow to the back of his head put him to sleep.

Shawn turned away from the action to stare at his daughter, growing weak in the knees. It was a mistake to bring her here, regardless of her talent. If the bullet had hit her head, or if Claire hadn't been there to save her…

"I'm okay, Dad," Emily said, looking into her father's eyes. She held out a hand and he pulled her to her feet. "Let's do what we came here to do. Let's get my big brother back."

"You're right," said Shawn. "Let's get Ben and get out of here."

Kingfisher kicked open the door to the north and immediately walked through. "He's in here," said the giant, beckoning them to follow.

The room, nearly as large as the library, was filled with long couches upon which lay all manner of plush pillows and silk blankets. In the center of the room stood a huge hot tub, in which sat a bearded man with long, dirty blond hair. He was wearing a straw hat and was surrounded by five naked women. The women, looking scared, were huddled against each other and the man, who was smiling.

"Hey, Shawn," said the man, tipping the brim of his hat. "I knew you'd find me eventually, but we really need to talk about your timing."

# Chapter 2

Shawn stared at the man he hadn't seen in five years. Ben had been Emily's age when they last saw each other, and now he was 24. He'd gone from being a teenager to an adult, all the while possessed by the demon Azazel. He was ashamed that he didn't recognize his own son.

He wanted nothing more than to rip the demon from his son's body and strangle it until it was dead, though of course he knew that wasn't possible. Shawn hadn't prayed since he was a little boy, but now he prayed with all his heart that Ben was still somewhere inside the body the demon now wore.

"Hello, Azazel," he finally said. "It's been a long time."

"What do you want?" asked the demon, pulling away from a startled brunette to lean forward in the hot tub.

"I want my son back," Shawn said, the jaguar's tooth digging into his palm as his hands balled up into fists.

"Give me my brother back, you son of a bitch!" Emily yelled, pushing past her father to stare at the demon.

"If you try anything, I'll simply use my powers to escape. You know that, right?"

"Yes, I know," Shawn said to Azazel, as he took Emily by the shoulders and pulled her into a hug. "That's why we're not here to fight you."

"Then why didn't you just knock, instead of assaulting the guards?

"We were pretty sure you wouldn't have let us in," interjected Claire.

"Good point," admitted the demon. "So, if you're not here to try to capture me, then what do you want?"

"We're here to…" Shawn stopped talking in mid-sentence, staring at his son. Something was wrong. Azazel was doing his best to sound imperious, but there was a nervousness beneath his words. He strode over to the hot tub, reached in, and grabbed the man's right hand, knocking off his hat in the process. His hand was pink and healthy.

Ben's right hand had been severed by David Dowd in 1977 and replaced by some sort of black mechanical hand that Ben had called forth from an alternate universe. There were other differences, too, now that he studied the man, though most were camouflaged by the scraggly beard and long hair. "You're not Ben."

The man's eyes went wide for a moment, and then he smiled. "It worked for a little while, though, didn't it?"

"This isn't him?" asked Claire, her face a mask of confusion. "If that's not him, where is he?"

The whup-whup-whup sound of helicopter blades sounded from outside, drowning out the rest of Claire's words and drawing everyone's attention to the back of the building. This man was just a decoy. Shawn felt like he'd been punched in the stomach.

"Oh, hell no!" shouted Emily, breaking past Shawn to run for the back door.

Kingfisher and Claire took off after her. Shawn hesitated before finally turning to Mr. Quarry, who nodded.

"He won't go anywhere," Quarry said, "Miss Pahari and I will make sure of that. Go."

Shawn took off after his daughter as the sound from the helicopter grew louder. He only hoped they wouldn't be too late.

***

Emily Spencer burst from the back door of the hunting lodge, the frigid wind hitting her so hard she felt her eyes blur. A helipad stood some 50 yards from the lodge, upon which sat a helicopter. Both had been painted white, effectively blending into the snowy landscape. They were essentially invisible from satellite imagery, which must be why Claire hadn't mentioned them.

Azazel, wearing the skin of her brother Ben, grinned at her as the helicopter began to rise. He wasn't flying the copter, which meant there must be a pilot. She didn't see anyone else inside.

Mr. Kingfisher ran past her, leaping for the helicopter, his fingertips just missing the landing gear. He landed on his feet, a cat-like grace she hadn't expected from the giant.

Claire appeared seconds later, a pistol in her hands. She aimed carefully at the copter and pulled the trigger, but nothing happened. She glanced toward Kingfisher and cursed.

"I can't control it, Ms. Locke," Kingfisher said, looking back and forth between the rapidly ascending helicopter and Claire. "You know that."

Emily tensed. It was now or never. And then her father was there, grabbing her by the shoulder. "No, Em, don't. It's too dangerous. We'll have another chance."

"This has been our first chance in five years, Dad. In five years! It might be our only chance. I'm not letting it slip past our fingers." She pulled away from him, and she *jumped*.

Emily appeared a fraction of a second later inside the helicopter, startling her demon-possessed brother. He was dressed in jeans and a leather jacket and wearing snow boots. He was also clean-shaven, unlike his double in the hot tub. She didn't give him a chance to say or do anything, much less to use his powers against her. Instead, she simply grabbed his wrist, thought of her destination, and disappeared again, taking him with her.

She appeared back on the ground, next to her father, the cold wind once again surrounding her. It hadn't worked. Her heart sank, and she felt like throwing up. Releasing Azazel, she watched as he tumbled face-first into the snow with a satisfying thump. The man rolled over on his back and grinned, even as the helicopter disappeared into the distance.

"I always wondered what your power was," he said, sitting up on his elbows. "Ben never knew."

"No one knew but Mom and Dad," said Emily, flatly.

Kingfisher was upon him in a second, yanking Azazel up by his arm. The demon offered no resistance and let the giant pull him to his feet.

"You tried to take me somewhere else, didn't you," asked Azazel, ignoring Kingfisher while staring at Emily, "but my powers circumvented it?"

"We still captured your ass," Emily yelled, despair filling her head. She'd had one chance at this, and she'd blown it.

"You've come a long way and broken through a lot of firewalls to find me," said Azazel, turning his head toward Emily's father. "What do you want?"

"To offer you a trade."

Azazel laughed out loud. "A trade? What do you have that I could possibly even want?"

"The jaguar's tooth and…me."

"But, Dad," Emily interjected, and was immediately cut off.

"He knows what you can do now, Em. I promised you I'd get your brother back one way or the other, and I will. This is the only way."

Their original plan was for Emily to get hold of Azazel and teleport him to the spirit room that lay hidden at the top floor of the Huffman Heights apartment building in Carthage, Illinois, where Katy could use her powers to forcibly separate Azazel from Ben's body.

The element of surprise, however, had been lost when she'd had to retrieve him from the helicopter, and he'd apparently used his abilities to shift her away from her intended destination and instead toward the ground. He'd be ready now, and could use his powers against her, so that was no longer a viable option.

"Why would I want your body," asked Azazel, "when I already have his?"

"Because, as far as I can tell, I'm immortal, or at least closer to living forever than my son is. And because I have this." Shawn opened his hand to reveal the jaguar's tooth. "And you no longer have the nickels. Am I right? I can't sense them anywhere near here, though you could always have them hidden in an old jar of pennies, I suppose."

Azazel stared at him for a moment. "Can we talk about it inside? I'm freezing my ass off out here."

# Chapter 3

The air was still, and an eerie calm filled the room as Emily, her father, and the others led Azazel back into the hunting lodge. All the guards they'd subdued earlier stood facing the east wall, their hands at their sides. The man who'd pretended to be Ben, dressed only in wet boxer shorts, stood with them, along with the women who'd been in the hot tub. They all stared ahead as if in some sort of trance. A trance, Emily imagined, induced by Mr. Quarry's magic.

"I see you've made friends!" Azazel said, looking around the room. "Claire Locke, the doorway between life and death. Hot. Too bad she's into girls. And then there's Mr. Kingfisher and Mr. Quarry, supernatural bounty hunters of a sort, along with their new charge, Miss Pahari. I'm glad you could all come to the party."

"How do you know—" Pahari started to ask but was silenced by a quick shake of Kingfisher's head.

"So, talk," said Azazel, turning to face Shawn, "sell me on this grand plan you have."

"It's pretty simple, really. Me and the jaguar's tooth for my son. It's clear that whatever plan you had for him didn't work out, otherwise you wouldn't be hiding out here in the middle of nowhere."

Azazel ignored the assertion. "Even with the tooth and your longevity, why should I take your offer? I'm happy with this body. Your party has quite a bit of power at their disposal, I can't deny that, but it's nothing compared to what I can do with your son's talents. You know that, right?"

"I thought so, but now I'm not so sure. Why the ruse, Azazel? Why did you need time to get away? Your stand-in clearly knew who we were, which meant you had time to react, and your reaction was to run. Why is that?"

The demon remained silent.

"I'll tell you what I think, Azazel. I think Ben has been fighting you all along, tooth and nail, and that your ability to use his powers isn't nearly what you claim. You took us all by surprise when you stole his body five years ago, and took Ben by surprise, too. Five years later, I think he's clamped down pretty hard on what you can and can't do."

"But you're not entirely sure, are you? Hence the offer for a body swap."

"Hence the offer for a body swap," Shawn repeated, staring his demon-possessed son in the eyes. "It's either that or we take our chances capturing you and exorcising your sorry ass from my son. Which one will it be?"

Azazel stroked his chin, seeming to consider the offer. "And I get the tooth, correct?"

"Yes, you get the tooth."

"What about Jenny? Do I get her, too?"

Emily lunged forward and slapped Azazel hard across the cheek. "Thanks, demon, for giving me an excuse to do something I've wanted to do for years."

Azazel licked his lips. "I wonder how you'd be in the sack, little one?"

"Oh, cut the crap," said her father, stepping between Azazel and Emily. "I know what you're trying to do. Do we have a deal or not? The longer this goes on, the more inclined I am to try our chances with the exorcism."

Azazel stared at him, before slowly smiling. "We have a deal, Mr. Spencer, with two conditions. First, strip. I don't want any tricks; I need to see what you have on your person."

"And the second?" Shawn asked, already starting to remove his parka.

"Everyone here will take a vow not to look for me ever again. And by now you know how that works. Say it three times, and you're bound to it."

"Dad—" Emily started to interject, but her father silenced her.

"Hush, Emily. It's a deal. My life for Ben's, and no one will come looking for you."

He removed everything he was wearing, save for his boxer shorts, Azazel searching each piece of discarded clothing in turn before patting him down. Apparently satisfied, the demon nodded before turning to Emily.

"Say 'I promise not to look for Azazel,' and then repeat it twice."

She met the demon's eyes and did as he ordered, loathing him as the words passed her lips.

"And now the rest of you."

One by one, starting with Claire and ending with Nadine Pahari, they all repeated the vow. Emily knew from the extensive research that she and Katy had done after Ben's abduction that, due to some arcane magical rules that she still didn't understand, any promise repeated three times to or about a demon or an angel was very difficult if not impossible to break. But if things went according to plan, it shouldn't matter.

"And now my turn," Shawn said, as soon as he was dressed again. "Conditional upon his releasing my son Benjamin Spencer, I give my body and the jaguar's tooth to Azazel." He repeated the words twice more.

"It's done," said Azazel, reaching out to take his hand.

"Wait," said Emily, putting herself between the two men. It was now or never.

She threw her arms around her father's neck, hugging him tight. She had to blink back tears at the thought that she might never see him again.

He returned the hug, pulling her tight, and then she did one of the most difficult things she'd ever done. She let him go.

"I love you, Daddy, and I'm so sorry."

"Touching," said Azazel, pushing Emily to one side and grabbing Shawn's hand.

Though she couldn't see it happen, Emily knew in an instant that Azazel had left her brother's body and entered the body of her father. Ben dropped to his knees, a look of anguish passing over his face.

She turned away from her brother to stare at Azazel, looking out at her from her father's eyes. It was up to her now. She'd failed once, she couldn't fail a second time.

"You can go now," said Azazel, stepping back from Ben. "Take your prize, and get out of my—"

They'd never hear what he was going to say. Emily shoved him hard in the chest, sending him stumbling backwards, stepping on the foldable mesh pentagram she'd dropped behind him just a moment ago.

Her father vanished, taking the demon inside with him.

"Em," Ben whispered, looking up at her, his lips seemingly struggling to form words. "You...you shouldn't have come for me, not if it meant losing Dad."

"He's not lost," she said, dropping to her knees beside him, "just misplaced for a while."

She pulled Ben into an embrace, tears coursing down both their cheeks. "Ben, I've missed you so much."

"I've missed you, too, Em."

"Were you conscious inside, with that...thing?" asked Emily, finally releasing him.

"Conscious and powerless, for the most part. Everything he did, every disgusting thing...I was there, along for the ride. I tried to fight him, I really did, but in the end, it was like being a fish in a bowl. He was just too powerful."

"Guys," interjected Claire, stepping forward to put a hand on Emily's shoulder, "we really need to get going."

"You're right," Emily said. "Ben first, then I'll be back for each of you."

"Wait," said Ben. "Where did Dad go? Where did you send him?"

"I'll explain when we're out of the Yukon and back home." Turning to the others, she said, "Be right back, guys."

Taking hold of Ben's hand, she thought about home and disappeared.

# Chapter 4

Katy Ruskin paced the sparsely furnished living room of her little second floor apartment in Huffman Heights in Carthage, Illinois, filled only with spare furniture from her mother's home, wishing for the umpteenth time this afternoon that she could have gone with Shawn and Emily. She understood why she couldn't go, logically, but emotionally...she wanted nothing more than to slap that awful, demonic grin off Azazel's face.

The face that he shared with Ben, the man who, over five years ago, she'd fallen in love with. If they did get him back, how would she ever know for sure who was actually inside his body?

She felt suddenly ashamed. She *would* know, wouldn't she? Ben was, after all, the father of her child. How could she not know who the father of her child was?

Like Ben, Katy had supernatural powers that were passed on to her because of a magical battle their parents had been involved in years before she was born. She could enter other people's dreams and control them, and, when she entered a hidden room on the third floor of the very building she was in now, she could alter the fabric of reality itself—but only in that room.

After Ben was taken, she'd spent countless nights trying to enter his dreams, all to no avail. It was like he had ceased to exist. In the past, all she'd had to do to enter someone's dream was either think of them while both she and her target were asleep or visit the spirit room. His dreams, if indeed he still dreamed, were locked to her. She'd even tried to amplify her abilities with the jaguar's tooth, but it hadn't helped.

She had, however, learned to do a lot of other things with the tooth, things that even Shawn had never learned to do with the nickel. She'd sworn never to let anyone hurt her or the people she loved ever again, and that meant learning to better use the resources she had available to her, both magically and physically.

Katy looked at the time on her cell phone. It was almost three in the afternoon, which meant it was approaching noon in the Northwestern part of Canada, where the Yukon was located. It was early April, but according to The Weather Channel app on her iPhone, Whitehorse (the closest city she could find to where Shawn and the rest currently were) was experiencing an unusually frigid cold front. She hoped everyone was okay.

"I just got her to sleep," said Jenny, walking into the room. "She knows something's going on, even if she doesn't know exactly what."

Jenny Spencer, Ben's mother, sat beside Katy on the couch and took the mother of her granddaughter into her arms. Katy started to tremble and then the tears began, and try as she might, she just couldn't stop crying.

"I'm sorry I'm such a mess," she finally said into Jenny's shoulder.

"Ben might be coming home today. My little boy, all grown up. You think I'm not a mess, too? I'm just a little better at hiding it than you are."

Katy laughed before pulling away. She stared at Jenny. Her red hair was cut short now, and her green eyes seemed to contain a wisdom that hadn't been present during Katy and Ben's time travel trip to 1977, but otherwise Jenny looked like the same person she always had. Katy was fast approaching 30, while Jenny was almost 60. Soon enough, Katy would take on the gray hair and wrinkles that came with life, while Jenny seemed to be perpetually stuck at 29. Serious weirdness, but nothing she wasn't already used to.

"We should hear something soon, right?" Katy asked. "I mean, it's been two days, and Dad's been in that room waiting for, what, almost five hours?"

"Just about," said Jenny, looking at her antique Mickey Mouse watch. "Shawn said to give it an eight-hour window, but you know Fred, he'll stay in there until Ben comes home or someone tells him otherwise."

"The silence is killing me."

The last five years had been both the most joyful and most heart-breaking of Katy's life. The birth of her daughter had, of course, been a wonderful blessing, but it was tempered by Ben's absence. They had already missed out on so much time together, and Ben had missed seeing his daughter grow from a baby into a precocious child.

Ever since Azazel had tricked Ben into giving him his body, her life had been dedicated to getting him back. When her daughter was born, she'd shifted most of her focus to her little girl, but the net effect was that she didn't have anything left for herself. She'd been running on fumes for five years.

"How've you been sleeping?"

Katy had suffered insomnia most of her life, prior to her time travel trip to 1977, a side-effect of the nightmares she'd had as a child that came from her connection to the spirit room. After Ben had been kidnapped, both the nightmares and the insomnia came back with a vengeance.

She'd once again managed to master the nightmares, but still had trouble sleeping upon occasion. It had been better as of late, however, when she finally let herself believe that the attempt to rescue Ben might actually be successful.

"Better," she finally said.

"How's your mom been?" asked Jenny, in a less-than-subtle attempt to change the subject.

"Better as well," Katy said. "Thanks for asking."

Unlike her father, Katy's mother didn't have the gift of longevity. She was in her late-sixties and had slipped and broken her wrist last week. Katy offered to take her into the spirit room to heal her, but she had declined, saying that if she were going to get old, she may as well get used to it.

"Mommy, are you okay?" asked Hope, coming out of the bedroom. "I heard you crying."

Katy looked to Jenny, who shrugged. "Well, she was asleep with Hercules when I left her, or so I thought."

The little girl climbed onto her mother's lap. "Mommy's okay," Katy said, hugging her daughter hard, the girl's long, dark brown tresses falling down over her face as she returned the embrace. "Sorry if I woke you, my little Hope."

The little girl smiled. "It's okay, Mommy. Daddy will probably be home soon anyway."

A shiver traveled down Katy's spine. "How do you know that?"

"My friend told me."

Hope had an imaginary friend, or at least Katy thought they were imaginary. Having an imaginary friend wasn't at all unusual for a four-year-old, though in her family it might be cause for concern. No matter how many different ways Katy asked, however, Hope would never reveal her friend's name.

"What exactly did your friend tell you, sweetie?" asked Katy, pulling back to look into her daughter's green eyes.

"Just that Daddy might be coming home today, that's all."

Jenny's face turned white, but she otherwise remained silent.

This had been going on for the last year, ever since Hope turned three. Hope's imaginary friend would tell her things she couldn't possibly know. Mostly it was just little things, like when a friend was coming over, but once it had been the numbers for the Illinois state lottery. Katy had played the numbers on a lark and won thirty-two million dollars, about half of which she donated to charity.

She knew her daughter probably had some sort of magical talent, based simply on who her parents and grandparents were, but she didn't think it was talking to spirits. Claire Locke, who could see and communicate with ghosts, had been here the last time Hope spoke to her imaginary friend. Katy asked Claire if there were any spirits hanging around, and she'd said no, or at least none that she could see.

"I sure hope your friend is right," Katy finally replied, shoving the mystery of the imaginary playmate aside for the time being, "because I know your daddy loves you and misses you very much."

Katy made the decision early on to be honest with her daughter, at least as honest as someone could be with a child. Hope always knew she had a father, and that her father had left her through no choice of his own. She'd gone as far as to promise that Ben would eventually come home, though she'd been careful never to say when. Hope didn't know about the current rescue operation—or at least she wasn't supposed to know.

"Tell Grandpa Fred I love him," Hope said out of nowhere.

Before Katy could respond, her cell phone rang. She looked at the caller ID. The display read "Daddy" and showed a picture of her father's face. Once again, she felt goosebumps raise on her skin. Was her daughter prescient?

"Hello?" she said, tentatively.

"Nothing yet, Katy-bear," he said, using her childhood nickname, "Just checking in. Have you heard anything?"

"Hope says she loves you, and, nope, I haven't heard a thing."

"Shawn?" She heard her father say into his cell phone, and then silence.

"Dad?" Katy asked. She heard a gunshot echo through the phone. "Dad!"

"Grandpa Fred needs you," said Hope, a faraway look in her eyes, "and so does Grandpa Shawn and Daddy. Hurry, Mommy!"

"I've got her," Jenny said. "Go!"

Katy rose from the couch without a word, shoved the cell phone into her pocket, and raced out the door.

# Chapter 5

Fred Ruskin sat in a green and yellow lawn chair, a pistol in one hand and an old, dog-eared paperback copy of *Iron Mike* in the other, hidden from the rest of the house. He was in the secret room on the third floor of Huffman Heights, a little nook behind the staircase, the only light provided by a portable lantern he'd brought into the room.

Until three days ago, the room he was in had only been accessible by stepping onto the pentagram that lay in the center of the room on the other side of the wall while possessing one of two special necklaces. That pentagram would, in turn, teleport the user to the five-pointed star that sat on the floor at Ruskin's feet, just a few feet from the shimmering curtain of light that led into the spirit room.

The diminutive Mr. Quarry had, however, managed to duplicate the pentagram in the other room as well as one of the necklaces. The new portal was a third the size of the original and much more portable. Where the original pentagram was made of marble and weighed a good hundred pounds, the new one was made of a foldable mesh and weighed less than the pistol in his hand.

With any luck, Shawn wouldn't even have to use the devices Quarry had made. The plan was for Emily to grab Azazel and teleport him to this room, after which Ruskin would shove him through the spirit door, where Katy could deal with him later. Though they'd argued against it at first, Shawn and Jenny eventually came to believe that using Emily's powers was their best chance at rescuing Ben. Only a handful of people knew what Emily could do, and the hope was that she could take Azazel by surprise before he could use the abilities he'd stolen from Ben to re-shape reality.

Taking out his phone, he decided to call Katy to see if she'd heard anything. She answered on the first ring.

"Hello?" He heard her voice echo over the phone.

"Nothing yet, Katy-bear," he said, "just checking in. Have you heard anything?"

"Hope says she loves you, and, nope, I haven't heard anything."

One instant he was alone in the room, and the next Shawn Spencer appeared on the pentagram, staring at him, looking lost and confused. He was wearing a white parka and his boots were wet with snow.

"…house," Shawn said, blinking, staring with wide eyes at Ruskin.

"Shawn?" he asked, the cell phone falling from his fingers into his lap.

Shawn was on him in a second, punching him in the side of the jaw, knocking the wind out of him with a knee to the stomach. Ruskin felt the chair falling backwards, and himself with it, as Shawn leaped atop him, wrenching the gun from his fingers.

"Where am I?" Shawn yelled, pointing the gun at Ruskin's head. "Tell me!"

Ruskin kicked out his size-thirteen foot, connecting the steel-toed boot he wore hard between Shawn's legs. The gun fired, and the bullet screamed past the former Hancock County sheriff's head, lodging in the floor just a few inches from his ear. Shawn fell on top of him, and then they were wrestling, each trying to get the upper hand on the other.

Ruskin brought a huge fist down on Shawn's wrist, sending the gun clattering to the ground. Shawn ignored the weapon and instead wrapped his hands around Ruskin's throat. The old sheriff felt something sharp dig into his flesh, and then he was gasping for air, blood squirting through Shawn's fingers to stain the walls that surrounded them.

As his eyes clouded and he gasped in vain for breath, Ruskin thought he saw Shawn stumble backwards and disappear. He had just enough time to wonder where he'd gone before everything went dark.

***

Katy sprinted up the stairs, slipping the pentagram necklace, the one that was a twin to the necklace her father currently possessed, around her neck. She'd heard him arguing with someone, and then a gun shot. She hoped with everything in her that he wasn't dead.

She'd left Jenny and Hope alone in her apartment, without a word of explanation as to her flight out the door. She briefly felt a twinge of guilt about that, but if Ben had come through the portal and was still controlled by Azazel, she wanted to put herself between him and Hope. She'd never allow anyone to hurt her little girl, not even the man she loved.

Katy nearly ran into Shawn as she reached the top of the stairs. Shawn's hands and white parka were covered in blood, and his face was pale. He stopped on his heels, looked past her, and then turned to stare into her eyes.

"Katy! Thank God. Azazel shot your father before he could push him into the spirit room. I was coming to look for you. You need to heal Fred."

She felt like she'd been punched in the stomach. "Is he…is he…"

"He's not dead yet, but he will be if we don't get in there. Where's Jenny?"

"She's down in my apartment with Hope."

He looked confused for a moment before nodding. "Hope. Is she okay?"

"She's fine, why wouldn't she be? And where's Emily? Where's Claire?"

"Claire's still in the Yukon, with the others. Emily's in there with Fred. Azazel shoved her head into the wall as we came through, and then wrestled Fred's gun away from him and shot him with it. Hurry, Katy. They need you. Go!"

Why hadn't he mentioned Emily before? She stared at him and felt the hairs on her arms and the back of her neck raise as a slow, crooked smile crept across his face.

"You can try to stop me," Azazel said from inside Shawn's body, "or you can save your father. You don't have time to do both, and there's no guarantee you can do either. I promise, I have no intention of hurting Jenny or your daughter. Let me escape and I'll do no further harm to you or your family. So, Katy Ruskin, what's it going to be?"

She struggled with the decision for a second but knew what she had to do. "Fine. Go. But I will find you," Katy whispered, between gritted teeth, "and I will destroy you."

"Just leave me alone," he said, as he turned to head down the stairs. "That's all I've ever really wanted."

She turned away from the demon and ran for the pentagram, disappearing as her foot touched the marble, reappearing on the other side.

Her father lay sprawled upon the remains of the lawn chair he'd taken into the room with him, blood pumping from a small, jagged hole in his neck. Jesus.

Katy dropped to her knees beside him, removing her own shirt to press against his neck.

"Shawn," he gurgled, his eyes abruptly opening, "he's...he's..."

"I know, Daddy. I know. Don't worry about that right now. Shh. Here," she said, taking his hand and pressing it against the shirt that even now was turning a deep shade of crimson, "hold on to this, if you can. I've got to get you into the spirit room."

He said nothing but winked at her before closing his eyes altogether. His lips were turning blue, and his whole body began to tremble.

"Come on, Dad," she said, rising from her knees to take hold of his feet. She slowly dragged him toward the curtain of shimmering light. God, he was heavy. "Hang in there for just a few more seconds."

And then she was pulling, pulling him through the curtain, and into the little cabin in the woods that existed nowhere except inside her own mind, and yet felt and looked as real as any place she'd ever visited.

Katy dropped to her knees again, pulling the blood-soaked shirt from her father's neck. He was in her realm now, and there was no way in hell she was going to let him die.

She held his right hand with her left, placing her other hand on his throat. Concentrating, she willed the skin to knit together, to heal, to become whole, but it wasn't working. Why the hell wasn't it working?

Katy jerked back as something poked the palm of her hand. Kneeling closer to her father, she noticed something sticking out of the wound. It looked like stone. She grasped the object with her thumb and forefinger and gave it a gentle pull. Blood gushed harder from the wound as the object dislodged from his skin, covering them both.

She held the jaguar's tooth, one of the five legendary talismans, in the palm of her hand. It was the very same tooth she'd given Shawn before he and the others left for the Yukon. Her father hadn't been shot. Instead, Azazel had stabbed him with the tooth, and it had gotten lodged in his neck.

Katy dropped the tooth to the hardwood floor of the cabin, once again reaching out to touch her father's throat. She watched as skin knit and healed, and in a few seconds his flesh was as good as new.

"Thank you, Katy," Fred whispered, raising his free hand to touch her face.

"Shh, Daddy, be quiet. Rest. You've lost a lot of blood."

She concentrated and the blood that covered her shirt, them, and the floor of her imaginary cabin vanished. She quickly slid the shirt on over her head and rose to her feet, but not before plucking the tooth from where she'd let it drop.

"I'm fine, and there's no time to rest. Azazel…he's inside Shawn now. He's the one who did this."

"I know, Dad," she said, looking down at her father. "I'm going to go find him and, somehow, some way, I'm going to end this."

"I don't think he meant to stab me," he said, surprising Katy. "He looked as startled as I was by all that blood, and he seemed more scared than anything else. If you do find him…remember, Shawn is in there, too."

A sudden thought struck her. "Is Ben okay?"

"I don't know, sweetie. Azazel came through alone. But him being in Shawn's body must mean that Ben is free, right?"

She felt momentarily elated at the thought of having Ben home again, but the feeling was immediately dampened by guilt over Ben's father taking his place. It was their backup plan, for Shawn to get Azazel to trade Ben's body for the tooth and his own body, but things had already gone awry.

"I've gotta go," she said. "Hope would never forgive me if anything happened to either of her grandpas."

Her father struggled to his feet, shaking off Katy's assistance. "I'm fine. Go. Find Shawn and bring him back, but please be careful. I'll let Jenny know what's happened, and I'll keep them safe."

Katy hesitated for a second, before giving her father a quick hug and a kiss on the cheek. "Thanks, Dad," she said, before disappearing through the curtain of light.

# Chapter 6

Emily and Ben appeared in the only unoccupied apartment in Huffman Heights, on the second floor, just down the hall from Katy's apartment. The little living room was empty, and in an instant Emily knew something had gone horribly wrong. This is where they were supposed to meet.

Ben's hand gripped hers, his eyes finding her own. Just then, Fred Ruskin flung the door open and hurried inside. He looked pale and out of breath.

"Where's Dad?" she asked, her stomach feeling hollow as the words left her mouth.

"He surprised me," Fred said, looking down at his feet. "He got away. Katy—"

"Katy?" Ben asked, still looking lost. "Where is she?"

Ruskin looked at Emily, who shook her head. A lot had changed in the five years since Ben had been taken from them, and they had all agreed that reintroducing him to the life he'd left behind should be done gradually, particularly when it came to Katy and the daughter he didn't even know existed.

"Where is she?" Ben repeated, his voice growing louder, more desperate. "Where's Katy?"

"Katy went after him. She's very resourceful," said Fred, forestalling Ben's objections. "She can take care of herself. More than take care of herself, actually."

"You let her go alone?" Ben asked, shouting now.

"I wasn't in much of a position to help her, son. Azazel got the jump on me. Nearly killed me. Katy got me into the spirit room just in time and healed me."

"It's okay, big brother," Emily finally said. "We'll find her."

"Why couldn't you just forget about me?" Ben shouted, whirling to face her. "Losing Dad, putting Katy in danger...it wasn't worth it. Not for me. It just wasn't worth it."

"What do you mean, 'it wasn't worth it?'" she said, fighting to keep the anger she felt out of her voice. "Who in the hell are you to decide what you...what your life...Do you have any idea what we've all been through the last...what Katy...?"

"How long was I gone?"

She stared at him. He didn't know?

He must have seen the confusion on her face. "Em, how long was I gone?"

"Ben, it doesn't matter right now," interjected Ruskin. "What matters is finding Shawn and Katy."

Ben ignored him. "How long was I gone, Emily? Tell me. Tell me!"

"Five years," she said softly, reaching out to take his hand.

He looked like someone had punched him in the gut. Pulling away from her, he began walking toward the door.

"Where are you going?" she asked, staring down at her empty hand.

"To find Katy," he said, "and to get Dad back."

# Chapter 7

Katy burst out of the apartment building, looking up and down Randolph Street for any sign of Shawn. Nothing. He could be anywhere. Cursing under her breath, her heart beating staccato in her chest, she sprinted to the parking lot and climbed into her blue Kia Sportage.

Peeling out of the parking lot, she raced down Randolph to Main Street, all the while looking for Shawn. No luck. She turned around from Main and drove the opposite way to Highway 136. Still no sign of him. He could be anywhere.

"Shit!" she screamed into the empty car. "Shit, shit, shit!"

Katy went stock still. The tooth. She had the tooth. Surely, its magic could help her. She removed the jaguar's tooth from her pocket. Concentrating on the talisman, she closed her eyes, whispered, *"Invenire daemonium,"* and thought of Azazel. Nothing.

Inspired by Jenny's prowess with Latin during her time in 1977, Katy began researching the language as it related to magic after Ben's kidnapping and found that, while it certainly wasn't necessary, using Latin words and phrases did seem to help her focus the power of the tooth.

*"Invenire daemonium"* simply meant "find the demon" in Latin.

The phone rang, startling her. She looked at the caller ID. It was her father. She thumbed the answer button.

"Still looking, Dad," she said, through gritted teeth.

"So is Ben. We couldn't stop him."

Her stomach fluttered, and her throat went dry. Ben. She had loved this man, missed this man, for five years. She'd given birth to his child. She wanted to see him so badly that her heart ached, but she was also terrified. They'd both been through so much since he'd been taken from her life. Would he even remember what he'd felt for her?

"Katy, are you there? Katy?"

"I'm here, Dad," she finally said, shifting the Sportage into drive and speeding back toward Huffman Heights. And there he was. Ben Spencer, the man she loved, looking up and down Randolph Street just as she'd done only moments earlier.

She couldn't breathe for a moment, but then forced herself to squeal to a stop beside him. Their gaze met, and tears formed unbidden in her eyes. Blinking, she forced them back. There was no time. They had to find Shawn. She could fall apart later.

Quickly composing herself, she rolled down the window. "Get in."

"Katy?" said her father's voice over the phone.

"Sorry, Daddy, I gotta go."

Ben stared at her through the open car window, seemingly not comprehending. Finally, wordlessly, he circled the SUV and climbed into the passenger's seat. He was so close that she could easily touch him, though she forced herself not to, not yet.

"We have to find your father, Ben." She choked out the words.

Ben reached a hand toward her, held it there for a moment, and then let it drop. Instead, he took the seat belt and buckled himself into the car.

He looked like he wanted, needed, to say something, but instead simply nodded. They stayed that way for a second or two, until finally he spoke: "I'm so sorry."

She blinked. "For what? None of this is your fault, and we don't have time for this now. Where would Azazel go? Do you have any idea?"

"No clue," he said, his face falling. "He…had full access to me, to my memories, but I could only catch glimpses into his. Toward the end, I just sort of…drifted away."

She wanted to know more, but they were wasting precious time and didn't even have a plan of action. If only there was a way to track Azazel. And then she remembered the pentagram charm Mr. Quarry had surgically implanted behind Shawn's left shoulder blade a week ago, so that he could be teleported into the spirit room if things went bad—which had obviously happened.

"What are you thinking?" Ben asked, staring at her.

She smiled but said nothing, instead focusing on the pentagram. Magic called to magic, so this might work. The tooth grew warm in her hand, and an image began to appear in her mind. She could see Azazel running down the side of the road, past a row of houses. She caught a street sign. Marion. He seemed to be moving with a purpose, but where was he going?

He had to know by now that he was carrying the talisman, and that it could be used to track him. After all, he more than likely had access to all of Shawn's memories, just as he had with Ben's. But what could he do? That's why they had implanted it in his shoulder blade. It would be almost impossible for him to remove without help.

There was something about that neighborhood…and then she made the connection. The bastard was heading for the little veterinary clinic on Quincy Street where she and Shawn had taken Hercules last year. That had to be it! If he could force Dr. Maynard to remove the pentagram, there was no way she'd be able to track him.

"I think I know where he's headed," she said, shifting the car into drive. "Let's go get your father back."

It took them less than three minutes to get there. Katy parked at the curb, leapt out of the car, and ran for the little red brick building. She heard the door slam and knew that Ben was just a few steps behind.

The door to Maynard's Veterinary Clinic was locked, despite the accompanying sign proclaiming the business open for two and a half more hours. Katy touched the doorknob, letting the magic of the jaguar's tooth flow through her. The lock clicked open.

She pushed the door, but it still wouldn't budge. It must be deadbolted. Katy closed her eyes, visualizing the thumb-latch on the other side, sliding it to the right.

The door swung open now, leading into a small lobby. A bell above the door sounded as the door opened, making Katy flinch, but there was no Azazel there to greet them. Ben pushed in front of her, quickly walking through the entrance. She reached for his arm, but he pulled away before she could touch him, barreling into the clinic. Swearing under her breath, she followed him inside.

Various posters of dogs and cats selling pet food and medicine lined the walls of the lobby, an empty receptionist desk taking up most of the left half of the room. A single closed door marked "Examination Room" lay before them. Katy's steps clacked against the wooden floor as she moved to follow Ben toward the closed door, but a moan from behind the abandoned receptionist's desk caught her attention.

An older woman with graying hair lay on her back, rubbing the side of her head. Her chair had been knocked down and was lying on the floor beside her. She looked up with a start, scooting away from them on her bottom.

Katy knelt beside the woman, putting a hand on her knee. "It's okay," she whispered, "we're not here to hurt you. What happened?"

"You're Fred Ruskin's girl, aren't you?" said the woman, staring up at Katy. "You were in here last year with that horrible Shawn Spencer. That's the man who attacked me! You need to call 911."

"We don't have time for this," Ben said, turning away from them.

Katy ignored Ben. She remembered the woman now, from their trip with Hercules. Mrs. Schroeder. "Is he...is Shawn still here?"

"I don't know where he is!" Mrs. Schroeder said, her voice getting louder. "You have to call the police before he hurts Dr. Maynard. He ripped the landline out of the wall, but my cellphone is in my purse."

Katy reached out a hand to touch the woman's cheek, where already a bruise was forming. She closed her eyes, holding the jaguar's tooth in her other hand, concentrating. She willed the woman to sleep. A few seconds later she felt her go limp. It was done.

She heard a door slam open and whirled to see Ben backing away from the entrance into the examination room, hands in the air. It was a shirtless, demon-possessed Shawn, and he had a shotgun trained on his son. Damnit, why couldn't Ben have waited for her?

"I just want to be left alone," Azazel said. "Why must you people keep hounding me?"

"Because you have my dad's body!" Ben shouted. "Because you stole five years of my life, you son of a bitch, and because you're responsible for every bad thing that's ever happened to my family."

"No, no, I'm not," said Azazel, gesturing at Ben with the shotgun. "That's not true. None of this is my fault. I mean, some of it was, in the beginning. I'll admit that. But not anymore! I just want to go on living, being human. And Shawn made a deal. A deal! But it was all a trick."

"Like you tricked me into giving you my body?"

"I had to! Don't you see? Don't you understand?"

The demon was rambling now, gesturing with the weapon. He shoved the shotgun towards Ben's chest, and Ben scurried backwards. Katy wasn't sure either of them even noticed her.

Why weren't Ben's luck abilities working? In the past, anyone trying to assail Ben like that would have accidentally shot themselves, slipped and knocked themselves out, or any of a myriad of other possible scenarios. Had Azazel somehow stripped him of his powers?

She wasn't going to wait to find out. Katy sprang into action, leaping into the air to kick the shotgun from the startled demon's grasp. The weapon spun through the air, crashing against the far wall and clattering to the floor. She followed up with a spin kick to his stomach, sending him reeling away from Ben and crashing into something in the other room.

Katy sprinted past a startled Ben and through the doorway of the examination room. Azazel lay sprawled partway across a table covered with white paper, holding his stomach.

"Where did you learn to fight like that?" Ben asked from behind her.

"You've been away a long time," she said curtly, instantly regretting it. "I was never again going to let myself be put into a position where I couldn't protect myself or the people I love, especially after…"

She almost said, *"Especially after having Hope,"* but managed to stop herself. He'd know about his daughter soon enough, but now wasn't the time and Dr. Maynard's office certainly wasn't the place.

"After what?" Ben asked.

"Oh, someone doesn't know something that maybe he sho-ou-uld," said the demon in a sing-song voice, still holding his stomach. "But Shawn does. I guess we all have to have a little…hope, huh?"

"What're you talking about?" asked Ben, his eyes darting between Katy and the demon.

"No more games," Katy shouted, grabbing Azazel and forcibly turning him over onto his stomach. She twisted one of his arms behind his back and pushed him hard into the table, forcing an audible gasp from the demon. "You're coming with us, and there isn't a damned thing you can do about it."

"Things have changed a lot since you've been gone, Benny Boy. Your grandfather kicked the bucket, and Katy here—Ow!"

Katy twisted his arm, hard, interrupting his words.

"My grandfather?" asked Ben. "Which one?"

"Your mom's father, Paul," Katy said softly, ignoring the demon as he started to laugh. "He passed away in his sleep last year. No disease or anything, just old age. He was nearly 80."

Ben stumbled against the wall, and Katy's heart ached for him. She wanted more than anything to go to him, to hold him, to let him feel his grief, but there just wasn't time.

"Not now, Ben," she said. "I'm so sorry, but we just don't have time. We need to get Azazel back to the house."

Searching the little veterinary office for something to bind Azazel's arms, Ben found a cache of brand-new dog leashes in one of the drawers. After binding and gagging him, they began the search for Dr. Melvin Maynard.

The search wasn't difficult. They found Maynard cowering in the supply closet, alone and frightened. The old man had been about to carve the pentagram out of Azazel's shoulder when Katy and Ben opened the front door, and the demon had thrown him into the closet and told him he'd kill him if he made so much as a peep.

Using the tooth to alter his memories, Katy convinced the veterinarian that the person who had barged into his office and demanded he cut out a piece of metal from Shawn's shoulder wasn't in fact Shawn Spencer but rather a crazy drifter who claimed that the government had implanted a tracking chip under his skin. It was a strange story, to be sure, but it was close enough to what really happened to make sense.

Before today she'd never used the talisman to alter people's memories but found it surprisingly easy. She wondered what else she could do that she hadn't yet discovered, but reminded herself that using magic wasn't always the best solution. Regardless, she'd have to do the same thing to Mrs. Schroeder.

"Let's get going," she said, pushing the bound and gagged Shawn in front of her.

"What else changed since I was gone?" asked Ben. "Did anyone else die?"

"No one else died. There are a few things you don't know yet, but I'll explain everything as soon as I can. Nothing else bad happened, I promise. Azazel was just trying to spook you, to get under your skin. Speaking of which, keep an eye on him for a minute, will you?"

Not waiting for Ben to reply, she walked over to Mrs. Schroeder, knelt beside her, and used the tooth to alter the woman's memories just enough to replace Shawn's face with that of her imaginary drifter. There, that was one problem solved. If only everything were that easy.

On the short drive back to the apartments, with Azazel bound and gagged in the back, Katy began to fill in some of the gaps for Ben. Shawn and Jenny purchased Huffman Heights from Shawn's father almost five years ago, she explained, just a few months after Ben was abducted. As their plan to rescue him came together, they realized that having immediate and full access to the spirit room that lay hidden on the third floor of the old mansion was critical. If they were going to separate the demon from Ben, it had to be done there, and it had to be done by Katy, who's powers increased exponentially while inside the room.

Immediately after buying the property, they terminated all the tenant's leases, set them up in other apartments around town, and gave each a check that would cover rent at their new building for double the time they had left on their lease at Huffman Heights. No one complained about the deal. Soon thereafter, Shawn, Jenny, Emily, and Katy all moved from Chicago to Carthage and into the building, where their primary focus was rescuing Ben.

They had also revamped the entire first floor, creating an entrance foyer, a communal living room, a library, a kitchen, and a dining room. The four second floor apartments still had small kitchens, living rooms, and dining rooms, she explained, but they rarely used them, instead preferring to cook and eat as a group.

"You gave up five years of your lives for me," he said, arms crossed in front of him, staring at the road. "Why?"

She felt a spark of anger. "Why? Because we love you, that's why! Do you know how devastated your mom and dad were when Azazel took you? And Emily? She almost had a breakdown. And me. Me, Ben. I love you. I wanted to make a life with you. We..." she said, faltering. "We all love you."

"The things he made me do," whispered Ben. "If you knew the things he made me do, you wouldn't love me. You couldn't."

She pulled into the parking lot of Huffman Heights to find her father pacing in front of the building, waiting for them, but neither her nor Ben moved to get out of the car. "Whatever he made you do, Ben, that's on him, not you. Him!"

"We'd better get this over with," he said, finally opening the door and sliding out of the vehicle.

"Thank goodness you found him," said her father, meeting Katy at the door of the Sportage.

Fred Ruskin opened the side door and hauled the demon out of the back seat. He had an old pair of his police issue handcuffs ready and snapped them onto Azazel's wrists, above where the dog leash already bound his hands.

"Ben!" yelled Jenny, running from the front door of the apartments to embrace her son.

Ben pulled away, recoiling from his mother. "I'm sorry, I just...I can't do this right now," he said, his arms hovering for a moment before dropping to his side, "not while that thing is inside Dad."

"Your father did what he had to do to get you home," she said. "I promise you we will get him back."

"I need time alone, time to think."

"But Ben—"

"Leave me alone!" he yelled, causing Jenny to flinch.

Ben took off in a run, heading behind the apartments.

"Ben!" she yelled, but he didn't even look back.

Katy started to go after him, but her father grabbed her wrist. "He'll be fine. He's home now, even if he doesn't know it yet. He just needs a little time. The best thing we can do for him now is to get Shawn back."

Katy looked over her shoulder at Jenny as she followed her father and Azazel into the apartments, hoping with all her heart that her father was right and that the demon could be separated from Shawn.

# Chapter 8

Fred and Katy Ruskin, father and daughter, walked up the stairs to the third floor of the old mansion turned apartment building in silence, Azazel between them. The demon didn't once try to escape, trudging one foot after another as if he'd lost all hope. Maybe he had, or maybe he was just playing them. Katy held the jaguar's tooth tight in her fist, just in case.

Katy went first, stepping onto the marble pentagram inlaid into the floor at the back half of the third story of the house, followed by Azazel, and then her father. Anger flared in her chest when she spied the broken lawn chair covered in her father's blood, but she tamped it down, concentrating on the task at hand.

Azazel's eyes grew large as he saw the shimmering curtain, and he shoved himself backwards, into Katy's father. The former Sheriff was ready this time, however, and quickly subdued him. The demon struggled to speak. Katy finally removed the gag, ignoring her father's protests.

"What?" she asked.

"They're going to come for you, you know," he said in a rush. "Get me a body, anyone's body, and I'll tell you everything. I don't care anymore. I'll give up Shawn and take the new one. Just don't make me go into that room."

Katy remembered how in 1977 the demon Leonard, inhabiting Brody Huffman's body, had done everything he could to avoid entering the spirit room. Maybe this would be easier than she thought.

Without another word, she maneuvered around the demon and shoved him screaming through the shimmering curtain of lights, leaping in after.

The demon was still screaming as they tumbled through the curtain into her little cabin in the middle of the woods. Shawn Spencer fell to his knees as a misty white burst of energy poured out of his mouth, coalescing just a few feet away as it formed his identical, albeit transparent, doppelgänger.

"Bitch," said the spirit, as he too fell to his knees. "That hurt."

Katy hadn't had to perform any sort of exorcism, after all. The room had done it for her.

"Well, that wasn't fun," said Shawn, as Fred, who'd followed Katy into the room, helped him to his feet and removed the handcuffs and dog leash from around his wrists. "Someone want to clue me into what's going on here? I remember bits and pieces, but it's all murky."

"We did it, Shawn," said Katy. "Ben's home. Your body is your own again. We're all safe."

"Hardly," said Azazel, rising to his feet. "Shawn Spencer, your body is still mine. You gave it to me. Once I get out of here, I'll simply reclaim it."

"Not gonna happen," Katy said, as she willed an open Mason jar to appear in one hand and reached out to grab the spirit's wrist in another.

She yanked the demon towards her, lifting him high into the air before shoving him hard down into the jar. He turned to mist again as he filled the glass container, and then she conjured a lid for the jar, screwing it on tight. She placed the jar on a nearby bookshelf before turning to face Shawn and her father. She curtsied, flashing them both a big smile.

"Amazing," said Shawn, a smile dancing across his own lips. "Though Azazel won't give up, you know."

"For now," offered Fred, "it doesn't look like he has much say in the matter. Now, Shawn, let's get you to that boy of yours. You two have a lot of catching up to do."

# Chapter 9

Ben ran until his calves ached and his lungs were on fire. Was any of this real, or was it all in his mind? He stood gasping for breath in someone's front yard on Fayette Street, unsure where to go next. He'd all but given up ever escaping Azazel when his father and the others had rescued him. He should be elated, but instead he felt disoriented, confused, and inexplicably angry.

He closed his eyes, trying not to scream. The breeze on his skin, the sounds of the birds in the trees, even the clothing he wore—it felt overwhelming. When Azazel had been in control of his body, he'd still been able to feel, but everything seemed muted somehow. Food didn't taste quite the same, and even the snow in the Yukon hadn't felt nearly as cold as it should have. But this? This felt almost *too* real.

Ben shook his head, attempting to will away the confusion he felt. So much had happened over the last five years, while he was locked away inside his own body. Emily grew up, his Grandfather Paul died, and now Ben's father had been stolen by the same demon responsible for taking everything else from him.

Moss Ridge Cemetery, the place where most of his family, and presumably his grandfather Paul, were buried, was less than a mile from where he stood. Almost before he thought about it, he began walking north along the sidewalk, parallel with Country Road, toward the cemetery.

A crow sounded in the distance, and he startled, nearly diving to the ground. Jesus, was this what his life was going to be like from now on, fearing every little thing? If it was, he wasn't sure he could take it. He felt like he was going to crawl out of his skin. He lowered his eyes and stared at the sidewalk, concentrating on walking, and almost before he knew it, he was making his way through the wrought iron gates of the cemetery.

Not much had changed since the last time he'd been here. Maybe a few more graves, but that was it. He wandered through the grounds, reading various gravestones, until he finally found the one he was looking for.

"'Here lies Paul McGee,'" he read aloud, staring down at the simple grave marker, "'beloved husband, father, and grandfather. He will be forever missed.'"

He felt as though there were a huge, gaping hole in his chest where his heart had once been and had no idea what he could do to ever fill it up again, or if filling it up was even possible. Feeling a nearly unbearable weight on his shoulders, Ben dropped to his knees, reached out a trembling hand, and touched the marble gravestone.

After that, things got a little strange.

***

Margaret Ruskin and Jacob Wang stood beside Paul McGee's grave, watching Ben Spencer as he entered the cemetery. Margaret's hand found Jacob's, and he squeezed her fingers. She was in love with Jacob Wang, something she hadn't expected and certainly hadn't thought possible, but also something she fully welcomed with an open heart. Death wasn't the end, after all.

"Well, he's finally here," Jacob whispered into her ear. "Are you ready?"

Jacob had been twelve when he died and was the only spirit she'd ever known in her well over half a century in the cemetery who had grown from a child into an adult. It shouldn't have been able to happen, but it did. If that was possible, who knew what else this world may hold in store for them?

"As ready as I'm going to be," she finally replied, not bothering to whisper. It's not like Ben could hear them anyway.

Ben wandered through the grounds, looking at the various gravestones, until he finally found the one Margaret knew he was looking for. "'Here lies Paul McGee,'" he read aloud, "'beloved husband, father, and grandfather. He will be forever missed.'"

Jacob walked through Ben, turned around, and walked back to Margaret. "I never get tired of that."

Margaret rolled her eyes at him. Okay, so maybe he hadn't completely grown up, after all. "Stop messing around and help me get Paul," she said, smiling.

"Your wish is my command, my queen," said Jacob, as they both sank into the ground.

Seconds later they reappeared, with Paul McGee in tow. He was wearing his favorite blue suit, the one he'd been buried in. He'd learn to change that in time, if he so wished, but he still wasn't used to being dead.

"I was trying to sleep," he complained, glaring at Margaret. "What's the—oh!" He stared at Ben, who was kneeling before his grave. "I guess it's time, isn't it?"

"I'm sorry I wasn't there, Grandpa Paul," Ben whispered, his head bent. "I've missed so much over the last five years. Everything and everyone I loved is so different."

Paul reached out to touch Ben's cheek, frowning as his hand passed through the man's skull. He slowly shook his head. He was learning.

"How long has it been since I died, Margaret?" He asked.

"Maybe a year, give or take. None of us are very good with time, Paul."

It was true. For spirits, time was much more fluid than it was for the living. Consequently, time seemed to slip away from them, at times passing alternately slowly or much more quickly than it did for those who still breathed oxygen. Some of them, like Margaret, could even see a little into the future, because for them whatever was going to happen already had.

"How am I going to do it, Grandpa Paul?" Ben asked the gravestone, tears in his eyes. "They rescued me. I'm back! But I don't feel back. I feel like I'm still hiding out somewhere inside my body, and someone else has hold of the reins."

"Oh, my poor boy," said Paul, staring down at his grandson. "They've taken so much from you, from all of us."

Margaret wished Claire were here. Her mere presence would have made all of this so much easier, but Paul could still talk to his grandson. It was just going to take a lot more energy. Margaret had learned much in her many years at the cemetery, and she would make this happen even if after she had to sleep for a week.

Smiling, Margaret reached out to take Paul's hand and he squeezed her fingers, his eyes never once leaving his grandson's face. He tried again to touch Ben with his free hand, placing a hand on Ben's shoulder, and his hand again passed through Ben's body. Ben's head slowly turned toward his shoulder, and he shivered, his eyes growing wide.

"The connection has been made," Margaret said, as she felt a heart she didn't possess beat faster.

Ben stood up, his eyes scanning the graveyard. "Is someone else out here?" he asked aloud, turning in a slow circle.

Still holding Margaret's hand, Paul stepped in front of Ben and reached his other hand out to touch his grandson's cheek. Ben went still, his eyes losing focus for a moment before shifting to stare into Paul's.

"Grandpa Paul?" asked Ben. He looked the ghost up and down. "How is this possible?" He turned to stare at Margaret. "And who are you?"

"This is Margaret," said Paul, enunciating like he was talking to someone hard of hearing. "She's my sister, and she was married to Fred Ruskin."

"Grandpa Paul?" Ben said, his eyes going back and forth between the two spirits. "I can see your lips moving, but I can't hear you."

"He's kept himself guarded against the demon for so long that he's closed himself off. This would be easier if he had one of the talismans, but it's still doable. Jacob?" asked Margaret, and the third ghost stepped forward to take her hand.

And that's when everything changed.

***

Ben couldn't believe it. His grandfather, Paul McGee, was standing right in front of him, and beside him, holding his hand, stood a beautiful woman with long, flowing red hair wearing a blue dress. Was he dreaming? But he knew he wasn't. This was really his grandfather, or at least his grandfather's ghost.

Grandpa Paul said something, but no sound escaped the old man's lips.

"Grandpa Paul?" Ben said, his eyes shifting between his grandfather and the woman holding his grandfather's hand. "I can see your lips moving, but I can't hear you."

The woman said something, but he couldn't hear her either. He gasped as a tall, dark-haired Asian man blinked into existence beside the woman, holding her other hand. His grandfather's hand moved to rest on Ben's shoulder, and he could swear he felt something, like a hummingbird alighting on his arm.

"Try again, Paul," said the woman, and this time Ben could hear her, though he had to strain.

"I said, this is my sister, Margaret. Your great-aunt. She was also married to Fred Ruskin. She and Jacob are helping me contact you. Can you hear me?"

Shivers ran down Ben's spine. His grandfather was speaking to him from beyond the grave. And Margaret was his great aunt. He knew that his late great-aunt Margaret had been married to Fred Ruskin, and that she and her daughter had been murdered by a serial killer a long time ago, but beyond that had gleaned very little. Fred never liked to talk about it, and Grandpa Paul looked so sad whenever her name was brought up that he had never been able to bear asking him questions about her.

"I can hear you, Grandpa Paul," he finally replied. "I'm sorry I wasn't here."

"You couldn't be here," said Paul, "and if you could have been, what could you have done anyway? I was an old man, lived longer than most. I died in my sleep. It was my time to be with my sister."

He turned to smile at Margaret, squeezing her hand.

"I could have at least said goodbye."

Paul smiled. "Isn't that what we're doing right now, saying good-bye?"

Ben couldn't help but smile. He supposed it was. "Is it all over, Grandpa Paul? Is Azazel finished with me?"

Paul turned to Margaret, who nodded.

"He is, but there are others. Michael, for one, and another even more powerful," she said. "You have a long road ahead of you, Ben, you all do, and how it all turns out…I can't see it."

"Michael really did betray us?" Ben felt his emotions turn to anger. "All the time Azazel had control of my body, he never met with Michael. I'd hoped the demon was lying."

"Azazel wasn't lying," Margaret said, "and Michael didn't betray any of you, because he was never on your side to begin with. But enough about that. You'll find out more in time. Right now, you're what's important. You and your grandfather, and we don't have much time."

"What do you mean?"

"I'm strong, but I can't do this forever," she said. "Neither can Jacob, and without us you won't be able to see or hear your grandfather."

A tremor of fear ran through Ben. "Grandpa Paul," he said, reaching for the old man, watching helplessly as his hand passed through Paul's chest. "I love you so much. We all do. Emily, Mom—"

"I know that, Ben," interrupted the ghost, "I was blessed with more love than I knew what to do with, and I love all of you just as much. When Tanner was taken from us, I shut down for a very long time. He was my son. But I had a wife, and a daughter. Was my grief more important than they were? No, it wasn't."

Tanner was his mother's brother and his father's childhood best friend, murdered by an ancient priest and the priest's monster when he was just a boy. His parents still had a hard time talking about Tanner's death.

"The best way for me to honor Tanner," Paul continued, "was to be there for your Grandma Abby and your mother and father. To let go of the pain and learn to live again. So that's what I did, and that's what you're going to do, too."

"I don't know if I can. I've lost five years of my life, Grandpa. Five years with Katy. We had something really, really special, and that's gone now."

"And you're angry."

"You're damned right I'm angry."

"So angry that you're willing to lose even more time with the woman you love?" Paul asked.

"Shit," said Jacob, the first words the ghost had spoken. "I'm—"

Ben would never know what Jacob was going to say, for at that moment he disappeared. One moment he was there, and the next he was gone.

Margaret looked at the hand Jacob had just been holding, shrugged, and then blew Ben a kiss. She said something Ben couldn't quite make out, but he thought it might have been "time to rest," and then she, too, disappeared. Grandpa Paul reached out to take Ben into a ghostly embrace, disappearing just as his arms encircled his grandson.

Ben was all alone again.

"I don't know if I can do it, Grandpa Paul," he said to the space where his grandfather had been just seconds earlier. "I don't know which way is up anymore, and if I lose Dad, too…I just don't know."

"What don't you know?" asked a voice from behind him.

Ben whirled, coming face to face with his sister.

"Hi, Em," he said, staring down at his feet. "What are you doing here?"

"Looking for you, stupid," she said, reaching out to take his hand. He didn't pull away. "After Katy told me Azazel told you about Grandpa Paul, I had a feeling you might be here. Who were you talking to?"

"I'm sorry I ran off," he said, ignoring the question. "This is just all so…so weird, for me. You're grown up, Grandpa Paul's gone, and Katy…"

"What about Katy? She's still in love with you, you know. She never stopped loving you. We lived together for a while, in Chicago, before we all moved here. When she wasn't…" Emily looked like she said something she wasn't supposed to have said. "Well, anyway, all she could think about was you. All we've been doing for the past five years is trying to get you home. And here you are!"

Ben squeezed her fingers. "Thank you. But what aren't you telling me? I got the same feeling from Katy."

Emily started to say something, seemed to think better of it, and instead pulled Ben into an embrace. "Just shut up, big brother, and let me take you home, okay?"

They vanished from the cemetery, leaving only the ghosts behind.

# Chapter 10

Ben sat beside his mother on the long brown couch that occupied most of the living room's south wall, while Hercules curiously sniffed his feet. He still couldn't get over the huge border collie's existence. Both he and Emily had begged their father for a pet for as long as he could remember, but he'd always said no, finally citing the murder of his cat Samson by the monstrous fetch when he was a teenager as an excuse. He asked what changed his father's mind about pets, but his mother shrugged off the question, promising to explain later.

The dog barked and growled at him when he and Emily first appeared in the living room but had gotten over his anger once he realized Ben wasn't a threat. Something had changed in Ben. He felt more a part of the world around him now and hadn't even startled at the dog's barks.

Jenny whispered something to Emily just a few minutes after they'd arrived, and she'd run off, leaving Ben confused. They definitely weren't telling him everything.

Claire Locke, the woman who, his mother explained, had spearheaded his rescue, sat in a chair she'd pulled in from the little dining room off to the north. Every once in a while, he'd catch her staring at him, but when he looked back, she'd always look away. Jenny said something about Claire being related to Katy's old roommate Mel, but Ben wasn't really paying attention. All he could think about was Katy.

The giant Kingfisher and his partners Mr. Quarry and Miss Pahari had apparently departed shortly after Emily teleported them back from the Yukon. When Ben asked about them, Claire said they weren't much for goodbyes.

"Are you sure you're okay?" asked Jenny, interrupting his thoughts. "You can rest, you know. Your dad would understand."

"He might never understand anything ever again," he said sharply, causing her to flinch. "He gave up everything for me. You all did. Is Dad even still writing, or did he give that up, too?"

"He hasn't written anything since you were taken from us, but that's not your fault. Now that you're back, I'm sure he'll—"

"He might not be coming back at all. Why he did such a stupid, pointless thing is beyond me."

"Because I love you," said Shawn as he walked through the front door, followed by Fred and Katy Ruskin. "But as you can see, I'm here. We beat Azazel, Ben. We won."

Ben stood up from the couch, fists clenched at his side. He wanted to punch someone, anyone, though he couldn't understand why. Grandpa Paul had told him he needed to let go of the anger, but he couldn't seem to do that. If he was finally free from the demon who'd held him prisoner for the last five years, why couldn't he let go of the impotent rage he felt?

His father, tears in his eyes, walked across the room to pull him into an embrace. "I'm so happy you're home, Ben."

Something broke in him then, like a dam holding back an ocean. It was real. It was all real. The demon Azazel stole half a decade of his life, but he was home now, with his family. His vision blurred as tears formed in his eyes and he began sobbing, almost howling with pain, anger, and loss, but also with blessed relief.

His mother was up in an instant, embracing him along with his father, and they stood that way for a long time, holding each other, safe in the comfort of one another's arms.

"What he did to you was awful, but he's never going to do that to anyone else ever again," said Shawn. "Katy made sure of that."

Katy! He'd been such a shit to her in the car. She was the woman he loved, and she'd put her life on hold for him, done lord knows what just for the chance to bring him home. He slipped through his parent's arms and, crossing the room, stood before her. Tentatively, he held out his left hand, his real hand, and just as tentatively she took it.

Despite being mere inches from her in the car, this was the first time they'd actually touched since his return. She looked both the same and different than she had five years ago. Her hair was longer. He was shaking.

"I'm so, so sorry," he said, fighting the almost overwhelming urge to avert his gaze from her own in shame. "I'm...I'm broken right now, Katy, and I think I might be broken for a good long while, but if you'll give me the chance, if you can forgive me for going away, I'd like to—"

She interrupted him with a kiss, long and hard, a kiss that he wanted to go on forever. "Do you still love me?" she asked, after finally pulling away.

The taste of her lips still lingered on his. "I love you more than anything," he answered, and meant it.

"Then you're never out of chances with me, Ben Spencer."

The front door banged open and there was his sister Emily, along with a beautiful little brown-haired girl he didn't know. The girl looked maybe three or four years old. She wore a dress adorned with cartoon characters he didn't recognize, and sported light-up tennis shoes.

"I'm sorry," said Emily, out of breath. "She got away from me and I couldn't catch her before she got here. I'm so sorry."

"Hi Mommy," the little girl said, looking at Katy. "Is this him?"

Ben stared at the little girl, then turned to Katy, his stomach turning to ice. "You have a daughter?"

"No, Ben," she said, squeezing his hand. "*We* have a daughter. And yes, Hope, this is your daddy."

He felt himself go weak in the knees, and it was all he could do just to stand. The little girl had Katy's brown hair and delicate features, and his green eyes. They had a daughter. He flashed back to the one and only time they'd made love, that night in the cabin inside the spirit room, during their time travel trip to 1977.

"Hi Daddy," said Hope, peering up at him.

Still holding Katy's hand, he dropped to his knees in front of the little girl. "Hello, sweetheart," Ben said, his voice shaking. "Your name is Hope, huh? That's a beautiful name, and you're a beautiful little girl."

"Thank you, Daddy."

He had a daughter and hadn't even known it. He'd missed out on so much time with her. It must have been hell for Katy, pregnant and alone. But she wasn't alone, not really. She had Ben's sister and parents as well as her own parents. They'd all worked together to raise and take care of this precious little girl while he could not.

His mind was racing, and beneath it all was the same white-hot fury his grandfather had recognized. Azazel had stolen so much from him, far beyond time. He was determined not to lose one more moment with this precious little girl and the people they both loved, and so he closed his eyes and let go of the anger as best he could. He knew he'd have to deal with it eventually, but not now, not today.

He looked up at Katy, who had tears in her eyes. Katy, Hope, Emily, his parents, his surviving grandparents, Fred, and Candy. Even Hercules. This was his family.

"Can I hug you, Hope?" he asked, once again staring into the eyes of his little girl.

In response, she ran up to him and threw herself into his arms, hugging him for all she was worth. In an instant, he gave her his heart.

He was finally home.

# Chapter 11

Emily stood with her parents, Fred Ruskin, and Claire Locke at the entrance to Huffman Heights, ignoring the others as they talked. She'd wanted nothing more than to rescue Ben from Azazel, and they'd finally done that, but she was still one brother short. If Colin were here, everything would be perfect.

Colin, Ben's twin brother, had been gone even longer than Ben, though he'd left of his own volition. He and Ben had never gotten along, and their relationship took a turn for the worse when they were both interested in a girl named Burgundy. The girl chose Ben, and Colin had left home soon thereafter.

Katy said that Colin hadn't existed before her and Ben time traveled to 1977, but Emily didn't care. If they'd done something to alter the past and somehow caused Mom to get pregnant with twins instead of just Ben, well, so what? Colin and Ben had been her twin big brothers all her life. For her, the past hadn't been altered at all. Couldn't it be *Katy* whose memories had been altered?

When Katy had tried to explain that Colin shouldn't exist, Emily's parents shut her down, and Katy rarely brought it up again after that. Emily had listened, though, and believed that, if nothing else, Katy believed the story. The fact that Ben hadn't once asked about his twin since returning home only served to add credibility to what Katy had said. There'd always been problems between Ben and Colin, though, even before Burgundy came along.

For whatever reason, Colin had no magical abilities and had always been jealous of Ben's. That girl choosing Ben over Colin had ruined whatever relationship they had left.

She'd only seen Colin a handful of times since, though they had managed to stay in communication via email, texts, and the occasional phone call. It wasn't the same, though. In effect, she'd lost both her brothers. She had Ben back now, so if there were any justice in the world, maybe Colin would soon follow. Once Ben saw Colin, he'd have to remember him. Wouldn't he?

"Sorry again about what happened in the Yukon," said Claire, interrupting her thoughts.

"What?"

"With you getting shot. It should never have happened."

"Oh, it's fine. You healed me. It doesn't even hurt anymore. There's not even a scar," Emily said. "It was a small price to pay for rescuing Ben. Thanks, by the way. For everything."

"Anytime," said Claire, giving Emily a quick hug. "If you need anything, just let me know. And keep an eye on Sabrina and Farris once I leave town, okay?"

Sabrina was Claire's youngest sister, and Farris was Sabrina's boyfriend. Emily's parents had insisted she continue going to school after they'd moved to Carthage from Chicago, and Sabrina had befriended her on day one. They'd graduated high school together last year, but only recently put two and two together and discovered that both their families were touched by magic.

"Absolutely," she said, pulling Claire in for a longer hug.

"We owe you, big time," Shawn said to Claire. "If you ever need anything, anything at all, just let us know, okay?"

"You paid me, remember? We're square."

Claire normally charged for her services, and this time was no different. The payment, however, was just $1.00, while Kingfisher and Quarry required 24 hours possession of the jaguar's tooth. Why, she wasn't sure, but they had gladly paid both fees.

"Some payment," Shawn said, shaking his head. "Are you sure you won't let me pay you for real?"

"Tell you what," Claire said, "next time I'm in town, you spring for Ruskin's Pizzeria. Pepperoni, mushrooms, and extra cheese. Deal?"

Shawn sighed, a weary smile on his face. "It's a deal, Claire."

"Seriously, though, thank you," said Jenny, hugging Claire. "You brought our son back to us. Thank you."

They watched as Claire climbed into her rented Lincoln Navigator, turned to wave goodbye, and drove off down Randolph Street. Emily had never been to Arkansas and so couldn't teleport Claire home, but had been to Tulsa, Oklahoma, which was just two hours from the Arkansas border. She'd offered to teleport Claire to Tulsa, but Claire had begged off, instead deciding to spend a few days with Sabrina and Farris before enjoying a leisurely drive back home to her wife and son.

"Let's go check on Ben," Shawn said, turning to head for the door.

Emily bit her lip, trying to work up the courage to bring up what she knew was a sore subject. Finally, she just said it.

"How do we tell him about Colin?"

Shawn paused at the doorway before turning around. "I don't know, sweetheart. I'm hoping we won't have to, that Katy's wrong."

"Do you really think she's wrong?" asked Jenny, taking her husband's hand. "Really?"

Shawn sighed. "No, I don't. I believe her."

"But what if it were her memories that were altered?" interrupted Emily. "Occam's razor, remember? Whatever is the simplest answer is probably the correct answer."

"My sweet girl," said Jenny, looking into her daughter's eyes, "since when has anything with our family ever been simple?"

# Chapter 12

Ben held his daughter in his arms. He could hardly believe it; he and Katy had created a child together. He finally released her, wiping away tears with the back of his hand.

"Why are you crying, Daddy?" she asked.

"I'm just so happy to see you, Hope. I've…missed you so, so much. I'm sorry I was gone for such a long time."

"That's okay, Daddy. Mommy said it wasn't your fault. Besides, I knew you were coming home today."

Ben looked up at Katy. What had they told her?

"Hope's imaginary friend sometimes tells her things," Katy said, arching an eyebrow. "Isn't that right, pumpkin?"

"Sometimes," she agreed, "but not always."

Ben felt the hairs on his arms stand. "What's your friend's name, Hope?"

"I can't tell you that," Hope said, her eyes downcast. "At least not yet. Is that okay, Daddy?"

Everyone else had left the room to give their little family time to catch up. Everyone, that was, except for Hercules. Ben finally understood why his father had relented and taken in another pet after all these years. Who could say no to this beautiful little girl?

"Yes, Hope," he finally replied, "that's okay. At least for now. So…tell me about Hercules."

"He's the best doggie in the whole wide world!" Hope shouted, giggling.

"We adopted him for Hope's third birthday," Katy said, as they moved from the floor to the couch, the dog following. "She'd wanted a dog for as long as she could talk, and one day her Grandpa Shawn brought home this scraggly little collie pup from the animal shelter. He was the runt of the litter, the worker at the shelter told Shawn, and he's grown up to be this huge, beautiful boy you see before you. That was a little over a year ago. The name 'Hercules' was supposed to be ironic, because he started out so small, but he really grew into the name."

Ben reached a tentative hand toward the dog, who sniffed for a moment before nuzzling his fingers.

"He likes you, Daddy," said Hope, sitting on Ben's lap. "I knew he would!"

"I like him, too, sweetie. He's a very good boy."

"Can we come in?" asked his father from the doorway. He stood with Ben's mother and Emily.

Ben waved them into the living room.

"Wow, I wish Colin were here to see this," said Emily, looking at them with tears in her eyes. She immediately covered her mouth, looking like she'd said something she shouldn't have.

A shiver travelled down Ben's spine. Who was Colin?

Katy glared at Emily. "I thought we agreed not to tell him until the time was right."

"We did," said Shawn, turning to stare at Emily.

Ben could see Emily's face turning red, the way that it always did when she was embarrassed or when she got caught doing something she shouldn't have been doing.

"Tell me what? And who's Colin?" asked Ben.

"I didn't mean to, all right?" Emily said, looking at everyone but Ben. "I was thinking it in my head, and it just popped out. I'm sorry."

Hope climbed up from Ben's lap and hugged Hercules.

"Em!" Ben yelled, and her head swiveled to face him. "Who. Is. Colin?"

"Lower your voice," Katy said. "You're scaring Hope."

"I'm not scared, Mommy."

"Your brother," Emily finally said, eyes downcast.

What the hell? "Brother? Since when do I have a brother? Unless—you two had a baby while I was gone?" He looked at Shawn and Jenny.

"No!" said Jenny. "I mean, three children are enough, and I—"

"Three?" Ben asked. "Please, someone explain this to me."

"Uncle Colin," Hope said. "He's your brother, Daddy, though he wasn't always. You'll meet him soon."

That shiver again. He had a brother who hadn't always been his brother. What did that even mean?

Katy sighed, throwing one last glare at Emily. "Emily, can you take Hope to her room to play, please? Hercules, too."

"I swear to God, Katy, I didn't mean—"

"I know, Em. What's done is done, and we can't put the djinni back in the bottle. Besides, I was going to tell him tonight anyway."

Hope walked over to Emily and took her hand. "Come on, Auntie Em, let's go upstairs and play knights. You too, Hercules."

The dog walked to her side, nuzzling her hand and causing her to giggle.

"Okay, Hope," Emily said, looking at Ben and the little girl. She looked like she wanted to say something else, but instead turned for the door.

Ben waited until they'd left before saying, "Auntie Em?"

"We watched the *Wizard of Oz* the other day," Jenny said, by way of explanation. "She has your sense of humor, Ben."

"Okay, tell me about this Colin. I don't have a brother. I've never had a brother, but Emily claims I do."

Katy started to answer, but Jenny interrupted her. "Let's talk in the dining room. We have some leftover Thai food that your sister picked up from New York City two nights ago, we can heat that up. It was really good, and I bet you're hungry."

From New York City? And then Ben remembered Emily's ability. It must be nice, having a teleporter in the family. His stomach grumbled at the thought of food, and he realized he was starving.

They adjourned to the dining room while Shawn set about heating up the food. Soon, wonderful smells from the kitchen began to make Ben's mouth water. It'd been five years since he last ate, or at least it felt that way, and it was then that he realized just how much he was looking forward to eating under his own power again.

"It was the time travel, Ben," Katy said, as she sat down beside him in the dining room. "We must have done something, changed something, somehow, and the result was your twin brother."

"We're identical twins?"

"Oh, no," Jenny said quickly. "You were fraternal twins. You were born just a few minutes apart. You first, and then Colin."

None of this made any sense. What could they have changed that would cause his mother to give birth to twins?

"Jenny," Shawn called from the kitchen, "the food's ready. Can you set the table?"

Jenny stood up from the table, pausing to give Ben a quick hug.

"Don't worry, we'll get all this figured out," she said as she exited the room.

Ben waited until his mother had left the dining room before turning to Katy. "What's to figure out? I don't have a brother. I've never had a brother. He doesn't exist."

"He's never existed for us, Ben, but he certainly exists for your parents and Emily. When we left our time to visit 1977, you didn't have a brother, but when we came back, you did. The first time they mentioned Colin it scared the hell out of me."

"Have you met him?"

"No. The story is, you and he had a falling out over that Burgundy chick you used to date, and he left home, travelled around the world for a while, and eventually wound up in Toronto. That was five years ago, around the time we went to 1977. Apparently, you two had problems even before that, because he was jealous of your abilities, abilities he doesn't share.

"Emily and your parents visited him in Canada twice, and I think they talk to him on the phone from time to time, but that's it. They've tried to get him to come home a few times, but he's always refused."

"Jesus. What did they say when you told them he didn't exist?"

"They kind of freaked out, to be honest. They remembered meeting us in 1977, so they knew we time travelled, but they still didn't believe me. They thought my memories had somehow been changed."

"But that doesn't make any sense."

"To us, maybe not," Katy said, "but to them, it makes perfect sense. I mean, if someone tried to tell me that Hope shouldn't exist, I wouldn't exactly welcome that news with open arms, you know?"

"Did anything else change?"

"A few other things," Katy admitted, "most notably, my dad is now a multimillionaire."

"Seriously? How did that happen?"

"It was that Microsoft duffle bag you brought back to 1977, doofus. He bought Microsoft stock and made a ton of money. Used it to turn his little pizza restaurant into a chain. There are almost 4,000 Ruskin's Pizzerias across the country and in Canada."

Ben started to say something but fell silent when his mother, carrying plates, silverware, glasses, and a pitcher of water, entered the room. His father trailed behind her, balancing four steaming bowls on a platter. Jenny set the table and Shawn deposited the food in the center.

"We have Evil Jungle Prince, Pineapple Curry, Pad Thai, and Avocado Curry," Shawn said. "It's all delicious, but I especially like the Avocado Curry. Just the right amount of spice. You'll love it."

His father was right; the Avocado Curry was delicious, but the Evil Jungle Prince was amazing. He tried everything but Pad Thai, savoring each spicy bite. Food had never tasted this good before, especially now that he could eat what *he* wanted, under his own power.

Emily and Hope joined them just a few minutes into supper, and Jenny made her granddaughter a peanut butter and jelly sandwich with a side of carrots. Emily apologized to Ben once again for springing the news of Colin's existence on him, but Ben waved it off. It wasn't her fault, and he didn't want any of them keeping secrets from him.

Once they'd finished eating, his mother presented him with something all-too familiar: the family photo album. What looked the same as it always had on the outside, however, was anything but inside.

Where he had previously appeared in photos by himself, now many of those same photos showed a boy who his parents identified as Colin. There were also solo photos of Colin, and family photos including all five of them.

He flipped though the album, feeling a strange sense of dread settle in on him. This was real. He had a brother he didn't even remember. There were the two of them in baby clothes, and there they were on their first day of Kindergarten in Chicago. It went on and on, and, like a train wreck, Ben couldn't bring himself to look away.

He also couldn't help noticing that very few photos of him and Colin together existed past the age at which Ben had gotten his powers. That tied into what Katy said about Colin's anger at Ben's abilities, and, according to his parents, his disdain for the supernatural.

"Does Colin know I'm home?" Ben asked, once he'd gone through the entire album.

"Not yet," said Shawn. "Do you want me not to tell him?"

"We don't have to if you don't want to," Jenny added.

"Actually, it's just the opposite. I think it's about time I met my twin brother."

# Chapter 13

The weather in Toronto during April was always unpredictable. Sometimes it snowed, sometimes it rained, sometimes it was scorching hot, and sometimes—like today—the weather was perfect. The sun was shining, there wasn't a cloud in the sky, and it was a cool 22° Celsius, all of which made for a pleasant walk from the University of Toronto to The Queen and Beaver Public House less than a mile away, where Colin Spencer was meeting his girlfriend Natsumi Hashimoto for lunch.

Colin adored Canada. Moving from Chicago to Toronto was the best decision he'd ever made, even if the decision had originally been a knee jerk reaction to a stupid argument he'd had with his twin brother. Sure, he missed his family, especially his little sister, but he was making a life for himself here, a life as far away from magic and the supernatural as possible.

He enjoyed working at Chapters, a huge bookstore right in the middle of Toronto, and made enough money to afford a small off-campus apartment with Natsumi. He was also attending university, working on his master's degree in political science, which made for a delicate balancing act. He was on the cusp of having everything he'd ever wanted, though he still missed Ben.

They hadn't always been at odds. They'd been as close as twin brothers could be until around age 12, when Ben first began exhibiting his abilities. Suddenly, Ben was winning every video game they played, was making all A's in school, and could never be beat at Monopoly. He constantly found money on the street and won every competition he entered, and, inexplicably, even a few he didn't.

Neither of them understood what was happening until their parents sat them down and told them all about the supernatural world they'd been born into. Ben's powers were a result of their father using the combined strength of five magical talismans to heal himself, their mother, and Fred Ruskin. The magic he'd used on them had been inherited by Ben, but apparently not by Colin.

Ben had been born just a few minutes before Colin. Had their births been reversed, Colin was sure he would have been the one to inherit magic instead of his unworthy twin. The rift between them started that day, and eventually widened to a chasm.

He realized now he'd been unfair to his brother. It wasn't Ben's fault he had these abilities any more than it was Colin's fault that he didn't. In many ways, those talents had handicapped Ben. If everything came easy, how could you ever take pride in your accomplishments? Every good grade Colin achieved, every competition he won, he knew he'd earned. Ben didn't have that. It was what it was.

Colin left home less than a month before Ben was kidnapped by a demon named Azazel. They'd both been interested in Burgundy, a girl they'd gone to high school with, and she'd chosen Ben. It was a stupid argument, and one he wished never happened. He'd give anything to be able to share these newfound insights with his brother, to be able to apologize for how he'd acted, but it'd been five years since Ben was taken, and he may never have that chance.

That was a large part of why he'd never returned home, despite the pleas of his sister and their parents. He loved Canada, to be sure, but he was ashamed of how he'd acted, ashamed that he'd let his own jealousy hurt his relationship with his twin brother. He'd grown up but had yet to forgive himself.

Colin looked up. Lost in his thoughts, he'd walked straight past the restaurant. Laughing at himself, shaking his head, he turned around and walked right into Natsumi.

"First you walk past me, then you nearly run me over," Natsumi said, the sunlight sparkling off her deep brown eyes and jet-black hair. "Whatever am I going to do with you, Colin Spencer?"

"Absolutely anything you want," he said, leaning in to kiss her. "Sorry. I was daydreaming, I guess."

"No biggie. C'mon, let's go eat."

She took his hand and half-led, half-dragged him into the restaurant. Soon they were seated and had placed their orders, with Natsumi ordering the quiche of the day and Colin opting for the fish and chips.

"How were classes this morning?" Natsumi asked, between drinks of apple cider.

"Not bad," Colin replied, "though Professor Franklin seemed out of it again today. I really do think he's going to retire soon, if not at the end of this semester, then the next."

They'd met two years ago in Franklin's Social Policy class. The old man was brilliant and had taken Colin under his wing, but at age 72 he seemed to finally be losing a step. Colin had always imagined Franklin attending his and Natsumi's wedding one day, if indeed they got married, and would be sad to see him go.

He was in love with Natsumi and had been from the moment he first saw her in that classroom. The feelings he'd had for Burgundy and every other girl he'd ever been interested in paled in comparison. Simply put, she made him shine.

"That's too bad about Professor Franklin," Natsumi said, frowning, "though I guess we all get old eventually."

*Except for my parents*, Colin almost said, but held his tongue. He'd yet to share any of his family's experiences with magic and the supernatural with her, though he knew if he wanted to have a life with her, he'd have to have that conversation eventually.

Natsumi had met Colin's parents and sister twice, the second time about six months ago, when they'd came for a visit. She'd remarked upon how young his parents looked but didn't seem to suspect anything but good genes. Natsumi and Emily had become Facebook friends, but he didn't think they talked much if at all.

She knew Colin's twin had gone missing five years ago but had no idea he'd lost his body to a demon. That one would be even harder to explain than his fountain of youth parents. Whenever he did reveal his family's supernatural past to Natsumi, he'd have to do it in small doses lest she think him insane.

"You're being quiet," Natsumi said. "What're you thinking about?"

"Honestly? My brother." said Colin.

"Oh, honey," she said, reaching across the table to take his hand. "I can't even imagine losing one of my sisters like that, let alone a twin."

"It's okay."

"Why don't you go visit? I think it'd be good for you, and I know for a fact that Emily would love that."

He started to respond but was interrupted by a beep from his cell phone. Speak of the devil. It was a text from Emily. He read her message, then reread it three more times, trying to comprehend what it said.

"Oh my God!" he whispered, still staring at his phone.

"What? What's wrong? Who's it from?"

"It was from Emily. Ben…I can't believe it…"

"What? Colin, you're scaring me."

"It's Ben, Sumi. They found my brother. He's safe. My brother's home!"

# Chapter 14

**Eighteen Years Ago**

It was a bright and beautiful spring day when death visited Janna Sparks' little town of Sarcoxie, Missouri for the second time in less than a week. Janna's father, Edward Sparks, died unexpectedly in a three-car pile-up on Center Street last Tuesday, leaving her a twenty-nine-year-old orphan. She'd buried him on Saturday, beside her mother Lorene, who passed away from a heart attack while visiting her parents in Springfield when Janna was just five.

Janna sat on the porch swing in front of the house she'd grown up in, holding a small geode in the palm of her hand. Aside from the house and everything inside, this was the sole inheritance from her father. She poked the stone with her finger, waiting for it to do something. She could sense the power buried beneath the surface, calling to her, but had no idea how to access it.

Today was Sunday, the day after she had put her father in the ground. She'd taken last week off from her job as a fourth-grade schoolteacher at Sarcoxie Elementary so that she could plan her father's funeral and wasn't looking forward to going back tomorrow.

Her longtime boyfriend, another teacher at the school, suggested she take a leave of absence to let herself grieve. She knew, however, that she needed to get back into the swing of things, lest she allow herself to fully sink into the depths of depression that even now threatened to engulf her.

She folded her fist around the stone, closed her eyes, and thought of her father. Janna had first removed the stone from the small copper keepsake box it usually rested in last Wednesday, after recovering it from the safe her father had installed in the back of his bedroom closet. She'd only seen the stone a handful of times before, and even then, only for a few seconds at a time. She'd never even touched it before then.

She wondered if her father's angel had welcomed him into heaven, and if her mother had been there beside him? The thought, at least, made her smile.

"He told me copper would keep it safe from those who might seek to use its power unwisely," her father explained to her, on her sixteenth birthday, the day he'd revealed to her the story of how he'd acquired the stone, "and that I should only use it when absolutely necessary."

The archangel Michael came to him in the summer of 1975, her father claimed, when he was Janna's age, telling him a story of five talismans that could destroy the world if they fell into the wrong hands. Ernie had been chosen to become one of the five great protectors, and it was now his life's duty to keep the geode safe, and only use the talisman if absolutely necessary.

"Okay, Daddy, so what mysterious powers does the geode have?" she remembered asking him at the time, laughing, thinking it was either a joke or he was going crazy.

The story became all too real when a bowl of oranges on the coffee table levitated halfway to the ceiling, spun around in lazy circles, and landed on the fireplace mantle. That was the first and last time he'd ever used the geode in her presence, forever after relegating it to its copper keepsake box.

"You believe me now?" he asked, putting the geode back in the box and closing the lid.

She believed him. Janna was to become the protector, he explained, after he passed. That's why he risked using the stone to show her its powers. She had to believe, and now she did. He promised her, however, that he wouldn't be leaving her any time soon. That was over thirteen years ago, but it still seemed like yesterday.

Janna realized she was crying. Wiping away tears with the back of her hand, she pushed her dark brown cornrows back from her face and rose from the porch swing. She looked around the yard, finding it deserted, and concentrated on the geode still in her hand. The copper box sitting on the little table beside the swing hovered a few inches off the ground, shook, and then fell with a clatter back to the table.

She removed a red velvet cloth from the box, wrapped the stone in its folds, and placed the package back inside the box. Inside the house again, she was headed for her father's bedroom to return the box to the safe when the doorbell rang.

Janna twirled on her heels, startled, her heart beating heavy in her chest. She glanced at the clock on the wall; it was just a few minutes before ten. Who could be bothering her this early on a Sunday morning? Forcing herself to calm, she laughed at her paranoia. It was probably just a salesman or something else equally innocuous. Her father's many dire warnings that eventually someone might come for the geode had her spooked, especially after his untimely death.

She peeked out the eyehole and could see only a bouquet of red roses. Janna smiled. It had to be Drew. He'd been so good to her through all of this. He'd held her all night the day her father died and had been with her every step of the way since.

Janna opened the door, startled to see a huge white man holding the bouquet of flowers. Janna was 5'6", which was about average for a woman, but this man was at least a good foot taller than her. He was bald with a full white beard and had a black eye patch over his left eye. He looked to be in his early-to-mid sixties, though she had never been very good at judging age. He was wearing gloves, though it wasn't even remotely cold.

"Can I help you?" She asked, ready to slam the door shut again at the first sign of trouble.

"I'm sorry for your loss," he said, looking down at her with his one good eye. "Here, these are for you."

"Did you know my father?" Janna asked, not taking the flowers.

The man shrugged and let his arm fall to his side. "Not exactly," he said. "May I come in?"

Not exactly? "I don't think so, mister," said Janna, pushing the door closed with her foot. "Sorry, but I'm busy. You can leave the flowers outside, on the table by the door."

He stuck a huge foot between the door and the frame before it could fully close, and then shoved the door hard into her, sending her sprawling. She stumbled backwards, her hip on fire from where the door struck her. The box fell from her fingers to land upside down on the hardwood floor below.

"Get out!" she yelled, backpedaling. She reached into her pocket to pull out her cellphone. "I'm calling 911 now."

He was on her in an instant, snatching the phone from her hand and hurling it against the wall. It shattered in an explosion of plastic and metal, littering the floor.

"I don't want to hurt you," he said, laying a huge hand on her shoulder. "I'm here for the geode. Let me have it, and I'll leave you alone. Please!"

Her heart raced. She kicked the man hard between the legs, scrambling away from his grip as he winced in pain and stumbled into the wall. Snatching the box from the ground, she turned and sprinted for her father's bedroom.

Janna closed and locked the door behind her before running to the closet, but the door splintered and flew open just as she reached the safe.

"I had a vision, in 1977, long before you were born," said his voice, from behind her. "It was your father, using the geode. He was outside getting his mail when some asshole hit a cat with his pickup. He ran back into the house, got the geode from where he kept it hidden, and used it to heal the cat. I saw the address on a piece of mail he held in his hand. If he'd moved, I never would have found him, because I don't have visions anymore."

She frantically spun the combination, praying to whoever would listen to get it open before he reached her. And then she remembered she held a weapon far more powerful than the pistol. Abandoning the safe, she opened the copper box just as she felt a sharp pain shoot through her back.

Gasping, Janna sparks looked down at her chest to see the tip of a long sword poking through. Blood gushed from the wound, and she knew she was dying. She tried turning around again, planning to do something, anything, to prevent the man from stealing the geode, but she couldn't move. The box tumbled from her fingers to land on the floor somewhere.

"Why?" she asked, as the world began to slip away.

"I'm sorry. I didn't want to hurt you," he whispered, pulling the sword from her body. He gently took her into his arms, walked over to her father's bed, and laid her on the green comforter. Tears trickled down his cheek from his one good eye, which she noticed was a dark blue. "I hope you can forgive me."

She thought again of her father's angel, and how she had failed him along with her father, and then she thought about the blood she was getting on the comforter. It would take a lot of washing to get that much blood out. Her vision was blurry, but she sensed the man sitting on the bed beside her, and then felt his massive hands wrapping around her neck. She heard a sharp crack echo through the bedroom and all her pain went away, blessedly away, and that was all she knew.

# Chapter 15

Katy woke at just past four in the morning, knowing exactly what she needed to do. She'd known it, in fact, ever since Azazel was ripped from Shawn's body in the spirit room. Ben, sound asleep beside her, didn't even stir when she rolled out of bed. She stared at his sleeping form and couldn't help but smile. Though she'd never given up, a part of her had been convinced that she'd never see him again. If not for Claire Locke, she might have been right.

Last night had been wonderful. After Hope had fallen asleep, she'd dragged Ben into her bedroom, and they'd made love. It had been frantic at first, hurried and awkward, but round two was much more relaxed. They'd taken their time, getting to know each other's bodies all over again, and it was amazing. They'd fallen asleep in each other's arms, exhausted but happy.

She put on the clothes she had so hurriedly shed last night, a smile coming unbidden to her lips as she remembered Ben's eyes on her as she undressed. She shook her head. She'd have time to savor those memories later, and to make a million new ones. For now, though, she had a mission, perhaps the most important mission of her life.

Forcing herself to walk from the room, ignoring the inexplicable but all-too-real feeling that he might not be there when she got back, she padded down the hallway to check on Hope.

Posters from Hope's favorite cartoons adorned the walls, and a huge, intricate Victorian dollhouse that both of Hope's great-grandfathers and Katy's father had worked together to build filled nearly a quarter of her bedroom and stretched halfway to the ceiling. Though Hope certainly didn't have a normal childhood by any stretch of the imagination, she was very much loved and adored by all the adults in her life. Katy had to believe that was enough for now.

Crossing over to the little girl's bed, she pulled back the Paw Patrol comforter and kissed her daughter on the forehead. Hope smiled in her sleep before turning over on her side to hug her plush Peppa Pig. Katy looked down at her daughter for a while longer, sure her heart would burst with love. Without Hope, she wasn't sure she could have made it through the last four years.

Her daughter gave her a purpose beyond rescuing Ben, which had probably saved her sanity if not her life. Because of that, however, she'd been burning the candle at both ends, studying martial arts, training with the jaguar's tooth, and researching the supernatural when not investigating leads on Ben and taking care of Hope.

She still couldn't believe that Ben was finally back. Introducing him to his daughter yesterday afternoon had been beyond amazing, as was their time together last night, and that's why she needed to do everything in her power to make sure that no one ever again took Ben from them. Demons and angels had been fucking with both their families for far too long, and it needed to stop.

Leaving Hope's room, she paused only to grab her leather jacket before heading out the door.

Everything was just as she'd left it in her little cabin inside the spirit room, including the old Mason jar sitting on the bookshelf. She steeled herself before picking up the jar, balancing it in her hand. The container glowed but had no weight to it. It was now or never. She glanced at the bound and gagged old man standing beside her before unscrewing the lid.

A bright white amorphous mist poured from the jar, collecting on the floor at her feet before growing to form the shape of a man. He looked like Ben for a moment before Katy waved her hand and changed him to resemble Tom Logan, the man whose body Azazel had stolen years ago before taking Ben's.

"What do you want?" asked the demonic spirit, ghostly hands clenched in fists.

"To take you up on your offer," said Katy.

The spirit's eyes grew wide as he turned to stare at Katy's companion, and she followed his gaze. The man was probably sixty or seventy years old, had stringy white hair, and wore a pair of threadbare jeans and a stained sweatshirt that hung from his skeletal frame. His feet were bare, and he looked confused.

"This is the best you could do?" asked Azazel, the hint of a smile on his lips. "That's not good enough."

"It's going to have to be good enough. It was difficult tracking down someone that no one would miss, and I'm not going to do it again. This goes against everything I believe, but I've got to keep my family safe, and to do that I need information."

The demon tilted his head, studying the man. "Will he agree to give me his body? It looks like you brought him here by force."

"He already gave me his body. It was easy. I offered him $10,000 in exchange for saying, 'I give my body to Katy Ruskin,' three times. He didn't even hesitate."

"Clever," Azazel said, grinning. "Yes, he is now yours to do with as you wish. Give him to me and I'll tell you all you want to know."

"No, Azazel. You tell me everything, and I mean everything, and then you get the body…the man, I mean. This is non-negotiable, and you need to do it before I change my mind."

He seemed to consider. "And Ben and his parents, they know about this? Your father?"

She looked away from the demon, shame passing over her face. "No, they don't, and they're never going to. Part of the deal is that you take that money I gave him and get the hell out of Carthage and never look back. Last chance, Azazel. I'm starting to have second thoughts."

"Fine," he said, folding his non-corporal arms in front of his chest. "You have me at a disadvantage. I agree to the trade."

"Say it three times."

"What?"

"Say 'I give up any claim I have to Shawn Spencer, and I agree to answer all of Katy Ruskin's questions honestly and fully, leaving nothing out, in exchange for Herman Andrews, whose body I'll get after I've answered all of Katy's questions.' Say it three times."

He laughed before repeating her long and cumbersome sentence three times, as instructed. After, he added, "Okay, what do you want to know?"

"Was Michael really involved in your plan to take Ben?"

"Intimately."

Katy's heart sank. Her father so wanted to believe that the archangel wasn't involved in this whole mess. This was going to break his heart, not to mention Shawn's and Jenny's.

"Why did you fuse the two versions of the nickel?" She finally asked.

"We thought we could use them to end the world as you know it, but we were mistaken."

End the world? "Why do you want to end the world?"

"I don't," he said, smiling, "at least not any longer."

"Don't fuck with me, Azazel. Why do your friends want to end the world?"

"I wouldn't call them friends, exactly, more like kin, but they want to end the world as you know it because it's gotten out of control. It wasn't supposed to be this way. Your kind has destroyed the oceans, ruined the lands, and forced countless species into extinction. Soon enough, you'll find some way to destroy yourselves and take the planet with you."

Katy knew he was probably right. Sure, many people were working to stop the needless destruction of the planet's resources, but just when there seemed to be some headway, something would change, and humanity would backslide.

"And you could have prevented this?"

"Of course, we could have prevented this! We were supposed to rule, but we're losing power as fewer and fewer people believe in us."

"In angels and demons, you mean?" She motioned for the old man to sit on the couch, then followed suit. They were going to be here for a while.

"Oh, Katy Ruskin, you still haven't figured it out, have you?"

"Figured what out?"

"It's a long story," Azazel said, as he began to tell his tale.

# Chapter 16

**Almost 4000 years ago**

The Norse demigod Thor floated among the clouds, miles above the surface of the planet. Others of his kind grouped around him, including the Egyptian gods Anubis and Osiris, the Greek deities Aphrodite, Cronos, and Nike, and the Hindu gods Vishnu and Brahma. Huitzilopochtli, the Aztec sun god of war, was also there, along with Venus, the Roman goddess of love, Eshu, the African trickster god, and thousands of others, representing every major and minor religion on Earth.

"I don't see why this is even necessary," said Vishnu, stroking his long, white beard with his fourth hand, in a language they all understood.

"It might not be, for you," said Giltine, the Baltic goddess of death, "but my believers are dying out, and I, for one, want to hear what Odin has to say."

Laima, the goddess of fortune and pregnancy, echoed her sister's sentiment.

Odin, the all-knowing father of the Norse deities, sat astride Sleipnir, his eight-legged horse, in the middle of this gathering of gods. He had called them all here because he knew that change was in the air, and, if they ignored it, their power and influence would suffer.

"Hear me, brothers and sisters, sons and daughters, brethren one and all," he said, straightening the huge, wide-brimmed hat he wore, "I have seen the future, and it is not ours. The Jewish superstitions have taken foothold, and we must adapt if we are to survive."

"I'm tired of following the humans," said Ishtar, the Mesopotamian sky goddess of sex and war, "how much longer will we allow them to run rampant over this world before we reclaim what is rightfully ours?"

Izanagi, the Japanese god of creation, nodded in agreement. "Why must we bend ourselves to appease them?"

"It is what we have always done," Danu, the Celtic mother goddess, interjected. "Their belief feeds us, gives us energy, and makes us stronger. We must go where that energy leads us. We have done it before, and, I imagine, will do it again."

Yen-Lo-Wang, the Chinese deity of death, raised a huge bronze sword in the air. "No more changes. I don't like to remember."

Odin sighed. "None of us do, Yen-Lo-Wang, but this will be the final change."

A murmur went through the crowd.

"At last," shouted Thor, gesturing with his mighty hammer Mjölnir as he spoke. Thunder rumbled in the distance. "But how can this be, All-Father?"

"Can it really be true?" asked Tinia, the king of the Etruscan pantheon.

"I don't want to change," complained Yen-Lo-Wang again.

Some agreed with the Japanese god, while others shouted him down.

"Enough!" bellowed Odin, and silence filled the skies.

"Those who want to retain their identities will not be forced to change," he said, "but if you lose too many believers, you will also lose strength and then be unable to change. You know this, for it is as it has always been. We have lost other kin."

"You said this would be the final change," prodded Zeus, the leader of the Greek gods, who had, up until now, remained quiet.

"Men move on, form new beliefs. We change with them," added Hades, the Greek god of the underworld and Zeus' brother. "How can this be the last iteration?"

More murmurs arose from the crowd, and Odin held up a hand to silence them.

"It's simple," he said. "When we first came here, before humanity arose, we learned of certain things that had been set in motion, certain objects of power hidden around the globe that preceded even us. Do you remember?"

Mama-Quilla, the Incan moon goddess, tilted her head in thought before finally nodding. "So long ago, but I remember."

"I also remember," said Perchta, the Germanic goddess of fertility. "Though even a moment ago, I did not."

"I remember as well," admitted Yen-Lo-Wang, surprise in his eyes. "Though not until you spoke of it."

"But we can't use those talismans," added Manjusri, the Tibetan god of wisdom. "Can we?"

"No, we cannot," said Odin, "But the humans can, and, through them, we will make use of the objects. It will take many millennia of manipulation, an eternity to them, but just the blink of an eye for us."

"And when will we set this in motion?" asked Thor.

"Soon, my son. Patience is paramount. Ahpuc," he said, turning to face the Mayan god of hell, "you will lead one of your priests to the first talisman, which I have already recovered and changed into the tooth of a jaguar. Close your eyes and you will see the location."

Ahpuc closed his eyes. "It is beneath a Monkey Puzzle tree, close to the priest's home."

"Exactly. Lead the priest to that spot, and everything will begin. In a mere four millennia, give or take, we will have the ability to eradicate the humans from this planet and the power of their beliefs will be fully ours. We will no longer need them."

"And then what?" asked Perchta.

More murmurs, this time silenced by a wave of Odin's hand.

"We will start over," Odin said, "and, this time, we'll get it right."

# Chapter 17

Katy couldn't believe it. Angels, demons, all of it. It was all just a scam so that these beings, whatever they were, could gain power from humanity's worship, and eventually destroy them.

"You were the Mayan god Ahpuc?" She finally asked.

"One of my many names, yes. I was Ahpuc, god of death and disaster. Before that, I was Ereshkigal, Sumerian goddess of the underworld, and before that—"

"Wait a minute," Katy interrupted, "you were a goddess?"

Azazel smiled. "Gender is meaningless to us, Katy Ruskin. I became whatever I needed to become."

"What…are you? I mean, really?"

"We are called Vīrya."

"Vīrya?" she asked, doing her best to pronounce the word correctly.

He nodded. "It's from the oldest language in the world, Sanskrit. It essentially means 'energy.' Before language existed, we didn't have a name."

"Where are you from?"

"That's a harder question to answer. We've existed for as long as we can remember, before your kind even crawled out of the oceans and swamps. We were here, formless, shapeless, simply existing and observing. Once your kind developed consciousness, however, we found we could draw sustenance from you, from the beliefs you formed, and so we began to change, to fit those beliefs, to grow more powerful."

"To pretend to be something you weren't."

"Not exactly. When we become one of your gods, we inhabit the role to the fullest. For almost 2,000 years, I truly believed I was Ahpuc, the Mayan god of death. I bestowed favors upon those who worshipped me and punished those who displeased me. But it was the Mayans who gave me the power to do those things. Without them, I had nothing. They created us, and only as their beliefs began to wane would we in turn begin to remember what we truly were."

"What do you really look like?"

"It's been so long that I honestly don't remember, but here's one of the forms I like to use when I wish to terrify your kind."

Azazel changed into a seven-foot-tall *thing*, a bulbous creature covered in yellow, oozing lesions, its face an open maw of needle-sharp teeth that dripped green venom and blood.

"Or sometimes this one."

Now he was a green creature with glowing red eyes and massive wings and tentacles coming out of his face, a perfect representation of Lovecraft's Cthulhu. She wondered whether Lovecraft had inspired Azazel's image, or perhaps Azazel has inspired Lovecraft.

The thing reached for her, and she returned him to his human form with a wave of her hand.

"Enough. You said you weren't able to use the nickel to change the world. What *can* it do?"

"Almost anything you could imagine. Think of the power you feel when you connect to the jaguar's tooth, and then multiply that by a thousand. No, a million. Near limitless power, in the right hands, but it comes with a price."

"And what price might that be?"

"Death, more than likely, at least for a human. If we had been able to use it for what we wanted, Ben Spencer's body more than likely would have been destroyed."

She felt her face flush with anger, but she tamped it down. "Who has the nickel now?"

"Probably Father. I haven't seen it since our experiment failed."

"By father, you mean Odin?"

"Yes."

"Tell me about Odin. He's the most powerful among you, right?"

"Correct, though he's no more Odin than I am Azazel, Eblis, Ahpuc, or any of the other names I've used."

"What does he call himself now?"

"Jehovah. Beelzebub. God. Satan. He's all of them, wrapped up into one. He's the only one of us able to take on several aspects at the same time."

"What's his real name?"

"He's never told me. If we reveal our true names, they can be used against us. As you well know."

"Okay, what do *you* call him? Other than 'father?'"

Azazel said something she couldn't even pronounce.

"Write it down for me, as best you can, in English."

A pad of paper and a pencil appeared in her hand. She gave them to Azazel who scribbled something on the paper. "Atenanunaki."

"Aten-an-unaki?" she asked, sounding it out.

"Close enough. He also goes by Elohim. That one's not quite as old, but it's easier to pronounce."

"Does he control you?"

"No, though perhaps he could if he wanted to. He's our…father, in a sense, though he did not create us. He took on the role of a God before any of us even knew how. He's the most powerful of our brethren, by far."

"Let's go back to the nickel. You said, 'in the right hands, it has near limitless power,' or words to that affect. What does that mean, exactly? 'The right hands?'"

Azazel sighed. "Because I fused the two versions of the nickel while in Ben Spencer's body, using his ability to see into and manipulate alternate realities, only he—or someone using his body—can access its power. It's locked for anyone else. Even my father."

"So, the nickel is essentially useless to anyone but Ben?"

"Not 'essentially,'" Azazel replied, "it *is* useless."

She stared at him. "Could Ben 'un-fuse' the nickel?"

"Probably, but why would he want to? All that power…"

"Power isn't the most important thing."

"Katy Ruskin, power is *everything*."

They sat in silence for a moment or two, Katy trying to digest everything she'd just learned, until finally he spoke.

"Is that all the questions you had?"

"Not by a longshot," she responded, forcing herself to think. "If you're not really a demon, why does the whole 'rule of three' thing work on you? Why did it work on Ben, for that matter, when you took his body?"

"I honestly don't know," Azazel admitted. "Perhaps simply because everyone believes it will. We are all bound by what we believe, are we not?"

"I suppose so. Can you be hurt?"

"We don't exist in the physical world, so how could we be hurt? If we're inhabiting a human body and that body is killed, we simply move out of it. We can, however, be trapped. My being here is proof of that, as is what you did to poor Leonard when you imprisoned him within that green hunk of plastic in 1977. Colin Wainwright figured out that much, as have other humans from time to time."

They had indeed trapped Leonard, who had been part of the murderous fetch, in a green hunk of plastic, a prize from a box of Freakies cereal she'd purchased during their time travel trip to 1977. Even now, the "Boss Moss" toy sat upon the shelf beside Azazel's jar, in a jar of its own.

"You answered my question with a question," she said. "Can you be hurt? Or, to put it more bluntly, can you be killed? Not your host, but you."

Azazel smiled. "No, I don't believe so."

"But you don't know for sure?"

"Many have tried in the past, and thus far no one has succeeded. If used correctly, however, I believe the fused nickel could bind us even without using a spirit room. Doing so, however, would require completely merging with the power it holds. As I said before, it would probably destroy its user."

She dreaded the answer to the next question but made herself ask it anyway. "You took Ben because of his abilities. Is our daughter one of your targets?"

"Has your daughter exhibited abilities?"

"No." She wasn't going to mention Hope's imaginary friend, nor her uncanny sense of predicting lottery numbers.

"Then she's probably safe. That may not always be the case, however."

Katy took a deep breath. She would die before she let anything happen to Hope. Having Ben taken from her was the hardest thing she'd ever gone through, and she imagined losing Hope would be a thousand times worse.

"How many of you are there?" She finally asked.

"That's a hard question to answer. Probably no more than ten thousand."

"Probably? Why don't you know?"

"We haven't all toed the line, as it were. Some refused to change when mankind's beliefs changed and suffered for it. They lost power and fell asleep. Others ignored the summons altogether. Still others merged with humans and lost themselves inside, forgetting who they were. And a few...well, we don't know what happened to them. They went off to explore and got lost."

"Got lost where?"

Azazel shrugged.

"Can you procreate?"

Azazel laughed. "No, Katy Ruskin, we cannot."

"Are there any real gods out there? Does God exist?"

"I have no idea. There is something else, that much we can sense, but we've never been able to contact or communicate with it. It remains as much a mystery to us as we remain a mystery to you, or as much a mystery as you most likely remain to ants."

Azazel turned from her to stare at her companion, who sat unmoving beside her. She concentrated, willing her creation to breathe. She was getting off track and the illusion she'd created was suffering as a result.

"The talismans...did your kind create them?"

He turned back to face her. "No, they've always existed, though not necessarily in the forms they're in now. We believe they were used to create the world and to shape consciousness, or perhaps to bend a world that already existed. We've directed their use before, but we have no idea who or what created them or where they came from."

"'Create the world?' My God..."

Azazel smiled. "Perhaps."

Katy ignored the implication. "If the talismans created the world, can they be used to destroy it?"

"No, at least not in any way we've discovered. What was created is not so easily destroyed, even using the same tools. That's why we fused the nickels."

"Earlier, you said you've 'directed their use'? You can't use them yourselves?"

"Not in our natural state, no. If we take possession of one of you, then yes, we can use the items, but even that can sometimes be problematic. As we've found out with the nickel."

"What were your plans for Ben?"

"His abilities to travel through time are something we lack. We are anchored to the here and now. We thought we could break that barrier by using him, but...we were wrong. I tried, and nearly lost control of his body. We would have tried again, but the attempt almost killed him. After that, things were never the same."

"What do you mean, 'almost killed him?'" Katy felt like she might vomit.

"His heart stopped during the attempt, but we were able to revive him. His ability to see and bend causality in his favor, his 'luck,' as he thinks of it...none of it worked reliably after that. We'd miscalculated, and badly. We'd ruined the vessel. Even his ability to access the fused nickel was lost. All of our manipulations were for naught."

"So, Ben is no longer a target?"

"As far as I know, no, he isn't. When the experiment failed, I left. I isolated myself in the Yukon, as you well know. Not once did Father send anyone after me."

She breathed a sigh of relief. If Ben was no longer a target, and Hope wasn't either, perhaps these demons and angels had finally given up on their mad plan.

"Why did you need to go back in time?"

"We didn't *need* to, Katy Ruskin, we wanted to. As I said earlier, your kind has all but destroyed the planet. We wanted to prevent as much of that destruction as we could."

She couldn't argue with him on that score. Thousands of animals extinct, the oceans polluted, the ozone layer depleted...still, she had hope that humanity would eventually wise up and start taking care of the planet upon which they lived. They may have been poor caretakers, but that didn't mean they deserved to be eradicated from Earth.

"Since they can't use the fused nickel nor go back in time, their plans are finished, right?"

Azazel laughed. "They have more contingencies than you could ever possibly imagine. They will find a way."

"But earlier, you said, 'All our manipulations were for naught.' What did you mean by that?"

He sighed. "A deal is a deal, but you aren't going to like it. Pacal, Colin Wainwright, Shawn Spencer, Jenny McGee, your father…everything was planned, with the result being Ben Spencer and his ability to travel through time and touch all possible realities, neither of which we can do. Even with the power of the five talismans together, we couldn't remake existence the way we needed to. We tried, when we had Pacal."

A feeling of dread settled over Katy. "Why us?"

"Why not you? We did the same with others, but the Spencer family were the first to come to fruition."

"Everything was a lie?"

"Nothing was a lie, Katy Ruskin. You all made choices. It's just that those choices were based on criteria we designed."

Dread turned to anger. "What would have happened had Shawn chosen to keep the talismans united in 1975?"

"We don't know, but what we believe would have happened was that the power would have corrupted him much in the same way that it did Pacal, and that he would have risen to take control of North America. There would have eventually been a thermonuclear war, we believe. The war would have killed off most of humanity and done immeasurable damage to the planet and everything on it, setting back our progress thousands of years. Destroying the world is a misnomer. We never sought to destroy the world, just to reshape it more to our pleasing."

"And yet you did it anyway?" she asked, incredulous. "Why risk it?"

"It was a calculated risk. When you've existed for as long as we have, you learn to calculate the odds. We've rarely been wrong."

"But you were wrong about Ben. What would time travel give you that having all five talismans wouldn't?"

"It wasn't just time travel," admitted Azazel, "but also the fusing of the nickels. That single talisman, as it stands now, is infinitely more powerful than all of the other four talismans combined a thousand-fold. It should not exist. It could not exist, were it not for Ben Spencer's abilities to hold two versions of the same object at the same time. But once I used his body to fuse both versions of the nickel together, it *did* exist, and…" He stopped talking, once again staring at Herman Andrews. "Is he dead? Why isn't he breathing?"

Oh shit! She concentrated again, forcing her creation to breathe, but it was too late.

"This…isn't real, is it? You lied to me. This isn't real."

She waved her hand, and the imaginary old man disappeared. "I'm afraid not, Azazel. Remember, I control the spirit room. I needed information, but I wasn't about to give you someone's life for it."

Katy expected a tirade of curses and threats from the demon, but he surprised her by laughing instead. "You humans never cease to amaze me. That was good, Katy Ruskin. Very good. You played me, and I fell for it. You even got me to give up my right to Shawn Spencer's body. Bravo!"

"You're not angry?"

"Oh, I'm not happy, but I also recognize the irony. One good manipulation deserves another, after all, and I'll eventually get my body, one way or the other. What else do you want to know? I'll answer three more of your questions, for free. I'll be your djinni in a bottle, Katy Ruskin!"

She stared at him. "I don't get it. You're not getting a new body. You want to remake humanity. Why would you help me?"

"You do me a disservice. I did want to remake humanity, until I lived as a human for five years. It was the best five years of my entire existence, and it was gone in an instant. I could eat, I could touch. I could sleep, I could make love. I could dream, I could feel. No, Katy Ruskin, I no longer wish to remake humanity. Instead, I want to help you save it."

# Chapter 18

Sunlight slipped through the blinds that adorned the windows in the bedroom, and Katy glanced at the clock that sat on her bedside table. It was 6:32 in the morning. She'd gotten back from her excursion into the spirit room at just past five but was never able to fall back asleep. She'd learned a lot from Azazel, though still didn't have a clue how to stop Michael and the rest of his pretend pantheon of angels and demons.

She still couldn't believe she'd wasted the first of the last three questions Azazel had promised to answer by asking him why he wanted to help. She'd posed better questions the second and third times around, however, and as a result had gained information she might be able to use to her advantage in the future.

Though Michael had indeed helped orchestrate everything that happened to her and Ben's families, he wasn't the only one manipulating humanity. Nearly all the so-called gods were influencing humans around the globe in their attempt to remake the world, each a contingency plan for all the others.

Elohim, who had also gone by many names throughout history, was the most powerful of Azazel's kind. He was, for all intents and purposes, both God and Satan. The Alpha and the Omega. But how could he take on two roles at once? She had no clue, because she'd run out of questions, and try as she might, she couldn't get anything further out of Azazel.

She thought back to something Azazel said last night, about making love, and her stomach grew sour. Ben tried to tell her, had told her that

Azazel used his body to do all sorts of things, but she wouldn't listen. Had he used Ben's body to have sex? If that was true, she knew it wasn't Ben's fault, but it also left her feeling angry and confused.

Katy jumped as she felt a hand touch her shoulder, but of course it was only Ben. She quelled her anger, bent down, and kissed him softly on the lips. She still hadn't quite wrapped her head around the fact that they had him home again, and that Hope finally had a father. Everything else would work itself out. It had to.

"I had the most awful dream last night," Ben said. "Azazel managed to take control of me again and made me do…things. Awful, Terrible, disgusting things."

"It was just a dream," she said, kissing him a second time. "You're free from Azazel, and he's never going to take you away from us ever again."

"How can you be so sure?"

Truth be told, she wasn't sure. But that wasn't what he needed to hear right now. He also didn't need to hear that she'd just spent an hour talking to Azazel. She'd tell him, and everyone else, later, after she'd processed what she'd learned.

"Because we all worked too hard getting you back to let you go again," she finally said. "And tonight, I'll dreamwalk with you if you want, and if the nightmare happens again, we'll deal with it. Together. You're never going to be alone again."

"I love you, Katherine Grace Ruskin," Ben said, his fingertips tracing her shoulder.

"And I love you, Benjamin Tanner Spencer," she said, looking deep into his eyes, "and I'm so happy to have you back."

"Last night was nice."

"It sure was. Speaking of which, I have something to ask you, and I'm not asking to hurt you, it's just—"

"Shoot," he said, interrupting her.

"When Azazel had control over you, did he make you sleep with other women?"

Ben turned away, and her heart sank. "He used my body to have sex, yes. But he didn't 'make me' do anything, because he didn't need to. He was in control; he did what he wanted. I tried to tell you this last night, before we made love, and…"

"And I wouldn't listen," Katy said, interrupting. "I know it wasn't you, Ben. It was him. He did this. It's just…"

"It feels like a betrayal. I get it."

"I didn't even look at another man while you were gone," she said, an irrational surge of anger causing her to raise her voice. She shifted in the bed, pulling away from him, the closeness they'd just shared all but forgotten.

"You think I wanted him to do those things? Katy, I tried to stop him! I fought him every step of the way, but there was nothing I could do. Nothing. I finally just gave up and tried to go away, but that wouldn't work either."

Katy closed her eyes and took a deep breath. She knew he was telling the truth but couldn't stop picturing him with untold faceless women involved in countless sexual acts.

"How many?" she finally asked, regretting it the instant the question left her lips.

"How many what?"

"How many women, damn it! How many women did you…did he sleep with?"

"I didn't keep count!" he shouted.

"There were that many, huh?"

"Katy!" He reached out to take her hand, but she shrugged it off. "Please. I love you."

"I just need a little time. Okay?"

"Believe me, if I could go back in time and erase it all…" he said, but then trailed off. He stared at her in silence, unblinking.

"What?" She finally asked.

"I don't know. I just remembered something I'd forgotten, but I don't know how I ever could have forgotten it in the first place. It just doesn't make sense."

"What did you remember?"

"Not too long after Azazel took me, he tried to use my body to go back in time. It didn't work, but somehow, I went back in time without him. Or at least I think I did. For just a second or two, I was free of him. Maybe longer. The next thing I knew, I was…rubber-banding back to the present, and then he was in control again."

"What happened after that?"

"Nothing. He never tried time travelling with me again. None of my powers really worked after that."

Azazel had told her that Ben almost died in the experiment, but he never said anything about him actually travelling through time. In fact, he said it didn't work at all. But if Ben hadn't remembered until now, that made sense. If he didn't know what happened, Azazel wouldn't know, either.

"What do you remember? Where did you go?"

"I don't know. I'm not even sure it really happened. Just a second ago, I had a memory of lying in the grass somewhere, finally free. And then the image was gone."

She took his hand. "Listen, Ben. I love you. None of this was your fault, and I'm sorry if I made you feel like it was. These last five years, I've missed you so much. But I had Emily, Mom and Dad, your parents, Mel, and then Hope. As awful as it was for me, I know it was a million times worse for you, because you didn't have anyone."

"At least it's over now," he said, squeezing her hand.

She didn't have the heart to tell him that it wasn't over yet, after all, and it might be only the beginning.

# Chapter 19

The tiger licked the knight's face, rousing him from his slumber. He yawned, stretched, and sat up, ruffling the big cat's head. He didn't need to sleep, not really, but what else was he going to do when not guarding his charge? He'd read every book in the house at least twice, and there was no television. God, what he wouldn't give for a television.

"Hey, kitty," said the knight, "anything interesting happen while I was out?"

The tiger gave a good-natured growl, which the knight took as him saying no, nothing at all happened that was even remotely interesting, but thanks for asking.

The knight snatched last night's reading material, *20,000 Leagues Under the Sea*, from the nightstand beside his bed, and then made his way down the grand staircase at the end of the hall outside his bedroom, the tiger slinking behind him.

They walked down the stairs together, the knight leading and the tiger following, finally winding up in the kitchen. There was a huge pink wedding cake and a roast turkey in a silver pan waiting for them on the little wooden table that stood opposite the stove, as there were many days, though yesterday it had been pepperoni pizza, and the day before tacos.

There wasn't much variety to their meals, but that was okay. Neither the knight nor the tiger needed to eat any more than they needed to sleep, but both did so out of habit and because they enjoyed it.

The knight broke a drumstick off the turkey and then gave the rest of the bird to the tiger, who began tearing into his breakfast. Once they were done, they'd share the cake for dessert.

While the tiger gnawed through the turkey, the knight walked over to the refrigerator and snatched a Coke. The refrigerator always felt a bit incongruous in the old-timey Victorian house, but he wasn't about to complain. He liked his pop cold.

He popped the top on the Coke and drank half of it in one long swig. It tasted wonderful, just the way he remembered it from his childhood. He took a bite from the turkey leg before sitting down at the table. He knew he should enjoy this leisurely breakfast, a calm before the storm he knew was coming, but he felt uncharacteristically ill at ease. Maybe the storm was closer than he realized.

The knight sighed and rose from the table. Sword ready at his belt, he strode over to the window to check on his charge. But all was well, at least for now.

He went back to the kitchen, sat down at the table, and delved back into the adventures of Captain Nemo. This was his third time reading the book, and he really needed to see about restocking the library shelves.

# Chapter 20

Colin sat in the living room of his and Natsumi's tiny apartment, looking up flight information to Quincy, Illinois on his laptop. He had barely been able to contain himself as he drove himself and Natsumi home from university, thoughts flying though his head a mile a minute. He felt like an enormous, stultifying weight had been lifted from his shoulders, a weight he hadn't fully realized was there until this morning.

He had a lot to apologize for, and not only to Ben. He'd run off in the night like a petulant child, not even telling Emily or his parents good-bye. He regretted that almost as much as he regretted the bad blood between him and his twin brother.

Colin had never really admitted it to himself, but a part of him always felt that if he'd been there, if he hadn't left home the way he did, he might have done something to help Ben, to prevent him from being taken. True or not, that guilt had slowly been eating away at him for the last five years, and now it was finally time to make things right.

But it wouldn't be cheap. The least-expensive roundtrip flight he could find was $626. It was doable, just barely, but would leave him dead broke.

"Have you texted anymore to Emily?" Natsumi asked, walking into the living room. She had mail in her hands.

Colin had immediately responded to Emily's text at the restaurant, telling her that he was going to try to get a flight home as soon as he okayed it with school and his boss at the bookstore, but had yet to respond to her follow up texts. He wasn't sure where he was going to get the money for a plane ticket, but he'd think of something. If nothing else, he suspected his father would be happy to foot the bill.

"Not yet," he admitted. "I wanted to get a flight before I wrote anything more, and honestly I just don't know what to say. I've been such a jerk to them, refusing to come home."

"Well, you're going home now."

"Yeah, I guess I am."

"Do you want me to come with you?" asked Natsumi, repeating the same offer she'd made in the restaurant after he'd received Emily's text. "I will, you know."

"You're incredible for offering, but I think this is something I need to do alone," he said. "There'll be other trips, and if you'll take a raincheck, I'd love for you to go with me next time."

"It's a deal," she said, as she began to sort through the mail.

"I probably need to talk to Dad before I book a flight. These are all so damned expensive."

She didn't say anything.

"What's wrong?" Colin asked.

"Oh, nothing," she finally replied. "There's a letter for you, but it's just your name, no address and no stamp. Strange."

"Let me see," he said, taking the letter from her.

It was indeed strange. The envelope contained only his name, written in a swoopy cursive. No address, and no stamp. He opened the envelope, took out a folded piece of paper inside, and that's when everything changed.

# Chapter 21

It was so strange being in this old house again. It looked nothing like it did five years ago, when it had been an apartment building, nor like the version of the house Ben had visited in 1977, when the renovations were just beginning. It would take a while to get used to this third version of the house. In some ways, he felt like a man out of time.

The morning hadn't started out well, with Katy upset with him about the things Azazel had done with his body. He understood her feelings, but it was also frustrating. He'd lost half a decade of his life to Azazel and had hated every second of it. The demon used his body to have sex with at least a dozen women. He hadn't enjoyed it; far from it, it disgusted him.

Ben stood next to the marble pentagram that was inlaid into the floor of the building's third story. He was at once both so close and so far from the creature who had stolen his life. He held in his fist one of the pentacle necklaces that would allow him to teleport into the room that held the door to the spirit room but wasn't sure he wanted to use it.

He wanted to confront Azazel, to scream at him, to ask him why he'd done what he'd done. Even though he was no longer bound to the demon, though, Azazel still terrified him. He'd have to face him sooner or later, he knew, but it didn't have to be today. Hell, it didn't even have to be tomorrow.

He walked away from that confrontation, back down the stairs, past his and Katy's apartment and outside to the balcony. In 1977, the stone balcony was old and falling apart. It had been restored and remodeled, however, several times over. The broken marble railing had been replaced by stainless steel and was higher than it had been during his trip back in time. Safety first.

He gazed out at the giant oak tree that took up most of the view from the balcony. The tree's branches were no longer encroaching on the balcony, like they had in October of 1977, and they looked like they'd recently been trimmed. It was taller than it had been in 1977, of course, but no less beautiful.

Part of him felt like he was trapped in 1977. If they hadn't traveled to the past, Azazel would never have been able to possess him, and he wouldn't have a twin brother. On the other hand, if their time travel trip hadn't taken place, he and Katy probably wouldn't have fallen in love, Hope definitely wouldn't have been born, and several people he loved would be dead, including Katy's father and sister and his grandmother.

If he had to do it all over again, even knowing Azazel would take possession of his body, he'd still go back in time. Katy and Hope were his world now, and he loved them both with every fiber of his being. He had missed out on five years of their lives but planned to more than make it up to them.

Ben left the balcony and headed downstairs, refamiliarizing himself with the building. The downstairs included a large kitchen, an even bigger dining room, a spacious living room, a library filled with books, and a foyer. This was all different than it had been five years ago, when the first floor of the house contained four small, one-bedroom apartments.

He walked through the kitchen and down the steps to the cellar, through which he and Katy had first entered the house that night in 1977, the night he almost shot a homeless drifter named Jeremiah Watson. He sometimes wondered what had happened to the old man after their chance meeting.

1977 was also when he learned the full extent of his powers. After "Reverend" David Dowd cut his hand off with a Samurai sword, Ben lay bleeding and paralyzed on the ground. The 18-year-old version of his father had saved him, however, using the nickel to heal him just enough to allow him to access his abilities.

That was the second time he'd seen the gossamer threads, the visual representation of all the different possible timelines coexisting with our own, but the first time he'd been able to fully interact with them.

He'd been able to touch the threads, to weave them together to create a reality where his missing hand was replaced by an obsidian mechanical hand from an advanced alternate reality, where Dowd's attempt to behead Ben's father was unsuccessful, and where Dowd had never suffered the accident that had left him disfigured both physically and mentally but gifted him with psychic powers.

Ben made sure to leave the man's memories alone, however, wanting him to remember everything he'd done. Had that been a mistake? Dowd had been operating with a mind warped by brain damage, so wasn't fully in control of himself or his actions. Now that Ben had been controlled by Azazel for five years, he had a different perspective and maybe a little more compassion for the self-proclaimed reverend.

He exited the cellar, going outside. The sun was bright in the cerulean blue sky, the grass was a healthy shade of green, and a gentle breeze caressed his skin. It was a beautiful day, something he wasn't sure he would have been able to fully appreciate before he'd lost five years of his life to Azazel.

Ben had taken his time on this planet for granted, not realizing what a gift it was simply to exist and to make his own choices. To walk where he wanted to walk, to eat what he wanted to eat, and to love who he wanted to love.

And that brought him back around to Katy and Hope. They were his family, and he wanted to spend the rest of his life with them. There was no way in hell he was ever going to let anyone separate them, ever again. He walked back into the house, his mind made up, knowing exactly what he wanted to do next.

# Chapter 22

Emily lay in bed inside her little second-floor apartment, listening to music through her earbuds, feeling embarrassed and ashamed. She couldn't believe she'd blurted that out about Colin last night. What was even worse was that, almost the moment they'd gotten Ben home, she'd texted Colin to let him know Ben was alive and safe. She wanted so much to bring her family back together again that she hadn't even thought of what Ben might want. Luckily, Ben ended up wanting to see his brother, but that didn't make her actions any more excusable.

A part of her resented both her brothers for disappearing when she was only 13, causing her to grow up faster than any girl should. In many ways, however, she was still a little girl. She'd only just started dating when Ben was taken, and she'd put having any sort of a love life on hold indefinitely. Not only was she still a virgin, but she'd only once even kissed a boy.

She was eighteen now, however, officially an adult, and she needed to put that resentment in the past. She needed to grow up and start making better decisions. She needed to think more with her head and less with her heart.

Emily's cellphone beeped, interrupting *Games*, a song by Tessa Violet, and she rolled over to snatch it from the bedside table. She looked at the screen. It was a text from Colin. She held her breath and read the message, thumbs moving furiously in reply.

Colin: I'm glad he's back, Em, I really am. I'm ready to put our differences aside and reunite with my brother. I've missed you, Mom, and
Dad so much, and I've missed Ben, too. I think it's finally time to come
home.

Emily: That's fantastic!! When??

Colin: Soon, hopefully. I'm still waiting to hear back from work and
the university about time off.

Emily: Is Sumi coming with you? Please say yes!

Colin: Sorry to disappoint, sis, but she's not. Maybe next time. Besides, I'm not even sure I can afford one plane ticket, let alone two.

Emily: Forget plane tickets, I can come get you.

Colin: What do you mean, come get me?

Emily: Shit! Sorry, but I can teleport. I'm sorry I never told you.

Colin: Teleport?! You got powers, too, huh? Why didn't you ever tell
me?

Emily: It's complicated. I'll explain when I see you in person.

Colin: I'm not so sure about teleporting. I think I'd rather fly.

Emily: You know Dad will pay for it. He'd love to have you home.
Mom, too. We all would! And you'd finally get to meet your niece.

Colin: If I can't pay for it myself, I'll ask him.

Emily: He'd be thrilled to do it, I promise. In fact, I think he's going
to call you today. Do me a favor and don't tell him I told you Ben's
home, okay?

Colin: Sure, but how come?

Emily: He wanted to surprise you.

Colin: If you say so. Okay, I'm gonna go online and check out flights.
I'll text you as soon as I know something.

Emily: You'd better. Love you!

Colin: Love you too, little sis, and I can't wait to see you!

She hated lying to her brother about the reason she didn't want him to tell Dad that he already knew about Ben, but Colin wouldn't understand. No one had ever told him that, according to Katy (and now Ben) he shouldn't exist, and she didn't want to be the one to broach that subject.

Unlike Ben and herself, Colin didn't seem to have any powers, and had always resented Ben because he'd been born first. According to Colin's theory, had he been born first, he would have been the one gifted with the ability to always win at Monopoly and get all A's in school without even trying, not to mention winning the lottery whenever he wanted.

Learning that he might not even exist had it not been for his brother mucking around with the timeline would only make things worse. Sure, he'd find out eventually, but better here where they could talk to him than through texting while he was in Canada.

Emily set the phone aside and rolled out of bed. Soon, she'd have both her brothers home again, and they could all get on with their lives. It was wonderful to have good news for a change.

The little electric doorbell she'd installed in the front door of her apartment rang, startling her. Still in her pajamas, she hurried to the front door and peered out the peephole. It was Ben. She felt herself tense up. Did he somehow know she'd been talking to Colin?

But no. That was a silly thought. Still, she hoped he wasn't mad at her about yesterday, about her once again opening her big mouth. She steeled herself and opened the door.

"Good morning," he said, pulling her into an embrace. "How's my favorite sister?"

"Umm, fine, I guess?" she answered, returning the embrace. He seemed happier than he had last night, which she instantly decided was a very good thing.

"I have a favor to ask, and it just might be the most important favor I've ever asked anyone."

"I'm listening," she said, cocking her head as he explained exactly what this favor entailed.

When he was done, she smiled and said, "You got it, big brother. This is gonna be fun."

# Chapter 23

It was just past one in the afternoon by the time Katy and Ben had finished eating lunch with their daughter, Ben's sister and parents, and Katy's parents in the downstairs dining room. She was about to send Hope off to play with Hercules before explaining all she'd learned early this morning from Azazel, but just as she began to speak, she was interrupted by Ben.

"I want you all to know how incredibly happy I am to be home," Ben said, "and how floored I am that you basically gave up five years of your life for me, and how sorry I am for how I acted yesterday."

"Ben," said Shawn, "you were trapped in your own body by that monster. No one blames you."

Ben waved away the excuse. "I know, but that's not really the point. I'm free now. Free! Free to start living my life again. Free to watch my little girl grow up," he paused to smile at Hope, "and free to ask her mother to be my wife."

Katy stared at Ben, eyes wide, as he stood up out of his chair and dropped to his knee beside her. Was he proposing? He had something in his hand, and he held it out to her. A beautiful princess-cut diamond ring set in white gold, which was her favorite. He was proposing!

"Katy," he said, looking into her eyes, "I've loved you for as long as I can remember. I crushed on you as a kid, dreamed about you as a teenager, and I'm madly in love with you as an adult. We've survived demons, serial killers, time travel, and being apart for five years. We made a beautiful little girl together. You are my life, and now I want to make it official. Katy Ruskin, will you marry me?"

All thoughts of angels and demons fell away as Katy stared into the eyes of the man she loved, her heart pounding and her eyes filling with tears. She knew she should stop this, should tell him and everyone else what she'd learned, but she couldn't. She just couldn't. It would have to wait. Stopping Elohim and Michael was imperative, but this was important, too.

She reached out a trembling hand to touch his, and then whispered, "Yes, Ben. Yes, of course I'll marry you."

The room erupted into spontaneous applause as Ben slipped the ring on Katy's finger. Hope squealed with delight and joined the clapping as Ben rose from the ground to take Katy into his arms. They kissed, and for just a moment it was only her and Ben in the room as all their troubles fell away.

Breathless, she stared into Ben's eyes. "I love you so much, and I'll be proud to call you my husband."

"Mommy and Daddy are getting married!" Hope yelled, and everyone laughed.

"So...who all here knew about this?" Katy asked, eyes moving from person to person.

"Guilty as charged," said her father. "Ben asked your mother and me for your hand in marriage this morning. I always knew I liked him."

"Of course, we said yes," her mother added, smiling.

"I knew! I knew!" yelled Hope.

"Even you, Hope?" asked Katy, sticking her tongue out at her daughter, causing the little girl to giggle.

"Even me!"

"And Emily helped me get the ring," chimed in Ben. "She took me shopping in Chicago this morning. Teleportation comes in handy."

Emily beamed, then ran over and hugged Katy. "Oh my God, oh my God, oh my God!" the younger woman exclaimed. "We're actually going to be sisters."

"We were sisters long before today," Katy said, as she returned Emily's embrace, "but I'll be happy as hell to make it official."

"Well, I for one didn't know," said Jenny, pretend-glaring at Ben, "but I can think of no one I'd rather have as my daughter-in-law than you, Katy."

"I'll second that," Shawn added. "It's about time this family had something to celebrate."

That brought Katy's thoughts back to what she'd learned in the spirit room last night, but she quelled the memory. She would deal with it, she would, but didn't they all deserve a break?

"So, soon-to-be husband," she said, turning to Ben, "when are we doing this? I suspect you already have plans."

He smiled, and she melted. "You know me too well. Emily and I came up with a plan, of sorts. What are you doing the day after tomorrow, and are you up for a trip to Las Vegas?"

# Chapter 24

Cellphone in hand, Shawn paced the length of his and Jenny's apartment, wondering what to say to Colin. He loved all three of his children equally, but they'd just got Ben back and he didn't want to risk losing him all over again.

He thought back to the summer of 1977, when he'd met his eldest son decades before he was born. Ben never mentioned having a twin brother during his and Katy's time-travel excursion, but neither did he mention having a sister, so that didn't really prove anything.

Ben and Katy claimed that Colin was somehow a result of them going back in time. Even if that was true, so what? Colin was every bit as alive as Ben, even if Ben didn't remember his brother.

Shawn sighed. All this pondering was getting him nowhere. He took a deep breath and hit Colin's number on his contact list.

"Hey, Dad," Colin answered on the second ring. "What's up?"

He suddenly didn't know what to say.

"Dad? Are you there?"

"Colin," he finally said, "your brother's home."

"Yeah, Emily told me yesterday."

Shawn sighed. Of course, she did. He knew he should be upset with her, but in a way, he was relieved Colin already knew.

"Did she also tell that Ben and Katy are getting married in Las Vegas?"

"What? No, she didn't. That's amazing! Hope must be thrilled."

Though he'd never met Hope or even seen Katy in over five years, Colin knew all about Ben's future wife and the child his twin had fathered. It gave Shawn no small amount of hope that Colin seemed excited about Ben and Katy getting married.

"Yes, she's so excited, and I was hoping you might come home after the wedding. I—"

"After?" Colin asked, cutting him off. "When is the wedding?"

"Sunday, in Las Vegas. Things move fast around here. I'd love for you to be there, but it's short notice and honestly, I just thought it might be better to wait. You and your brother have a lot to talk about."

"No, that makes sense, Dad, and I do want to come home. It's been way too long."

Shawn felt tears well up in his eyes at the thought of finally having both his boys home. He shook his head. There'd be time cry later, once he had all three of his children safe and together.

"So maybe in a week?" he finally asked.

"I want to. I need to see if I can get time off, permission from university, and then there's the matter of the plane fare," Colin said over the cell phone connection. "I've already checked, and flights aren't cheap."

"I'll take care of the flight, Colin. It'll be my pleasure. And before you argue, I'm not going to take no for an answer. Let me do this for you. For you, for Ben, for Emily, for your mother, for all of us."

No one spoke for a second or two, until finally Shawn heard Colin sigh and then say: "Okay, Dad, I'll allow it, but just this once."

They both laughed. Colin had always been fiercely independent, and the fact that he was letting Shawn buy the plane ticket without a big argument was huge.

"It'll be so great to have you home. And I'm more than happy to get Natsumi a ticket as well. We'd love to see her again."

"Just me this time, Dad, but Sumi definitely wants to come next time. And there will be a next time, I promise. As for this time, how about next Wednesday? That'll give me time to square things away, and Ben and Katy time to enjoy their wedding."

"I'll make the reservation now and email you the confirmation. I'll make sure the return flight is open-ended, so you can leave whenever you want. It'll be so great to have you home, Colin. Your mother will be over the moon."

"I can't wait to see Ben. We have a lot to talk about."

# Chapter 25

The day passed quickly as they made plans for the wedding, and that night, Katy dreamwalked.

Katy had been able to enter other people's dreams ever since she hit puberty at age 11. That was her ability, passed down to her through her father's magically enhanced genes. She was tied into the spirt room on some level even she didn't understand and could visit it in her dreams and from there enter the dreams of almost anyone she'd ever met.

The room hadn't changed since she'd had her conversation with Azazel last night, though why she thought it might she hadn't a clue. It made her nervous having Azazel in her imaginary little cabin in the woods, even if he was currently secure inside the mason jar where she'd left him.

Katy's cabin was decorated with masterpieces of art from all around the world, art that, in real life, was in museums and private collections of the very wealthy. She changed the artwork often and thought she might again sometime soon.

There, on a pedestal against the south wall, was a bust of the Egyptian goddess Nefertiti from 1345 BC. Beside it stood Gian Lorenzo Bernini's *Ecstasy of Saint Teresa,* and to the left Marcel Duchamp's *Bicycle Wheel.*

The opposite wall held four very special paintings: Georges Suerat's *A Sunday Afternoon on the Island of La Grande Jatte,* Vincent Van Gogh's *Café Terrace at Night,* Claude Monet's *Water Lillies,* and Johannes Vermeer's *Girl with a Pearl Earring.*

Katy had been pursuing her master's degree in art history when Aza-zel, posing as Michael, had entered their lives and coerced them into going back in time in a successful effort to gain possession of Ben's body and steal the nickel. She'd never finished her degree, having instead de-voted her time to raising her daughter and trying to rescue Ben, but she still loved art.

Sitting down on the large, overstuffed leather couch that took up nearly a third of the living room, she picked up the remote control for the 72" flat screen television opposite the couch and thumbed the power button. The screen instantly filled with a scene of a snowy forest. Her "dream screensaver," of sorts.

She pressed the button on the remote with Melissa Fleming's face on it and Mel appeared on the screen, supplanting the snow-covered woods. Mel was dreaming about high school again, as she often did. She was barefoot and clad only in her bra and panties and kept trying to cover herself up with books. Students filled the hallway, but no one seemed to notice.

She and Mel had been best friends ever since their first year in college together, and she wanted nothing more than to have her best friend at her side the day she got married. She'd tried to call Mel just an hour after Ben proposed, but it went straight to voice mail. Her texts and PMs had also gone unanswered. This was the surest way to contact her, and so Katy thought about the school, disappeared from the couch, and ap-peared beside the startled woman.

"Katy? Am I dreaming?"

"Guessed it in one, dude," Katy said, smiling.

"A little help here, please?"

"Oh, right." Katy waved her hand and a cute floral print dress sud-denly covered Mel. "Better?"

"Much," Mel said, throwing herself at Katy.

Katy returned the embrace, and then asked, "Why didn't you call me back? Or answer my texts?"

"Broke my phone earlier tonight," Mel said, disengaging from the hug. "Dropped it in the toilet. Smooth, huh?"

"Super smooth. But why didn't you answer my PMs? Did you drop Facebook in the toilet, too?"

"Some days I wish. But no. Shane and I were out late with some friends, and I never got around to logging into my laptop once we got home. Why? What's up?"

Katy peered around the high school, stepping back as a hurrying student nearly collided into her.

"First, let's get you out of her. Wanna come to the cabin?"

"Always," Mel said.

Katy took Mel's hand, thought about her little imaginary cabin in the woods, and then they were there. She led Mel over to the couch and the two sat down. She summoned up a couple of mugs of hot chocolate, handing one over to Mel.

"This is the best, you know," Mel said, after taking a sip. "You can eat and drink all you want here and never gain a pound."

"It's one of my favorite parts," agreed Katy.

"Well? This must be important, with all the phone calls and texts I've yet to see. The suspense is killing me. What's up?"

"Ben's back."

"Oh my God! Seriously? When? How? I'm so happy for you, Katy! Does he know about Hope yet?"

"Yesterday," Katy admitted, "I meant to call you then, but I got…sidetracked."

"Oh, I bet you did," said Mel. "How many times did you get 'sidetracked'?"

"Three," Katy said. If she could have blushed in her dream world, she'd be bright red. "But I didn't dreamwalk to brag about my suddenly hot and heavy love life."

"Oh, yes, you did!"

"Okay, maybe a little. Oh, and he knows about Hope and loves her to pieces. She was so happy! She absolutely adores him."

"I bet. Wow. Ben's a daddy!"

"As to the how, it's long and involved, but suffice it to say that he's no longer demon infested. In fact, the demon is trapped right over there."

She pointed to the Mason jar on the shelf, the one that stood next to a similar jar that held the green 'Boss Moss' figure that trapped Leonard.

"Seriously? He can't get out?"

"Nope, he can't get out. And he's not *really* here, anyway. We're just in a facsimile of the spirit room of sorts, one that exists only in my head."

"You know this is über-confusing, right?"

Katy laughed. "I guess it doesn't really matter. Bottom line is, we're safe. Azazel can't get out, unless I let him out."

Mel stared at her, smiling.

"What? Do I have spinach on my teeth or something?"

"So, when's the date?"

Katy stared at her. "Am I really that obvious?"

"Girl, look at what you're wearing."

Katy looked down. She was wearing a long, flowing wedding dress, subconsciously weaved from the stuff of dreams. She shook her head and instantly changed into a blue top with a black skirt.

"Aww. I liked it!"

"You'll get to see the real dress if you come to the wedding."

"When is it?"

"That's the thing," Katy said, biting her lip. "It's incredibly short notice."

"How short a notice?"

"It's...Sunday, Mel. I'm getting married tomorrow."

"Sunday? Way to give a girl a heart attack! There's no way I can drive to Carthage in time, or get a dress, or anything."

"Well, first of all, I already have a dress for you. Second of all, it's not in Carthage. It's in Las Vegas, and—"

"Las Vegas? That's, what, a million miles away?"

"You didn't let me finish," said Katy, with a grin. "Remember Emily?"

"Ben's little sister? Sure."

"She can teleport."

Mel's eyes went wide. "Why does no one ever tell me these things? And why does everyone on Earth seem to have supernatural powers except for me?"

"We didn't tell anyone, and I don't know. She was instrumental in the plan to rescue Ben, and we had to keep it a secret."

"You didn't trust me? Your best friend?"

"It wasn't like that," Katy explained. "We just couldn't, and..."

"I know, I know. I'm just busting your balls."

"Bitch," Katy said, laughing. "Claire helped, too, you know. Without your big sister, we'd still be looking for Ben. We owe her big time."

"I knew she was working on a 'project' with you guys. She wouldn't say what, though."

"Well, now you know."

"Now I know," Mel repeated. "So, what time is Emily picking me up?"

"You're coming?"

"Of course, I'm coming! You think I'm letting my bestie get married without me? No way! Shane won't be able to, though. He has a show in Ft. Worth Sunday afternoon."

Shane Sullivan, Mel's boyfriend, was a professional wrestler. He and Mel had met when Mel did a story for the Dallas Morning News on pro wrestling a few years back and had been dating ever since. Katy thought it was weird at first, Mel dating a wrestler, but the two seemed to really love each other and had made it work. She was sorry he wouldn't be able to make it for the wedding and expressed as much.

"Oh, it's okay," Mel said. "It'll still be fun! Where are you getting married?"

"The Luxor hotel."

"That big pyramid?"

"That big pyramid."

"Very cool! How did you arrange that, with such short notice? Oh, I forgot who I'm talking to. Mr. Lucky, right?"

Katy had also wondered about that. It had been awfully lucky that someone had cancelled right before Ben called them, leaving an open spot. Normally, the wedding chapel was reserved weeks if not months in advance. Ben's powers didn't work anymore, so it was probably just a coincidence, but it did give her pause.

"So…will you be my maid of honor?" Katy finally asked, getting the topic off Ben. "If you don't mind."

"Mind? I'd be pissed if you didn't ask."

"I know this. So?"

"So? Duh! Of course, I'll be your maid of honor, silly girl!"

"Yay! The wedding is going to be small, obviously, but it'll be so cool to have you there. I can't wait!"

"I can't wait to see you. And Ben! It'll be so great to see Ben! He's…24 now, right? You cradle robber, you!"

Katy grinned. She never planned on marrying a younger man (or even getting married in the first place) but you couldn't help who you fell in love with.

The two talked for a few more minutes, making plans, and then it was time for Mel to get some real sleep. She hugged Mel one last time.

"It'll be so great to see you," she said, before sending Mel back to her own dreams, taking a breath, and switching the channel on her dream television.

She had one more stop to make tonight before allowing herself to drift off to sleep, and this one probably wasn't going to be nearly as easy.

# Chapter 26

Ben lay in darkness, unable to move. He could hear voices around him as well as sense movement, though both were somehow muted. Something pinned his arms to his sides, holding him down. Was he on a bed?

And then he realized his body wasn't immobile, after all; he just wasn't the one controlling it. He opened his eyes, and a young blonde woman stared down at him, her lips parted, her piercing blue eyes fixed on his own.

"This feels so good," she whispered, closing her eyes, as she rocked her hips back and forth against his own.

"It's amazing," he heard himself say. "Humans take so much for granted."

But it wasn't him talking, not really. It was his lips forming the words, his voice, but he wasn't in control. The demon Azazel possessed his body, and no matter how hard Ben fought back, he couldn't do a thing to stop him.

*Let me go!* Ben screamed in his mind, willing his arms to push this woman off him, to get up and run from the room as fast and as far away as he possibly could, but his limbs wouldn't obey him.

*Sit back and enjoy it, Bennie-boy,* a voice whispered back in his head, *and shut the fuck up.*

He felt his right hand, the one that had been replaced be a mechanical hand from an alternate universe, run down the woman's back, and then both his hands were grabbing her hips, pulling her down hard against him, emitting a squeal of pleasure from her as he thrust his hips up to meet hers.

*Please,* he pleaded, begging the demon, *kill me or let me go.*

Azazel ignored him, continuing to have sex with the blonde. Ben felt his hands cup her breasts, squeezing them, as the woman atop him moved faster.

*I don't want to do this!* Ben shouted in his mind, but nothing changed. He wasn't in control of his body, and never would be again. Katy, Hope, his parents, Em…he'd never see them again. He was, for all intents and purposes, dead.

He closed his eyes, the eyes in his mind, and tried in vain to block everything out, to ignore the unwanted sensations, to fall deeper into the darkness that every day, every hour, every second since Azazel stole his body threatened to consume his soul.

He wanted nothing more than to cease to exist.

\*\*\*

Yawning, Katy thought back to her conversation with Azazel. Neither Ben nor Hope appeared to be on Elohim's radar, so everyone was safe, at least for now. She felt guilty for not telling Ben about her conversation with the demon, but in the end, she didn't think it would matter.

They needed to stop the faux angels and demons, to be sure, but she didn't even know how to begin going about that, and she didn't think a few days would matter one way or the other. At least, that was her hope.

Pushing away her guilt for now, Katy flipped the imaginary television in her equally imaginary cabin in the woods to Ben and immediately felt sick to her stomach. Ben was having sex with some blonde woman. She was riding him, and he was massaging her breasts, fondling her nipples until they looked rock hard.

"What in the actual fuck?" she said out loud, suddenly awake.

She felt tears threatening to flow from her eyes but took a deep breath and managed to keep from crying, at least for now. She thought back five years ago, just before their trip to 1977, when Katy had dreamwalked into Ben's dream and found him having sex with a dream version of herself.

"This feels so good," Ben's lover moaned, moving up and down on top of him.

*You can't control your dreams*, he'd said, or words to that effect, and that was true. But Jesus, they'd made love three times since he'd returned home, and he'd just asked her to marry him. If he was going to dream about sex, why weren't his dreams about her?

Fuming, she was about to switch off the imaginary television, her entryway into the dream world of others, and just go to sleep when she heard Ben say, "It's amazing. Humans take so much for granted."

That wasn't Ben.

Katy phased into Ben's dream and immediately took stock of her surroundings. She stood in a large room, entirely empty save for a small bed in the middle. The room was covered in shadows and there was no light, though she could see the bed and its occupants clearly. The floor was concrete, as were the walls. It looked like the most miserable, depressing place Katy had ever seen.

"Okay, bitch," she said, walking over to the bed, "get off my soon-to-be husband."

The woman immediately vanished, as did the bed. Ben stood there in that dark void, dressed only in a pair of blue boxer shorts, looking confused and afraid.

"Katy?" he asked. "Is that really you? How did you find me?"

"Honey," she said, taking his hand, "it's really me, and you're dreaming. Let's get you out of here, okay?"

"This is a dream?"

One moment they were in the void, and the next they were standing in her little imaginary cabin in the woods, the place they had first made love. Of course, they weren't *really* in the spirit room, just her mind's recreation of the spirit room.

She led Ben over to the couch and pulled him down beside her, their knees touching. He wouldn't look at her.

"I'm…sorry you had to see that," he whispered.

"It's okay, Ben," she said, taking his face in her hands and forcing him to meet her gaze. "Azazel was controlling you, wasn't he?"

He nodded. "It was Azazel, and the woman was one of his demons, I think. I tried to fight him, screamed at him to stop, and he just taunted me. I'm so sorry."

Katy felt like an ass for their argument yesterday morning. None of this was his fault. Ben was a victim and didn't deserve her anger; instead, he deserved her love and support.

"None of this was your fault," she finally said, squeezing his hands.

"When I realized I couldn't stop him from using my body to do…things I didn't want to do," he continued, "I just sealed myself off as best I could, but he'd yank me right out of whatever hiding space I'd found in my mind and make me watch."

"That son of a bitch."

"All of that stuff pretty much happened during the first year or so. After that, thank God, he mostly left me alone inside my brain. I think that's why I didn't realize five years had passed. I was huddled down somewhere deep in my mind, buried in darkness, just trying to disappear."

Her heart broke for him. "Ben, I'm so sorry about yesterday. I didn't understand, but now I do. None of this, absolutely none of it, is your fault. Repeat, it is not your fault. It was all Azazel. Every single thing he used your body to do is on him, not on you."

"In my head, I know you're right," he said, "but in my heart, I still feel guilty. I feel disgusted with myself. Not just for the sex and the other things he did, but for losing my body to him to begin with."

Katy pulled him close, wrapping her arms around him, and he began to cry. Finally, she allowed her own tears to flow, but this time not from anger or jealousy but with compassion for the incredible pain these parasites had caused the man she loved.

She once again second guessed her decision to keep what she'd learned from Azazel to herself but was sure it could wait a couple days longer. They deserved a brief respite from worrying about demons, didn't they, as well as a chance at the happiness they were so long denied?

Katy decided then and there that she would do everything she could to kill every last one of them, these false angels and demons. And if she truly couldn't kill them without sacrificing herself in the process, she'd trap them in 10,000 mason jars and bury them deep in the yard behind her imaginary cabin.

"I promise you," she finally said, "nothing like this will ever happen to you again. You're safe. You're home."

"I've had dreams about him every night since I've been back," said Ben. "I tried to tell you yesterday. They just won't stop, and I don't know how to make them stop."

"Oh, they'll stop," she said, already formulating a plan, "and no demon or angel will ever take advantage of you ever again."

# Chapter 27

Hope's bedroom always brought joy to Emily. The posters depicting characters from *Sesame Street*, *Dinosaur Train*, *Word Girl*, and other shows Hope liked reminded her of her own childhood, while the huge Victorian dollhouse was fun and simply amazing.

Emily walked into Hope's bedroom with a present for her and found her and Katy playing with the dollhouse while Hercules slept in the sunshine coming in from the window. She stood there for just a moment, watching them, a mother and daughter together. Perfect. She absolutely loved having a niece and was bound and determined to spoil the little girl rotten if she could.

"Hey, dude," said Katy, when she finally looked up. "What's up?"

She hid the present behind her back. For months she'd been ordering 1:12 scale dollhouse furniture and other accessories off eBay and Wish, because she loved helping Hope fill the rooms in her dollhouse.

"Auntie Em!" yelled Hope, running over to hug Emily.

"I thought I might play with Hope for a while, if that's okay with you," she said, hugging Hope.

Last week Hope had mentioned something about wanting a television for the living room of the dollhouse, so Emily bought one on eBay and it finally showed up in the mail today. It wouldn't exactly go with the Victorian design of the house, but so what? Neither did the refrigerator, or the dolls living in the dwelling, for that matter.

"Sure thing," Katy said, standing up. "What's behind your back?"

"I got my precocious little niece a present," said Emily, revealing a pink and gold gift bag.

"You really don't have to keep doing that," Katy said. "She has enough toys to last a lifetime."

"I do not!" said Hope, and both women laughed.

"Anyway, I can watch her for a while, if you have anything you need to do." Emily said, tilting her head at Hope. "I've been wanting some dollhouse time anyway."

"Are you sure? I do need to go get my make-up sorted for the wedding. Your mom promised to help me with that."

"I'm absolutely, 100% sure," Emily said, grinning. "Go, go, go."

Katy kissed her daughter on the forehead, gave Emily a quick hug, then headed off to find Jenny.

"What's in the bag, Auntie Em?" asked Hope, looking up at her with her big, green eyes, and Emily thought she might melt.

"A surprise for your dollhouse. Want to open it?"

"Yes, please."

Hope snatched the bag from Emily and reached inside to pull out the miniature widescreen television, complete with an appropriately sized remote control, in a plastic baggie. The little girl's eyes grew wide when she saw the television, and Emily knew she had done good.

"Oh, thank you," Hope said. "Thank you, thank you!"

She flung her arms around Emily's neck and hugged her tight, and Emily returned the hug in kind. "I love you, kiddo," she said, into Hope's ear, "so, so, so, so much."

"I love you that much too, Auntie Em. They're going to be so excited!"

Emily felt a chill go up her spine. "Who's 'they'? Your imaginary friend?"

Hope bit her lip, looking like she'd revealed too much. "Just my dolls," she finally said, ripping open the plastic bag.

They had been quizzing her about her imaginary friend for months but never made any headway. Emily researched the concept via Google and had found an article from The Atlantic about a 2004 study that said, by age 7, 65% of all children would have had an imaginary friend.

If they were a normal family, she wouldn't have thought anything of it. Hope's imaginary friend, however, gave her information she couldn't possibly know, such as winning lottery numbers and when Ben would finally return home.

Perhaps Hope had the power to see into the future, and the "imaginary friend" was her way of coping with the things she saw. The only hole in that theory was that she, Katy, and Ben had all discovered their abilities around puberty, not as toddlers.

"There!" announced Hope, as she sat the television on a little wooden table in the living room of the dollhouse.

"That's the perfect spot," Emily said. "Now, Hope, did your imaginary friend ask for the television?"

"No, she didn't."

"But she still talks to you, right?"

Hope looked at the floor before finally speaking. "She still talks to me. Is that okay? I know you and Mommy don't like her."

She pulled Hope into another hug. "Oh, sweetie. Of course, it's okay. And we don't dislike your friend, we don't even know her and we're just curious about her. We'd love to know her name."

"You already do," said Hope cryptically, then went back to playing with the dollhouse.

This was progress. At least she finally knew Hope's imaginary friend was female, which is more than she knew 5 minutes ago. But how did they "already know" her name?

Emily helped Hope rearrange one of the many bedrooms in the doll-house, adding lacy white curtains she'd also purchased from eBay a couple of weeks ago to the window, and two plastic bedside tables on both sides of the little bed.

Emily's phone beeped, and she jumped, earning a giggle from Hope. It was a Facebook message. She hoped it was from Sumi, who she'd been trying to reach for the last two days without success.

The message, however, was from Sabrina, confirming that she and Ferris would happily travel "Emily style" to Las Vegas on Sunday for Ben and Katy's wedding. She responded with a smiley face, then sent Sumi yet another message before delving back into the dollhouse with Hope.

# Chapter 28

Ben fell asleep exhausted but happy that night, looking forward to his and Katy's wedding on Sunday. Once again, like almost every night since he'd been rescued, he dreamed…

Ben and Katy appeared in a burst of light in the middle of the garage of his parent's home in Chicago. Azazel was there waiting for them, in the guise of the angel Michael, but they were ready. Ben immediately began the spell that Jenny had prepared during their time travel trip to 1977, and Katy leveled the gun at the demon's chest.

"*Redimio vox Eblis!*" he shouted, as she pulled the trigger in an explosion of noise and gunpowder.

Her aim was true; a small hole appeared in his chest, and he staggered back against the wall, his face turning white. And then he began to laugh, a long, maniacal laugh that echoed through the garage.

"Oh, that was good!" he said, smiling. "You've far smarter than I gave you credit for. Your father would be proud."

"*Redimio vox Eblis!*" he repeated, gripping the nickel tight in his fist. "*Redimio vox Eblis!*" Why wasn't this working?

"The rule of three only works," said Azazel, as the blood drained from his face, "if the wizard knows the subject's true name, which you do not. In any event, you cannot bind someone when you yourself have already been bound."

"But he's *not* bound," Katy argued. "We removed the last part of the incantation. He never said it a third time!"

"What do you want?" asked Ben, putting himself between Katy and the demon. "The nickel? Here, take it." He held the coin out to Azazel, who backed away.

"Ben," Azazel said, "keep the nickel, and please take my hand." He held his hand out towards Ben.

He felt his body moving despite himself. His heart pounding wildly in his chest, he could do nothing as he watched himself reach out to clasp the demon's hand.

"Oh my God," he said, thinking back to the cabin. He had read aloud the words Jenny had translated into English even if he hadn't been casting the spell. He'd bound himself to Azazel without realizing it.

"That's right," the demon whispered. "You said the words. You're mine now, Ben Spencer. I'm sure we're going to have a grand old time together."

And then Azazel was falling to the ground, his legs crumpling under his own weight. The trench coat flopped open to reveal a University of Chicago sweater. He took one final, shuddering breath, and then Tom Logan, the body Azazel had stolen in order to play the role of Michael, lay still.

Time seemed to slow, and Ben watched as a shadowy form stepped out of Logan's body and slowly moved towards him.

"That's about enough of that," said Katy, stepping between him and the demon.

This wasn't how it happened, was it? Ben stared at Katy, confused. She no longer looked like the woman he'd gone back in time with. Her hair was longer, and she seemed more confident of herself, and maybe a little older, too.

"Ben," she continued, "Repeat these words after me: '*Daemonium, et abierunt.*'"

"What? I don't understand what's going on. Why is he…just frozen like that?" He asked, gesturing to the shadowy form, which was hovering just a foot or so from Katy.

"Say the words three times, and then I'll explain everything. '*Daemonium, et abierunt.*' Do it for me, Ben. Do it now."

"*Daemonium, et abierunt,*" he said, "*Daemonium, et abierunt. Daemonium, et abierunt.*"

The demon vanished, and they stood alone in the garage.

Katy reached out to touch his cheek, and he kissed her hand. A glowing blue aura appeared suddenly around him, shimmered, and was gone.

"I'm dreaming again, aren't I?"

"You are," she said. "I had to see exactly how one of the dreams started before I could help you. What I've done is place a protective aura around you that should keep the dreams away. However, if you *do* have them again, all you'll need to do is say those three words three times and he won't be able to hurt you."

"Are you sure?"

"Positive, dude."

"I love you," said Ben, and she smiled.

"Not those words, silly, though I do love hearing them."

"But what if I don't remember the words?" Ben asked.

"You will. You'll never forget them."

"How do you know I won't forget them?"

"Because I said so. They're a part of you now, Ben. The phrase will make Azazel disappear, and your dreams will be your own again."

"Speaking of which, can you get us out of this garage?" he asked.

"Gladly." She snapped her fingers, and they were in her little dream cabin, standing beside the imaginary bed where they'd first made love, where Hope had been conceived.

The room was darkened, lit only by candles, and the covers had been pulled back. Katy was wearing a beautiful blue negligee trimmed in lace.

"Why, Miss Ruskin, are you planning to seduce me?" Ben asked, smiling.

"Why yes, doofus, I am," she replied, taking him by the hand and leading him to the bed. "Do you have a problem with that?"

"Absolutely none whatsoever," he said, as they fell into each other's arms.

# Chapter 29

Katy lay in bed, snuggled close to Ben. They were back in the real world now, having exhausted themselves in their shared dream. She smiled, remembering everything they'd just done.

She hoped the words she'd given Ben, which were just "demon, be gone" in Latin, would help. She thought they would. Likewise, the blue aura, which was just an impromptu light effect she'd come up with to make everything seem more official. She hated being anything less than 100% honest with Ben, but this was truly for his own good.

Azazel had told her that the "rule of three" worked because everyone thought it would work, so why not this? If Ben really and truly believed saying the Latin phrase *"Daemonium, et abierunt"* would protect him from the demon in his dreams, then it should work.

His demon wasn't real, of course, and was more than likely post-traumatic stress disorder haunting his dreams. Real, honest-to-goodness therapy was probably in order, but sadly there just wasn't time for that right now. Also, what therapist would believe his abduction and imprisonment actually happened?

She looked at Ben, sound asleep, and was overwhelmed by the love she felt for him. She'd never given up hope of getting him back from Azazel, not even when lead after frustrating lead ended in disappointment. And now here he was, sleeping next to her, and tomorrow they'd be married.

Once they were married, she promised herself, she'd tell him, tell everybody, about Azazel and everything he'd said. But that was then, and this was now, and she really wanted to live in the moment. She smiled to herself as she imagined getting married on Sunday in Las Vegas, and then drifted off to sleep.

# Chapter 30

The one major drawback to Emily's power was that she had to have physically visited a place (or at least seen the place from a distance, like the top of a hill) first to be able to teleport there later. Fortunately, she had been to Nevada once, and once was enough for her powers to work.

Unfortunately, the only time she'd been there had been during a layover on a trip with her mother from Chicago to San Diego. She was just 11 at the time, before her powers kicked in, and the only place they'd had time to visit in the 45-minute layover was a fast-food restaurant and the restroom.

Which is how she found herself with her brother in the women's restroom on a Saturday morning in the McCarran International Airport in Paradise, Nevada, which, according to Google Maps, was just about five minutes south of Las Vegas. They'd received several confused stares when walking out of the bathroom, but beyond that everything had gone smoothly.

"I miss having abilities," said Ben as they walked through the airport, heading toward the rental cars. "I know that sounds bad. I mean, I should just be grateful to be free of Azazel, and I am, but...what if I lose my title as King of Monopoly?"

Emily punched him in the arm. Growing up, he'd won every game of Monopoly they'd played, because his ability to subconsciously bend causality in his favor almost always guaranteed he'd get the best possible dice rolls and draw the most lucrative Chance and Community Chest cards. Emily had been resigned to it early on, but Colin complained every single time.

"Guess you'd better not gamble while we're here, then," she said, which earned her a begrudging laugh.

She thought back to the Yukon, when she'd tried to teleport Ben to the entrance of the spirit room and instead wound up on the ground. If his powers weren't working, how did that happen? She voiced her question, and he raised an eyebrow.

"I hadn't really thought about that, but you're right. Do you have any change on you?"

She reached into her purse and came up with a handful of quarters, nickels, dimes, and pennies. She held her hand out, palm up, and Ben snatched a quarter from the pile.

He flipped the quarter, called it heads in mid-air, slapped it on the back of his hand, and it was indeed heads. He flipped it again, once more calling heads, and it was heads again. The third flip, however, ended up being tails. He did the experiment a few more times and sometimes got it right and sometimes wrong, all within the margin of chance.

He looked at her, shrugged, and handed back the coin. In the past, the quarter would have come up heads (or tails, if he'd called tails) every single time. His powers really did seem to be gone.

"So much for that," he said, as they resumed their walk through the airport.

They'd had a busy two days. Yesterday morning, they'd gone to the DMV in Carthage to renew his Illinois driver's license, which had expired while he'd been gone. After that, she'd helped Ben go through five years' worth of unopened mail, searching for new versions of his bank debit card and two credit cards, all of which had expired while he'd been controlled by Azazel.

Once he had his cards in hand and activated, she'd teleported him to Chicago. They'd visited three jewelry stores before Ben had found the perfect engagement ring, having already purchased white gold wedding bands at the first store.

She'd heard from Colin via Facebook Messenger later that afternoon that Dad had called him and booked a flight for him. Her other brother would be home Wednesday, which was just three days from now. She'd thought about asking Ben to hold off on the wedding until then, but in the end, had decided not to even bring it up.

Ben still insisted that he wanted to see his brother but didn't want him at the wedding. The thought made Emily sad, but in the end, it was Ben's decision.

Yesterday, she'd teleported her mother and Katy to Chicago to go wedding dress shopping. In the end, this would be a quickie wedding, but Katy still wanted to find the perfect dress for the occasion. The dress she'd ended up purchasing had been amazing, and Emily was sure it was going to knock Ben's socks off.

"Wow, it's hot out here," said Ben, as they walked to their rental car from Enterprise, bringing her thoughts back to the present.

"It sure is," she said.

Emily decided she liked the dry heat of Las Vegas. It was a nice break from the humid weather they were having in Illinois, and she said as much.

"Anything is better than being trapped inside your own body in the Yukon," Ben agreed.

She thought about that, and how awful it must have been for him to have had five years of his life stolen. She reached out to squeeze his shoulder and he looked back, startled, and smiled.

"This is weird for me, Emily," Ben said, as they finally climbed into their little Nissan Versa rental and set off for the Luxor hotel. "You were 13 when I left, and now you're 18, almost 19. You're all grown up. You're an adult."

"I don't feel like an adult," she admitted.

"You're no longer my bratty little sister, that's for sure."

"I don't know about that. I felt like shit when I blurted that out about Colin yesterday. I wasn't even thinking. I get that you don't remember him, or that he didn't exist in the original timeline, or whatever, but for me—"

"For you," he said, interrupting, "he's real. I get it, and I'm not mad. It just takes some getting used to. Hell, I wish Dad hadn't even told him about Katy and I getting married."

"He didn't invite him, Ben."

"And thank goodness for that. What if—"

"You're worried he's part of some nefarious, demonic plot," she said, interrupting him this time.

"Well, yeah."

"He isn't. He's real, and he's my brother, sure as you are. You guys are twins. He's a good man, Ben, I promise, even if you two didn't always get along."

"We *never* got along because he didn't exist," Ben said, "at least not for me."

"Can you just give him a chance? For *me?*"

Ben sighed. "I'll do my best."

They drove the rest of the way in silence, Emily regretting once again that she'd brought up Colin, until finally they pulled into the parking lot of the Luxor. Her brothers would see each other soon enough, and hopefully figure all of this out.

The Luxor was a giant, black pyramid-shaped building right in the middle of Las Vegas, and the theme of the hotel and the casino that was inside it was, of course, Egyptian. There was a huge sphinx outside the hotel, and Egyptian-style statues, sarcophaguses, and other paraphernalia filled the hotel itself.

Ben checked them into the hotel, claiming the four rooms he'd re-served for them yesterday. One room for their parents and Hope, one for Katy's parents, one for her, and one for Ben and Katy, which the hotel concierge upgraded to the honeymoon suite free of charge. All their rooms were on the 27th floor of the 30-story hotel and overlooked the casino.

At 18, Emily wouldn't be allowed in the casino, but that was okay. There was still plenty to do. She vowed to return when she was 21, however, because the constant cling and clang of the slot machines as they passed the casino on their way to the elevators was almost hypnotic.

They finally reached her room, and Emily used the card they'd given her at the front desk to open the door. Ben followed her inside as she walked to the window. The room was beautiful, and the view was amazing. In the distance she could see the Excalibur hotel and casino, Caesar's Palace, and part of the Vegas strip itself.

"Wow," Ben said, joining her by the window. "Katy's going to love this."

"Yeah, she really is," said Emily. "And what's more important, big brother, is that she loves you, and you two are finally going to be together. For what it's worth, I'm very proud of you."

"It's worth a lot, Em," he said, hugging her. "Thanks, and ditto."

"Thanks, Ben. And now I guess it's time to get everyone else. Remember, you can't see Katy before the wedding."

"We still have to go get the marriage license," Ben said. "There's no way *not* to see her."

"But you shouldn't see her until then," Emily insisted.

"Yeah, yeah. I'll be in my room. Send Dad and Fred over when you get them, okay?"

She promised she would and then disappeared, reappearing moments later with her mother.

"I never get tired of this," Jenny said. "It always makes me a little dizzy, though."

"Not me," Emily said, grinning, as she disappeared and reappeared at the apartments in Carthage.

"Ready, Hope?" she asked her niece, crouching down beside her.

"Yep!" the little girl said, leaping into Emily's arms. "Bye-bye, Hercules!"

The dog barked in response as they vanished and reappeared in her hotel room in Las Vegas.

Emily continued the jumps, until the room contained Hope, Jenny, Fred and Candy Ruskin, Katy and her half-sister Samantha, all of Emily's surviving grandparents, her best friend Sabrina and her boyfriend Farris, Claire Locke, and Claire's sister and Katy's former college roommate, Melissa Fleming.

She was already exhausted but having fun, and her teleporting duties weren't over yet. As soon as Claire received word that her wife and son had arrived in Tulsa, Emily would fetch them as well. After the wedding and reception, she'd take everyone who wasn't spending the night in Vegas back home again, and then port back to Carthage to feed Hercules and take him outside to do his business.

She loved it. Her ability was simple, and nothing in comparison to the powers Ben had lost, or Katy's dreamwalking abilities, but it came in very handy for travelling.

"You are fucking amazing," Sabrina whispered to her, giving her a big hug, "and I'm so lucky to have you as my best friend."

Emily blushed, her freckled face turning almost as red as her hair. "Thanks, 'Brina!"

"Wouldn't say it if it weren't true."

Everyone but Sabrina, Farris, Claire, and Emily had gone off to their rooms or to explore the hotel.

"Get a room, you two," said Farris, grinning.

Sabrina turned to look at him, arching an eyebrow. "And how do you know we haven't?"

Emily's blush deepened. Sabrina and Ferris had been sexually active for a couple of years now, but Emily was still a virgin. At this point, she'd be happy to "get a room" with just about anyone.

And then she had a thought. What happens in Vegas stays in Vegas, as the old saying went. Maybe she could have a little adventure in Las Vegas, after all.

# Chapter 31

**Seven Years Ago**

Alejandro Torres loved spring in Malinalco, Mexico, the small resort town he'd lived in his entire 72 years on this planet. The daytime temperature in the Spring rarely got above 25° Celsius, while the nights cooled to around 10°. He'd periodically traveled through Mexico and even into the United States and Canada, but this was still his favorite spot on Earth. He was going to miss it.

His thoughts drifted back many Springs ago, to 1975, the year the angel came to him and entrusted the small, brown twig into his care. He'd been a young man then, married three years, with one child and a baby on the way. His father had passed the year previous, and he'd taken over the family tour guide business, dragging white visitors around to the religious and historical sites.

"*Alejandro,*" Lucia had said, "*Oí un ruido en el patio trasero. ¿Puedes ver?*"

She'd heard a noise in the backyard and wanted him to investigate. They had a small garden behind their house and a neighborhood dog seemed determined to shit in it at least once a day.

"*Estaré de vuelta en un minuto,*" he'd said, expecting it to be that damned dog again.

He opened the screen door, let himself outside, and quietly closed it behind him. Little Juan Pablo had just gone to bed, and he didn't want to wake the boy.

He clicked on the green flashlight he'd taken from the kitchen, illuminating the night in front of him. Scanning the yard and finding nothing, he was about to go back inside when he heard a noise from the garden.

"*Ese maldito perro*," he muttered under his breath, walking toward the garden. But it was no dog.

Before him stood a tall blond man in white flowing robes, a silver halo hovering over his head. A pair of gigantic white wings protruded from his back, as though he had just flown down from the heavens. The man shrugged his shoulders and the wings disappeared behind him.

"*Dios mío*," he whispered, falling to his knees before the angel.

"*No soy Dios, Alejandro, sólo soy un ángel*," the being replied. "*Me llamo Miguel.*"

The angel said his name was Miguel. San Miguel, the archangel? Could it be true?

"*¿El Arcángel San Miguel?*" Alejandro asked, his eyes full of tears, "*¿Me estoy muriendo?*" He was sure he was dying.

The angel laughed, and it was the most beautiful sound Alejandro had ever heard. Miguel reached out his hand and Alejandro took it, allowing the angel to pull him to his feet.

"*No, amigo mío, no te estás muriendo*," the angel said, shaking his head.

He had come all the way from heaven, Miguel said, because he needed Alejandro's help. There were five sacred objects of power, and Alejandro was destined to be the guardian of one of them. If the objects were ever to fall into the wrong hands, the angel explained, they could be used to bring about the apocalypse.

"*¿Pero por qué yo?*"

Of all the people in the world, who was he to be the guardian of anything?

San Miguel told Alejandro that he had a pure heart and would never abuse the power that was about to be bestowed upon him. The simple twig, the angel confided, had the power to heal flesh and move mountains, but if it was ever combined with the other talismans, hordes of demons from hell could use the magic to remake the world in *El Diablo's* image.

Alejandro could use the twig at his own discretion, but only occasionally, and never in public. In the nearly half a century he'd been the keeper of the object, he'd only dared use it twelve times, all in the name of healing. The first time had been just three years after he'd gotten it, when his *tío* Sebastián had fallen from the roof of Alejandro's house while helping him repair some storm damage.

His *tío*, his uncle, had landed on his head, breaking his neck instantly. As he lay there dying, Alejandro had rushed into the house and fetched the little copper box that had once belonged to his grandmother from beneath a loose floorboard under his bed. Running to his uncle's side, he'd yanked the twig from inside the box, fallen to his knees beside the dying man, and taken Sebastián's neck in his hands and prayed with all his might that his uncle might be healed. And it had worked!

*Tío* Sebastián had gone on to lead a long and healthy life, passing away in his sleep at the ripe old age of 84 just three years ago. He'd had minor neck and back problems after the fall, and had never walked quite the same again, but he'd lived. And each time Alejandro used the twig after that, his ability to harness the power within had only gotten better.

He'd finally used it a thirteenth time just a few days ago. His granddaughter Camila had just given birth to a beautiful baby girl of her own, but something had gone wrong during childbirth. The baby was fine, but Camila wouldn't stop bleeding. The doctors said she was going to die, it was just a matter of time, but Alejandro had snuck into the hospital after hours and healed Camila. It was a miracle, the doctors proclaimed, and she was released from the hospital the very next afternoon. Even now, Alejandro imagined, she was at home with her husband and their new baby girl, who they'd named Lucia, marveling over the second chance they'd been given.

Alejandro had kept the twig a secret all these years, even from his now-deceased wife and their five children and grandchildren. No one knew the power that Alejandro kept hidden beneath a loose floorboard under his bed, not even the hulking stranger with the salt-and-pepper beard and long hair to match who stood above him. But the stranger knew something and was seemingly willing to do whatever was necessary to steal the twig.

"I don't want to hurt you," said the man standing before him, "I just want what's mine."

Alejandro had pretended not to understand English when the huge *gringo* dressed all in black and wearing an eye patch had showed up at his door five minutes ago, demanding the twig, but the stranger was having none of it. He knew about the tours, he said, and that it was mostly Americans, and surely Alejandro had picked up a little English over the years.

It was true. He spoke English fluently, and finally admitted as much after the man had shouldered his way into Alejandro's home.

"I still don't understand what you're asking for, *Señor...*" he paused, hoping to get the man's name.

Alejandro looked around his small house. There, on the far wall opposite the fireplace, were photos of him and Lucia on their wedding day, all five of their children, eighteen grandchildren, and five great-grandchildren. He'd yet to add Camila's precious bundle of joy, little baby Lucia, to the wall, and now he knew he may never get the chance.

"Dowd," the man finally said, staring down at him with one eye. "My name is David Dowd, and you know exactly what I'm asking for. You have the twig, and I need it. I don't want to hurt you, I truly don't, but I will if I have to."

Alejandro was an old man. He knew his beloved Lucia was waiting for him in heaven, and he didn't fear death. He told Dowd as much, and his blood chilled when the tall man smiled.

"I wouldn't expect anything less. You've lived a long and fruitful life, *Señor* Torres," Dowd offered, "but your beautiful new great-granddaughter, on the other hand…"

Alejandro stared at the man, seething, the muscles in his neck tensing up. How dare he threaten little Lucia? He knew then and there that he was going to die today, and he intended to take the tall demon with him. The man looked to be about half Alejandro's age and much larger and stronger, but still he had to try.

Dowd smiled, and Alejandro swung a right hook at his chin. Dowd caught his fist in his hand, as effortlessly as a grown man might fend off a toddler. The big man squeezed Alejandro's hand, and he thought his fingers might snap. It was all he could do not to howl in pain.

"It doesn't have to be this way," the man continued, letting go of Alejandro's fist. "I've killed far too many. I don't want to hurt you, or your great-granddaughter. I don't want to hurt anyone. I just want to forget, but without your twig, there's no way I'm going to be able to do that. I've been looking for it for over ten years. The geode just wasn't enough."

Geode? Dowd was talking nonsense, but maybe he could use the man's madness to his advantage. He rubbed his hurt hand, and then slumped his shoulders and hung his head, giving the appearance of defeat. He couldn't defeat Dowd with his fists, but there might be another way.

"Don't hurt little Lucia or anyone else," he said in a voice barely above a whisper, "and you can have the twig."

"I meant what I said," reiterated Dowd. "I wish you and your family no harm. I just want what's rightfully mine. I need it, if I'm ever going to be whole again."

"Follow me," Alejandro said, leading the man through the house and into kitchen, where he retrieved a screwdriver. "It's under a floorboard beneath my bed. I need this to pry it open."

Dowd nodded, eyes drawn to the screwdriver. "Just don't think about putting that into my neck."

Alejandro had indeed thought about that very thing, about sinking it into Dowd's jugular up to the hilt, but knew he'd be dead before the metal even reached the man's neck.

He walked through the house and into his bedroom, Dowd just behind him. He kneeled on creaking knees beside the queen-sized bed he used to share with his wife, not even needing to look as he maneuvered the screwdriver into the crack between the loose floorboard and the rest of the floor.

His fingers still hurt, so he used the palm of his hand to leverage the board loose. It released with a little pop, and then he passed the screwdriver to his left hand and slowly sat it on the bed. He glanced up at Dowd, who was smiling.

His fingers found the little copper box, and he deftly turned it on its side, slid open the container, and plucked the twig from the box, dropping it into the hole. Swiveling on his knees, he presented the empty box to Dowd.

"Take it," he said, feigning defeat, "and get out of my house."

"Gladly," said Dowd, snatching the box from his hand.

It was then that Alejandro snaked his hand back into the hole and snatched the twig. He'd only ever before used the talisman to heal, but he knew it could also hurt. If he could incapacitate the man long enough to escape, he might have a chance.

Dowd's smile turned to a frown as he opened the empty box.

"Where is it?" he asked, as Alejandro connected with the twig in his mind, harnessing its power, and *pushed*.

Dowd flew backwards, crashing into the old dresser that stood behind him. The wood gave way and the giant fell to the floor amidst a tangle of broken boards and Alejandro's clothing.

Using the bed to help him to his feet, Alejandro ran past the startled Dowd and into the living room, whirling to slam the bedroom door closed behind him. He paused, knowing that what he did next could mean life or death for him and his family.

Alejandro ran through the living room and into the kitchen, heading for the broom closet. His hip slammed into the small breakfast table that crowded the middle of the room and he nearly fell.

"*Señor* Torres," came Dowd's voice from the living room, "stop. I don't want to hurt you, but I will have the twig. One way or the other, I will reclaim what's mine."

He yanked open the broom closet, reached inside, and pulled out his old shotgun. His hand fumbled on the top shelf, searching, finally finding the box of shotgun shells. He managed to load one of the shells into the shotgun just as Dowd kicked open the door to the kitchen. Alejandro spun on his heels, levelling the weapon at the giant.

"I've never killed a man, *Señor* Dowd, but I will not let you harm my family, nor will I let you have the talisman. The archangel Miguel himself gave it to me to guard, and you can't have it."

Dowd stood motionless, hands raised in supplication.

"There's no such thing as angels, *Señor* Torres. Whoever gave it to you wasn't an angel. That shit isn't real."

Alejandro blinked, his finger tightening on the trigger. "Blasphemer!"

"I used to believe in fairy tales," Dowd said, his hands still out, "and I used to preach the word of the Lord. I even led a congregation, but then a man named Ben Spencer took everything from me and made me see the truth. There are no angels, no heaven or hell, and certainly no God."

Alejandro prayed that the same God that Dowd denounced would forgive him as he pulled the trigger. The shotgun boomed, and he stumbled backwards from the force, slamming hard into the kitchen counter.

The shotgun pellets hovered uselessly in the air, just inches from Dowd's outstretched hands. Dowd smiled, and the pellets fell harmlessly to the kitchen's tile floor.

"*¡Dios mío!* How? Why aren't you dead?"

"I already have one of the artifacts, *Señor* Torres. A second will make me more powerful still. You can't win this fight, and I meant what I said earlier. I don't want to hurt you. I don't want to hurt anyone. I've hurt so many people in my lifetime, the guilt is almost unbearable."

"Then why? Why do you want this power?"

"I don't *want* it, *Señor* Torres, I *need* it. Now give me the twig."

Dowd took one step, and then another, closing the distance between them. Alejandro threw the shotgun at him, but he knocked it away as though it were nothing.

Alejandro closed his fist around the twig and willed Dowd back, but it didn't work this time. The man just kept coming. He decided to try something else. He imagined Dowd unable to breathe, willing his thoughts into the twig.

Dowd gasped, clutching at his throat. It was working! He held his fist out at the man, concentrating harder than he'd ever concentrated before.

The giant reached behind his back and then a silver sword was flashing down through the air, sliding through Alejandro's wrist like butter. Alejandro screamed, staring at the bleeding stump where his right hand used to be.

"I didn't want to do that," Dowd said, kneeling to retrieve Alejandro's hand from the blood-covered tile, "but you left me no choice."

He pried the stick from Alejandro's ruined hand, then set the extremity carefully upon the breakfast table. Dowd closed his eyes as Alejandro sank to the floor, and the old man could swear the demon was glowing.

"Finally," said Dowd, as he reached down to heal Alejandro's bleeding wrist.

One moment he was in the worst pain he'd ever experienced in his life, and the next he simply wasn't. He watched in amazement as skin knitted together and grew over the stump. He could almost feel his fingers and thumb, though he knew they were no longer there.

"Why…" Alejandro stuttered, struggling to get the words out. "Why did you heal me?"

"I told you," Dowd answered, as he turned to leave, "that I didn't want to hurt you. I have what I came for, and now I'll leave you in peace. Enjoy your beautiful great-granddaughter, *Señor* Torres. No harm will come to her, at least not from me."

And with that, Dowd disappeared through the kitchen door and out of Alejandro's life. Alejandro had been wrong. He wasn't going to die today, after all. As tears streamed down his face and he imagined the apocalypse that must surely come, he prayed that the *arcángel San Miguel* could forgive him.

# Chapter 32

Ben stood on the altar in the small Luxor chapel, wearing his rented tuxedo, waiting for Katy. He'd faced down serial killers, battled demented preachers, and traveled in time, but standing here waiting for Katy made him more nervous than all three of those things combined.

A small balding man with a warm smile and a booming voice, their officiant Mr. Marshall, stood on a little pedestal slightly above them.

This was a small wedding, certainly much smaller than Katy deserved, but he had a feeling if they didn't do it now, they might never get around to it. Michael would be coming for him sooner rather than later, he was almost certain of it, and he'd be ready, but not before he married the woman of his dreams.

He looked at the small group of people currently occupying the chapel. His maternal grandmother Abby, his paternal grandparents Henry and Ellen, Candy Ruskin, Katy's sister Sam, Emily's friends Farris Hale and Sabrina Locke, whom he'd only just met yesterday, and Sabrina's sister and his rescuer Claire, who they'd managed to get in touch with just an hour before she was due to leave Carthage.

Claire's wife Leesie sat beside her, and they'd even found a role for their little boy, Jimmy, in the wedding itself. It was a tiny wedding party, to be sure, but he was proud to have every single one of them there.

Ben did feel a pang of sadness that Grandpa Paul wasn't sitting beside Grandma Abby, though seeing his spirit two days ago at the cemetery had helped bring him closure. He almost felt his grandfather was there with him, which brought a smile to his lips.

Processional music began to play, and Ben's father came down the aisle, accompanying Katy's best friend, old roommate, and maid of honor, Melissa Fleming, as well as her three bridesmaids: Katy's older sister Samantha, Ben's mother Jenny, and Ben's little sister Emily. The wedding party was clearly weighted on the bride's side, but that was okay. Fred Ruskin would help balance it out later.

Shawn took his place beside Ben as his best man while Mel, Jenny, Samantha, and Emily stood opposite them. All four were dressed in pink, and Emily couldn't stop smiling. Ben caught her eye and winked, which only caused her smile to widen.

Next came Hope, their flower girl, and Jimmy Locke, their im-promptu ring bearer, walking together down the aisle. Ben had a mo-mentary sense of *déjà vu* watching Hope and Jimmy together but didn't know why. The two had never even met before today. He shook his head and the moment passed.

Hope was dressed in a beautiful pink dress and carried a basket of rose petals, which she tossed to either side of the path. His precious daughter, the one whom he hadn't even known existed until three days ago, was smiling at him, and he blinked back tears. Jimmy carried a blue silk pillow upon which lay two white gold wedding bands, and these he handed to Marshall.

"I love you, Hope," he whispered, as he dropped to his knees for a moment to hug her.

"I love you, too, Daddy," she said, kissing him on the cheek.

He turned to address Jimmy. "And thank you, Jimmy, for helping out. Your mommy Claire is an amazing person, and I know she's very proud of you."

The little boy smiled shyly, then scampered away with Hope as she grabbed his hand and led him to their seats in the chapel.

Mr. Marshall gave one ring to Ben's father and the other to Mel, and then asked everyone to stand as the wedding march began to play. Ben felt his heartbeat quicken. It was now or never.

Fred Ruskin appeared at the far end of the aisle, escorting the woman Ben was about to marry. Katy wore a long, flowing white wedding dress, which was sleeveless, the train trailing behind her. Her hands were covered in short, white fingerless gloves made of delicate lace, and a gauzy white veil covered her face. She carried a bouquet of red and white roses.

Someone new caught Ben's eye, a man entering the chapel from one of the side doors, distracting his attention from his bride. Who enters a wedding chapel in the middle of the ceremony? It irritated him. He wondered for a moment who the man was, for he looked vaguely familiar, but then dismissed the question. It had to be one of the Luxor employees he'd seen earlier helping to prepare the chapel. And then Katy was standing before him, and the man at the back of the chapel was all but forgotten.

Mr. Marshall cleared his throat and said, "We are here today to celebrate the relationship of Katherine Grace Ruskin and Benjamin Tanner Spencer, and to be witnesses to the commitment that they share to one another." He paused, looking out over the small crowd. "Together, you are a gathering of the most important people in Ben and Katy's lives, and they've brought you here to publicly recognize the special part that you all share in their love.

"And because you are the important people in their lives, if anyone can show just cause why Katy and Ben should not be lawfully joined together, let them speak now or forever hold their peace."

Ben half-expected the man at the back of the chapel to say something, but of course he remained silent.

Marshall waited a few seconds before continuing. "Speaking of important people, no one has played a greater role in influencing the lives of Katy and Ben than their parents. With that said, who gives Katy's hand to Ben?"

"Her mother and I," said Fred. He took Katy's hand, kissed it, and placed it into Ben's. The old man had tears in his eyes but was smiling. Then he placed a hand on Ben's shoulder and took his place next to

Shawn, as Ben's groomsman. Katy squeezed Ben's fingers, and he could just make out her smile beneath the veil.

"The road that brought Katy and Ben here today hasn't been easy," Marshall continued. "It's been filled with challenges and obstacles they weren't necessarily prepared for. But together they've taken on each challenge, overcome each obstacle, and have used those experiences not to weaken but to strengthen their love.

"And now, Katy and Ben have asked me to read a poem, one of my favorites, from Emily Dickinson. It's titled, '*Hope is the Thing with Feathers*.'"

Ben heard Hope giggle at the mention of her name and felt weak in the knees with the love he felt for her. His beautiful little girl. He hadn't been able to be there for the first four years of her life, but he would damned well be there for her for the rest of *his* life.

"Hope is the thing with feathers," began Marshall, "that perches in the soul, and sings the tune without the words, and never stops at all.

"And sweetest in the gale is heard, and sore must be the storm that could abash the little bird that kept so many warm.

"I've heard it in the chilliest land, and on the strangest sea, yet never, in extremity, it asked a crumb of me.

"And now, Katy and Ben have asked to read their own vows. Katy?"

Katy cleared her throat before beginning. "Ben…I've known you since I was a little girl. First you were like my brother, then I fell in love with you, and now you're the man I want to spend the rest of my life with. Together, we brought a wonderful little girl into the world, and together, we'll raise her. I will love you with every bit of my heart and soul, and I'll honor and cherish you for the rest of my life. Notice I didn't say 'obey.'" Everyone laughed at that, including Ben. "Ben Spencer, this has been a long time coming, and I can't wait to be your wife."

"Ben?" asked Marshall.

"Katy…I tried to write vows, but all the things I want to say to you would take days if not weeks. I'll spend the rest of my life saying all of it to you, but for today…I'll just say that you are my heart, my soul, and my life. You and Hope complete me in a way I never thought possible. I'll love, honor, and cherish you until the day I die, and longer, if possible. I'll protect you and our little girl from anyone and everyone who means us harm, and I'll spend the rest of my life loving you both. And Katy, I can't wait to be your husband."

"Katy and Ben will now exchange rings to symbolize their commitment," Marshall said. "Rings are derived from humble beginnings of imperfect metal to create something striking where once there was nothing at all. It is customarily worn on the ring finger as it is the only finger with a vein running directly to the heart. The wearing of the rings is a visible, outward sign that they have committed themselves to one another."

Shawn gave Ben the bride's ring, while Mel passed the groom's ring to Katy.

"Ben, please take Katy's hand and repeat these words. 'I give you this ring, as a symbol of my love, for today and tomorrow, and for all the days to come. Wear it as a sign of what we've promised here today, and know that my love is present, even when I'm away.'"

Ben repeated the words, fumbling only once.

"Now place the ring on her finger."

Ben slid the wedding band onto Katy's ring finger, next to the engagement ring he'd given her just yesterday.

"And now Katy, repeat after me—"

"I give you this ring," Katy said, interrupting Marshall. "as a symbol of my love, for today and tomorrow, and for all the days to come. Wear it as a sign of what we've promised here today, and know that my love is present, even when I'm away."

"Great memory," Marshall commented, earning laughter from the audience. "Now place the ring on his finger."

Katy did as she was instructed.

"Katy and Ben," Marshall continued, "you have professed your love by exchanging your vows, and you have symbolized your commitment by exchanging rings. There is just one more question I need each of you to answer.

"Katherine Grace Ruskin, do you take Ben to be your lawfully wedded husband, to live together in the covenant of marriage? Do you promise to love him, comfort him, honor and keep him, in sickness and in health, and, forsaking all others, be faithful to him as long as you both shall live?"

"I do," said Katy, her voice shaking.

"And do you, Benjamin Tanner Spencer, take Katy to be your lawfully wedded wife, to live together in the covenant of marriage? Do you promise to love her, comfort her, honor and keep her, in sickness and in health, and, forsaking all others, be faithful to her as long as you both shall live?"

"I do," Ben said.

"Then by the power vested in me by the great state of Nevada, I pronounce you husband and wife. Ben, you may kiss your bride."

Ben pulled the gauzy veil from Katy's face. Tears ran down her cheeks. "I love you so much," she said, as he took her face in his hands and kissed her. Cheers and clapping filled the little Luxor chapel, but Ben barely noticed it, lost in the kiss with his beautiful bride.

"Ladies and gentlemen," Marshall said, in a booming voice, "it's my great honor and privilege to be the first to present to you Mr. and Mrs. Ruskin-Spencer!"

Everyone clapped and cheered as Ben and Katy kissed again, lost in each other's embrace.

# Chapter 33

Emily stood apart from her family at the wedding reception in the Cleopatra Ballroom, yet another of the many spaces in the labyrinth known as the Luxor, watching as her brother and his bride danced.

Everything was decorated in ancient Egyptian motif and looked stunningly beautiful. Though their party was small, and the room had been adjusted accordingly, the ballroom could easily have held at least 100 people. Even then, she was sure all eyes would have been on Katy and Ben. After all they had been through the last five years, they finally got their happy ending.

Ironically, she'd been the one to catch the wedding bouquet when Katy tossed it into the air after the wedding. It was ironic because she'd never felt more alone. She didn't even have a boyfriend, much less a potential husband in her life. There was no way in hell she was getting married any time soon.

*I'm Gonna Be (500 Miles)* was playing over the loudspeaker, but not the original by The Proclaimers. This version, according to one of the waiters she'd asked, was by a group called Sleeping at Last. It was slower and more soulful than the original, and the perfect song for her brother and new sister-in-law.

As happy as she was for them, she also couldn't help but feel a little jealous, and the feeling shamed her. Turning away from the dance floor, she startled herself as she walked straight into someone.

"Oh! I'm so sorry, I wasn't..." she said, her mouth dropping open in surprise as she stared into the face of her brother.

"I forgive you, sis," Colin said, flashing her an easy smile.

"Colin!" she screamed, throwing herself into his arms. "What are you doing here?"

"I couldn't miss my twin brother's wedding," he said, "even if I wasn't actually invited."

"But how?"

"Dad called two days and told me about the wedding. He bought me a flight to Quincy for this coming Wednesday, but I managed to swap it for a cheaper, standby flight to Las Vegas and, well, here we are. I got in just about an hour before the ceremony and barely made it here in time."

"No one knew you were coming?"

"Nope. And other than you, no one even knows I'm here yet."

"Why didn't you say something?"

"Honestly? I didn't want to upset Ben, but I really wanted to see my brother and Katy tie the knot. Think he'll be mad?"

"Not at all," Emily lied. "He'll be thrilled to see you."

Emily noticed a different song was playing now, one she didn't recognize. She looked toward where Ben and Katy had been dancing earlier but didn't see them.

"I'm not sure that's the case, but hopefully it won't come to blows. Hey, I'm kidding."

"You'd better be."

"Emily," said a voice from behind her, "are you going—Colin?" It was their father.

"The one and only, Dad," Colin said, smiling. "Surprise!"

Emily watched as the two embraced, holding back tears. Ben was going to be pissed, no doubt about it, but it was so good to have Colin with them again. And he'd come to watch his brother get married. That had to count for something, didn't it?

"Not that I'm not thrilled to see you, but...what are you doing here?" He held his son at arm's length, his gaze shifting slowly from Colin to Emily.

"Don't blame her, Dad," Colin said. "I swapped the ticket you bought me for a flight to Vegas. I wanted to see my twin get married...even if he didn't want me here."

"It's not that he didn't want you here," Emily said, "it's that—"

"I saw you in the back of the chapel earlier," said Ben, walking up to them, interrupting Emily. "Who are you?"

"You're kidding, right?" Colin asked.

"Oh shit," Emily said.

"Does someone want to tell me what's going on here?"

"Ben," said Shawn, "it's Colin. Your brother."

"You really don't know who I am?" asked Colin. "C'mon, it hasn't been that long."

"You said you weren't inviting him," said Ben, turning to stare at his father.

"He didn't," Colin said. "No one invited me. I just wanted to see you get married. Can't we let the past go, Ben? I'm sorry I was such a prick to you, and I want to make amends."

"That's just it," Ben said, turning back to Colin. "The past. Before I time travelled to the past five years ago, I didn't have a brother."

# Chapter 34

The Pyramid Café was filled with gamblers taking a break from the casino and tourists exploring the giant black pyramid, but Shawn, Colin, and Emily managed to find a table in the back. A few minutes later, someone showed up to take their order.

"A water, a Coke, and an Ace Blood Orange Cider, right?" asked the perky blonde waitress. "Are you sure you don't want anything to eat? Not even some nachos and cheese?"

"No, thanks. We're good," Colin said. Shawn nodded, and the waitress left to fetch their drinks.

Colin stormed off just a few minutes after Ben confronted him in the ballroom, but Shawn and Emily had chased after him and finally managed to calm him down. At first Colin said he was going home, back to Canada, but he'd finally agreed to sit down and talk it over with his father and sister.

"He thinks I'm not real, huh?" asked Colin, as soon as the waitress was out of earshot. "Is he fucking nuts?"

Shawn hated this. He believed Ben, he really did, but he didn't want to think that, but for a trip back in time, Colin might not exist. It was one thing when Katy insisted that Colin wasn't alive in her original timeline, but quite another when Ben returned to confirm her story.

"He isn't saying you're not real," Shawn finally said, putting his hand on his Colin's shoulder, "but that you didn't exist before he went back in time and changed something. I promise you, Colin, you're as real as Ben, as Emily, as me, as any of us."

"No shit, I'm real. If he really thinks otherwise, he needs to have his head examined. I'm serious."

"The thing is," Emily said, "Katy doesn't remember you, either."

"But that's…insane. I've known Katy all my life!"

"We didn't believe her, at first," Shawn said, "but—"

"But what?" Colin yelled, standing up from the table.

"Colin, sit down," Shawn said.

"But what, Dad?"

"Sit down and we'll talk."

"Fine," said Colin, settling back into his seat. "Talk."

"When Ben came back and said the same thing, that you hadn't existed before he and Katy travelled back in time, we had to consider that there might be some truth to what she'd been saying."

"That's bullshit!" Colin said, standing up from the table again.

"Is everything all right?" asked the waitress, materializing at the table with their drinks.

"Better now," said Colin, snatching his cider from the tray, downing it in three large gulps. "Could I get another, please?"

"Umm, sure," she said, deftly depositing Emily's Coke and Shawn's water on the table. "Anything else?"

"We're good, thanks," said Shawn, watching as the waitress disappeared into the crowd.

He wished Jenny were here. She'd always been able to get through to Colin, even when no one else could. But Jenny was upstairs with Hope, so it was up to him and Emily.

"Colin," said Emily, "sit your ass the fuck down, okay?"

Both Shawn and Colin stared at her, looked at each other, and began to laugh. The laughter was contagious, and soon Emily joined in.

"What?" she finally asked, when they were done laughing.

"You're just so cute when you're angry," said Colin, sitting back down.

Emily punched him in the arm. "Dork."

He held up his hands in surrender.

"Hey," said Emily, reaching out to take his right hand. "What's that squiggle? Is it a tattoo?"

He stared at her for a second. "Oh, sorry, I almost forgot about that. Yeah, it's a tattoo. Well, it will be once it's finished."

It looked like someone had doodled a squiggly line on the palm of Colin's hand. Shawn wasn't really into the idea of tattoos, but if Colin wanted one, more power to him.

"What'll it be when it's finished?" asked Emily.

"A Japanese symbol for love. Sumi and I are getting matching tattoos."

"How romantic."

Colin sighed. "Look, I'm sorry for getting so upset. I know none of this is your fault. Hell, it's not even Ben's fault. I just…thinking that my entire existence might be a cosmic mistake is hard to wrap my head around, you know?"

"You're not a 'cosmic mistake,' Colin," said Shawn. "You're alive, you're real, and you're my son. Your mother and I love you with all our hearts, every bit as much as we love Ben, and we're so happy you're here."

"That makes three of us," Emily said. "Besides, you're not the only thing that supposedly changed."

Colin arched an eyebrow. "What else?"

"Katy's Dad. According to Katy and Ben, he just owned a single Ruskin's Pizzeria before they went back in time. Now, he has a chain of restaurants and is a multi-millionaire."

The waitress brought Colin's second cider, and this one he drank much more slowly.

"He's had that chain of restaurants ever since I could remember," Colin said, as soon as the waitress left.

"It's the same for us, Colin," said Shawn.

"This is making my head hurt."

"Mine, too," said Emily, "so let's forget about it all for a little while. Sabrina, Farris, and I are going to see the Blue Man Group tonight, before I take them home. Wanna come? Please?"

Colin smiled. "Sure, sis. That sounds fun."

"Great!"

"I'll talk to Ben," Shawn said.

"Dad, it's his wedding night. It can wait."

"Are you sure?"

"I'm sure. I put in for a week off work and took a leave from university, so we have time. I'll come back with you to Carthage, and we'll figure everything out and make this work."

Shawn hoped with everything in him that his son was right, but he couldn't help thinking that their troubles were just beginning.

# Chapter 35

Ben, Katy, and Hope were standing in front of the window in Ben and Katy's hotel room. Ben and Hope were still dressed in their clothes from the wedding, minus Ben's jacket, while Katy had swapped her wedding dress for a black mini-skirt and red blouse.

"Move just a little to your right, Ben," said Jenny, camera in hand.

Ben moved dutifully to the right, doing his best to smile. He was still more than a little upset (not to mention weirded out) by his time-travel accident twin showing up for the wedding. Why had his father even told Colin they were getting married today, much less where?

"Okay, perfect," Jenny said. "Smiles, everyone, and say cheese!"

"Cheese!" Ben, Katy, and Hope all said in unison.

"There! Perfect."

"It had better be," said Ben. "That was, what, the tenth shot?"

Katy punched him in the arm, causing Hope to giggle.

"Ow! What was that for?"

"Be nice to your mother," Katy said, smiling. "Besides, it's your wedding day."

"I know, I'm just—"

"Upset about Colin. Yeah, I get it."

"I think this one turned out perfect," Jenny said, ignoring the mention of her other son, turning the screen on her digital camera to face Ben.

He stared at the photo, and the strangest feeling overcame him. It looked so familiar, like he'd seen it before, but he couldn't have. His mother had just snapped the photo.

"Are you okay, Ben?" asked Jenny. "You look like you've seen a ghost."

He shook his head and turned his gaze from the camera. "I'm all right, it's just...I don't know. That picture looks so familiar. It gave me a major case of *déjà vu*. Can I see it again?"

"Of course." Jenny handed him the camera.

"Hmm. Nothing now. Oh, well. It's a great picture." He passed the camera back to Jenny.

"I'll have it framed for you," she said.

At her words, Ben felt *déjà vu* all over again, but forced his thoughts past it. "Thank you," he finally said.

"I can't tell you what it meant to me to have you standing up there with me," said Katy, pulling Jenny into an embrace. "Best friend, and now mother-in-law. Between you, Shawn, Hope, and Ben, I feel like the luckiest girl in the world. I love you, Jenny."

"I love you, too," said Jenny, "but you're about to make me cry. How about Grandpa Shawn and I take Hope to M&M's World like we promised and give you two some alone time?"

"I like the blue ones the best!" yelled Hope.

"I know you do, sweetie," said Katy, dropping to her knees beside her daughter, "but don't eat too many, okay? Promise?"

"I promise, Mommy," Hope said, throwing herself into Katy's arms.

"Bring me back some?" asked Ben, smiling.

"I will, Daddy," she promised, hugging Ben, and he thought his heart might burst with the love he felt for this little pixie of a girl.

Once Jenny and Hope were gone, Katy turned to Ben. "Colin worries me, too, but he may just be an anomaly, like my father getting rich off Microsoft and pizza. Different from our original timeline, but not necessarily part of some demonic plan."

"I sure hope so," said Ben, not for a moment believing it to be true.

"Plus, this is our wedding night," she said, putting her arms around his neck, "and I'll be more than a little disappointed if I can't get your mind off Colin."

She pulled him close, kissing him softly. He returned the kiss with passion, has arms wrapped around her waist as he pulled her even closer.

"My mind is officially off what's-his-name," he said, when the kiss was finished.

"Good," she murmured, as she took his hand and led him to the king-sized bed that dominated their suite.

She pushed him onto the bed, climbing onto his lap and straddling his hips as his fingers quickly undid the buttons on her blouse. She pulled off his shirt, buttons ripping as she cast it aside, her lips finding his skin.

"I love you, Katy," he whispered into her ear, "and nothing's ever going to come between us again."

She stiffened and slowly pulled away from him. "Shit. You just had to say that, didn't you?"

"Say what?"

"Shit. Shit. Shit!"

"What? What'd I say?"

"It isn't you, Ben," she said, rolling off him, "it's me. I have something to tell you, and you're not going to like it."


Ben listened as Katy told him about her journey into the spirit room two nights ago, the trick she'd pulled on Azazel, and what she'd learned as a result, his mood growing sour. When she was finished, he said nothing, only stared at her.

"Look, I'm sorry, okay?"

"You didn't think I needed to know all of this?" He finally asked.

"Yes, of course I did, and I was going to tell you—I was going to tell everyone, in fact—but then you asked me to marry you, and…"

"And it seemed less important, somehow?"

"No, damn it! I was just happy, okay? You were happy, our parents were happy, Hope was ecstatic, and I just…I just…"

"You decided to put it off and enjoy the moment," he said, his tone softening. "I get it, I'm just not happy about it."

"At least we know they're no longer after you."

"Which is great news. I just wish I'd known about that two days ago."

"Still love me?"

"Still love you."

"Do you want to have sex now?"

That earned her a smile. "Of course I want to have sex now, but what are going to do about Michael and…and Atenanunaki, or Elohim, or whatever his name is? What are we going to do about all of it?"

Katy sighed. "It's waited this long. Tomorrow, once we're home, we'll tell everyone and figure it all out. Okay?"

"But don't you think—"

She silenced him with a kiss, long and deep. Afterwards, she asked him, "Think what?"

"That we should shut up and enjoy our wedding night," Ben said, trailing little kisses down her throat as his fingers undid the catch on her bra.

"Ben Spencer," she whispered, "that's the smartest thing you ever said."

# Chapter 36

Emily lay alone in her queen-sized bed in her hotel room in Las Vegas, unable to sleep. The day had been wonderful, and she was sorry it was over. After the wedding reception, she, Sabrina, Farris, and Colin had gone to see the Blue Man Group in the Luxor Theater, which was every bit as entertaining as she'd heard, and then ate dinner at the buffet inside the hotel.

After that, she'd teleported Sabrina and Farris home and walked Colin back to the room he'd rented, and that's when the loneliness set in. She'd already fed Hercules earlier in the day, right after the wedding reception, but decided to go visit him again and let him out one final time for the night.

The huge Border Collie had been ecstatic to see her, which helped to abate her blue mood, but now two hours later it was back with a vengeance. She rolled over and stared at the clock: 2:02 a.m. Jesus, why couldn't she sleep?

Scratch that, she knew why she couldn't sleep. As wonderful as last night had been, it was irritating as well. Ben had Katy. Sabrina had Farris. Colin had Natsumi waiting for him back in Canada. It was like all three couples had their own special language, little memories and quips that made them laugh or blush that no one else understood. She craved that intimacy. When was it going to be her turn?

She'd hoped to find a guy in Vegas, someone she could drag back to her room and have her way with, but none of the men she'd run into seemed even remotely interesting. She'd been hit on twice since being here, but both were overbearing frat boys, and she couldn't see losing her virginity to a guy like that.

Making a decision, she rolled out of bed and to her feet. There was no use lying in bed if she couldn't sleep. Sure, she might not be able to visit the casino, but she could explore the rest of the hotel.

She quickly changed from her pajamas into the little black dress she'd worn earlier tonight to the show, slipping on her matching heels. She knew her parents wouldn't approve of this, but hell, she was 18 and legally an adult. She could make her own decisions. Besides, being barred from the casino, bars, and nightclubs, what sort of trouble could she get herself into?

Emily stared at the entrance to the casino, which occupied almost the entirety of the first floor of the Luxor. The rest of the hotel had proved boring. She'd even visited the Centra, a 24-hour nightclub across from the front desk, but had been carded almost immediately and asked to leave.

The same thing would happen, she guessed, were she to walk into the casino. That's why she didn't intend to walk. If she timed things just right, she could teleport from the shadowy corner of the lobby where she now stood to between the Monopoly and the Alice in Wonderland slot machines that stood against the far wall of the casino.

The Luxor was still busy, though nowhere nearly as crowded as it had been this afternoon or even just a few hours ago. She watched as people walked in and out of the casino, some with huge smiles on their faces and others looking like they'd just lost their best friend. She waited until there was a lull in the foot traffic, and then…

There! She teleported, immediately appearing between the two machines, her heart beating wildly in her chest. She'd teleported thousands of times before, and probably covered thousands if not hundreds of thousands of miles, but never to somewhere she wasn't legally allowed to be. Emily cast furtive glances all around her, but as far as she could tell she hadn't been noticed.

The beeps and chimes of the machines and the whirling of the wheels within them was almost as overwhelming as it was alluring. The slots seemed to call to her, begging her to play them. She reached into her little black purse, pulled out a quarter, and kissed it. She may not have Ben's luck, but she had close to $300 and intended to make the most of it.

She stepped out from between the two machines intending to spend the quarter and immediately walked into a cocktail waitress carrying a tray of drinks. The waitress, no doubt used to the crowds, deftly pivoted away from her, managing not to spill any of the drinks.

"I'm so sorry," Emily blurted out.

"No problem," said the waitress, an easy smile on her lips. "I can't believe I didn't see you. Would you care for a drink? I have Pepsi, Sprite, and water, on the house, or I can get you something from the bar if you prefer."

Emily blinked. "Umm, how about a water?"

"You got it," she said, taking one of the drinks from the tray and handing it to Emily. "If you need something stronger later, I'll be around."

"Thank you," said Emily, her heart in her throat.

She leaned against the Alice in Wonderland slot machine as the waitress walked away, trying to stave off panic. That had been too close, but she'd done it. She'd passed for a grown-up. She finished the water in three long gulps, tossing the plastic cup into a nearby trash can.

She still had the quarter she'd taken from her purse in her hand, but quickly realized it was useless. In the movies and on television the slot machines always accepted coins, but that didn't appear to be the case in real life, at least not at this casino.

According to the instructions on the machine, it only accepted paper money. This machine still only cost a quarter to play, but the minimum you could insert was a dollar. When you were ready to quit playing, you could "cash out" and the machine would print you a ticket that you could then trade for cash at one of the many kiosks located in the casino.

She looked in her purse, and the smallest bill she had was a five. Inserting the money into the Alice in Wonderland machine, she watched as the digital display told her that she could play the machine up to 20 times. Almost without thinking, she pressed the button. Emily watched, fascinated, as the three pictures (called reels, she'd read) spun and came up one at a time.

The first reel came up as the Cheshire Cat, while the other two continued to spin. A few seconds later, another Cheshire Cat appeared. Was she going to win? She held her breath as the last reel slowed, biting her lower lip. There was the Cheshire Cat! But no, it didn't stop there, instead turning over to reveal the dreaded Mad Hatter.

She'd lost. She felt inexplicably sad, though realistically it was only a quarter. She had 19 "virtual quarters" left, and more where that came from.

Emily glanced at her watch. It was almost 3:30 in the morning. She played her remaining turns, one after another, losing every time. By the time she was down to her second-to-last turn, she decided this wasn't all it was cracked up to be. She dutifully pressed the button and watched as three Alice symbols came up and the sound of the machine changed to a triumphant flurry of beeps and chimes and lights.

She'd won, and the machine happily informed her that her prize was $16! Not bad for a $4.75 investment. And to think she'd been about to give up just a few minutes earlier.

Emily spent the next forty-five minutes going from machine to machine, winning some and losing some but mostly breaking even, avoiding people whenever possible and eventually working up her nerve to move up to the dollar slots. On the other side of the casino from where she'd started, she spied a Family Guy dollar slot machine. Eager to give it a try, she inserted a twenty and on her fifth spin got three Brian symbols, winning $218. She'd never been so happy to see that sarcastic white dog in her life!

"Damn, baby," said a voice from behind her, "that's some good luck there."

Emily whirled around, coming face-to-face with a short bald man wearing a disheveled blazer. He looked to be about forty, and his face was covered in stubble. His breath reeked of so much alcohol that it made Emily's eyes water. He stepped toward her, and she automatically stepped backwards, bumping into the machine.

"Yeah, thanks," she said. "Beginner's luck, I guess."

"Maybe you wanna share some of that luck?" he asked, slurring his words.

"I really need to get going. My boyfriend's probably looking for me."

"He let a pretty young thing like you out of his sight? You don't need him. C'mon, let's go party, okay?"

"I really need to go," said Emily, finally maneuvering away from him.

"You don't gotta be rude," he said, grabbing her wrist. "All I wanna do is party."

Emily was just about to teleport back to her hotel room, witnesses and security cameras be damned, when a slender blonde woman inserted herself between the two of them.

"I think you're bothering her, asshole," the woman said in a slight southern accent, poking the man in the chest. "Why don't you take a hike?"

"What's it to you, bitch?" the man spat, slapping away her hand. "Why don't *you* take a hike, unless you wanna join the party?"

Before Emily even knew what was happening, the blonde had taken hold of the man's hand and twisted his fingers apart, causing him to scream in pain. A security guard ran over, and the man took off, holding his hand and yelling obscenities over his shoulder.

"Are you okay?" the blonde asked Emily, as the guard took off after the drunk.

"Umm. Yeah, I am, thanks to you." She stared into the woman's deep blue eyes for a second before turning away in embarrassment.

"No problem," she said, blushing. "I've been in way too many situations like that. Get some whisky into one of these assholes and he turns into…well…I don't know. A super asshole, I guess?"

Emily laughed. "I guess so. My name's Emily, by the way."

"Nice to meet you, Emily," she said, "I'm Cassie. So, how much did you win?"

"$218."

"That's amazing!" said Cassie. "How long have you been playing?"

"Just a couple hours now," she said, glancing down at her watch. Shit, it was almost four. "Speaking of which, I'd better get going."

"Darn," Cassie said. "I was hoping you'd let me buy you a drink. I did pretty well tonight myself and would love to celebrate."

*But I'm not old enough to drink*, Emily nearly blurted out. Then again, why not? If Cassie bought the drinks, would they even bother carding her? And if they did, what's the worst that could happen? They'd just make her leave.

She stared at Cassie, taking her in. She was probably in her early twenties, not that much older than Emily herself. She wore a red skirt and a short black top showing off her full breasts and pierced belly button, and she wore green tennis shoes.

"Sure, Cassie," she finally said, "I definitely have time for a drink, especially for the woman who slayed the super asshole and saved me from having my night ruined."

Cassie laughed. "That's me, the asshole slayer."

"So…where to?" asked Emily, feeling adventurous for the first time in a long while.

"How about the Aurora? But don't forget to cash out first. We wouldn't want that idiot to come back and snatch your winnings."

Emily pressed the button on the Family Guy machine to cash out, took the ticket, and followed Cassie to the kiosk to claim her winnings. Five minutes later and $218 richer, Emily and Cassie found themselves at the Aurora.

There were less than a dozen people in the night club, and most seemed to be drinking away their losses. Emily and Cassie sat at a dimly lit booth in the back, as far away from the bartender as possible.

"What brings you to Vegas?" asked Cassie, as she poured each of them a glass of red wine from the bottle of Cabernet Sauvignon she'd purchased at the bar.

"My brother's wedding," Emily said, taking the proffered glass. "How about you?"

"My sister's wedding!" exclaimed Cassie.

"Seriously?"

"Seriously," Cassie said, holding out her glass of wine. "Let's make a toast to siblings getting hitched and chance meetings in casinos."

Emily laughed and clinked her glass against Cassie's. "To siblings getting hitched and chance meetings in casinos!"

She sipped the wine slowly, trying not to look stupid. She'd tried alcohol twice before—once with Sabrina and Farris, and another time when she was just 14 and still living in Chicago—but this was the first time she'd drank wine. It tasted surprisingly good, and before Emily knew it, she had drained the whole glass.

"Ben—that's my brother—got married in the hotel, in the Luxor chapel. Did your sister get married there, too?"

"No," Cassie said, as she refilled both of their glasses, "she got married in the Little White Chapel, just down the road. Where did ya'll fly in from?"

They didn't fly, but she couldn't tell Cassie that. "Illinois. A tiny town called Carthage. You?"

"I'm also from Illinois!"

"Seriously?"

"Nope. But wouldn't it be funny if I were?"

Emily laughed. "It would be. But where are you really from?"

"Saraland, Alabama. Saraland is small, kind of a suburb of Mobile."

"I know where Mobile is, but I've never been to Alabama. I'd love to visit one day."

Taking another sip of wine, Emily was shocked to realize she'd drained almost half the glass. She looked up to see Cassie staring at her.

"What?"

"You're really pretty. Did you know that?"

"Hardly," Emily said, but she could feel herself blush. "Any chance I had at being pretty went away with all the freckles."

"Don't do that," Cassie said, frowning.

"Do what?"

"Put yourself down like that. You're beyond pretty, Emily. You're gorgeous. And that hair! I've always wanted red hair, but the only way I could ever get it was from a bottle. Yours is natural. You're lucky."

"You're the one who's lucky, Cassie," said Emily, meeting the other woman's gaze. "Blonde hair, beautiful blue eyes, flawless skin. I bet you have the boys beating down your door."

"It's not the boys I'm worried about," she said, leaning across the table to kiss Emily's lips.

Cassie's lips were so soft. Emily closed her eyes for a moment, enjoying the taste of their kiss, before suddenly jerking away.

"What?" asked Cassie, hurt flashing across her face.

"I'm so sorry. I'm just not...I mean..."

"I'm the one who should be sorry," Cassie said. "I misjudged the situation. I really like you, and us meeting like this was so cool, and I really hope you don't hate me now."

Emily felt tingly as she stared into Cassie's deep blue eyes, and her stomach flip-flopped. Maybe it was the wine talking, but...

Aw, what the hell? Pulse quickening, she leaned across the table and took Cassie's face into her hands, kissing her deeply. Finally, after what felt like hours of pure bliss but was probably mere seconds, Cassie was the one who pulled away.

"Are you sure?" she asked. "I don't want you to do anything you don't..."

"I'm sure," Emily said, interrupting her, kissing Cassie again.

This time, neither of them pulled away.

# Chapter 37

What was that awful sound? Emily tried ignoring it, but it just wouldn't stop. It was making her head pound. Please, she thought, just ten more minutes of sleep, but her eyes opened almost despite herself. She sat up in bed, shielding her gaze from the sun streaming in through the huge bay window, grabbed her cell phone from the nightstand, and answered.

"What?" she yelled into the phone.

"Emily, are you okay?" It was her mother. "We're all in Ben and Katy's room, waiting to go home. You were supposed to be here fifteen minutes ago."

Emily looked at the clock on the nightstand. It was 11:15 in the morning. Shit.

"Sorry, Mom," she managed to say, "I lost track of time and just got out of the shower. I'll be there in a few minutes." She hung up before her mother could respond.

"Hmm?" said a voice beside Emily.

She turned to stare at a half-naked blonde woman lying arms akimbo in the sheets, and last night came rushing back with a vengeance. Half-drunk, she'd led Cassie to her room where they ripped each other's clothes off and made love. The hair on her arms stood up as she remembered Cassie starting with her lips and slowly kissing and nibbling her way down Emily's entire body...

Well, she was no longer a virgin. Losing her virginity to a woman in Las Vegas wasn't exactly how she would have planned it, but she wouldn't change a thing. Was she a lesbian now? Emily hadn't a clue. She'd always thought of herself as straight, but last night had been incredible. She shook her head. There was no time. She'd have to figure it all out later.

"Hey, Emily," Cassie whispered, smiling up at her.

"Hey, Cassie. I'm late."

"You think you're pregnant? I don't think that's possible." Cassie sat up in bed, not even bothering to cover her breasts.

Emily laughed. "No, not that kind of 'late'. My family…shit. We're leaving today, and I was supposed to meet them fifteen minutes ago. Shit, shit, shit!"

Emily got out of bed, only to discover that she was completely naked. Her bra and panties were on the floor, her blouse was on the couch, and her skirt was inexplicably hanging from one of the light fixtures beside the bed. Blushing, she quickly got dressed.

"I didn't know you were leaving today," said Cassie, the disappointment in her voice making Emily's stomach flip-flop. "We're here for two more days."

"I know, and I'm sorry," Emily said, while searching for her shoes, "but maybe I can come visit you in Alabama or something. I have a lot of frequent flier miles. I mean, if you want."

"I want," Cassie said, a smile on her lips.

Emily stopped what she was doing, walked over to the bed, and kissed Cassie. The kiss lingered for a few minutes, until finally Cassie pulled away.

"I don't want this to stop, but I also don't want you missing your flight. Well, okay, I kind of do want you missing your flight, but you know what I mean."

Emily sighed. "Yeah, I do. Okay. Give me your phone number?" Cassie rattled off ten digits, which Emily carefully typed into her phone. "Got it. Here, I'm texting you, so you have mine."

Somewhere across the room, a phone beeped.

"I'll miss you, you know," said Cassie. "That's probably weird, and I shouldn't even say it, especially since we barely know each other."

"Say cheese," said Emily, as she took a quick photo of Cassie with her phone.

"Morning face," Cassie yelped, covering her face with her hands. "No cheese for you."

"I'll miss you, too, by the way," Emily said, laughing, as she picked up the small travel bag that held her bridesmaid dress and the change of clothing she'd intended to wear this morning. "I'll text you when I'm home, okay?"

"You'd better," said Cassie, blowing her a kiss as she walked out the door.

The rest of the morning passed in a blur. First, Emily teleported Leesie, Claire, and Jimmy back to the hotel Leesie had rented in Tulsa, leaving her rental car in Carthage for Sabrina to return. Then she took Mel back to Dallas, and after that took Katy's sister Samantha back to Chicago. Finally, she teleported Fred and Candy Ruskin, her parents, and Colin (who had finally agreed to travel "Emily-style") back to Carthage, leaving her alone with Ben and Katy.

"You seem happy," said Katy, while Ben was in the bathroom packing up his toiletries. "What's going on?"

Emily blushed. Was she that obvious?

"I met someone last night," Emily said.

"Seriously? Good for you! What's his name?"

"Whoever said it was a guy?"

Katy arched an eyebrow. "Okay, what's *her* name?"

"Cassie. It just sort of…happened. And I'll probably never see her again, honestly."

"Why not?"

"She lives in Alabama, for one thing. It's funny, she's in Vegas for her sister's wedding. They'll be here for two more days."

Katy bit her lip. "Well…it's not like you can't come back to the hotel, you know, after you take us home."

"I thought about that, but what will Mom and Dad think?"

"Dude, you're 18. A legal adult. Do you like this girl?"

"Yeah, I really do."

"Then go for it. Life is short, you've gotta take your happiness wherever you can find it."

"I'll second that," said Ben, emerging from the bathroom. "What are you talking about?"

"Just girl talk," Katy said, which earned a laugh from Emily.

"You ready?" she asked her brother.

He was, and she took him home.

# Chapter 38

The knight sat in the little library off the dining room, reading *Tales of the Neverwar*, one of the new novels that had mysteriously appeared on the shelves this morning. It was like the food that periodically showed up in the kitchen. One day the cupboards were bare, and the next they were stuffed to overflowing. It didn't make any sense, but he wasn't complaining, either.

Was their charge responsible for these boons, or were their origins more celestial in nature? He supposed it didn't matter. One way or another, it would all be coming to an end soon enough anyway. He just hoped they could keep their charge safe.

"Hey, kitty," he said, as the huge tiger he lived with sauntered into the library. "What's up?"

The tiger stood on his hind legs, put his front paws on the knight's lap, and licked the knight's face. The knight ruffled the huge cat's fur for a few minutes, eliciting a nearly deafening purr from deep within its chest.

As one, the knight and the tiger spun their heads to stare at the south wall of the house. Instantly, the knight was on his feet, the tiger standing next to him, both ready to defend their charge.

Something was happening, something that could cause a lot of problems down the road, if it were all allowed to play out. There were only so much he and the cat could do to protect those they loved. It was frustrating, but it was what it was.

"Are you ready to go on patrol, tiger?"

The huge animal licked his hand, which he took as a yes. Gathering his sword, the knight and the tiger prepared to leave their home and confront whatever danger lay beyond.

# Chapter 39

Though it had taken Shawn a long time to warm up to the idea of getting a dog, he'd fallen in love with Hercules the moment he saw the scrawny puppy at the shelter. He'd probably always be a cat person at heart, but he loved Hercules just as fiercely as he'd loved Samson.

He'd just returned from taking Hercules for a walk when they both heard a sharp bang from the other side of the front door. The border collie instantly raised his hackles, a low growl rumbling deep in his chest.

"It's okay, boy," said Shawn, ruffling the dog's head.

But it wasn't okay. The door burst open just as Shawn approached it, wood splintering, and a man dressed all in black hurried through the entrance. Shawn instinctively jumped back while Hercules sprinted for the door.

The border collie leapt for the man's throat, settling for his forearm as the intruder moved to protect himself. The dog bit down hard, eliciting a grunt of pain from the man.

Three other men, all dressed the same, poured through the doorway, and one cracked Hercules across the head with the butt of his rifle. The dog refused to let go, though, and growled fiercely as his prey shook his arm, trying to get free.

"Fucking dog," said the man who had hit Hercules.

He pointed the rifle at the collie and pulled the trigger, shooting him point blank in the side. Hercules released his hold on the other man's forearm as he crumpled to the ground, not moving.

"No!" screamed Shawn, staring at the dog, for a moment not comprehending what had just happened.

The memories of finding his cat Samson dead all those years ago, murdered by the fetch, memories he'd thought he'd dealt with, all came flooding back. The blood, there had been so much blood.

"We're here for Ben Spencer," one of the men said, "no one has to get hurt."

He was on the man in a second, white hot fury coursing through his veins, red blinding his vision. He punched the man hard in the face, once, twice, three times, and then someone else was pulling him off, shoving him angrily to the floor.

Shawn rolled to his feet and tackled the second man, slamming him into the wall, throwing wild punches. Then he was on the floor again, his shoulder in agony. He'd been shot. He tried to struggle to his feet, but someone kneed him in the stomach, knocking the wind out of him.

"Stay the fuck down," the man who'd hit him said, "or I'll put you down just like I did your stupid dog."

Shawn stared at Hercules, just a few feet away from him. The dog was still breathing, sucking in shallow, desperate breaths. He started to push himself to his feet again when Katy burst into the foyer.

"Katy, no!" he yelled, as the man who'd shot Hercules levelled a rifle at her, preparing to murder his daughter-in-law.

And that's when Katy used the tooth.

# Chapter 40

Katy sat beside Ben at the small dining table inside Emily's apartment, listening to the two brothers argue. Ben, Colin, and Emily had been hashing everything out for the last half-hour, and at least twice Katy thought her new husband and his alternate-reality brother might come to blows.

Earlier this evening, after supper, Katy had called her father and mother over to the apartments, sat everyone down, and told them about her discussion with Azazel. They had been upset with her at first, for not telling them earlier, but Ben defended her, and eventually everything was smoothed over. They all agreed they had to be on their toes, and Shawn wondered aloud if he should hire security for the house.

After they were finished, Emily suggested that she, Ben, and Colin adjourn to Emily's apartment to hash out the issues between the two "brothers." Katy hadn't thought it was a good idea, but she'd been overruled by Ben and Colin. Now she wondered if Emily regretted suggesting the discussion.

"For the last time," Ben said to Colin, "you didn't exist before I went back in time, and you shouldn't exist now."

"Ben," said Emily, turning to glare at her brother, "that's an awful thing to say."

Ben looked exasperated. "It isn't awful, and it isn't nice; it's just the truth."

Katy stared across the table at Colin. He and Ben had the same eyes and similar facial features. Perhaps something they did in 1977 really did change the timeline and, much like her father's multi-million-dollar business, this was the result.

"It's all right, sis," Colin said, "I get that he's angry, I really do."

"You're not real," said Ben, flatly. "Emily thinks you're real, Mom and Dad think you're real, but you're not real."

"Enough," said Colin, standing up from the table. "I'm every bit as 'real' as you are, asshole."

Ben stood up from the table as well, fist cocked back, and Katy was sure they were going to fight. Katy was moving between them when a loud crash echoed through the room, followed by the sound of gunshots.

"What was that?" Emily asked, eyes wide.

Hope! Katy's heart raced. Hope was upstairs with Jenny, so she had to put herself between whoever had just invaded the apartment building and her daughter. In an instant she was running towards the sound, Ben and Colin just a step behind.

Four men dressed head to toe in black camouflage and carrying assault rifles stood just inside the entryway to the building. The door lay splintered behind them.

"Katy, no!" yelled Shawn.

He was lying on the tile floor, in a pool of his own blood, holding his shoulder. Hercules lay beside him, bleeding from his side. His breathing was labored and shallow, but at least he was still alive.

"Get down on the ground!" barked one of the mercenaries, his face bloodied and bruised, pointing his rifle at her. "No one else has to get hurt."

Katy was already moving, the jaguar tooth gripped tight in her hand. She dropped to one knee, imagining a great wind pushing out from her hands, rushing toward the man who stood above Shawn.

"*Ventus,*" she whispered, using the Latin word for wind to focus the magic.

The mystical gale caught the man, flinging him across the room and hard into the wall. He crumpled to the floor, not moving.

"Shit!" said one of the other mercenaries, turning his rifle on Katy.

"Get down!" Ben yelled, tackling her just as the man fired, the bullet missing them by mere inches.

"Hey, that's him," said the man. "Don't shoot him, we need him."

Emily materialized beside the front door, holding an aluminum baseball bat. She swung the bat at the man's head, hitting him hard. He stumbled, turned to face her, but she teleported behind him and swung the bat into the other side of his head. He crumpled to the floor, out like a light, or worse.

One of the two remaining invaders pulled something from his jacket and threw it at Emily. It was a small green net that expanded as it soared through the air, releasing something gelatinous as it flew towards her, covering her. She stumbled and fell, the bat rolling away from her, and the more she moved, the tighter the net seemed to become.

"I can't teleport," she yelled, her voice shaking.

The mercenary, a blond man, walked over to her and held his rifle to her head. "Benjamin Spencer, if you don't want to see your sister's brains splattered all over the wall, you're coming with us. And Katy, drop the talisman. Now. You have three seconds."

The tooth held incredible power, but there was no way she could do anything before the bastard shot Emily in the head. She dropped the jaguar's tooth to the floor, raising her hands into the air.

The other remaining invader, a bald man, held his rifle on Colin, who also had his hands in the air.

"Take me," said Colin, "and leave my sister alone."

"You're not going to take either of my sons," Shawn said, struggling to rise from the floor. "And you're not going to kill my daughter. Whatever you're being paid, I'll double it."

"You couldn't afford it," said the blond man. "Now, Ben, before we blow her brains out."

"What do you want with me? Why can't you just leave us alone?"

"Michael wants to have a word with you. After that, you'll be free to go."

"That's bullshit," Emily said, still struggling against the net. "You're not taking my brother anywhere."

"I'll come with you," said Ben, walking towards the man. "Just don't hurt anyone else."

The mercenary pointed the rifle at Ben, and that's when Colin made his move. He dove toward the ground, rolled, and came up with Emily's bat. The bald mercenary shot at him, hitting him in the lower leg. Colin stumbled but swung the bat low, hitting the man between his legs. He dropped the rifle and fell to the floor, crying out in pain.

The blond man turned to aim his rifle at Colin, but Ben tackled him. They both tumbled over Emily, crashing to the floor as they fought for the weapon. The mercenary quickly gained control, rolling Ben onto his back, hands wrapped around his throat.

Katy picked up the tooth, concentrating, and the man floated away from Ben and into the air, arms pinned at his sides, helpless. Ben stared up at him, and then at Katy.

She caught Colin out of the corner of her eye, aiming one of the rifles at her. She flinched as the rifle barked, but the bullet shot past her and into the forehead of the man she had earlier flung into the wall. The mercenary had been about to stab her with a very sharp-looking hunting knife. The weapon tumbled from the man's hand as he fell backwards, dead.

"This might be over for us, but it isn't over," said the blond mercenary, still floating in the air.

He rolled his jaw and then bit something, and seconds later was frothing at the mouth, his eyes rolling back in his head. Though they were unconscious, the two remaining mercenaries also had foam in their mouths. They jerked once, and then were silent.

Katy gasped, dropping the dead man to the floor.

"Jesus Christ," said Colin, staring at the motionless form of the blond mercenary. "He...he killed himself. And the other two...some automatic suicide pill tied to their leader? And the one I shot...I killed a man."

"You also got shot," Katy said. "Are you okay?"

Colin stared at her for a second, then shook his head. "The bullet missed. It went through my pants leg but didn't hit me. Didn't even graze me."

"But you have blood all over your pants."

He pulled up his pants to show his right leg; it was perfectly fine. "The blood must belong to the guy I hit with the bat."

Katy could have sworn he'd been shot in the leg. she shook her head. Colin had saved her life by shooting the man who was about to shoot her. He might not have been able to do that had he actually been shot.

"Guys," said Shawn from across the room, "I'm glad Colin wasn't shot, but I think Hercules is dying, and I'm not doing that great myself."

"You two need to help me get your father and Hercules up to the spirit room," Katy said. "Now!"

There was no way in hell she was going to let Hercules die.

"Hey, can someone get this thing off of me?" complained Emily, still trapped in the net.

# Chapter 41

In Hope's bedroom, Jenny and Hope were playing with the doll-house when the mercenaries broke into Huffman Heights. They'd locked the doors and kept on playing, Jenny doing everything she could to distract Hope and keep her safe without scaring her.

Ben didn't know what he'd do if he lost his little girl. He'd only known her a few days, but already loved her with the intensity of a thousand suns and would kill or die to protect her.

Jenny decided to call Grandpa Fred and Grandma Candy to ask if they wouldn't mind taking her and Hope to visit Hope's favorite doll-house store in Quincy, and of course they said yes. Jenny and Hope exited through the back of the apartments, to avoid Hope seeing the massacre that had taken place in the apartment building's foyer. That gave the rest of them at least two hours to rid the house of the aftermath of the attack.

Katy had immediately taken Shawn and Hercules into the spirit room to heal them, while Emily, after they'd managed to get her out of the net, teleported the bodies of the dead mercenaries to the Yukon. That was the best they could come up with, once they had all agreed that involving the police wasn't a good idea.

They'd searched each man before Emily teleported them, one by one, to the frozen tundra, finding absolutely nothing to identify any of them. Their fingerprints had even been removed, probably with acid.

Ben wished there had been some way to track them, to find out where Michael was holed up. It was time to take the fight to the enemy and end this once and for all, before anyone else got hurt.

Why did Michael want him? According to what Katy had said about her conversation with Azazel, Michael and Elohim were no longer interested in him. But perhaps they knew something Azazel didn't, or Azazel had been lying despite his oath to tell the truth.

He stared at the man who claimed to be his brother, watching him as he pushed a mop across the hardwood floor. Could he be wrong about Colin? He had offered himself up to the kidnappers and, when that didn't work, risked his life by attacking one with Emily's baseball bat and then shooting the other one sneaking up behind Katy.

"You saved Katy's life," said Ben, holding out his hand. "Thank you."

Colin stared at it, then pulled Ben into an awkward hug. Ben resisted at first, before finally hugging him back.

"I can't believe I killed that man," said Colin. "I feel sick to my stomach."

"He was going to kill Katy. You didn't have a choice," Ben said, pushing his own mop across another part of the floor.

"You really don't remember me, not at all?" asked Colin.

"I don't. I wish I did, but I don't."

"What happened to the version of you I grew up with?"

Ben shrugged his shoulders. "I don't understand this any more than you do."

"Remember what you did with me in 1977?" asked Katy, walking down the stairs. "I'd only remembered the reality that the demon Leonard had helped create, where my father was dead. You touched me and suddenly I remembered both realities."

"Could you maybe do that to yourself?" asked Colin.

"Maybe if I still had my powers." Ben said. "But I don't, so the point is moot."

Colin didn't respond, just continued cleaning the floor, but Ben could see the hurt in his eyes. He felt guilty for all the cruel things he'd said to him earlier.

Ben always wanted a brother, and now he had one, albeit in the most unconventional way possible. Ben accepted Katy's father's wealth easily enough, also a product of their trip to the past. Was this really any different? Fred becoming wealthy and owning a chain of pizza restaurants wasn't a bad thing, and Ben having a twin brother didn't have to be bad, either.

"Listen, Colin" Ben said, coming to a decision. "I'm sorry for the shit I said earlier."

"It's okay," Colin said, turning to face Ben. "I didn't exist before you time traveled. I get it. I don't like it, but I get it."

"But none of this is your fault, and like everyone has been trying to tell me, you're just as real as I am. This reality is just as real as the reality that existed before we made the jump. So, let's call a truce and start over, okay...brother?"

Colin looked like he might cry. "I'd really like that, brother."

He pulled Ben into another hug, and this time Ben didn't resist.

# Chapter 42

Shawn was fuming. How dare mercenaries invade his home, and not only shoot him and nearly murder his dog, but also threaten to kill Emily and attempt to kidnap his son? Beneath that anger, however, was a stronger emotion, and that was fear. He'd lost his best friend Tanner at age 15, during that fateful summer of 1975. He lost his cat Samson to the murderous fetch not long after, and he and Jenny, not to mention Fred Ruskin, had nearly been killed by a deranged Mayan priest who had ultimately been controlled by the demon Azazel, and then that same demon had stolen his son away from him five years ago.

Until yesterday, he'd thought at least the archangel Michael was on their side. But no, even that was a lie. There were no angels, nor demons, just beings called the Vīrya pretending to be those things to gain power from the humans who believed in them, and Michael had been plotting against Shawn and his family all along.

Hercules, fully healed, lay at Shawn's feet. He bent down and stroked the dog's fur, feeling thankful the border collie was still with them. The dog had attempted to protect Shawn when the men broke into Huffman Heights and had taken a bullet for his trouble. If not for Katy, Hercules might not have made it. He was a good boy, and Shawn loved him fiercely.

"Nickel for your thoughts?" asked Jenny, coming into the room.

Substituting a nickel for the penny in the classic phrase was their private joke, and the reference brought a smile to his lips. He sighed, and said, "I just don't know what to do."

"I know you're angry," said Jenny, sitting beside him on their bed, "but we can't afford to dwell on the past. What's done is done. What we need to do is figure out how to protect Ben from these…things."

"And how do we do that?" he snapped, instantly regretting it. "Sorry, sorry. None of this is your fault, and I shouldn't take it out on you."

She reached out to take his hand. "I'm scared, too. We all are. We finally get Ben back, and now this."

"I wish I still had the nickel," Shawn said. "At least then we'd have some protection against them. I know Katy has the jaguar's tooth, and honestly she's probably learned to use it better than I ever could, but…I just hate feeling so helpless, so out of control."

"The cameras should help with that, I'd imagine," said Jenny.

This morning, Emily had teleported Shawn to three different Best Buys in Chicago, where he'd purchased a total of 32 Blink security cameras. He'd also bought 5 Amazon Echo Shows, to use as monitors for the cameras, and they'd installed the Blink apps on all their phones.

Fred, Ben, and Colin had helped him attach the cameras all over the inside and outside of the house, on all three floors and even the roof. They'd also upgraded their internet service, not to mention the modem and router, so they now had a cool 1GB of wi-fi bandwidth with which to monitor the cameras. The entire project had taken them nearly six hours.

He'd briefly considered hiring ADT or another home security company to outfit the whole building, but there just wasn't time to schedule an appointment and then wait for them to show up and do the job. Plus, he wasn't sure he wanted people he didn't know having access to Huffman Heights.

"Well, now at least we'll be able to see them coming," Shawn said, getting up to pace the room, "but what we'll do once they get here, I have no idea."

Hercules suddenly growled, and Shawn tensed up. But it was just Colin, standing in the doorway.

"I think I do," said Colin. "Sorry, I wasn't trying to eavesdrop, I just wanted to talk."

"It's okay, come on in," Jenny said, and Shawn nodded his acquiescence. "Hercules, be nice."

The dog stopped growling and settled for just staring at Colin. Hercules had taken to Ben right away but seemed to dislike his brother. Maybe it was just a case of too many people, too soon. Being shot probably hadn't helped, either.

"What's on your mind?" asked Shawn.

"Yesterday before the attack, you'd mentioned the possibility of hiring security guards," he said, staring at Hercules. "Are you still up for that?"

"I'm just not sure," said Shawn, "for two reasons. First, what if someone sees Emily teleport or Katy use the tooth? Do we really need that scrutiny? Second, and this is a bigger concern, how do we know we can trust them?"

"I can't really answer your first objection, but I have an idea about the second."

"We're all ears," Jenny said.

"Okay. Well, a good friend of mine at the university is from Chicago, and his father runs a security company. They've provided guards for a lot of Chicago politicians and visiting celebrities. They even kept Taylor Swift safe the last time she was there.

"They're also very discreet, according to my friend Brandon, and Brandon's father, who I've met, by the way, seems like a really stand-up guy. Former air force major. I took the liberty of texting my friend—I didn't tell him anything, I promise—and asked about the business. He said their guys are willing to travel as long as they're put up at a decent hotel and given a per diem for food and stuff."

"Huh," Shawn said, thinking it over.

It would be good to add an extra layer of security. If they'd had guards yesterday, those mercenaries might never have gotten inside the house. Azazel's guards in the Yukon had almost enabled him to escape. If nothing else, they'd have an extra buffer of safety between Ben and the supernatural beings that sought to capture him.

He'd talked to Mr. Kingfisher about using some of their mirror wards to hide the house from their enemies, but the giant had informed him that the magic wouldn't work on supernatural beings. He now regretted not pushing Kingfisher further, because the wards definitely would have worked on the mercenaries. He made a mental note to reach out to Claire Locke to see if she could contact Kingfisher and Quarry on his behalf.

"I think we should at least give them a call," offered Jenny.

"What's the name of the business?" Shawn asked, setting aside for now thoughts of supernatural solutions.

"Oslov Security. That's Brandon's last name, by the way. His father is Jack Oslov. Mr. Oslov told me he started the business something like 20 years ago, right after he got out of the air force."

"Okay. Let me Google them, and if everything seems on the up-and-up, I'll give them a call tomorrow. It couldn't hurt to hear what they have to say."

"Good," Colin said. "I just got my brother back, and I don't want to lose him again."

"Colin," said Jenny, rising from the bed to pull her son into a hug, "We're so glad to have you home, too, even if it's just for a little while, and so happy you and Ben are getting along. You're just as important to us as Ben or Emily. Never forget that."

"I'll second that," said Shawn, a lump in his throat. "We love you, Colin, and together, we're going to get through this."

*I hope*, he added silently, reaching down to ruffle Hercules' fur.

# Chapter 43

The cling and clang of the slot machines coming from the casino inside the Luxor called to Emily, but she walked on past, ignoring their siren song. She was here for one thing and one thing only, and that was to see Cassie.

They'd been texting nearly nonstop since Ben and Katy's wedding two days ago, and Emily finally decided to throw caution to the wind and once again teleport to Las Vegas. Surely there would be no mercenaries waiting for her in the neon capital of the world, and if there were, well, she'd just teleport them to the Yukon along with the others who'd tried to kidnap Ben. As long as they didn't have any of those damned nets.

She stood outside the entrance to the Aurora, the club where she and Cassie had first kissed two days ago, dressed in a short blue skirt, a white blouse, and strappy black heels. The club only had a couple dozen people in it, but she couldn't see Cassie anywhere.

She'd texted Cassie just ten minutes ago, from her bedroom in her little apartment in Huffman Heights, and asked her if she might be up for a drink or three. Cassie had thought she was kidding, of course, but Emily swore that if she walked down to the Aurora, she would more than make it worth her while.

"Oh my God," said a voice from behind her, "oh my God, oh my God, oh my God, you're really here!"

Emily whirled around and there was Cassie, dressed in a black and white checkered miniskirt with a tight black crop top. She looked stunning, and she smelled of roses and vanilla.

Cassie jumped into her arms, and Emily felt those now-familiar flip-flops fill her stomach. The two kissed, a long, deep kiss that was perfect.

"I'm really here," Emily said, when the kiss ended.

"But how? I mean, you just left two days ago. Or did you not leave, after all?"

"Oh, I did leave, but I missed you," said Emily, feeling herself blush at her own words, "so I came back."

Cassie folded her arms over her chest and cocked her head to the side. "Just for little ole me?"

"Just for little ole you."

"I'm flattered. But seriously, that flight had to cost you a bundle. Are you fabulously rich, or something?"

"I wish," Emily said, laughing. "Frequent flier miles work wonders."

She hated lying to Cassie, but she couldn't very well tell her she could teleport. That would open a whole different can of worms. Besides, Cassie would probably think she was insane. She was going with the little white lie, at least for now.

"We're leaving tomorrow, you know."

"I do know."

"And you still came."

"And I still came."

"I know we barely know each other," Cassie said, "but I could definitely fall for you."

"Same," said Emily, butterflies dancing in her stomach.

"So…wanna get that drink?"

Shit. Last night had been one thing, but she was already lying to Cassie about how she got here. She didn't want to build a relationship based on yet another lie.

"I need to tell you something," Emily said, biting her lip. "I'm not actually old enough to drink, the other night notwithstanding."

"Okay. How old are you, exactly?"

"Eighteen. I'll turn nineteen in a couple of months. I'm so sorry I didn't tell you when we first met."

Cassie laughed. "Whew. I thought you were going to tell me you were fourteen or something. Now, that would have been awkward."

"You're not mad?"

"Honey, I just turned twenty-two last month. You said you're almost nineteen. Three years and change isn't a big deal for me, as long as it isn't for you. Is it?"

"Not at all."

"Well, there you go, then. We're fine, but let's not tempt fate at the bar. How about you go get comfy in my room, while I grab us a bottle of wine to go?" Cassie asked, reaching into her purse to remove her hotel keycard. "It's room 2817, on the 28th floor."

"Sounds great to me," said Emily, taking the card before pulling Cassie in for another lingering kiss.

Cassie's room—no, it was a suite—was huge, much bigger than Emily's room had been. It was a corner suite, and the view outside the slanted window was amazing. She could see for miles, or at least it seemed that way.

Emily glanced at the king-sized bed and for a moment thought about getting naked and waiting for Cassie under the covers, but she didn't want to be presumptuous. Instead, she wandered around aimlessly, exploring the suite.

It really was luxurious, with a small dining area in the kitchen, a gorgeous soaking tub in the bathroom, and a comfy-looking purple couch and writing desk in the sitting room. There was a book lying open on the writing desk. Curious, Emily picked it up and began to read:

> Dear Diary, I met the most amazing woman today, while in Las Vegas for Meleah's wedding. Her name is Emily, and she has gorgeous red hair and beautiful green eyes, but more than that, she's smart, fearless, and funny as hell. After a few drinks, we went back to her hotel room and made love. It was amazing! She lives in Illinois, though, and left the next morning, so I may never see her again. That would make me very sad.

Emily blushed and put down the diary, embarrassed to have read Cassie's private thoughts, but also flattered. She could definitely fall in love with this girl, if she hadn't already.

She'd always been attracted to women as well as men, but never really explored that side of herself. Hell, she'd barely even explored her heterosexual side. She supposed it didn't really matter, in the end. She liked Cassie and Cassie liked her, and she was excited to see where this relationship might take them.

A knock reverberated through the suite, and for a moment Emily wondered who it was, but of course it was Cassie. She had given Emily her keycard, so there was no way for her to enter the room.

Emily rushed to open the door and felt her heart race as Cassie's smile greeted her on the other side. She was carrying a bottle of wine and two wine glasses.

"Hey, you," Emily said, returning the smile, as she took the two glasses from Cassie.

"Sorry it took a while," said Cassie, walking into the little kitchen. "There was a couple ahead of me who seemed determined to talk the bartender's ear off."

"No worries. I love this room, by the way. Especially the soaking tub."

"Maybe we'll try it out later," Cassie said, as she de-corked the bottle of Buttercream Chardonnay she'd purchased from the bar. "I mean, if you think you might want to."

"I think I just might," said Emily.

Cassie poured the wine and then they made their way to the purple couch in the sitting room. Cassie lowered herself cross-legged onto the couch, and Emily did the same, facing her.

"Wow, this is good," Emily said, after taking a sip of the wine. "I haven't had a lot of alcohol, honestly, but this is probably my favorite yet."

"Here's to corrupting beautiful young women named Emily with alcohol," said Cassie, holding up her glass to Emily's.

Emily laughed and clinked her glass against Cassie's before taking another sip. "This really is delicious, but the company is even better."

Cassie sat her glass on the coffee table next to the couch and reached her hand out to caress Emily's cheek. "You really are beautiful, you know."

Emily drained her glass and then sat it beside Cassie's. She took Cassie's hand in her own hands and kissed her palm and then each finger in turn. Moaning, Cassie took one of Emily's hands and did the same, and then they were kissing, kissing deeply, bodies pressed close as they fumbled at each other's clothing.

"I want you so much," Cassie whispered into Emily's ear, gently sucking on the lobe.

"You smell so good," said Emily, as shivers of ecstasy travelled up her spine. "I want you, too."

"I'll race you to the bed," whispered Cassie, and then they were on their feet, giggling, sprinting towards the king-sized bed.

Emily won the race, but only because Cassie stopped to turn out the lights. Laughing, Emily pulled her blouse up and over her head, stepped out of her skirt, and dived under the covers.

With only moonlight from the slanted window to illuminate the bedroom, Emily watched as Cassie slowly stripped, first letting her miniskirt fall to the floor, and then her top. She wasn't wearing a bra or panties.

"Come to me," whispered Emily, her heart beating fast, throwing back the covers to reveal her own now-naked form.

"I thought you'd never ask," Cassie replied, as she crawled into bed, her lips meeting Emily's in a kiss that seemed to last all night.

# Chapter 44

Shawn couldn't believe it had actually come to this and that he was considering hiring a security firm to protect them from the Vīrya. He'd checked out Oslov Security's website, however, and everything seemed on the up and up, so he felt he owed it to Colin to at least see what they had to say.

Colin had texted him Jack Oslov's direct phone number, and also let Oslov know he'd be calling.

"Jack Oslov here," said the voice on the other end.

For some reason, Shawn had expected a Russian accent, but Oslov sounded as American as anyone. "Mr. Oslov? This is Shawn Spencer, Colin's father, and I wanted to talk to you about possibly providing security for my family."

"Ah, Mr. Spencer. I'm so glad to hear from you. Your son let me know you might be calling. What can I do for you?"

"Well, first of all, call me Shawn."

"And I'm Jack. Good. I hate formalities."

"Okay, Jack. I'm not sure how much Colin told you, but we find ourselves in the need of home security."

Shawn made up a story about a home invasion. They talked for a good five minutes about what sort of security he needed and what Oslov might provide, including alarms as well as actual security guards.

"Well, you're in luck. I have a team finishing up an assignment in Quincy. That's pretty close to Carthage, isn't it?"

"Sure is. Less than an hour from here."

"Good. If you're agreeable, I can send the team's captain—Corey Durst—out to see you tomorrow afternoon, so he can access your building and see how many guards you might need.

"One thought, though. Home invasions are usually a one-time occurrence, and from my research Carthage has a population of well under 3,000 people. Are you sure any of this is necessary? Don't get me wrong, I'll never turn down business, but this won't be cheap. I don't want you to have to spend anything more than absolutely necessary."

Shawn decided right then and there that he liked this man. Not many people would try to talk you out of giving them your business, even if they didn't think you needed it.

Unfortunately, they did need his services, even if he couldn't give Oslov the full story. Having someone to guard his home and family just might mean the difference between life and death.

"I really appreciate that, Jack, but it's as much for peace of mind as anything else. I'd definitely like to meet with Mr. Durst to hear what he has to say."

"Fair enough. I can get him out there around one o'clock tomorrow afternoon, if that works for you."

"Sounds perfect," Shawn said. "I really appreciate this, Jack."

Shawn gave him the address, exchanged goodbyes, and hung up the phone.

"Sounds like that went well," Jenny said.

"I think so. One of his security specialists, Corey Durst, is going to stop by tomorrow afternoon at 1:00 to evaluate the house and talk to us about the services they provide. I'd like you to be there, if that's okay."

"I wouldn't miss it for the world. Shawn, everything really will be all right. We're going to get on top of this, and we're going to protect our family from Michael and anyone else who wants to do us harm."

He pulled her into a hug. "I love you."

She held his face in her hands and kissed his lips. "And I love you, too. We've built an amazing family. Ben and Colin are finally home, Emily, Hope, and Katy are safe, and we're never going to let anyone hurt any of them ever again."

# Chapter 45

Katy walked through the shimmering curtain of light into the spirit room, determined to get some answers. Azazel had said that Elohim and the other angelic and demonic pretenders would have no use for a powerless Ben and thus would make no further attempts to capture him. He had either lied or been woefully uninformed.

"Wait up," said Ben, following her. "Are you sure about this?"

Katy whirled on Ben. "Look, I knew Azazel freaks you out. I get it. I'd be freaked out, too, after what he did to you. But I'm going to question him again, with or without you."

Ben stared at her for a moment before nodding. "Fine. Let's get it over with."

Katy walked over to the bookshelf, grabbed the illusionary mason jar that currently held Azazel, screwed off the lid, and turned the jar upside down. A glob of glowing energy fell to the floor, and then formed into Azazel.

"Couldn't get enough of me, huh?" the demon said, then raised his eyebrows when he saw Ben. "Bennie-boy, come to give me my body back? I knew you'd eventually come around."

"Fuck you," Ben said, swinging a fist at the demon's chin.

Making a split-second decision, Katy concentrated, using her connection to the room to turn Azazel solid for just a moment, long enough for Ben's fist to connect with the demon's jaw. Azazel tumbled backwards, tripped, and landed on the floor.

"That hurt! How did you do that?" he asked, holding his jaw, staring up at Ben. "How?"

"I…don't know," Ben said, staring at his hand.

"You both forget where we are. This is my realm, remember? After all you put Ben through, that's the very least of what you deserve."

"I didn't know you could do that," Ben said, staring at her.

*Me either*, she thought. But while beating the hell out of Azazel might be fun, that's not why they'd come into the spirit room.

"The other night, when we had our conversation," said Katy, getting back on track, "you said your 'kin' would have no reason to come after Ben. Earlier today, four men invaded our home, shot both Shawn and our dog, and almost kidnapped Ben. Were you lying to me?"

"Are they okay?"

"They're fine. Now answer the question."

"I didn't lie to you. I thought you were going to give me a body and let me leave this accursed place. I couldn't have lied to you, even if I wanted to. I told you the truth about everything. The only reason they might come after him is if he got his powers back."

"Which sadly hasn't happened," said Ben, glaring down at the demon. "You took that from me, too."

"I didn't—"

"Enough," said Katy, interrupting the demon. "The fact of the matter is, they did come for Ben. They almost killed his father, and they threw a net on Emily that glued her to the Goddamned floor so she couldn't teleport. Clearly, they knew about her ability."

Try as she might, Emily had never been able to teleport anything or anyone who weighed more than about double her own body weight. Once the net glued itself to her and in turn glued her to the hardwood floor on the apartment building's foyer, she was stuck.

Once everything was over, they'd had a devil of a time cutting her out of that net. 30 minutes into the process, however, the glue abruptly dissolved, and after that it was just a matter of untangling the cords.

"And you think I told them?" Azazel asked, seeming genuinely confused. "I haven't communicated with anyone. How could I? you have me trapped here. Maybe Jonathan Conroy—the helicopter pilot—told them, after he saw Emily teleport me to the ground? I was careful to only hire people who had no connection to Father, but perhaps I wasn't careful enough."

That seemed plausible. More than plausible, actually. Once Ben had been rescued, they hadn't really given the Yukon another thought. Perhaps that had been a mistake.

"If we were to go back to the hunting lodge in the Yukon, what do you think we'd find?" asked Katy.

"I don't know, and I don't care. I've answered more than enough of your questions, Katy Ruskin. Now, if you were to free me…" He let the implication that he'd be willing to answer more questions hang there.

"Not gonna happen, Azazel. Not now, not ever."

"Then I'm done answering your questions."

"You really are a piece of shit," Ben said. "Everything you told Katy about wanting to save the world was all a lie, wasn't it?"

"Don't waste your words, Ben," said Katy, "he's not worth it."

Katy made a show of angrily grabbing the Mason jar from the shelf and reached for Azazel, who quickly backed away.

"Wait a minute," yelled Azazel, "Just wait a minute, will you?"

"We're listening," Ben said.

"If I help you, would you at least leave me out of the jar? I hate it in there."

Katy looked at Ben. "What do you think?"

Ben leaned over and whispered something in her ear.

"Yeah, I can do that," Katy responded. "Okay, Azazel, here's what we'll do. You give us something we can use to find out what the hell is going on, and I'll create a room here just for you. You'll be locked in, but the room will be yours. If the information is especially good, I might be inclined to leave some books in your room for you to read, to help pass the time. Deal?"

"A room with a bed?"

"Yeah, sure. A room with a bed."

"Deal. In my bedroom at the lodge, there's a safe. It's hidden behind a Picasso hanging on the wall. Among other things, there's a small black notebook in there with all the contact information I have for Father and the others. Beyond that, I don't think you'll find much else in the lodge that'll do you any good but knock yourself out."

"What's the combination?" asked Katy.

"To what?"

"The safe."

Azazel smiled. "Ah. No combination, just Ben Spencer's left thumb print. You'll have to go along, Bennie-boy. I'm sure you'll love that."

"Why do you hate me?" asked Ben, staring at the demon.

Azazel stared back at him. "I don't hate you, Ben Spencer. You were just a means to an end."

"Then why do you taunt me every fucking chance you get? 'Bennie-boy' and all that other crap."

"Ben…" said Katy, laying one hand on his shoulder. He jerked away.

"This asshole stole five years of my life. He at least owes me an explanation."

The demon looked confused. "I'm…sorry. You get used to playing a role, and it's hard to stop. As I said, you were simply a means to an end. I don't hate you. If anything, I'm envious of you."

Katy stared at the demon. Was this more of his games, or was he being honest? There was no way to be sure, but she almost thought it was the latter.

"Something I've been wondering...those men, why would they risk their lives for...for your father?" asked Ben.

"They most likely came from the Society of the Great Exodus, a group of people who are convinced that if they free the 'demons' from hell, they'll get to help us rule the world. Probably one of them were my kind, inhabiting a host body from the Society."

"These people just give you their bodies?"

Azazel nodded. "If they serve us and especially if they give up their lives in service to us, they're certain they'll be rewarded when the 'great exodus' of devils and demons happens. Which of course will never happen, because we're already here. But they don't know that. The society has existed for hundreds of years and has served us well."

"You just use them?" Ben asked.

Azazel shrugged. "Essentially, yes. These aren't good people. They willingly serve us and give up their bodies for us, because they want to unleash hell on Earth. The fact that it will never happen doesn't make their desires any less heinous."

Katy couldn't argue with that. "So how can we stop them?"

"If you want to stop Father, you'll have to take the battle straight to him. Unfortunately, I have no idea how you could ever defeat him. Even if his plans are ruined, and without knowing what his plans are I have no idea how to tell you to do that, he'll never give up. Ever. This is all he's ever wanted, and he'll stop at nothing to get it.

"Unlike me, he doesn't enjoy being human. He tolerates it from time to time, because it's a means to an end, but he hates humanity, hates that we get our power from your beliefs, and he wants nothing more than to usurp humanity's place in the world."

"Yeah, well," said Katy with a bravado she didn't feel, "we're not going down without a fight. Now if you'll excuse us, Azazel, I think we have a date with the Yukon."

# Chapter 46

Ben and Emily appeared in the dimly lit Yukon hunting lodge, joining Katy, whom Emily had teleported inside just a few seconds earlier. Katy stood next to the hot tub, shining her flashlight inside. It was extremely cold in the building, probably below freezing, and the water in the hot tub had frozen solid. It was a good thing they'd worn their parkas.

Ben activated his flashlight and slowly waved it around the room. The lodge had clearly been abandoned, and the doors were wide open. No wonder the water had frozen. He flipped a light switch, but nothing happened. The power generators must have been disconnected. The place looked like it had been ransacked.

All three of them walked to the entrance. The paintings that had once adorned the walls were nowhere to be found, probably taken by the now-unemployed guards to sell for cash. The bookshelves had been tipped over, and books were scattered across the floor.

Everything looked stripped bare. Even the monitors for the cameras outside the lodge were gone. Hell, they'd probably also taken the cameras themselves. Little remained of value here, at least in the foyer.

Even with almost everything gone, however, the lodge felt way too familiar, and brought back awful memories. Ben fought the urge to throw up. He'd spent years here, a prisoner, with Azazel in control of his body. He shivered, and not just from the cold.

Katy walked over to Ben and wrapped her arms around him, and he returned the hug. "I'm okay," he whispered, though he wasn't, not really. "Let's just do this and get out of here."

"I don't think we'll find much, beyond his safe," Katy said. "If they took those paintings that you said were by the entrance, they probably took everything else of value as well."

"Those paintings were real," said Ben, "I can't believe they ran off with them. Stolen, of course, and replaced by forgeries. I'm sure they're worth a fortune, but I bet whoever took them will have a hell of a time selling them. But that's their problem, not ours."

"Where to first, big brother?" Emily asked.

"Let's open the safe in the bedroom first, and then check out the rest of the building," Ben said.

He took Katy by the hand and led her down the hallway and into a huge room near the end of the hunting lodge. Emily trailed not far behind.

"Wow, this is pretty fancy," said Emily, as they stepped into the bedroom.

It was most definitely fancy and had been left largely undisturbed. A giant, four-poster king-sized bed filled one end of the room, and a huge flat-screen television filled the other. A stately oak dresser stood against the east wall, beside a door to the master bathroom. More artwork filled the walls, including (according to Katy) paintings by Vermeer, Picasso, and Van Gogh.

"Why didn't they ransack this room?" Katy asked.

"Because if Azazel ever came back there'd be hell to pay, that's why," said Ben. "Invading his personal space was very much against the rules and punishable by death."

Katy removed *Girl on the Ball*, the Picasso painting, from the wall and true to Azazel's word, there was the safe the demon had told them about.

Though the rest of the house was without power, a dim red light lit a panel large enough for a fingerprint.

Ben moved in front of Katy and pressed his left thumb to the glowing panel. The panel hummed for just a second, they heard something clink inside the safe, and then it opened.

There were several things inside: three large bundles of cash, the promised notebook, an old, yellowed piece of paper with something written on it, and a handgun.

Ben snatched the notebook and paper, leaving everything else in the safe. Emily grabbed the cash and the gun.

"Hey, a girl's gotta eat," she said, "and protect herself. Honestly, after that attack at the house, I wouldn't mind having a gun."

Katy and Ben looked at each other and shrugged.

"I'm probably going to come back and grab the paintings, too."

"Knock yourself out," Katy said.

"This is strange," said Ben, looking at the paper. "It's just a list of five names with the city, state, and country each person lives in, and the one on top is Dad."

Shawn Spencer—Carthage, Illinois, USA

Renjiro Hashimoto—Tokyo, Japan

Edward Sparks—Sarcoxie, Missouri, USA

Alejandro Torres—Malinalco, Mexico

Agatha Muir—Chelmsford, Essex, UK

"What in the hell?" asked Katy, taking the paper from Ben.

"Hashimoto?" Emily asked, peering over Katy's shoulder. "That's Sumi's last name. Natsumi Hashimoto, Colin's girlfriend. That's strange."

"I think Hashimoto is probably a fairly common Japanese name," said Katy, "but yeah, it's a little strange. We can research it when we get home."

"Dad told me stories about what happened in 1975," Ben said. "Michael named him the guardian of the nickel, or some such bullshit. Maybe this is a list of who has the other talismans?"

"Had, you mean," said Katy. "Your dad no longer has the nickel, and I have the tooth, which of course I got from David Dowd in 1977. But, yeah, it might be a list of the original so-called guardians. Some of them may even still have the talismans."

Ben flipped open the notebook, revealing dozens of handwritten addresses and phone numbers but no names to go along with them. "There are probably two or three dozen addresses here, from all over the world. But that's it. Just addresses, no names."

"You'd think Azazel could have told you that," said Emily.

Katy shrugged. "This is just standard operating procedure with him. He tells you as little as he can get away with, so you'll have to talk to him again and give him something else to get the whole story. I swear he enjoys the attention."

They left the bedroom to explore the rest of the lodge, including the guard barracks, a huge kitchen, a dining room, and a library, but found nothing of consequence. The guards had apparently stripped the lodge of anything of value outside of Azazel's room, including all the silverware and most of the food from the freezers.

"Where did those women who were in the hot tub stay?" Emily asked.

"They didn't," Ben said. "He'd fly them in on that helicopter from time to time, and they'd always leave the same night. It would not have worked out well if they lived here."

"Were they prostitutes?" asked Katy.

Ben nodded. "For Azazel, mostly, but also as rewards for the guards."

"That's disgusting," said Katy. "Morally, I have nothing against prostitution, but sex should never be used as a prize."

"I agree," said Ben. "The whole thing was beyond disgusting."

"At least we got what we came for," said Emily, in any obvious gambit to change the subject.

Ben couldn't argue with that. "You're right. I think it's time to go home."

# Chapter 47

## Three Days Ago

It was a foggy evening in London when David Dowd walked out of Heathrow Airport, travel bag slung over his shoulder, eager to find the third talisman.

He missed his sword, but there was no way around that. Even attempting to bring the weapon on the airplane would have brought him attention he didn't need. True, it wasn't the same sword he'd had before spending twenty-five years of his life in prison, but it had made for a faithful substitute.

Seven years. It had been seven long years since he'd found the twig, and eighteen since he'd obtained the geode. The maddening part was that he knew exactly where the jaguar's tooth was, but didn't dare attempt to retrieve it until he'd acquired the emerald. With any luck, he wouldn't even need the tooth or the nickel, wherever on earth it was.

Maybe the emerald would be enough.

Dowd was nearly 75 years old, though he didn't even look 40. The twig and the geode had been able to do that much for him, at least, though changing his appearance and physicality was more a matter of necessity than anything else. He would gladly live out his remaining years as a doddering old man if he could only fix the other parts of him that were broken.

Though it was almost eight at night local time, Heathrow was busy. Dowd had never visited Europe before, and wondered if it was always like this. As a child, before the explosion in the grain silo that left his face disfigured and his life forever changed, he'd often dreamed of exploring the world. Instead, he'd settled for preaching a religion he now no longer believed in and hurting those who didn't deserve it.

Ben Spencer had fixed his face, but not his soul. He shook his head, willing away the memories and the guilt and shame that came with them. He held no ill will towards Spencer. Nearly 25 years in prison had given him all the time he needed to work that out of his system. Spencer had done what he had to do, just as Dowd was doing now.

"Need a taxi, mate?" said a voice, startling him.

He blinked, staring at the black cab with a bright yellow "taxi" sign on the roof that idled in front of the airport and the short, stocky man wearing a brown cap that leaned out its window.

"I suppose I do," Dowd said slowly, walking toward the taxi.

The driver scuttled out of the cab and doffed his hat at Dowd. "And where might we be going?"

Dowd recited an address from memory.

"Chelmsford? That's almost two hours away. I don't usually go that far at night. You should have flown into Stansted if you were going to Chelmsford."

He'd finally had a vision of the emerald two days ago, when, inexplicably, it's guardian had used it to open an especially tight jar. It was the first time the talisman had been used since Dowd began using the geode to search for it and the other talismans 18 years earlier.

This was the only flight he could get on short of notice, but of course he couldn't tell that to the cabbie. Instead, he pulled out ten crisp American $100-dollar bills from his wallet.

One thing he didn't need to worry about was money. Before he'd gone to prison, he'd squirreled away nearly $50,000 from donations to his traveling church. 25 years in a savings account had almost doubled his money, and he'd lived very frugally ever since he was released from Western Illinois Correctional.

"Can you make an exception tonight?" Dowd asked, holding out the cash.

The cabbie's eyes grew wide. "That's…what, £750? A bit more?"

Dowd shrugged. He truly had no idea. He hadn't even bothered changing his money into pounds. He didn't plan on being in London that long.

"Is that enough?" Dowd finally asked, staring at the cabbie with his one good eye.

"More than enough, mate!" the little man said, thrusting his hand out to shake Dowd's hand. "Name's Roger, and it looks like I'll be your driver for this evening."

Dowd shook the man's hand and let him take his bag from him and stow it in what he referred to as the "boot" of the car. After the cabbie was finished, he opened the vehicle's back door for Dowd and motioned for the man to climb inside.

"Thank you," Dowd said, as he folded himself into the back seat.

"Watch your head there. You're a tall one, aren't you? I hope you'll be comfortable in there."

"I'll be fine."

That wasn't exactly true. By the time the ride was over, his back ached and his knees hurt, but it was a small price to pay for being that much closer to his destination.

The taxi pulled up to the curb beside a small house on Maltese Road and the driver was out of the car in a flash, retrieving Dowd's luggage from the boot of the car before zooming around to open the door for him.

"Doesn't look like they left the lights on for you, does it now?" Roger said, staring at the dark house while closing the door behind Dowd.

Dowd stretched his legs and worked out the kink in his back before finally saying, "No, doesn't look like it."

He glanced at his watch. It was just after 11, London time. He'd get in, take the emerald, and then go to ground somewhere and wait for his flight out of Heathrow tomorrow afternoon. He almost asked Roger to wait for him but decided against it. He'd have plenty of time to get back to the airport in the morning.

"If that'll be all, Mr. Cameron," said Roger, using the name Dowd had given him, the same name that matched his faked passport, "I'll be on my way then. I suspect the missus is wondering where I've gotten myself off to right about now." He stared at Down expectantly.

Oh, right, the money. Dowd retrieved the $1,000 from his wallet and folded it into the man's hand, adding an extra $200 as a tip.

Roger beamed. "You didn't have to do that, Mr. Cameron, but I'm dead chuffed that you did. When will you be going back? I can drive back out here to fetch you again, and in fact it'd be my pleasure."

"I'm not entirely sure."

The cabbie retrieved a business card from inside the cab and pressed it into Dowd's hand.

"Just call me, anytime, and I'll drop whatever I'm doing and zoom out here."

Dowd agreed, though he had no intention of calling the man. He'd make other arrangements. There was no sense in being too predictable. He paused by an old birch tree, one of many that filled the front yard, waiting for Roger to drive away, and once he was gone made his way to the front door of the house and knocked.

He waited 30 seconds and then knocked again, louder this time.

"I'm coming, I'm coming," he heard a woman's voice call from inside. "Calm yer tits!"

"I'm sorry it's so late," he said through the door, "but my car broke down and—"

"No, yer not," she said, "and no, it didn't. Yer here for the damned emerald, and it's about time, too."

Dowd took a step back from the door. He felt like running but forced himself to remain still. How could she know? The door creaked open, revealing a woman of about 80 in an old white night gown. She didn't look happy.

Dowd stood motionless, starting at her.

"What, are ye daft? Get yer giant ass in here before I catch me death of cold."

"Yes, of course," said Dowd, ducking under the threshold of the house and making his way inside.

"Yer from America, aren't you?" she asked, as she shut the door behind him.

"I am, ma'am. Miss…"

"Muir, you idiot. Mrs. Agatha Muir, but Agatha will do. So, have you come for the emerald, or haven't you?"

"I have, Mrs. Muir…Agatha. But how did you know?"

"I always knew you would come. It's been, what, some 45, 50 odd years since that pretend angel showed up and gave me the damned thing. I felt you searching for a long time, and I finally decided to let you find me."

"You used the emerald to open that jar, so I'd find you?"

"Yes, you ninny, I used the emerald to open that jar, so you'd find me. You couldn't seem to find me on yer own, so I figured you needed a wee bit of help."

"But…why?"

"What does it matter why, as long as you get what you came for? I have some tea brewing, and—"

She was interrupted by the shrill whistle of a tea pot.

"And there it is. Sit down while I fetch us some tea. And don't worry, I have no intention of running from the likes of you."

Dowd watched helplessly as she retreated into the kitchen. He turned to study the house. An old orange couch stood against one wall of the living room, facing an even older television on a wooden table. Bookcases filled the room, holding equal amounts of books and knick-knacks. Nothing out of the ordinary here, just the house of an old woman.

"An old woman who could kick yer ass, I'd wager," she said from behind him.

"You can read minds?" said Dowd, turning to face the old woman.

"Simple ones, like yours," she said. "Now sit down and share some tea with me before we get down to business."

Dowd sat down, watching carefully as she deposited a bamboo tray containing a china teapot, a container of sugar, a saucer of cream, and two chipped cups on the table. Was the tea poisoned?

"Stop being so suspicious," she said, looking at him through rheumy blue eyes. "I've yet to poison a guest, and I'm not about to start now."

Muir filled both cups with tea, motioning for Dowd to take one. Dowd took one of the cups, added two teaspoons of sugar and a splash of cream, and slowly sipped the hot liquid. It was good.

"You miss what you used to be, but what you used to be was a monster."

Dowd almost dropped his teacup. He wanted to argue with her, tell her she was wrong, but in his heart, he knew she was telling the truth. With one subtle difference. He was still a monster, but now he was a monster with a conscience.

"And you want that conscience gone," she said. "You want to rip it from yer heart as surely as you ripped yer eye from yer own skull in prison. You loathe what you used to be, feel ashamed of it, but at the same time yearn for it."

He touched his face, felt a tear trailing down his cheek, and realized he was crying.

"You can't escape the nightmares," said Muir. "Every night, you hear the screams of your victims. You want peace, but you think you don't deserve it. Benjamin Spencer took that blanket from you, the blanket of righteousness, of surety, the one that allowed you to hide from taking responsibility for your own actions for so much of your young life."

"The accident wasn't my fault," he managed to get out. "It turned me into a monster. It wasn't my fault."

"Perhaps," she said, "but what you did after was no one's fault but yer own. You used the powers yer so-called 'accident' gave you, and you used them poorly. You enslaved, you murdered, you destroyed, and somewhere in yer heart, despite what you want to believe, you knew. You knew, and you didn't care. Your injuries made you a monster on the outside, but you and only you made you a monster on the inside."

"No!" Dowd crushed the teacup in his massive hand, the hot liquid burning his skin. He didn't care. The pain only fueled his anger. He stood up, trembling with rage, wanting nothing more than to rip the woman's beating heart from her chest.

"It's a good thing you couldn't bring yer sword on the airplane, you might run me through like you did that poor woman in Missouri."

The anger drained from him in an instant, replaced by regret, regret so painful that it almost suffocated him. He stared at the old woman, defenseless beside him, and felt ashamed. He dropped back down to the couch, staring at his hands.

"I didn't want to kill her," he mumbled. "I needed her talisman. She left me no choice, and I—"

"You always have choices," she interrupted him. "You could have walked away. You could have lived the rest of your life doing good, trying to balance out the evil you did. You didn't, and that's on you."

He knew in his heart it was true, just as he knew that one way or the other, he'd be leaving with the emerald tonight. He was on a path, and there was no way he could step off that path.

"And there you go again," she said. "You have choices. You chose the path you're on, no one else. In Mexico, you chose to spare that old man's life. You cut his hand off, just like you did Benjamin Spencer's, but you healed him. You could have ended his life, but you didn't. Why do you think that is, David?"

She startled him by using his first name. He hadn't been called David in fifty years, and mostly thought of himself simply as Dowd. But he hadn't always been that way. Before the accident that left him disfigured but with psychic abilities when he was 12, he'd just been David. He'd had a mother, a sister. Friends.

"I didn't need to kill him," he finally responded.

"But when has that stopped you in the past?"

"I'm different now."

"That's true. Yer different. A better version of yourself, but yer still on the same path you put yourself on when 12-year-old you woke up from yer 'accident'. Is that what you want? What you truly want?"

"I…don't know."

"Is that why you ripped yer own eye out? To become a monster again?"

"I don't know!"

"The 'accident' gave you abilities most people only dream of, while at the same time warping your mind even as it warped your face. You heard voices that were not there, and you did their bidding, all in the name of a God you no longer believe in. Benjamin Spencer took that burden from you. He not only fixed your face; he fixed your brain."

"But he didn't take the guilt. He took everything from me but the guilt."

"And you want to kill him for it," Muir said.

"No! I just want him to change me back. I want this damned guilt to go away."

"Look inside yerself, David. You do want the guilt to go away, to be sure, but you also want revenge. You want revenge for him forcing you to grieve for the little boy that was lost in that so-called 'accident' so long ago, and for all the lives you took after."

Was it true? Was that what this was all about?

"It's always been about revenge," she said. "And not just against Ben. We both know yer injuries weren't an accident—"

"I don't want to talk about that!"

"But that's where the rage comes from, David. That's where it all started. Sure, the injuries changed you, changed your brain, but the rage was already there.'"

"Spencer should have just killed me."

"But he didn't. You have two of the five talismans," Muir continued, "and after tonight, you'll have three. That's more than any single person has had in a very long time. Still, it won't be enough to change you in the way you want."

"What will, then? What can take away the guilt?"

"Nothing can take away the guilt! And why should it? You did those things, David, and you deserve the guilt."

"But I—"

"I wasn't finished!" she said. "You'll always have the guilt, but you can learn to live with it, and the first step in learning to live with it is to ask for forgiveness."

"But ask who? Ben Spencer?"

"No, you ninny," she said softly, "yourself. Before anyone else can forgive you, you first have to forgive yourself."

"But…I don't think I can. I've done so many horrible, monstrous things. Killed so many people. Buried a girl alive. Murdered Janna Sparks in Missouri."

"Once the scales have been balanced, perhaps you'll be able to forgive yourself then."

Dowd felt like screaming, felt like crying, felt like running away, felt like strangling the woman to death. So many emotions ran through his mind he didn't know which way was up.

"But how?" He finally asked. "How do I balance the scales?"

"First, yer going to need this." She pulled a small emerald from her pocket and tossed it to him.

He snatched it out of the air without even thinking and immediately felt its power connect with the energy of the geode and the twig. The talismans were at once singing to each other and calling out for the other two that he didn't yet have. He felt a hunger rise in him, but pushed it down, struggled with it, and finally mastered it.

"How do I balance the scales, Agatha?" he repeated, searching her withered face.

She told him exactly what he needed to do.

"Thank you," he said, when she was finished.

She stood on tip toes, beckoning for him to stoop. As he did so, she kissed his cheek. His face turned red.

"There's hope for you yet, David," she whispered. "Now get out of here. It's a long flight back to the states, and you don't have much time. Oh, and come back once this is over, and we can share another cup of tea."

If he survived the coming storm, he thought he might do just that.

# Chapter 48

Emily lay in a queen-sized bed in the Peninsula, a gorgeous luxury hotel in Chicago, happier than she'd ever been. Cassie's room was amazingly luxurious, even better than her room at the Luxor had been, and the things they'd done last night...

Cassie texted her yesterday, just after they'd returned home from the lodge in the Yukon, to tell her that she'd accepted a last-minute gig in Chicago. She worked as a model for tech conventions, she'd explained when they were in Las Vegas, showing off gadgets such as new gaming rigs, smart watches, things like that. The assignment started Wednesday morning.

She wasn't sure how far Carthage was from Chicago, but she was hoping Emily might consider driving up so they could spend some time together. Chicago was only four hours from Carthage, Emily told her, but of course Emily didn't have a car. She did, however, have those fictitious frequent flier miles, and would be more than happy to use some of them on a quick trip to see Cassie.

She teleported to one of the many women's bathrooms inside the Chicago O'Hare airport last night, and Cassie picked her up in a little rented blue Subaru ten minutes later. Emily hated lying to Cassie, but still wasn't sure how to tell her that she could teleport. That would open up a whole can of worms about magic, demons, and angels that she wasn't quite ready to explain.

They'd had a late dinner at Mrs. Murphy & Sons Irish Bistro, where Emily drank a little too much, and then back to the hotel, where they'd made love multiple times late into the night.

Emily glanced at the clock on the bedside table. It was just a bit past eight in the morning. She needed to get home before anyone missed her.

"Hey, sleepyhead," said Cassie, coming out of the bathroom, clad only in a white towel.

"Hey yourself," she said. "Aren't you supposed to be getting dressed for work?"

"Just got a text, and the first presentation got bumped to 11. So, we have a little time. We could have breakfast, or maybe something else first…" She said, letting the towel slip from her body and pool on the floor at her feet.

Emily stared at her, feeling herself flush with desire. Every little inch of Cassie was amazingly beautiful, from the top of her head to the bottom of her toes. She wanted her, wanted her so much, but she needed to get home, dammit. She'd probably stayed here too long already. Then again, wasn't she allowed to have a life just like everyone else?

Emily knew she'd be missed if she stayed much longer, but so what? She was 18, almost 19, legally an adult. Ben had Katy, Colin had Sumi, and Sabrina had Farris, so why couldn't she have Cassie?

"I'll go with the 'something else' first," she finally said, making a decision, "and then maybe breakfast after."

"Good choice."

"I thought so," said Emily. "Now let me respond to a text from Ben real quick."

"Go for it."

*Out with a friend,* she typed, *I'll be home around 11.*

"All done," said Emily, patting the bed beside her. "Come here, you."

"I have a confession to make," Cassie whispered, as she slipped under the covers next to Emily. "I think I'm falling in love with you."

Emily felt her heart go into overdrive. "I'm so in love with you, Cassie," she whispered back, "I've just been afraid to say it. You're all I can think about. I think I fell for you the first moment I saw you."

They kissed then, a long, electric kiss that seemed to go on forever, and Emily wanted nothing more than to be with this woman for the rest of her life, to just stay in this hotel room with her for eternity, letting the rest of the world fall away.

"God, Emily, that feels so good," Cassie said. "I love your kisses."

"And I love to kiss you."

"I'd do anything for you, you know," Cassie whispered, as her kisses trailed down Emily's throat, to her breasts, her nipples, and slowly, ever so slowly, down her stomach.

"Cassie, that feels amazing. I'd do anything for you, too, anything, until the day I die."

"That feels really good to hear," said Cassie, as her kisses reached Emily's inner thighs, "though you really didn't have to add the dying part. I'd love to hear it again, though."

"You can hear it as many times as you want. I'd do anything for you until the day I die. Oh! That is so perfect."

Emily enjoyed the feeling of Cassie's lips and tongue exploring between her thighs and wrapped her legs around her lover's neck to pull her even closer. She began to moan and could feel an orgasm starting to build.

"Say it again, it makes me so fucking hot."

"Mmm. Say what again? This feels amazing."

"That you'd do anything for me until the day you die, anything at all, just like I'd do for you," Cassie whispered. "Please say it."

"Cassie…oh my lord. This feels amazing, don't stop."

"Say it, then. Tell me you'll do anything for me."

"I'd do anything for you, Cassie, anything at all, until the day I die," she moaned. "Now fuck me with your tongue."

She came just seconds later, an amazing orgasm that almost had her seeing stars. After it was all over, they lay there in each other's arms, enjoying just being together.

"Your turn," Emily finally said, as she began to nibble Cassie's ear, "I want to make you feel just as good as you made me feel."

Cassie didn't say anything and looked like she was about to start crying. The bottom fell out of Emily's stomach. "What's wrong? Are you okay?"

"I'm sorry," Cassie whispered.

"For what?"

"For this. Emily, slap yourself in the face," Cassie said, and Emily slapped herself hard on the cheek.

"What?" asked Emily, dumbfounded, staring at her hand. What the hell was happening?

"Sorry, I just had to make sure it worked."

"Make sure what worked?" She stared into Cassie's eyes, seeing a cruelty that hadn't been there just seconds earlier. It scared her.

"The binding," she said. "You're mine now, Emily Spencer, for always and forever, until your death do us part."

"I don't understand."

"Oh, I think you do. I think you know exactly what's going on."

Emily flashed back to the Yukon, where the demon Azazel had forced them all to say that they wouldn't come looking for him before he would agree to give up Ben's body and take her father's body instead.

They'd had to say it three times, just as the demon had to say that he gave up all rights to Ben's body three times. Anything said to, about, or by a demon three times was forever binding, an arcane rule that she didn't understand. She'd said she'd do anything for Cassie, three times.

"Got it in one," Cassie said, as Emily's face fell.

"You're...Azazel?"

Cassie laughed. "Hardly. Though I did fuck him a few times, when he was in your brother's body. I'm an angel, or at least I pretend to be one."

"But...why?" Emily asked, her eyes filling with tears. "Why are you doing this to me?"

"I really, really love you, Emily, for real. But this is bigger than the both of us put together. Daddy wants you to help us kidnap your little niece, and what Daddy wants, Daddy gets."

"I don't care who your 'Daddy' is, there's no way in hell I'm going to let you kidnap Hope," shouted Emily, reaching for her phone.

"Drop the phone and be quiet," Cassie said, and against her will Emily felt her hand drop the phone.

This was a nightmare. That was the only explanation for this heartless betrayal, but she knew it was all too real. She tried to curse Cassie, to cry out, but she couldn't make a sound. She was under the angel's control for now, maybe forever.

"I see you're finally starting to get it. Good. You are going to help me and Michael steal Hope, whether you like it or not. But first things first. You got to come, and now I wanna come, too. Go down on me, Emily, and make me scream."

# Chapter 49

David Dowd sat in a brown armchair in room 19 at the Prairie Winds hotel on East Highway 136, in Carthage, thinking about his past. He'd always told everyone he'd been in a grain silo explosion when he was 12 years old, but that wasn't true. If it had been true, he might not have turned out like this.

He'd grown up on a farm in the tiny town of Grainfield, Kansas, which was even smaller than Carthage. The population when he'd lived there had been around 400 souls, but the last time he checked, Grainfield was down to around half of that. His father, in addition to being a corn farmer, had also been a minister at the small Baptist church located in the middle of town.

He wasn't nearly as good at farming as he was at preaching, and as a consequence, they were about to lose the farm. His parents had been fighting almost non-stop for the last six months, each fight getting progressively worse. Isiah Dowd had taken to hitting Connie, his wife, when anything went wrong that he could remotely pin on her.

"Isiah," she said, for the second time in the last five minutes, "I can get a job. A bakery in Quinter is hiring, and—"

He grabbed her shoulders, shaking her. "How many times do I have to say this? No wife of mine is going to work. Colossians 3:18 says, *'Wives, submit to your husbands, as is fitting in the Lord.'* Providing for the family is my job, not yours."

"It wouldn't be the end of the world if I got a job."

"I said no!" he screamed in her face, still holding her by her shoulders. "You work at home, not at some fucking bakery. I work outside the home. I provide. That's how it works."

They were arguing in the kitchen. David and his 7-year-old sister Ruthie stood in the doorway to the living room, peeking around the corner, watching their third fight this week.

"If you provided better," Connie said, "we wouldn't be in this mess."

"What did you say?" Isiah asked, his voice low. "Ephesians 5:22 says, *'Wives, submit to your husbands, as to the Lord.'* What is wrong with you?"

"I'm sorry, but I don't want to lose my family's farm," she said, finally wrenching free from his grasp. "I grew up on this farm. And don't quote anymore silly, outdated scripture at me, Isiah, or so help me…"

His eyes raged, and he slapped her hard across the face, knocking her into the dining table. "How dare you mock scripture! Just who do you think you are?"

"I thought I was your wife," she said, holding her cheek, blood trickling between her fingers.

"You *are* my wife. Proverbs 12:4 says, *'An excellent wife is the crown of her husband, but she who brings shame is like rottenness in his bones.'* You are rotting my bones."

"Fuck you, Isiah," she said, as she pulled off her wedding ring and threw it at him. "You're a joke. My sister tried to warn me, but would I listen? No, not stupid Connie. Well, I'm done."

He pushed her into the dining table again, this time knocking over one of the chairs. He made a fist, cocked it back, and that's when Ruthie burst into the kitchen.

"Stop it, Daddy," she said, crying. "Don't hit Mommy."

David reached out to grab Ruthie, but she ran to her mother.

His father turned to stare at him. "David! Your mother and I were having a private conversation. Were you eavesdropping?"

"I'm scared," Ruthie said.

"It's okay," said Connie, hugging her. "Shh. Mommy's fine."

David's father grabbed him by the arm and drug him out of the kitchen and back into the living room. "David, I asked you a question. Were you eavesdropping? You and your sister do not need to see us fighting."

"You fight all the time," David said.

"Careful, mister. Exodus 20:12 says, *Honor your father and your mother.* I will not have my son behaving like a godless heathen. You aren't too big for me to put you over my knee, David."

At 12 years old, David was already 6' tall, three inches taller than his father. He wanted to challenge the man but was still terrified of him. He hadn't been whipped by that damned belt of his since he was 11 and didn't miss it.

"Yes sir," he finally said, looking at the floor.

The next night they were at it again. This time, they were in their bedroom. Connie was crying, screaming at Isiah to stop hitting her. Ruthie was hiding under her bed, terrified, but David was done hiding. He'd finally had enough. He grabbed his father's shotgun from the garage and burst into the room, levelling the gun at Isiah Dowd.

"Just stop," David said, his hands shaking. "If you don't stop, I swear to God I'm going to shoot you."

"David, no," screamed Connie.

He stared at his mother. She had a black eye and was bleeding from her mouth again, and it looked like she might be missing a tooth.

"Honor thy father and mother, David," Isiah yelled, wild-eyed. "Put that rifle down this instant, young man, or you're going straight to hell. Do you hear me, David? Straight to hell!"

"David, go to your room and lock the door," said Connie, tears running down her cheeks. "Please, David."

"Why do you let him do this to you?" he asked her, still pointing the shotgun at his father. "Why don't you call the police?"

"That's enough, David," Isiah yelled, walking straight up to him. "Give me the gun. Now!"

"Isiah, please, no," Connie pleaded, putting a hand on his shoulder.

He backhanded her across the face, and she tumbled to the floor. David pulled the trigger, but nothing happened. He pulled it again and again. Nothing.

"Did you think I'd keep a loaded shotgun in the house?" his father asked, yanking the weapon from his trembling hands. "Do you really think I'm that stupid? You thought it was loaded, and you tried to shoot me. You tried to kill your father."

"I'm sorry, Daddy," David said, backing away.

"Proverbs 13:14 says, *the one who will not use the rod hates his son, but the one who loves him disciplines him diligently.* I love you, David, and I will not spare the rod. You will be a man of God if I have to beat it into you."

He swung the butt of the shotgun at David, hitting him in the eye. It felt like his head was exploding. And then his father was on him, kicking him, bringing his heel down into David's face over and over. He was screaming, his mother was screaming, Ruthie was screaming, all the while his father kept saying, over and over, 'Spare the rod and spoil the child. Spare the rod and spoil the child."

The next thing he knew, he was waking up in the hospital. He'd been in a coma for over a month and had suffered extensive brain damage. His left eye was gone, and his face was permanently disfigured. He was lucky to be alive, they later told him, though he didn't feel lucky, not in the slightest.

He began to hear voices when no one was speaking shortly after waking up. Eventually he figured out he was hearing some of the nurse's thoughts, and that he could mentally "push" some of them to bring him extra food, fluff his pillow, and do other things that made his stay in the hospital a little easier. If they were upset or happy, worried or excited, he could drain them of those emotions, making his new abilities even stronger. He was amazed by these powers, once he finally accepted that he wasn't going insane.

Soon he was ready to be released, but where would he go? His father was in jail. Ruthie had been taken to an orphanage by the police, and shortly thereafter his mother had hung herself in the garage. Deidre Neill, his mother's sister, ended up taking him and his little sister into her home.

He had taken on his father's warped sense of religion, believing Jesus himself was talking to him. Deidre Neill wasn't Godly, Jesus whispered in his ear. She spared the rod when Ruthie misbehaved, which meant she didn't really love the little girl. Proverbs 22:6 said, *train up a child in the way he should go; even when he is old he will not depart from it.*

He wanted to be a man of God, just like his father. David had failed his father, and as a result Isiah Dowd would spend thirteen years in prison. If only he'd honored his father, his mother would still be alive, and they'd all still be together.

Two weeks into living with his aunt, Jesus had ordered him to punish the woman for her lack of faith by murdering her in her sleep. Instead of following the son of God's order, however, he had run away. He'd begun his lifelong history of self-flagellation after that, punishing himself for not being strong enough to follow the word of the Lord.

David had strayed from God's path, and he'd paid the price and lost everything. There was nothing he could do for his family now, but he could make sure others didn't follow in his footsteps. He'd preach His word, and if people didn't want to accept Jesus into their lives, well, he'd just have to make them.

For a time, after he'd woken from his coma, he'd shared the hospital room with a 14-year-old boy named Simon Todd. Simon had lost an arm and part of a leg in an explosion in a grain silo. Because he was ashamed of how he'd gotten his injuries, he'd stolen Simon's story and made it his own.

He shook his head, regretting that and all the other stupid, senseless things he'd done after he came out of the coma. He'd brought so much pain and misery into the world, all in a futile attempt to be like his abusive father.

David no longer believed in God, because what kind of god would allow him to do the things he'd done? What kind of god would allow his father to turn him into a monster?

Ben Spencer had healed his brain, but not his heart, not his soul.

He often thought about his little sister. He wondered what she'd done with her life, and if she were still alive. He could probably find out through the internet but resisted the urge. If she was dead, he wasn't sure he could bear to read her obituary.

He'd finally looked up his father just three days ago. Isiah Dowd had been released from prison after serving only 8 of his 14 months. He'd gone on to remarry but never had more children, thank God, nor did he regain custody of Ruthie. He'd died an old man, at the age of 73.

David looked at his watch, letting go for now thoughts of the past. It was almost time for him to go to Fred and Candy Ruskin's house. He'd done far too much evil in his lifetime, and now it was time to do a little good.

# Chapter 50

Fred and Candy Ruskin were eating lunch when it happened. The doorbell rang, and Fred got up from the kitchen table. He peered through the peephole, and a man and a woman stood at his door.

He rolled his eyes. They were dressed in suits so were probably Mormons, wanting to "spread the word" of their version of Jesus. Normally he wouldn't mind talking to them for a few minutes, but he didn't want to be late for Shawn's meeting with Oslov Security.

"Sorry, guys," he said, as he opened the door, "but I'm really busy today. Can you come back another time?"

The man, bald and probably in his early-to-mid-forties, held a gun pointed at Ruskin's chest. The woman, a blonde who was probably in her late thirties, also held a gun.

"Get inside," ordered the man, "now."

Ruskin backed up, hands in the air. He feared this was no mere robbery, and he hoped with all his heart that Candy would stay in the kitchen.

His cellphone, which he kept in the pocket of his jeans, began to ring, startling both him and the pair of robbers.

"Give me the phone," said the woman, holding out her hand.

He removed the phone from his pocket and passed it over to her, but not before glancing at the caller ID. It was Shawn. She dropped the phone to the ground and crushed it beneath her heel.

"What do you want?"

"Never mind that," said the woman, as she closed the door behind her. "Sit down in that recliner over there, keep your hands on your head, and shut up. My partner is going to check out your house, see if your lovely wife is home."

"I'm the only one here," Fred said, sitting down in the brown La-Z-Boy recliner with his hands on his head.

"I'm not certain I believe you," said the woman, as her partner left the living room and walked towards the bedrooms. "Besides, I told you to be quiet."

"I'll ask again," said Fred, "what do you want? If it's money, I have plenty. I'll give you $250,000 right now to take your partner and leave my home."

She laughed, then kicked him hard in the left kneecap. He bit his tongue to stop himself from screaming, but his knee felt like it was on fire.

"Open your mouth again and I'll shoot you in your other knee. Got it?"

Ruskin stared at the woman, finally nodding.

"Good. Now, we're just going to sit here for half an hour or so. We don't want your money, and as soon as I get the word, we'll leave. Nod if you understand."

Ruskin nodded once more.

"No one in either of the bedrooms or the bathrooms, I'm going to check out the rest of the house," said the bald man as he walked through the living room.

He hoped Candy had heard them talking and left the house through the back door, maybe even called the police. One thing he knew for certain is that he wasn't going to let anyone hurt his wife. If the man so much as laid a finger on her, he'd rip him apart.

Assuming, of course, that the blonde didn't kill him first.

"Hey, who're—" yelled the man's voice from the kitchen, and then silence.

"Shit," said the woman, gun still trained on Ruskin. "You stay here. Move, and I'll kill whoever else is in the house."

Ruskin scrambled up from the recliner, rushing the woman, but his knee gave out before he could reach her. He hit the floor hard, pain coursing through his damaged knee.

"Okay, I've had enough of this shit," said the woman, aiming the gun at Ruskin's head. "You were probably going to die tonight anyway, so let's just call it a day and get it over—"

The woman's eyes went wide, and she dropped the gun to the floor. A long silver blade stuck out from her chest, and blood dribbled from the wound. She gasped, then shuddered and fell to the floor, dead.

Ruskin looked up to see a huge man wearing a trench coat and holding a bloody sword looming over him. He had an eyepatch over one eye, and his other eye was trained on Ruskin. The stranger looked vaguely familiar, but he had no idea from where he might know the man.

"Are you hurt?" he asked.

"I'm fine. My wife, is she okay?"

"She's safe. She's still in the kitchen. Here, let me help you up."

He took the man's hand and managed to rise to his feet, though his knee was on fire. If his kneecap wasn't broken, it was almost surely dislocated.

"My kneecap might be broken," he said.

"Oh, Fred," said Candy, walking into the room, rushing to her husband's side, "what did they do to you?"

"It doesn't matter, as long as you're safe," he said, reaching out to squeeze her hand.

"We don't have much time. We have to get to Shawn Spencer's house," said the tall stranger, "if we don't, he and his whole family are going to be murdered, and they'll have sent a hell of a lot more than two people to do the job."

"Jesus. Okay, let's go," Fred said, picking up the dead woman's handgun. "One thing, though. Who are you?"

"You met me a long time ago. My name is David Dowd."

Ruskin blinked, stared at the man, and then aimed the pistol at him. "I knew I recognized you. What do you want?"

"I want to save your friends and your daughter," Dowd said. "If you still want to shoot me, you are more than welcome to do so after we've made sure they're safe."

Without waiting for an answer, Dowd turned and walked towards the door.

"Go, Fred," urged Candy, giving him a quick kiss on the lips. "Go save them."

Making a decision, lowering the gun, he said, "I will. I love you," and then limped after Dowd and out the door.

# Chapter 51

Shawn, Jenny, and Colin sat in the downstairs living room, discussing their security needs with Corey Durst. The man had arrived precisely at one o'clock, with another member of his team, Austin Gurley, in tow.

He'd called Fred last night and asked him to come to the meeting. Fred was a retired sheriff and knew more about security than Shawn would ever know. He'd agreed but failed to show up, which was very unlike Fred. Shawn tried calling him, but his calls went to voicemail.

"We can supply a security team to guard the house around the clock, three men per each 12-hour shift, for a total of six armed guards," said Durst. "Along with setting up alarms and using the Blink cameras you've already installed, we should be able to create a very safe environment for you and your family, Mr. Spencer."

Shawn hated the thought of having to hire security without giving them the full story, but there was just no way they were going to believe that supernatural beings had sent mercenaries to capture his son. Hell, if he hadn't witnessed it himself, he probably wouldn't believe it either.

He'd given them the same story he'd given Oslov, about a home invasion and robbery, and needing to feel safe in his own home again. He just hoped the guards would be ready for whatever came next, because he didn't doubt for a second that another attack was coming.

"Once Colin goes back to college, we'll have a spare room," Jenny said, "you can use it, if you want, though it's pretty small for six people."

"That isn't necessary, Mrs. Spencer, though it is a kind offer. We'll rent rooms at the Prairie Winds motel, more than likely. That's just a few minutes from here. We might, however, use your extra space as a break room of sorts, if that's okay?"

"Of course," said Shawn. "Whatever you need."

"I had a few questions," said Colin, reaching into his pocket. "Oh, shoot. I wrote down my concerns, but I must have left the piece of paper upstairs. I'll be right back."

Shawn watched Colin head for the stairs, proud of the help his son had so far provided. Colin and Ben were finally getting along again. Shawn hoped that would continue to be the case, and that this security team really could keep his family safe.

# Chapter 52

Ben sat in his and Katy's bedroom, with Hercules at his feet. His mother, father, and Colin were all downstairs meeting with a representative from the security company Colin had suggested, so now seemed like the perfect time to do a little research.

The list of names they'd found in Azazel's safe yesterday in hand, he scrolled through Google on his ancient Windows laptop computer. Deciding to search for the only other American name on the list first, he typed in "Edward Sparks" and "Sarcoxie" and was rewarded with an eighteen-year-old article from the Sarcoxie Record, the local newspaper in Sarcoxie, Missouri.

**From the Sarcoxie Record, Wednesday April 14, 2004**

Three-Car Accident Kills One, Puts One in Hospital
By Erin McDougall

A three-car pileup on Center street Tuesday left one dead, one in the hospital. Edward Sparks, 57, was pronounced dead at the scene. He is survived by his daughter, Janna Sparks, a schoolteacher at Sarcoxie Elementary.

Mackenzie Lodge suffered a broken leg and bruised ribs in the accident. The third driver, Olivia Baker, was unharmed.

No word yet on the cause of the accident, but police investigations are ongoing.

A quick search for "Janna Sparks" on the website revealed she'd been killed less than a week later herself, though it had been no accident.

**From the Sarcoxie Record, Tuesday April 20, 2004**

Sarcoxie Elementary Teacher Murdered
By Erin McDougall

Sarcoxie police are investigating a homicide thought to have been committed early Sunday morning. Janna Sparks, 29, a teacher at Sarcoxie Elementary School, was found dead in her home Monday afternoon by her boyfriend Andrew Ondalene, who also teaches at the school.

Sparks had just buried her father, Edward Sparks, the day before her murder. Edward Sparks died in a multi-car accident last Tuesday. According to the police, the two events do not appear to be related.

There was another article three weeks later by the same reporter, essentially saying there had been no progress in the investigation into Janna Sparks' murder. Ondalene had been cleared of any involvement in the crime, and Janna was buried in the Sarcoxie Cemetery, next to her parents.

There were many articles after that—Sarcoxie was a very small town, with a population under 2,000 people, and this was very big news—but apparently, the murder had never been solved. The articles never mentioned any possible motives, nor how she'd been killed. Presumably, the police had held back that information.

Had the demons killed Janna for one of the talismans? That just didn't make any sense. According to Azazel, they couldn't use the talismans by themselves, and why would Michael give away the objects if he or one of his "kin" were only going to start stealing them back 30 years later?

There must be something else at play here. Ben did a quick search of "Erin McDougall" and found she no longer worked for the Sarcoxie Record. McDougall was now employed by The Los Angeles Times, which was definitely a huge step up from the little Missouri newspaper.

McDougall's Twitter handle was easy enough to find, and so Ben sent her a quick DM. In the message, he claimed he was a college student writing a paper on unsolved murders and was curious if the case had ever been solved. He also asked how she'd been murdered and if it had been a robbery or something else.

He moved down the list, this time searching for Renjiro Hashimoto. According to an article from the *Dallas Morning News*, Hashimoto of Tokyo, Japan, and Hamari and Sara Nakamura, both from Dallas, Texas, had been murdered with a sword in a hotel room in Dallas in March of 1977. The perpetrator was never found.

Hashimoto must have had the jaguar's tooth, and David Dowd murdered him for it, using the same sword he'd used to sever Ben's hand. Given the timeline, and knowing Dowd had the tooth in 1977, it made sense.

A Google search of the name "David Dowd" yielded hundreds of results, so Ben added "prison" to the search and found the man he was looking for. David Allan Dowd had been tried and convicted of two counts of second-degree murder in February 1978 and been sentenced to 47 years in prison.

He'd been released for good behavior in December of 2003, at the age of 54. That had been almost 20 years ago, which would make him nearly 75 now. Surely the man was no longer a threat.

Ben almost regretted not killing Dowd when he'd had the chance. Instead, he'd used his ability to manipulate reality to fix Dowd's disfigured face and broken mind, negating the accident he'd been in that gave him his powers. Had that been a mistake?

A notification popped up on his screen. He tabbed over to Twitter, and was surprised to see McDougall had already answered his DM.

As far as I know, Sparks' murder was never solved. Nothing was stolen from her house. She was stabbed through the heart, with a dagger or sword or something, they never really knew what, and her neck was broken. The police kept that information private to help in the investigation, so don't quote me on that. It's been so long, though, I really don't see the harm in sharing that info. Good luck with your paper.

A sword? Son of a bitch. Could it really be Dowd, after all these years? He'd been stripped of his psychic abilities, though. How could he have found Janna Sparks without his powers?

Someone laid a hand on his shoulder and he jumped, nearly dropping the laptop to the floor.

"Sorry, didn't mean to startle you," said Katy, sitting on the bed beside him. "What are you doing?"

"It's okay. I'm researching that list of names we found. Renjiro Hashimoto was murdered in Dallas, Texas in March of 1977, killed with a sword. Edward Sparks died in a car crash, and his daughter Janna died less than a week later. She was also murdered, stabbed through the heart, probably with a sword."

Katy stared at him. "You don't think…?"

"I do think. David Dowd got out of prison just four months before she was killed, released for 'good behavior.' Good behavior, my ass."

"He'd be…what? Probably 70 or 80 years old by now."

Ben nodded. "He was 54 when he was released from prison, so yeah, almost 72."

"Even if he did murder those people, I can't imagine a 72-year-old man being much of a threat to anyone these days."

"What about a 72-year-old man with one of the talismans?"

Katy's eyes grew large. "Okay, I get your point. So, what about the rest of the names?"

"I was just about to Google them when you startled the hell out of me," he said, with a smile.

"Poor baby," Katy said, giving him a lingering kiss.

"More, please?"

"Maybe later, if you play your cards right. But right now, let's track down the rest of those names."

Ben typed in "Alejandro Torres, Malinalco Mexico" into the search engine and was quickly rewarded with a hit from *Mexico News Daily*. Thankfully, the article was written in English, because he never quite trusted Google's language translator and neither he nor Katy were fluent in Spanish.

Torres, apparently a long-time tourist guide, died of natural causes just last year at the age of 78. He was survived by 5 children and a host of grandchildren. There was a photo of him in the obituary, and his right hand was missing.

Had it been chopped off with a sword? That was Ben's first thought, but if that was the case, why hadn't Dowd murdered Torres like he did Janna Sparks? Try as they might, they could find no more information on Alejandro Torres.

They also struck out with Agatha Muir. The woman seemed to be a mystery insofar as finding any information about her on the Internet. Not even an address or telephone number.

"Were you able to find any connection between Hashimoto and Colin's girlfriend, Natsumi?"

Ben shook his head. "Nothing that I could see, but that doesn't mean it's not there. Let me search for her by herself."

He'd earlier searched for both of their names together, but now simply typed "Natsumi Hashimoto" into the Google search bar. He shook his head and blinked, a chill slowly running down his spine.

**From the Toronto Sun**

College Student Found Dead in Fireside Apartments
By Sara Kinsella

Natsumi Hashimoto, 23, a student at the University of Toronto, was found murdered in her apartment on Friday. Police say the crime most likely occurred 24-48 hours earlier but are awaiting the coroner's report before officially announcing a timeline.

Hashimoto's boyfriend, Colin Frederick Spencer, 24, a fellow student from Chicago, Illinois, USA, is wanted for questioning. Sources say Spencer shared Hashimoto's apartment with her and hasn't attended classes at University since Hashimoto was murdered.

# Chapter 53

**Seven Days Earlier**

Colin Spencer opened the curious letter with no postage Sumi had just brought in from the mail and removed the folded piece of paper inside. He unfolded the paper and stared at it, not comprehending. The entire piece of paper was blank, save for this strange, squiggly symbol in the very middle of the paper.

He blinked. The symbol was moving, somehow, sliding across the paper, sliding off the paper, caressing the palm of his hand—

No!

He didn't want this. He wanted nothing more than to throw the paper away, to destroy it, to shred it and burn it so he could never, ever see it again, but his hand wouldn't move. Instead, his fingers curled around the paper, and he began to remember...

This was wrong. He was Colin Frederick Spencer. He was Colin Frederick Spencer. He was Colin Fucking Spencer, Goddammit! He held fast to his identity as his consciousness was flooded with the memories of who—no, of *what*—he'd been before.

Enki, Durga, Kaescuchi, Zagreus, Xiuhtecuhtli, Thor, Michael...and so many more.

No!

No...

Yes.

"What's wrong?" Natsumi was asking him, over and over, and he realized he'd been screaming.

"Get...away from me," he whispered. "Please, while you still can."

"What are you talking about? Colin, you're scaring me."

Colin. That was his name, wasn't it? He held his head in his hands, screaming at the top of his lungs, trying in vain to hold on to the life he so desperately wanted. It wasn't enough. When he was finished screaming, he looked up into Sumi's terrified face.

"Leave," he said. "Leave, before it's too late."

"I'm not leaving, Colin. Tell me what's wrong."

He ignored her, staring at the palm of his left hand, where the strange symbol—it was his name, in a language he couldn't quite remember— had somehow tattooed itself. And it hurt, hurt like hell, hurt like nothing he'd ever felt before.

"Leave," he grunted again, pain searing through his body.

But she wouldn't leave. Instead, she sat on the couch beside him, and took him into her arms. He began sobbing hysterically into her shoulder, crying so hard his head felt like it might shatter.

"I don't want this," he finally whispered into her shoulder. "I don't want this. I don't want this. I don't want this!"

"What's happened, Colin?" she asked, pulling back to stare into his eyes. "Is it Ben?"

When wasn't it Ben? Of course, it was Ben! Colin, or what used to be Colin, began to laugh then, long and loud, a gamut of emotions running through his mind. It didn't matter what he wanted. Nothing mattered but what *father* wanted, and what father wanted, father got. This was all put in motion, all decided, a long, long time ago.

Or was it yesterday? He wasn't sure he could even tell the difference anymore.

Natsumi finally let go of his shoulders, fear in her eyes. She scurried away from him on the couch, but when she tried to stand up, he grabbed her wrist.

"Let go. You're hurting me!"

"I told you to leave before it was too late," he said, rising from the couch, "but you didn't listen, and now it's too late."

"Too late for what? Colin, let me take you to the hospital. And please, let go of my arm."

"My name's not Colin anymore," he said, smiling, and then said a name her precious human ears couldn't even comprehend.

"You are Colin. You are!" she screamed, tears rolling down her cheeks. "What's wrong with you?"

"I was never Colin," he yelled back at her, his hand suddenly around her throat. "Colin was just a mask I wore, like so many masks before, and now it's burning away, burning, burning, burning away."

She struggled to pull away, but he held fast to her wrist.

And then something was exploding over his head, and he stumbled back, in pain. Blood blurred his vision, and she held the remains of the glass vase that had occupied the coffee table just moments earlier.

He smiled, licking his lips, tasting the blood that ran down his face.

"Who…what…are you?" she choked out, backing away from him, holding the sharp glass out in front of her.

"I don't know!" he screamed, chasing after her.

Colin caught her just as she was running out the front door. His hand tangled in her long black hair and he pulled her back, making her head whiplash. He kicked the door shut with one foot, then spun her around to face him, pushing her up against the wall.

He reared back to hit her as an incredible pain surged through his body. He looked down to see the remainder of the vase sticking out of his stomach.

"Oh my God," Natsumi said, eyes wide, staring at his stomach. "I'm so sorry. I didn't mean…"

"Watch this," he said, as he yanked the vase from his stomach and then pulled off his shirt.

Blood gushed from the wound, but he ignored it. He pressed his left hand, the one with the tattoo, against his stomach, concentrating, and in a moment, he was healed. Not even a scar remained, only the blood.

Natsumi's hands went quickly to her mouth. "How…how is that possible? Am I dreaming? Is this just some horrible, awful nightmare?"

"I wish," he said, as he pointed the sharp glass at Natsumi.

"Please don't do this," Natsumi said, staring at the glass in his hand. "I don't want to die."

"I love you so much, Sumi, and I'm so, so sorry," he said, his eyes filling with tears.

He plunged the shard of glass deep into the center of Natsumi's chest, blood spraying everywhere. She tried to say something, failed, and fell to the floor, dead.

Colin screamed, and kept screaming for a very long time.

# Chapter 54

The knight sat on the couch in his living room, the tiger's head on his lap, watching old episodes of *The Twilight Zone* on the television set that had mysteriously appeared a day or two ago. He slowly stroked the tiger's soft fur, enjoying the throaty purr that emanated from the majestic beast.

This episode was about a clown, a ballet dancer, a hobo, a bagpipe player, and an army major trying to find their way out of a cylindrical enclosure of some sort. He was almost certain he remembered watching this one years ago, before he was drafted into knighthood, but he couldn't remember the ending.

In fact, a lot of his memories were fuzzy. He knew he hadn't always been here, in this house within a house, keeping watch over his charge, but whenever he tried to remember what came before his head hurt.

Once the little girl was safe and any threat to her had been eliminated, his duty would be finished. Perhaps after that, he'd remember everything. He looked forward to that day, but also dreaded it. Where did he and the tiger fit into this world, post-threat?

The knight smiled as the *Twilight Zone* episode came to an end. The bagpipe player, the ballet dancer, and everyone else turned out to be dolls trapped inside a Christmas collection barrel for a girls' orphanage.

His smile turned to a frown as a chill passed through him. This seemed familiar, somehow, these dolls who thought they were human, and not just in the sense that he'd long ago seen the episode.

And then the tiger was there, growling fiercely, and whatever memory he'd been dredging up was lost.

"What's going on, boy?" he asked, stroking the tiger's fur.

The tiger growled again. Something was happening.

Using the remote, the knight turned off the television and then rose from the couch. He grabbed his helmet, put it on his head, and withdrew his sword.

"This is it, isn't it?" he asked, already knowing the answer.

The tiger growled again, and together they left the confines of their home to protect their charge.

# Chapter 55

The world seemed to come to a halt as Emily walked into Hope's room, her heart thudding in her chest. She didn't want to do this, didn't want to help Colin kidnap her beautiful, innocent little niece, but she had no control over what she did next. Now she had a small idea of how Ben must have felt for those five years he'd been possessed by Azazel.

"You will do anything and everything Colin Spencer tells you to do," Cassie had instructed her yesterday before letting her teleport back to Carthage, "and you will tell no one about any of this. You will pretend everything is absolutely normal, until either he or I tell you to do otherwise. You will not do anything that could potentially interfere with serving myself or Colin Spencer."

Cassie kissed her then, a long and sensuous kiss, before sending her home. She wanted to bite the woman's lip off and spit blood in her face but was powerless against her.

She hated herself for willfully and naively falling into this trap. Cassie had seduced her, made her fall in love, and then ripped out her heart, all in the space of a week. She hated herself almost as much as she hated Cassie.

Emily tried telling Ben and Katy about what had happened the moment she'd returned to Carthage, but of course Cassie had forbidden her from revealing any of this. She tried to write it down, but her fingers wouldn't work. Katy asked her what was wrong, and she'd waved it off, mumbling something about having a headache.

Finally, in a fit of desperation and hopelessness, she'd tried to kill herself. She would do anything, absolutely anything within her power to prevent herself from stealing Hope away from Ben and Katy and delivering her into the hands of these monsters, but whatever magic bound her into Cassie's service also prevented her from downing a bottle of Tylenol or dragging a sharp knife across her wrist. Even in suicide, she was a failure.

She'd tried to take a nap, hoping against hope that she somehow wouldn't wake up, but she wasn't even able to fall asleep. They weren't going to let her die until they were finished with her.

Half an hour ago, Colin cornered her in her room and told her what to do. "Go into Hope's room at exactly 1:00 this afternoon, and I'll follow you in a few minutes. I'll pick her up and then you'll teleport us to Rand Park in Keokuk."

"But I can't teleport more than one person," she had responded.

"Yes, you can, and you will. You'll teleport us to Rand Park when I tell you to," he'd said, before walking out the door.

He no longer seemed like her brother, and instead, a being of pure ice, emotionless and straight to the point.

She couldn't even imagine how they'd enchanted Colin. Was Sumi one of them as well? Is that why she wasn't returning any of Emily's messages or phone calls? Sumi seemed amazing and so full of life the two times she'd seen her in person, and they had become fast friends. It couldn't be Sumi.

But it almost had to be Sumi, didn't it? It couldn't be Colin, it just couldn't. Her brother couldn't be in league with demons without being controlled like she was being controlled. That was almost unthinkable, and she felt guilty for even considering the possibility. None of this made any sense.

"Hi, Auntie Em," said Hope, looking up from her dollhouse.

Hope ran over to hug her, and she thought her heart would break. She willed herself to push the little girl away, to yell at her to run, but neither her body nor her mouth would cooperate. The most she could do was not return the hug, and even that took every ounce of willpower she had.

Hope looked up at her and whispered, "It's okay, Auntie Em. It's not your fault. I love you."

"What…what do you mean?"

"It's not your fault Uncle Colin is making you take me away."

Emily stared wide-eyed at the little girl. "How could you possibly know that?"

"My friend told me," Hope said, sounding sad.

Emily realized that Hope was wearing shoes as well as her little Mickey Mouse backpack that she sometimes used to lug her dolls around. She really must have known they were going somewhere.

"Who is your friend, Hope? How did she know? Can she…stop me?"

Hope stood silently and said nothing, and then Colin was there, scooping his niece into his arms. She didn't resist, but neither did she hug him like she'd hugged Emily.

"Your mommy and daddy are busy, and they asked Auntie Em and I to take you to the park to play," Colin said. "Won't that be fun?"

"Okay," said Hope, gamely.

"We're going there 'Emily-style.' Isn't that right, little sister?"

Emily felt herself open her mouth and say, "Yes, that's right."

"Put her down, Colin," said Ben's voice, from behind them.

Both Emily and Colin whirled to face their brother and Katy, who was right behind him. Hercules followed close behind her, growling and bearing his fangs.

"We're just taking her to the park, Ben. Nothing to get alarmed about," said Colin. "I think it's high time I spent some quality time with my niece, don't you?"

"Emily, Natsumi is dead," Ben said, looking at Emily and ignoring his twin. "She was murdered the day before Colin showed up in Las Vegas, and this son of a bitch did it."

Emily felt herself go weak in the knees. Natsumi! How was any of this possible? She turned to stare at Colin, and a slow smile spread over his face. It was then that she knew that, regardless of what skin he wore on the outside, her brother, the boy she'd grown up with, the man he'd become…was nowhere to be found.

Hercules growled at Colin, but Ben held him back. She thought back to the other times Hercules had been around Colin. The collie had always known what Emily was too stupid to see herself. Hercules tried to warn them, but they'd failed to listen, and now poor Hope was going to pay the price.

"Well, then," said Colin. "I knew that would probably come back to bite me in the ass. What can I say? I wasn't quite myself then. I should have disposed of her body."

"Why the charade, Colin?" asked Ben. "The attack, saving Katy…all of it was to get me to trust you, wasn't it?"

"I had to get you to stop watching me so closely, and to trust me around Hope."

"Colin," said Katy, her voice shaking, "put my daughter down."

"That's not going to happen. What is going to happen is that Emily, Hope, and I are going to leave."

"Why do the demons…why do *you* want my daughter?" asked Ben. "I thought you were after me."

"We were never after you. Without your abilities, you're useless. Emily, take my hand."

Emily felt hot tears streaming down her face. Try as she might, she couldn't refuse Colin's commands. She began walking towards Colin, one foot after the other, but then her feet wouldn't move. It was like she was standing in mud.

She looked at Katy, who was staring at her, clutching something in her hand. The Jaguar's tooth. *Please Katy*, she pled silently, *don't let me do this. Kill me if you have to, but don't let me do this!*

"Emily, why are you helping him?" Ben asked, and she felt like her heart might break.

"It's not her fault, Daddy," Hope said, from Colin's arms. "Uncle Colin is making her do it."

Colin slipped his hand around Hope's throat, and Emily wanted nothing more right then than to kill him. Hercules lunged forward, snapping at Colin, but Ben held tight to his collar.

"Keep that mutt away from me and let Emily move, or I'll snap your daughter's neck."

"If you hurt her…" Ben said.

"You'll do exactly nothing, because there's nothing you can do. Katy, last chance. Let Emily move, or I'll kill your daughter."

"You won't kill her. You need her for something," Katy said, but Emily could see she was shaking.

"Are you sure enough about that to risk her life?"

Katy stared defiantly at him for a few seconds before releasing her hold on Emily. Emily felt herself once again walking towards Colin, powerless to stop, reaching out to take his hand.

"We'll get them back," said Ben, "and then I'll kill you."

Colin laughed. "No, you won't. Emily, teleport us to the place I told you about earlier."

Emily fought herself. She couldn't resist his orders, but he hadn't said *when* she had to teleport them to Rand Park.

"You'll save me, Daddy," Hope said, staring at her father, "and then we'll play with my dollhouse."

"Now, Emily. Teleport us to the place I told you about earlier now."

She could hold off no longer. Emily thought of Rand Park in Keokuk, and she, Hope, and Colin vanished from the room.

# Chapter 56

Ben stared at his twin brother, wanting nothing more than to put him into the ground. He felt beyond stupid for trusting this man. No, this monster. Colin risking his life to save Katy, offering to take Ben's place with the mercenaries...all of it was just a ruse, designed to trick Ben into letting his guard down, so he could get to Hope. And it had worked.

He felt like his heart was being ripped out of his chest. Hope, his precious little girl, was being taken from him, and he couldn't do a damn thing about it. He'd known her just a week, but now couldn't imagine his life without her.

"You'll save me, Daddy," Hope said, staring into his eyes, "and then we'll play with my dollhouse."

Hope, Emily, and Colin vanished then, to God only knew where. Ben fell to his knees, shaking uncontrollably. Then he was face-first on the ground, immobile, as everything came flooding back to him.

**Four and a Half Years Ago**

Ben floated just beneath the surface, not in control of his own body, a rider on a ship he no longer captained. He stood inside a huge compound somewhere in California, surrounded by dozens or perhaps hundreds of other people. He felt his mouth open and heard words coming out, but the words didn't belong to him. They belonged to the demon Azazel, who had tricked Ben into giving away his life.

"So now what?" Azazel asked of a red-haired man in a gray suit. "And where's Michael?"

"Michael will be here when the time is right," said the man. "You, however, are the man of the hour. If this works…"

"Why wouldn't it work?" asked another man, this one short and bald. "You said it would work."

"It should," the redheaded man said, not missing a beat. "However, we always have contingencies. You know this."

"Papa always has contingencies," said a curvy blonde wearing a red skirt and an orange t-shirt that showed off her pierced belly button. "I've long given up worrying about them. Either it works, or it doesn't. In the meantime, Azazel," she said, turning to stare at Ben, "wanna fuck me?"

Ben felt a stirring in his groin mixed with disgust. The disgust, he realized, was his, while the desire was all Azazel's. He tried to close his eyes, to will everything away, but of course his body no longer obeyed him. He felt his mouth begin to say something, but whatever he'd been about to utter was cut off by the man in the suit.

"Cassiel, you've gotten a little too used to this human flesh, I believe. Then again, haven't we all? Alas, I have need of your brother. Run along."

Cassiel shrugged and took the hand of the bald man, who looked startled. "You'll do, I suppose," she said, as she led him off into the crowd.

"You have the talisman?" asked the ginger.

"Yes, father," Ben heard himself say, "of course." He looked down at his hand, which held the double-headed nickel, the one the demon had created from two alternate universe versions of the same coin.

"Give it to me," he said. "We don't want it lost if something goes awry."

Ben dutifully handed over the coin. "As you wish."

"Now reach into Benjamin Spencer's mind, find his ability to time travel, and picture this very house as it was two hours ago, before everyone arrived."

Ben felt his eyes close, and an image appear unbidden in his mind: the building where they currently stood, but empty of everyone save himself and the redheaded man standing before him. He tried to push down the power, to keep himself from activating the magic that lay dormant inside him, but it was useless. He wasn't in control anymore. He was merely an unwilling observer.

Time stood still around him, and then began to move backwards. There was Cassiel again, releasing the bald man's hand. God help him, Azazel was accessing his powers, going back in—

He felt an incredible searing pain, as the demon was torn from his body. He dropped to one knee. Blinking, he moved his fingers first, and then his hand. His body was his own again. He was free. His heart thudded hard in his chest. He was free!

Ben looked around the room. Cassiel was there, her mouth open, but she wasn't moving. Her father stared at the space Ben had occupied just moments ago, also frozen in place. A fly hovered motionless a few feet off the ground, even with the man's hip, as if caught in amber.

Pushing himself up on shaky legs, he placed both hands against the stucco wall, taking deep, gasping breaths. Something out of the corner of his eye caught his attention: the fly. Its wing moved, just a little, and Cassiel's lips were a bit closer together than they were a few seconds earlier.

He was catching up to the present.

Panicking, all Ben could think about was getting as far away from Azazel as he could, as quickly as possible. With nothing but escape in mind, he willed himself into the past. He instantly felt himself hurtling backwards through time, the world nothing but broken lines and blurs of color surrounding him, as everything else fell away.

Where was he? Ben opened his eyes but immediately closed them again, for the light was so bright that it stung and made his eyes water. He lay on something soft. A bed? No, he smelled soil, and felt a warm breeze on his skin. He was outside, which probably meant the light was the sun.

Shielding his eyes with one hand, he pushed off the ground with the other and squinted at the space in front of him. He was surrounded by tall sprouts of green and yellow grass for as far as the eye could see. Massive trees with long, willowy branches reached up to the sky in the distance. He sniffed the wind again, taking a deep breath. Something was different about the air, but he wasn't sure what. Maybe it was just because it had been so long since he'd controlled his own body.

Struggling to his feet, he surveyed the area. He was on a flat, grassy plain, but now he could see a large body of water in the distance, maybe a football field away. A lake? A huge pair of birds circled over the water, perhaps looking for lunch.

Something about the birds struck him as odd, and he squinted against the sun to stare at them. Their wings were larger than any he'd ever seen before, and their beaks were long and sharp.

A rush of noise from behind him made him drop to his knees as something threw itself over him, landing just a few feet away. His shoulder hurt, and he noticed blood trickling down his arm. Ben staggered backwards, staring straight into the face of some otherworldly creature.

The beast was half as tall as Ben was and had a lizard-like head. Its open mouth sported dozens of razor-sharp teeth. The creature was colored pale green, with light brown stripes, and looked like a mini-tyrannosaurus rex but with longer arms. It stood on its hind legs and wagged its tail menacingly as it circled him. It resembled a velociraptor from those *Jurassic Park* movies, he realized, but not quite as large.

Where in the hell was he?

A sharp pain shot through Ben's forehead and he felt an almost-irresistible urge to travel back to the future, to rejoin the demon to whom he was still bound. Whatever forces tied him to Azazel were attempting to call him home, to reunite host with parasite. He clamped down on the strange desire, attempting to ignore it, just as another creature, almost identical to the one circling him but a little smaller, shot out of the grass to lunge at his feet.

He closed his eyes, willing himself to Carthage, circa 1977, just as he'd done when he time travelled to the past with Katy on a journey to stop the Halloween murders. Why he thought of Carthage's past he had no idea, but his powers took him someplace else entirely.

A beautiful woman with long brown hair tied back in a ponytail stood above him, concern on her face. She looked to be in her early-to-mid-twenties, perhaps even younger. Her green eyes were tinted red, and he could see she'd been crying. His hand was grasping something, something he felt move, and then he realized she was holding his hand. He squeezed her fingers, causing the woman to jump.

"Oh! You're awake! Thank goodness, you're awake!"

"Where I am?" he whispered, blinking.

The last thing he remembered was the little dinosaur running at his legs and thinking of Carthage. Ben closed his eyes and opened them again, attempting to focus.

He was lying on a bed in a small room somewhere, the only other furniture the chair the woman beside him was sitting on and an end table beside the bed. The walls were painted light blue and were empty save for a photo of him in a tuxedo minus the jacket, a long-haired Katy in a red blouse and black mini-skirt, and a little girl wearing a white dress who stood between them. She looked maybe four or five years old, and he could immediately see a resemblance to the woman who currently held his hand. The photo hung beside a closed door.

"You're safe," she answered. "You're in Carthage, in the old Huffman Heights building."

He sat up in bed. Carthage? "This isn't 1977, is it?"

She laughed. "No, this definitely isn't 1977." She named a date nearly 70 years later. "But you're safe, I promise. Your shoulder was bleeding, but we fixed you up."

"How did I get here? I've never traveled into the future before. I was in the past, trying to get away from—"

"A group of velociraptors," she finished for him, smiling.

"How did you know?"

"Believe it or not," she said, "you told me."

"I don't understand. Who are you?"

"My name is Hope Ruskin-Spencer, and I'm your daughter."

Ben's mind was reeling. That little girl in the photo, it was her, and she was his daughter. He and Katy had made a child together, which must mean he'd successfully broken free of Azazel.

"But…how?" he finally asked, still trying to wrap his mind around the fact that he had fathered a child.

She frowned. "I don't know how much I should tell you. The last two times didn't work out so well."

"What do you mean?"

"We've called you here twice before, to keep you from rubber banding back to Azazel," she said, "and it didn't work out as we'd hoped. But this time…this time needs to work, because I'm not sure we can do it again."

"I'm trying to understand all of this, Hope. I really am, but it isn't easy. You saved me, but how? How did you call me here? And what happened the other two times?"

"First of all," she said, "I didn't save you. I just gave you a temporary reprieve. You can't stay here forever, I'm afraid. You're still bound to the demon, and you'll have to go back."

Ben felt his heart sink. "But why?"

"Because if you don't go back, everything could turn out even worse than it did the last time we tried this."

"When I was in the past…I felt the pull, the almost overwhelming need to go back to Azazel. Why don't I feel that here?"

"You're in the spirit room. Remember how my mother could control it? Not only can I control it, but I'm connected to it in ways that she never was or ever could be. As long as you're in here, you're safe."

"How are you doing this?"

"We used the room, and your connection to your artificial hand," she said, "to find you and pluck you out of the past at the only moment when you wouldn't be missed."

"You said that you can control the room better than Katy could. How?"

She looked Ben straight in the eyes. "I was created here, Dad. This room is part of me, and I'm part of this room."

Ben remembered back to that night in 1977, before going back to their time, when he and Katy finally made love. Their first and only time together. Hope was conceived in his past, not in his future, which meant there were no guarantees he'd ever escape the demon.

Ben stood up from the bed and resurveyed the room. "Where does that door go? Back to the house?"

"I'll explain everything, I promise," she said. "But first, I need to show you this."

Hope opened a drawer in the nightstand and pulled something out. It was his hand, the same black hand he'd called forth to replace the one David Dowd cut off in 1977. He looked at his own right hand, but it was still there.

"Am I…dead, in this timeline?"

"Yes," she said, "you died during a rescue attempt. You'd been controlled by Azazel for almost twelve years at that point."

His stomach went cold. "And Katy? Fred? My parents, my sister?"

"Emily is still alive," said Hope, "though everyone else eventually perished, along with half the planet."

"Azazel killed half the planet?" he asked, heart racing.

"No, Daddy," she said, her eyes downcast, "I did."

# Chapter 57

This couldn't be happening. In the original timeline, Hope said, she'd never even met Ben while he was in control of his own body. Their first attempt to rescue him hadn't been successful. Because Azazel had full use of Ben's powers, he'd murdered someone named Nadine Pahari and Ben's father Shawn before escaping.

Colin, Ben's twin brother who was somehow created because of their trip to 1977, had been estranged from the family but came back from Canada for his father's funeral. He ingratiated himself back into the grieving family, and never did they expect that he was actually one of the demons and that Colin had never really existed in the first place.

Ben and Katy's entire time travel journey to 1977 had been planned decades in advance by Elohim, the father of the Vīrya, the beings who masqueraded as demons and angels. Because Colin hadn't originally existed in the timeline, Elohim was able to use some cosmic loophole to implant the demon into the baby's body at the precise moment of his birth, destroying Colin's fledgling soul in the process. He grew up thinking he was Colin but had been activated by Elohim right after the attack on the compound where Azazel lived.

One night, about six months after Shawn's funeral, Colin assassinated Katy and kidnapped Hope. Hope hadn't seen the murder, and Colin had told her that her mommy abandoned her because she blamed Hope for her Grandpa Shawn's death, and so he was taking her to see her father.

Together, the demon masquerading as Colin, and Azazel (in the guise of Ben) spun a web of lies, ending with Hope despising her mother and her entire family, save for her father and uncle.

It had taken another seven years for Fred, Jenny, and Emily to track down Ben and Hope, and Ben perished in the ensuing battle. Azazel finally lost control of Ben's body minutes before he passed, giving Ben just enough time to tell Emily everything that had happened, including the tale of his all-too-brief sojourn into the prehistoric past and how that might be the key to saving everyone.

Six months later, the Gods (that's what they called themselves) gathered together nearly a mile above the surface of the Earth and, using a brainwashed twelve-year-old Hope and the fused nickel, cast a spell designed to enslave humanity. They were able to enchant almost all of the human population and immediately murdered half of them, citing population control. Those who, for whatever reason, they hadn't been able to take over (Ben's mother Jenny had hypothesized that, like her, the approximately 5% of humans who didn't fall under their sway had at some point in their lives been touched by magic) became the targets of their ire.

The "freewillers," as they took to calling themselves, continued to fight back, to little avail. The gods sent their enslaved humans out in hunting parties to murder those they couldn't control. Fred Ruskin was killed in an attack that took place almost a year to the day of the original enchantment, and Jenny died rescuing Hope less than a year after that.

Emily and sixteen-year-old Hope went underground then, after Emily managed to convince her that everything she'd been told by her "father" and "uncle" were lies, and hid from the Gods who still pursued them. They joined forces with a woman named Claire Locke and her son Jimmy, who was around Hope's age. Having lost her wife in the initial attack, Claire was eager to gain revenge against their supernatural oppressors. Nine years later, Claire herself died during a battle with Elohim.

After that, Emily took Hope and Jimmy into the spirit room, where they continued their research into time travel.

Hope was from that original timeline. The photo that hung on the wall, she explained, was from the timeline that had been created after that. She'd never actually met Ben until she called him to the spirit room.

"My God," Ben said, tears running down his cheeks, "I'm so sorry. What...what did they do to you?"

"It doesn't matter," said Hope.

"What do you mean, it doesn't matter? It does matter, it—"

"They did awful things to me, Okay?" Hope said, interrupting him. "They indoctrinated me and used me against the people I loved. My father and uncle, or so I thought, brainwashed me. Even though I know it wasn't my fault, not really, I'm ashamed of the things I did. But none of that matters if we can change the past."

"What...abilities do you have, that allowed them to use you to reshape the world?"

"I'm a conduit, of sorts," Hope said. "I have Mom's abilities to control this room, obviously, but beyond that I can harness energy that would pretty much kill anyone else. Other than you, I'm the only one in the world who can use the fused nickel, but unlike you, using it didn't destroy me."

"It's almost like you..." Ben trailed off.

"Almost like I was created to end the world?" She finished for him. "You're not wrong. We were all manipulated by these self-proclaimed Gods to get the results they wanted. You were their plan A, I was their plan B, and I'm sure they had other plans as well. The odds are stacked against us. But there's something else out there, too, something that's on our side. I'm almost sure of it."

Ben wasn't at all sure that was the case but didn't say anything. Azazel and the others seemed to be ahead of them at every step. If there were a force for good out there, what in the hell was taking it so long to intervene?

"I can also do a few things that I don't think they intended," she continued. "I can sense my other selves, past and present, and sometimes communicate with them, especially when they're younger. When your universe's version of me was little, I told her a number that she gave to Mom to win the lottery. That was a test of sorts, and it worked. I've been communicating with 'little Hope' ever since."

"Can you use that ability to help...fix things?"

"I guess we'll see."

"Tell me about the hand," he finally said, trying to ignore the hopelessness that threatened to drown him.

"It's the key to everything, really. It's taken us years to figure out, but we finally know how to use it. As you already know, you snatched it from an alternate version of our own universe, a place where science advanced at a much faster rate than it did here. But what you don't know is that it's much more than just a hand.

"It's actually an ingenious device that, were you actually living in the universe it came from, would allow you to connect seamlessly to the Ultranet—more or less their version of our Internet, but much more comprehensive—and download information, make holographic calls, and a bunch of other things. It would also allow you to monitor your health and heal you from minor injuries by altering your body's chemistry. Best of all, the hand would automatically make periodic changes to your body to prevent cancer and other diseases, keeping you in optimum health."

"Is that what fixed my arm?" he asked, looking at his torn shirt sleeve and the pink skin beneath. "That velociraptor got me pretty good, but it doesn't even hurt now."

"I healed your arm. Now let me finish," she said, with a lopsided smile that reminded him of Katy. "I said it would do all of those things, were you actually living in the world it came from. It needs to connect to the Ultranet, remember? The Ultranet doesn't exist in our universe. There, in that other universe, people voluntarily replace parts of their body to gain these abilities. Here, other than being a replacement hand that feels and operates exactly like a real hand, it's fairly useless. Or at least it was, until we figured all this out, and how to change it."

"Why is it black?"

"It doesn't have to be. It has the ability to match the skin tone of whoever is wearing it. But here, it just defaults to the stock color, which is obsidian. We think there's a way to force a match without being connected to the Ultranet, but figuring that out hasn't been our highest priority, obviously."

"You keep saying 'we' and 'us.' Who is 'us'?"

"You'll meet him soon enough. We've reprogrammed the hand, and before we send you back, we'll replace the hand you're using now with this one. The moment you start to manipulate casualty, the hand will send a dampening signal to your brain, disrupting that ability. It'll still work, but only for a few seconds. That feature was designed to help people with Parkinson's and other brain diseases."

"But why would I want to lose my abilities?"

"You won't lose them, you just won't be able to use them for a while, at least not until you repeat a certain phrase. Once your hand hears you say that phrase, it'll delete the subroutine we installed and go back to being just a very strange, fully functional hand. As to why this needs to be done, it's so the first rescue attempt works, and we don't have any casualties."

"But won't Azazel know this? He seems to know everything I know."

Hope smiled. "You're right, of course. But if you don't remember this little conversation, he won't either. The hand is set to alter your memories and block out everything we do today, and you won't remember any of it until the hand hears another key phrase, one that I'm not going to tell you. Now, let's make the switch."

Swapping the two hands was quick and painless. After that, Hope waved a hand over his shirt and the tears from the velociraptor knitted themselves together. She really did have her mother's powers to bend reality in the spirit room, and apparently much more.

"I have two more things to tell you before we do this," Hope said, "about Azazel. Given time, away from the influence of Elohim, we think he could grow to be an ally, of sorts, and—"

"An ally?" Ben asked incredulously. "Hope, he's a monster. He took everything from me!"

"Let me finish," she said, reaching out to touch his cheek. "I just said he could be an ally, not that you have to like him. Given time and space away from Elohim, he falls in love with being a human. We've seen it happen. He doesn't want humanity destroyed or enslaved. He wants to be one of us. You might be able to use that to your advantage."

Ben didn't like the idea of trusting Azazel, so he'd have to play his cards close to the vest and see what happened.

"And what's the second thing?" Ben asked.

"David Dowd," Hope said, "the man who took your hand in 1977. There's a chance he might show up at some point. If he does, he'll be on your side. It won't make sense to you, at least not at first, but give him the benefit of the doubt. Trust me."

"That makes about as much sense as Azazel, but okay. I do trust you, Hope."

"Good. And now we need to finish this up and wipe your memory."

He was about to ask how the hand had the power to wipe his memory when the room's only door opened, and in walked a tall, dark-haired man wearing a black trench coat. Hope stood up from beside the bed, walked over to the man, and kissed him on the lips.

"Dad, this is Jim Locke," she said. "He's my husband, and the one who helped me figure all this out."

"Pleased to meet you, sir," he said, walking over to the bed.

"Call me Ben," said Ben, shaking his hand. "You're probably older than me anyway."

"Okay, Ben."

"He didn't get to meet you the last time you were here," said Hope. "I didn't want to mess with your timeline too much. But this time, he's integral to our plans."

"Integral? How so?"

"This time, we're going to kill you."

Things had gone considerably better, Hope explained, after she had yanked him from the timeline the first time and altered his hand to block his powers, but not well enough to prevent the death of Fred Ruskin and Claire Locke in the Yukon rescue. Azazel had learned to jump incrementally backwards in time, in bursts lasting only a few seconds, bypassing the dampening affect provided by the hand and keeping control of Ben's body. They'd rescued Ben, but at a high cost.

Less than six months after Ben's rescue, much more quickly than the first time around, the Gods once again kidnapped Hope and flew more than a mile above the planet's surface. Linking hands, powered by the fused nickel, they repeated what they'd done in the original timeline, attempting to use Hope to help them enslave humanity.

Remembering how he defeated Aupuch in 1975 by substituting a common nickel for its magical double, Shawn intended to rescue Hope and sacrifice himself by inserting his own body into the link, hopefully short-circuiting the chain, ruining the ritual, and destroying the angels and demons in the process.

Before he could complete the task, however, he was murdered. Weeping over his father's body, Ben gathered the four talismans they'd managed to accumulate and flung himself into the sky, to take Shawn's place. The plan worked all too well. The gods were banished to another dimension when Ben disrupted the circuit, but the magical energy released in the resulting explosion was incredible. Nearly 90% of humanity was wiped out that day, including Ben and Hope, while the rest were left to deal with the ensuing chaos.

"You were very brave," said Hope. "You sacrificed yourself to save everyone. What happened wasn't your fault."

"90% of the population," he whispered, feeling a panic attack about to come on, "gone? Just like that?"

Hope nodded, and Jim took her hand. "Just like that. We can't fail a third time, Dad. We just can't."

"And that's why we've made some more modifications to the hand," Jim said. "Azazel shouldn't be able to access your abilities at all this time."

"We've covered the original timeline and the first time you sent me back in time." Ben said. "What happened the second time?"

"We screwed up, big time," said Hope. "We tried sending you back to *before* Azazel abducted you, so you could warn yourself, and the result wasn't pretty. We miscalculated and sent you back before your trip to 1977, before you learned to time travel, but you were still bound to Azazel. He was immediately sucked into your body, and the whole timeline you changed in 1977—"

"Never got changed," Ben finished for her, "and Katy and I never got together, and you were never born."

"Exactly. The whole thing was a mess, and the false gods eventually claimed the world anyway. It was a disaster."

"If you've brought me here before, why not again? Or as many times as it takes to get it right?"

"Because we're running out of time. We keep going back further, and taking you earlier, which effectively results in cancelling out the other trips. This isn't a perfect science, and there's not much room left for error. Eventually, we'll make an attempt before you arrived in the prehistoric past, which might result in bringing Azazel here, and—"

"And then he'd know," Ben finished for her. "Even if he were trapped in here, Michael or some of the others would know, and that would pretty much ruin everything."

"Exactly."

"So…how are you going to kill me?"

"That's where I come in, Ben," Jim said, stepping forward. "I am the gateway between life and death, as my mother was before me, and her father was before her, and his father…well, you get the idea. I can't explain why because I really don't understand it myself, but without the gateway, the door between life and death would be flung wide open, the dead would rise from their graves, and a bunch of other really bad shit would happen. So, I try not to die, especially since I haven't yet produced an heir to take my place."

Hope moved her hand to her stomach, smiling shyly. "Yet."

His daughter, the daughter he hadn't even known he had until just a few minutes ago, was pregnant. He was going to be a grandfather. The thought made his head spin.

"Anyway," Jim continued, "With that responsibility comes certain abilities. I can see and communicate with spirits, I can raise the dead, I can heal, and I can drain the life from people. Which is what I'm going to do to you. Not much, just enough to kill you."

"And then what?" asked Ben.

"Then we'll send you back to the past. The idea is that, once you rubber band back to Azazel, they'll revive you. They'll think they 'broke' you, because your powers won't work after that. It should make rescuing you a whole lot easier."

"If this all works, and I manage not to destroy the world, what'll happen to you?"

"Nothing, as long as we don't leave this room for more than a few hours. The world has changed around us before, but we've always been safe in here. There are other versions of us out there trying to fix things, and sometimes we even communicate, but mostly we just ignore them, and they ignore us. The spirit room has become our own little pocket universe. However, if we were to leave it for longer than a few hours…" she trailed off.

"We don't know what would happen," Jim finished for her, "and it doesn't matter, because we don't intend to leave. This is bigger than us, bigger than you, bigger than all of us."

Something had been bothering Ben. If his sister were alive, where was she?

"She left the spirit room a few weeks ago, and never returned," Hope said, after he asked. "I'd like to think she's still out there, somehow, fighting the good fight, but I really don't know."

"I guess we'd better get this show on the road," Ben said, pushing away the thought of his lost sister.

"The moment you die, I'll activate the hand, and you won't remember any of this. But at a certain point, someone's going to say something to you, something the hand is programmed to recognize, that will unlock your memories and bring them all flooding back.

"When that happens, say 'Hope Elizabeth Ruskin-Spencer loves James Gabriel Locke,' and you'll get your powers back, along with some information that I can't tell you now. You'll hear me talking to you, but it won't really be me, just a recording of sorts. Think you can remember that phrase?" Hope smiled, and Ben thought of Katy.

"Oh, I don't think I'll have any problems remembering that," said Ben, "and I can see that you do, and that he loves you, too. Take care of each other, okay?"

Hope wrapped her arms around him then, kissed him on the check, and said, "We will. I love you, Daddy."

"I love you, too, Hope," Ben said, and realized it was true.

He also realized something else. Hope said her last name was Ruskin-Spencer. Did that mean he and Katy would get married? But there was no time to ask.

"And now," said Jim Locke, reaching a hand to Ben's chest, "it's time for you to die. Good luck, Ben, and please don't take this the wrong way, but I hope I never see you again."

Ben had to laugh at that, and it was the last thing he did before his heart stopped and he died and forgot everything.

# Chapter 58

Ben's head hurt, and he felt like he'd been run over by a truck. All those memories had come flooding in, and he hadn't been able to handle them, had collapsed to the ground.

"Dad, this is Hope," said a voice in his head, "Once you say the key phrase, you'll get your abilities back, though it may take a while for you to relearn how to access some of them. Your subconscious ability to bend causality in your favor, however, should work right away."

"Hope?" he mumbled.

"If you're hearing this, that means they've kidnapped little me. I have no idea where they took me, though, so you're on your own from here. Good luck, I love you."

"I love you, too, Hope," he whispered.

He felt something like wet sandpaper rubbing his forehead. He tried to move away, but the wet sandpaper followed him.

"Ben, wake up," he heard someone pleading with him, over and over. "You've got to wake up."

He opened his eyes. It was Katy, and Hercules was licking his forehead. Everything came rushing back. Colin had used Emily to kidnap his and Katy's daughter, and they'd been powerless to stop him.

"Oh, thank god," Katy said, helping him to his feet. "We have to get Hope back."

Hercules woofed, nuzzling Ben's hand.

"'You'll save me, Daddy, and then we'll play with my dollhouse,'" he said, repeating the phrase Hope had said to him right before she'd been taken. "It must have been the phrase that unlocked my memories."

He hoped with all his heart that he could indeed save his daughter. There was another phrase he needed to say that would help him do that, that would unlock his long-dormant abilities. He concentrated, and it came to him.

"What are you talking about? What memories? Ben, I'm terrified."

He pulled her into his arms, and then she was crying, sobbing hysterically into his shoulder. They held each other like that for a minute, and then he whispered, "Hope Elizabeth Ruskin-Spencer loves James Gabriel Locke."

He felt something deep within him open up, an energy coursing through his veins that he hadn't felt in a very long time, and he knew his abilities had at long last returned.

She pulled away from him, staring. "What are you talking about? Jimmy Locke, Claire's little boy? What does he have to do with any of this?"

"It's a long story, and one we don't have time for right now."

"Your hand…" Katy said, staring at him.

Ben looked at his hands, and his right hand, previously jet black, was now the same color as his left hand, blending in seamlessly with the rest of his skin. Apparently Hope and Jim had figured out how to activate the color matching option in his cybernetic hand, after all.

Ben's mother walked into the room. "Ben, do you know where Colin is? He wasn't in his room, and…where are Emily and Hope?"

"Colin stole my daughter," said Katy, her voice shaking, "and he used Emily to do it."

"What are you talking about? Colin was just downstairs, with us."

"Your fake son stole my daughter! I should never have trusted him. I feel like such an idiot."

"Katy, you're scaring me," Jenny said. "Colin wouldn't…"

Ben started to say something just as a gunshot rang out from somewhere else in the house. He flashed back to the night of the mercenary attack. It almost felt like déjà vu, and he was not going to let his father get shot again. Pushing past Katy and his mother, he ran out of the apartment and towards the stairs.

# Chapter 59

Emily, Colin, and Hope appeared next to a tree in Rand Park, surrounded by children playing on the playground equipment and people walking their dogs. Emily immediately dropped to her knees and threw up all over the ground.

"Oh, come on," Colin said. "Are you really that weak?"

"You're a real piece of shit," said Emily, as she turned to stare into his eyes.

"Don't talk that way around your niece," Colin retorted. "It's just not very becoming. In fact, don't speak again until I tell you to."

Emily tried to respond, to tell him to go to hell, but her mouth wouldn't work. She began to cry.

"Don't worry, Auntie Em," said Hope, still in Colin's arms, "Mommy and Daddy will save us."

Colin laughed. "Sorry, little girl, but that's not going to happen. But I'll tell you what. You do exactly what I say, and eventually you'll get to see your mommy and daddy again. How does that sound?"

Hope began to scream, wailing at the top of her lungs, as she threw her backpack to the ground and pushed against Colin. "You're not my Daddy! Let me go!"

"Shut up," Colin said, under his breath, "or you'll never see your parents again."

People in the park were looking at them now. A young brown-haired woman, probably not much older than Emily, took out her cellphone, while a man in jogging shorts approached them, hands out.

"I don't know what's going on here," said the man, "but you need to put that little girl down."

"This is none of your business," Colin said to him, while simultaneously bending over to retrieve Hope's backpack. "Leave before you get hurt."

The man's eyes grew big. "That sounds like a threat to me. You need to put her down now, mister, before *you* get hurt."

"He's not my daddy and he's stealing me and my Auntie Em," yelled Hope at the top of her lungs,

Everyone in the park was staring at them now, some pointing cellphones at them, others moving closer. Emily said nothing, because she'd been ordered to be quiet, but inside she prayed that someone could help them.

"Miss, are you okay?" the jogger asked her. "Are you here against your will?"

"Emily," said Colin, grabbing her arm, "teleport us to Cassiel's room in Chicago. Now."

Cassiel? Who in the hell was Cassiel? She stared at Colin.

"You can speak. What's wrong?"

"Who's Cassiel?" she asked.

"You're not taking her anywhere," said the jogger.

"Cassie! Now shut the fuck up and teleport us to Cassie's room in Chicago, damnit, and do it now."

The jogger reached out and took her hand, but she was already starting to teleport. She fought against the command with everything in her, but it wasn't enough. She pictured the hotel room in Chicago and vanished, taking Colin, Hope, and the jogger with her.

# Chapter 60

Emily, Hope, Colin, and the jogger appeared in the middle of Cassie's hotel room in Chicago, startling Cassie, who was in the middle of packing her bag. She jumped back, letting out a little yelp.

"What happened?" she asked. "You weren't supposed to come here yet. You were supposed to—"

"What the fuck?" asked the jogger, eyes wide. "Where am I?"

Colin shoved Hope into Emily's arms, then moved fast as lightning behind the jogger and snapped his neck. He fell to the floor, eyes open in shock, dead.

Emily stared at the dead man who'd tried to help her, tears running down her cheeks. Her brother had just murdered a man in front of her and Hope. She hugged Hope tight.

"I know that, Cassiel," Colin said, stepping over the dead man. "It was an emergency."

"Well, lucky me. At least you brought me my little plaything. How're you doing, Emily?" She touched Emily tenderly on the cheek.

Emily tried to speak, to tell her to fuck off and die, but the words wouldn't come out of her mouth. She held Hope close, doing everything she could to prevent her niece from seeing the dead man.

"You can talk now," Colin said.

"You…you killed that man. Why?"

"Because he got in the way," Colin said.

"I hate to break it to you, my love, but humans are expendable," said Cassie. "At least most of them."

"Fuck you, Cassie," said Emily, as she sat Hope down behind her.

"You already did that, remember?" Cassie said, winking.

Emily wanted to strangle her, but of course she was forbidden to hurt either Cassie or Colin. Instead, she covered Hope's ears with her hands and then turned to stare at Cassie.

"I will kill you," she said, "and I'll enjoy it."

Colin and Cassie looked at each other and started laughing. Emily felt hot rage course through her body. She'd never really hated anyone before, not even Azazel, but she hated Cassie with her entire heart—almost as much as she loved her. And Colin...had everything been a lie?

"Were you ever really my brother?" asked Emily, whirling to face him, positioning herself between Hope and the man she'd thought was her sibling.

"Oh, I *am* your brother, at least physically. For 24 long years, I called myself Colin Spencer. I hated Ben, because he got the abilities I craved, because he stole the girl I loved, blah, blah, fucking blah. Typical teenage angst, and all that. And then last Wednesday, the day your precious big brother came home, I finally woke up and remembered everything."

"And then you murdered Sumi."

"That was a mistake. I loved Sumi, or at least the person I thought I was loved Sumi. She just happened to be there when I remembered, and...why am I telling you any of this? It doesn't matter."

"But it does matt—"

"I said, it doesn't matter."

"I guess Sumi was expendable," Emily said.

"Shut up!" He slapped her hard across the face.

Emily stumbled backwards, holding her cheek, glaring at Colin. She felt Hope grab her hand and turned to look at her. Little tears streamed down her cheeks and she looked terrified.

"Michael..." said Cassie, "take a breath and calm down."

Michael? Was the being who wore the guise of her brother Michael, the "archangel" her parents had told her about? The being who, until recently, they'd thought was their protector?

Colin stared at Cassie for a moment, and then smiled. "I almost forgot to do something."

He pulled out a cellphone, dialed, held the phone up to his mouth, and said, "Kill them all, then call the others and tell them to do the same."

"Kill who?" asked Emily, dreading the answer.

"Everyone you love," said the monster who she now no longer believed had ever really been her brother.

# Chapter 61

Shawn glanced at the stairs. Colin had been up there a long while now. How long did it take to find a piece of paper? He'd heard Hercules bark a few minutes ago and hoped the dog wasn't bothering Colin. Hercules seemed to love Ben, whom he'd only met a few days earlier, but just wasn't warming up to Colin, not at all.

"We can install the alarms tomorrow, if that sounds good," Durst said, drawing Shawn's attention back to the conversation, "and the security team can more than likely start the day after. Do you think that would work for you?"

Something felt wrong to Shawn, but he couldn't put his finger on just exactly what that wrongness was. Something just felt…off. Maybe it was just how easy it all seemed. Oslov just happened to have men in Quincy, and their job just happened to be coming to an end, making them available for this job.

Colin was the one who suggested them, though, and he trusted his son implicitly. Maybe he was just being paranoid, still shaken by everything that happened on Monday. Shawn looked at Jenny, who shrugged.

"I want to wait for my son to ask his questions before signing anything," he said, casting a furtive glance at the stairs again, "but yes, that sounds good to me."

"Of course," said Durst. "I'm happy to answer any questions Colin might have."

"I'm going to go see what's taking him so long," Jenny said, rising from the couch. "I'll be back as soon as I can."

The man's phone rang a moment later. Durst looked at the caller ID and said, "Sorry, I have to get this."

"It's okay," Shawn said slowly, the hairs on his arms standing at attention.

Durst listened to the phone, nodded, and said, "Consider it done," before standing up and pulling out a handgun.

Shawn rushed him, his ears ringing as a bullet whizzed by his head. He tackled the man, hurling them both over the side of the couch.

Gurley was on him in a second, pulling him off Durst. He wrapped his arms around Shawn's throat, putting him in a chokehold. Shawn elbowed Gurley in the ribs but couldn't break the hold, and his vision was starting to darken.

"Hold him still," said Durst, as he climbed to his feet, pistol still in hand.

Durst pressed the barrel of the weapon under Shawn's chin and was about to pull the trigger when the tip of something sharp and metallic shot through the man's chest. Durst's eyes grew big and he slumped to the floor, sliding off the sword.

"What the fuck?" said Gurley, loosening his grip on Shawn.

Shawn took advantage of the man's surprise, elbowing him again in the ribs and stomping down hard on his foot. Gurley yelped and Shawn, gasping for air, was finally able to pull free.

A huge man wearing a black trench coat and wielding a bloody sword stood before them. He had black hair and wore an eyepatch over one eye. He looked almost familiar to Shawn, but at the same time alien, like someone out of a movie or a dream.

"I don't know who you are," Gurley said, drawing his own gun from a holster inside his jacket, "but you just made a big mistake."

Shawn punched Gurley in the face, sending him stumbling backwards. He fired a shot into the ceiling, and then the stranger was upon him, burying his sword in Gurley's neck. Gurley made a gurgling noise and then fell to the floor, dead.

"Who are you?" asked Shawn, staring at the giant, and then it came to him. "Dowd?"

"There's more of them coming," yelled Fred Ruskin, hobbling through the front door, a gun in his hand. "At least six, maybe more, all from a van parked down the street."

Ruskin had blood on his shirt, but otherwise seemed unharmed.

"Fred?" asked Shawn. "What are you doing here?"

"You're right, I am David Dowd," the giant finally said, "but I promise I'm not here to hurt you or anyone in your family."

"David Dowd?" echoed Ben's voice, from the staircase.

*** 

Ben stood at the top of the stairs, staring down at the man who'd buried Katy alive and cut off his hand. Anger flooded his system, and then he remembered what his daughter had told him about Dowd during his just-remembered trip to the future five years ago:

*"There's a chance he might show up at some point. If he does, he'll be on your side. It won't make sense to you, at least not at first, but give him the benefit of the doubt."*

Katy stood beside him, with Jenny behind her. "Dowd? You son of a bitch," she yelled, "if you're helping them, I'll kill you."

She started down the stairs, but Ben held her back. "I can't explain how I know this, but he's here to help. You're going to have to trust me, at least for now."

Katy looked like she was going to argue when another gunshot echoed through the house. Two men dressed in black and holding guns burst through the door, and he could see more behind them.

Hercules bared his teeth, ready to run down the stairs, but Ben held him back. "Mom," he said, "keep Hercules safe. Hope would never forgive us if anything happened to him."

His mother took hold of Hercules' collar, holding him back.

"Ben, no!" she yelled as Ben leapt over the railing, did a flip, and hit a perfect landing next to Dowd.

There's no way he could have done that without his abilities to bend causality to his favor and choose just the right outcome. His powers were definitely back. That didn't mean he was invulnerable, however, as had been proven many times in the past.

Fred Ruskin dropped to one knee and shot one of the intruders in the stomach, then screamed in pain and toppled over to the floor.

"Dad!" screamed Katy, running down the stairs.

Dowd charged into the group of men, cutting the one Fred had shot nearly in half with his blade. The man fell to the floor, almost certainly dead. Then he was onto the next, knocking away the intruder's gun with his sword and then headbutting him into near unconsciousness before driving the sword through his chest.

Ben grabbed the coat rack that stood beside the downstairs closet and ran at one of the intruders, swung the rack at his feet, and knocked his legs out from under him. He brought the coat rack down on the back of the man's head, and the man moved no more.

"I'm okay," Fred said, holding his knee, as Katy dropped to a crouch beside him. "Stay with Hope, keep her safe."

"They took her, Dad," she said. "They stole my baby."

Four more men came through the door, and Dowd disemboweled one with a swing of his sword. One of the others, however, aimed his gun at Dowd and pulled the trigger before the big man could react. Ben jumped in front of Dowd, and the bullet ricocheted off the coat rack he was holding and buried itself into the intruder's forehead. He looked shocked, then slumped to the floor.

"Thank you," said Dowd, and Ben nodded.

The other two men, guns in hand, circled Dowd. Katy stood up and pointed her fist at one of the men and he flew straight up into the air, smashing his head hard against the ceiling, then dropped ten feet to the floor below with a heavy crunch. His gun skittered away from him, sliding somewhere under the couch, while the man lay unmoving.

Dowd charged at the remaining intruder, cleaving his head from his body with the sword. The man's head rolled off his shoulder, landing on the floor with a wet thunk, his body falling on top of it a second later.

"I counted six," Dowd said, wiping the bloody blade on the shirt of the man he'd just killed. "Ruskin said there may be more."

Shawn was beside Fred, helping him to his feet.

"It's my knee," Fred said. "Two of them attacked me at my house and damn near kicked my knee off."

"Is Mom okay?" asked Katy. "Please tell me she's okay."

"She's fine," said Fred, "She's safe."

"Thank God."

"I'll be back," said Dowd, walking over to the front door and exiting into the night.

"He saved our lives," Fred said, staring after the man as Shawn helped him to the couch. "If not for him, both Candy and I would probably be dead."

"You said to trust him, Ben. How did you know?" asked Katy.

"It's a long story. I'll tell you about it later. For now, though, just know that Dowd is on our side."

"Ben," asked his father, "your hand, it's no longer black. And your powers…are they back?"

"They are," he said, "and the hand changed to mimic my skin color. I'll explain more later, I promise. Right now, we have to get our daughter back."

"Can you time travel?" asked Katy. "Go back to just before he took her and kill the son of a bitch."

"That's the first thing I tried to do, but I can't, at least not yet. My abilities are back, but I'm having to learn how to use them all over again. There's also the chance that stopping him would mean Hope never said the phrase that triggered my memory, and then I'd never get my powers back in the first place."

Katy stared at him. "What phrase? What are you talking about?"

He started to answer but was interrupted by the ring of a cellphone. They all turned as one to face Shawn, who pulled his phone from his pocket and slowly held it up to his ear.

# Chapter 62

Shawn's phone rang, startling him. He pulled the phone from his pocket. It was his father. He almost didn't answer it, and then a thought fluttered unbidden into his head: what if they'd also attacked his parents?

"Dad," he said into the phone, "Are you okay—"

"We're fine. Shawn, do you know where Hope, Emily, and Colin are?" his father asked.

"No, actually, we don't. Why?"

"Turn on NBC. I'm pretty sure it's them. It's…really freaky, Shawn."

"Jenny," said Shawn, "please turn the TV on, channel 10. Dad, I'll call you back when I can."

They all watched as Jenny turned on the television and changed the channel to the local NBC affiliate on channel 10. The television showed a park filled with people, and it only took Shawn a few seconds to realize it was Rand Park in Keokuk, about a 20-minute drive from Carthage.

"…the strangest thing," said a man in overalls, being interviewed by WGEM's Morreen Klement, a reporter Shawn remembered seeing on the news before, "one minute they were there, and the next…they just up and vanished."

"Ran away, you mean?" asked Klement.

"No, ma'am. They were there one second and the next they were gone. The man said something to the woman and, poof, they were gone, and they took this other guy with them."

"We're talking to Harper Darland, of Keokuk, who claims he saw two men, a woman, and a small child vanish into thin air."

"It ain't no claim, Miss Klement. It happened. We all saw it. That woman over there, the one in the pink?" said Darland, pointing at a young pink-haired woman wearing a matching pink blouse, "She took a video."

"Thank you, Mr. Darland," said Klement, hurrying over to the woman in pink, who was talking to a newspaper reporter.

"Miss, miss," said Klement, pushing in front of the newspaper reporter, "can I ask you a few questions?"

"Hey!" said the reporter, a bald man who was probably in his 40s or 50s.

Klement ignored him. "Miss," she said, pushing the microphone at her, "what's your name?"

"Aubrey Daniels," said the woman, who was probably no older than Emily. "Do you want to see the video?"

"Yes, Miss Daniels, I think we'd all like to see the video. Mike," she said to someone, presumably the camera man, "can you get a close up on this?"

"You got it," said Mike's disembodied voice.

Daniels queued up the video on her phone, showing it to the camera man. "Ready?"

"We're ready," Klement said.

The camera zoomed in on the woman's phone, and the video began to play.

Colin and Emily were there, and Colin was holding Hope, who was crying and screaming. A man in a pair of jogging shorts approached them, and Colin leaned down to pick something up from the ground. It was Hope's Mickey Mouse backpack.

A few seconds later, Colin grabbed Emily's arm, said something to her, the jogger grabbed her other arm, and then all four of them vanished.

"Oh my God," Klement said. "This can't be real, right? It has to be a trick."

"It was real," said Daniels. "Everyone here saw it."

"What was the little girl saying? The audio isn't good."

"Something like, 'He's not my daddy and he's stealing me and my aunt,'" Daniels said. "It was really scary. I hope they're okay."

Shawn stared at the television. This couldn't be real. Colin kidnapped Hope and Emily? Colin loved his little sister, and loved Hope, too, even if he didn't know her very well yet. None of this could be real, unless what Katy had been telling them for 5 years was true, that Colin wasn't supposed to be born, and that his entire existence was due to the manipulations of demons and angels.

He just couldn't bring himself to believe such a thing. There had to be another answer. There just had to be.

He remembered being in the hospital with Jenny when she gave birth to the twins, remembered his knees almost buckling when he first saw Ben, and then, a few minutes later, Colin. He remembered their birthdays growing up, school events, everything. It couldn't all be a lie. Could it?

"They must be controlling him," Jenny said. "That's the only explanation that makes sense."

"He murdered Natsumi," Katy said, flatly.

"What are you talking about?"

"He murdered his girlfriend. We found the article on the internet, from a Canadian newspaper. He's wanted for questioning by the police."

"When we confronted him about it," said Ben, "he admitted it.

"That can't be right," Shawn said. "He loved Sumi. You could see it in his eyes whenever he talked about her."

"He admitted it, Dad! I know you don't want to believe it, but it's true. When we were upstairs, he threatened to break Hope's neck."

"Stop!" screamed Jenny. "Stop, stop, stop!"

Shawn went to her then, pulled her into his arms, and held her as she sobbed into his shoulder.

"I think…I think I can help," Ben said. "Something I did to Katy in 1977. She remembered the wrong timeline, the one where the Halloween murderer killed so many people, but I was able to help her remember the correct timeline, the timeline I remembered."

"Ben," Jenny said, pulling away from Shawn, "even if what you're saying is somehow true, I don't want to forget my son."

"Outside is clear," said David Dowd, walking into the living room. "I found the van. No license plates, and the van was empty…hey, what's this?"

Dowd bent over to retrieve a black cellphone from just under the edge of the couch. It must have been Durst's.

"Can I see?" asked Ben.

"Knock yourself out. It's locked, though."

Ben randomly pressed four numbers, unlocking the phone. Shawn had forgotten just how amazing Ben's abilities to bend randomness to his will were.

"There isn't much on here," he said, disappointed. "The phone appears to be brand new. Just…wait a second. Anyone recognize this number?" He read off a phone number, the only number ever to have called the phone.

"That's Colin's number," said Jenny, her face falling.

"What did the guy you were meeting with sound like?" Ben asked his father.

"What do you mean?"

"Did he have an accent? Deep voice or higher?"

"Not that I can remember, no. His voice was a little deeper than yours. Why?"

"Hell, I'll just wing it," Ben said. "Things usually turn out better when I do that, anyway, just let my ability take control."

Ben clicked speaker mode on the little black cellphone and dialed Colin's number. The phone rang three times, and then answered.

"Yes?" said Colin's voice.

"It's done," Ben said, "they're all dead."

"Good," said Colin, and hung up the phone.

Shawn felt the bottom drop out of his stomach. That was Colin's voice, and he'd been happy to believe they were all dead. He had to be possessed by a demon, as Ben had been. That was the only thing that made sense.

"I think we need to get to Rand Park in Keokuk," Fred said, breaking the tension, "and see if we can figure all of this out."

"Good idea," Shawn heard himself say, as if from a distance.

Fred tried to stand up, but his knee buckled.

"Dad," said Katy, "just stay here and I'll take you up to the spirit room and heal you after we find Hope."

"I can help him," said Dowd.

"I'm not letting you anywhere near my father."

"Please, let me heal him. I hurt all of you back in 1977, and I know I'll have to answer for that later, but for now let me help," Dowd said, kneeling down beside Ruskin.

"How can you heal him?"

Dowd pulled a necklace from around his neck, with a small silk bag attached. He emptied the contents of the bag into the palm of his hand, revealing a twig, a geode, and an emerald. "With these."

Shawn gasped when he saw the talismans. He had thought the talismans, other than the jaguar's tooth and the nickel, were long gone. He wondered how Dowd had gotten these items.

Katy glared at the huge man for a moment before nodding her head. "Okay, heal him."

Dowd touched Ruskin's knee and a moment later, Ruskin breathed a sigh of relief. "It doesn't even hurt anymore."

Dowd reached out a hand and Ruskin took it, hauling him to his feet.

"Ben, I'll call you once we get to Rand Park," Shawn said. "I promise you; we're going to get your little girl back."

"I'm coming with you."

"But Ben—"

"I'm coming with you," Ben said again, and Shawn nodded.

"All right."

"Jenny," said Fred, "can you go pick up Candy and bring her over here? At least until I can clean the house and get rid of those bodies."

"Of course," Jenny said, "and she can stay as long as she wants. You both can."

"I'll text when we get there," said Shawn, and then they were out the door.

# Chapter 63

Katy was sick with worry, not only for her daughter but for Ben, Shawn, and her father. She was afraid they might be walking into a trap in Keokuk, though realistically that didn't make sense. Colin thought they were all dead.

Jenny had gone to pick up Katy's mother, while she and Dowd tried to figure out what to do with the dead bodies of the security crew currently littering the foyer. Finally, they'd moved all but one of them into the cellar, choosing to deal with the bodies later.

"You got the talismans from Janna Sparks, Alejandro Torres, and Agatha Muir," said Katy, turning to stare at Dowd, as they walked up the stairs, "didn't you?"

"How do you know that?" Dowd asked.

"Answer my question," said Katy, "and then I'll answer yours."

Dowd nodded. "I stole the twig from Janna Sparks and the geode from Alejandro Torres. I murdered Janna and cut off Alejandro's hand, crimes that I'll have to pay for once this is over."

She hadn't expected him to admit it. "What about Agnes Muir?"

"Agnes Muir willingly gave me the emerald. She knew I was coming. She's the one who sent me here, to help you."

"But why?" asked Katy, as they walked up the cellar stairs. "How does she even know who we are?"

The giant shrugged. "I don't know the answer to either of those questions. Now will you answer mine? How did you know about them?"

"We found a list of the guardians of the talismans. We Googled them and found news articles about them. Sparks was killed with a sword, and Torres was missing a hand. We figured it was you."

"It was me."

"Okay, how about this question? Why do you care what happens to us? You cut off Ben's hand. You fucking buried me alive. You were a monster. Why are you suddenly pretending to be the good guy?"

"I never claimed to be the good guy, I'm just trying to no longer be the bad guy. Your husband changed me and then sent me to prison. For years, I was angry. I hated him for taking away my powers, but more importantly for fixing my brain, for making me see all the evil I'd done in the name of a god I no longer even believed in.

"I thought if I could just get those talismans, I could change myself back. Not just to regain my abilities, but to take way the guilt, the shame at what I'd done. That's all I thought about for years and years, so when I finally got out of prison, I followed a vision I'd had in 1977, and that led me to Janna Sparks in Missouri."

"And you murdered her for her talisman," Katy said.

"Yes, I murdered her for her talisman. I didn't want to, even then, but I needed the talisman, and so I killed her for it. I'd give anything to take it back."

"And yet you cut off Alejandro Torres' hand eleven years later, for the twig, right?"

Dowd nodded. "And I was prepared to do the same to Agnes Muir, if not worse, but with her I found something I didn't expect. Instead of fearing me, she…well, she laughed at me, and then she showed me compassion. She made me realize I no longer wanted to be a monster and that maybe I could, in some small way, atone for all the evil I'd done."

"Like burying me alive?"

"I know my apology will never make up for what I did, but I am sorry. I'm sorry for that, and for so much more."

Katy thought back to their time travel trip to 1977, and the insane preacher who had buried her alive and cut off Ben's hand. That man and the man standing before her right now didn't feel like the same person. Maybe he really had changed.

"You also saved my parents lives, probably saved all of our lives this evening," she said.

"I don't expect that to balance the scales, but hopefully it's a start."

"What happened to your eye?" she asked, changing the subject. "Ben healed you."

Dowd touched the patch over his left eye. "I wanted to be what I had been, a monster with no guilt. Three months into prison, I gouged my own eye out with a spoon. One of the stupidest things I've ever done."

"I think I can help with that," she said, deciding to choose compassion over hate. "I think I can give you back your eye."


At first Dowd refused her offer, saying he deserved the deformity for all the things he'd done, but eventually realized that was just another way of hanging on to who he used to be. Using the pentagram charm, she teleported him into the little alcove behind the stairs and together they walked through the curtain of lights.

"This is amazing," he said, looking around her little imaginary cabin in the woods inside the spirit room.

She nodded her head in agreement. "Okay, sit on the couch and take off the patch."

He did as he was instructed. His eye socket was a mess. Skin had grown over the hole, but there was scarring everywhere. She hoped she could do this.

"Ugly as hell, isn't it?" he asked.

"Well, you definitely did a number on yourself. But I can do a lot more in here than I could out there. Hold still."

Holding the jaguar's tooth in one hand, she touched his eye socket with the other, imagining him having two eyes. Skin began to separate and heal, and scars disappeared, but his eye socket remained empty.

"Here," he said, removing the necklace that held his talismans, "maybe these will help."

He held out the necklace with the little black bag to her, but she was almost afraid to take it from his hand. All five talismans together had nearly corrupted Shawn when he was 15 years old. What might four of them do to her?

"You trust me with these?" she finally asked.

"Probably more than I do myself."

"All right, then." She reached out to take the little silk bag.

*No fear*, she thought, emptying the contents of the bag into her hand, the hand that held the jaguar's tooth, and felt almost unbelievable power flow through her body. The moment the geode, the twig, and the emerald connected with her tooth, she truly felt like she could do anything.

She closed her eyes and imagined the molecules in the air around them merging together to form his missing eyeball. She felt the eye coming together in her hand, felt its weight in her palm, and opened her eyes. It was there, staring back at her.

She touched his eye socket with her hand and the eye immediately slid inside, filling the empty socket. He blinked, looked around the room, and began to cry.

"I have two eyes again," he said, tears running down both cheeks. "Oh, my lord, I can see. I can see. Thank you so much."

She ignored him, instead focusing on the power coursing through her veins. It felt amazing, like she could do anything. She never wanted to lose that feeling. The talismans weren't hers, though…

…then again, neither were the talismans his. He stole them, had killed and mutilated for them. He didn't deserve them, especially not after what he'd done to them back in 1977. He'd had her buried alive, very nearly killing her.

"It's addictive, isn't it?" he asked.

She looked up, startled. It most certainly was addictive. Sighing, Katy pulled herself back from the edge. She dropped the twig, the geode, and the emerald back into the little black bag, feeling the raw power they represented flowing out of her, and handed it and the necklace back to Dowd.

"It really is," she said, nodding her head. "Let's get downstairs and see if they're back yet."

# Chapter 64

Rand Park was still filled with many more people than normal, but less than there'd been when they'd seen the park on the news 30 minutes ago. The reporters mostly seemed to be gone, and parts of the park had been cordoned off from the public by yellow police tape.

They had driven to the park from Carthage, hoping to find something, anything, that might give them a clue where Colin had taken Ben's daughter and sister.

"It's that woman from the news," said Fred, pointing to a pink-haired woman in a pink blouse, blue jeans, and an old pair of Docs.

Ben rushed over to the woman, who was standing by a bush in the middle of the park. "Excuse me, ma'am. Aubrey Daniels, right? Could I talk to you for a minute?"

"You want to see the video, don't you?" Daniels asked. "Everyone wants to see the video."

"I'm the little girl's father, and these two are her grandfathers," he said, as Shawn and Fred caught up to him. "Her name is Hope, and the woman with them was my sister Emily. I was hoping you saw something else that might help us."

The woman's eyes grew big. "I'm so sorry. That man with her…he seemed awful."

"Trust me, he is," said Ben. "Can you think of anything, anything at all, that might help us?"

"I'm sorry, I already told the police and that reporter all I know. It was so strange. They just vanished. How did they do that?"

"Do you mind if we see the video again?" asked Ben, ignoring her question. "Maybe we missed something the first time."

"Oh, sure. Actually, give me your number and I'll send you a copy, then you'll have it for yourself."

Ben thought that was a good idea. He gave her his number, and a few seconds later she texted the video to him.

"Thanks, Miss Daniels."

"You can call me Aubrey, and of course. I hope you get your daughter back, and—oh! What's that?" She crouched down beside the bush and pulled out a little plastic helmet.

"That's from Hope's action figure, Galahad," said Ben.

It was from the Mego 8" Super Knights Sir Galahad figure from the early 1970s, identical to the one his mother's brother Tanner had briefly inhabited after he'd died. His father had won another one on eBay 5 years ago, just before Ben was taken by Azazel, but later ended up giving it to Hope.

"Well, then, this is yours," Daniels said, handing the helmet to Ben. "I hope you can give it back to her soon."

"Thanks, Aubrey," Ben said, shaking her hand. "You have my number. Please call if you remember anything else, anything at all."

"I will," she said. "I promise."

Ben stared down at the tiny helmet as Daniels walked away. Hope must have had the figure in her backpack, and it fell out.

"Can I see it?" asked Shawn.

He passed the helmet to his father. "Sure."

Shawn held the helmet in the palm of his hand, staring at it. "It's probably just what it seems, but…"

"But what?" Ben asked.

"The helmet brings back memories of that summer in 1975, when Tanner came back to life in the body of the Galahad action figure your mother put in his coffin with him."

"And you think he's back?"

Shawn shook his head. "I wish, but no. It just brought back memories, that's all. Come on, let's head home and figure this thing out so we can rescue Hope and Emily."

***

Jenny stood in the kitchen on the first floor of Huffman Heights, feeling like her heart had been ripped from her chest. She'd finally gotten one son back, only to lose the other. She was keeping it together, more or less, but had to fight the urge not to just burst into tears and huddle in a corner somewhere.

Had Colin really wanted them dead? None of this made any sense, unless he was possessed by one of the Vīrya. Neither Ben nor Katy seemed to think that was the case, however, but what other reason could there be for his actions?

She opened the refrigerator and pulled out a pitcher of iced tea as well as an 8-pack of bottled waters. She'd already put together a platter of fruits, vegetables, and little sandwiches. As soon as Shawn, Fred, and Ben got home, they needed to all sit down in the dining room and discuss next steps towards finding Hope.

Shawn walked into the kitchen, startling her, and she nearly dropped the pitcher of tea. She sat it and the pack of bottled waters on the counter and ran to him, holding him close. The tears started again, and she couldn't stop them, and soon they were both crying.

"It'll be okay," he said, whispering into her ear. "We're going to find them and figure out what the hell's going on."

"They can't be right about Colin, can they?"

"I hope not," Shawn said, pulling back from her. "We weren't able to find out much in Keokuk, but we did find this. We think it probably fell out of Hope's backpack."

He pulled out a small plastic helmet that belonged to Hope's Gala-had doll. She hated seeing the thing, because it always reminded her of Tanner, the big brother she'd lost to Aupuch and the Fetch in 1975.

"Well, that's strange," she finally said.

"Isn't it? It...brought back memories."

Jenny pulled Shawn into another hug. "I miss him every day, Shawn. Every single day. But he's not coming back."

"But how do we know that? He came back once, why not again?"

"If he was going to come back again, why wait almost 50 years?"

"Maybe because we didn't need him until now," Shawn said.

Jenny felt a spark of anger ignite into a flame inside her. "Didn't need him? Shawn! I needed him every single day of my life. I needed him when my Dad died. We needed him when Ben was stolen from us. He's not coming back."

Shawn looked like he was going to say something and then thought better of it, and finally just said, "I'm sorry. You're right."

She sighed. She didn't want to be right. She missed her brother with an ache that may never go away. He was stolen from them at the tender age of 16, before he'd even really had a chance to live. But none of that was Shawn's fault.

"Your goofy sense of optimism is one of the many reasons I love you," she finally said, pulling him in for a kiss. "I'm sorry I yelled."

"It's okay. I want to yell, scream, and punch things. Tanner, Ben, now Colin, Emily, and Hope...so many people taken from our lives. But we can't do anything about the past. Let's concentrate on getting our children and our granddaughter home, okay?"

"Okay," she said, kissing him again. "Now's let's get the drinks and food into the dining room and work on making this rescue a reality."

"It's a deal," he said, picking up the platter of sandwiches, fruits, and vegetables and following her out of the room.

# Chapter 65

Katy burst through the shimmering door into her imaginary cabin in the woods, full of anger. She waved a hand, and Azazel appeared before her. He looked startled.

"Hey," he said, "I was in my room."

"You no longer have a room, you fucking monster," she yelled into his face. "They took my daughter and tried to kill us."

"Someone took Hope? Who?"

"Your 'kin,' that's who. Don't pretend you don't know."

"I *don't* know," said Azazel.

"Ben's brother Colin is one of them. He did something to Emily and made her teleport them away. And then this fake security company tried to murder all of us."

"Slow down," Azazel said. "Ben's brother is a Vīrya?"

"Yes, he is. Ben didn't even have a brother before you tricked us into travelling to 1977."

"That…makes sense. I didn't know why I was tasked with impersonating Michael and sending you to the past. Someone must have hijacked his body *in utero*. Now why was a fake security company—"

"Colin brought them here," she said, interrupting him. "They were supposed to help keep us safe from your people, but instead they tried to kill us."

"And you think I had something to do with this?"

"I don't know!" she screamed. "We went to the lodge and got the book, but it's all addresses, no names. Where the hell is Elohim?"

"Addresses is all I ever had, and I wasn't even supposed to have that. He never stays in one place for long. He has houses everywhere, and he contacts you, not the other way around."

"Why won't you help us?"

"I'm trying," he said. "There's not much I can do from inside here."

"You're not getting out. You know you're never getting out, so just stop."

He spread his hands. "I know I'm never getting out. Truth be told, there's probably not much I could do out there, either."

"What do you mean?"

"When the time travel experiment with Ben Spencer failed…Father blamed me, even though I did everything according to his instructions. I became *persona non grata*, as it were. That's why I left."

"Your 'father' sounds like a real asshole."

Azazel laughed. "He wants what he wants, and he won't stop until he gets it. He's like a tidal wave, taking everyone else along for the ride."

"But why does he want Hope?"

"Let me think. You said before she hasn't exhibited any abilities. Has that changed?"

"I didn't tell you everything. Hope has…an imaginary friend who sometimes tells her things that come true. Would that qualify?"

"Maybe. Is that it?"

"As far as I can tell, that's it."

"You rescuing Ben…like I said, I didn't stay in communication with Father, or anyone, but you rescuing Ben may have sped up his timetable. He may have thought that…oh, shit."

"What? What aren't you telling me?" Katy asked.

"No one but Ben could use the nickel, and once he lost his abilities, even he wasn't able to use it. But Hope is his daughter. She may have the ability to access the fused talisman I created when I was in Ben's body."

"And if that happens…"

"She could change the world," Azazel finished for her.

# Chapter 66

Ben sat at the dining table in the large communal dining room on the first floor of Huffman Heights, Katy beside him. Shawn and Jenny sat across from them, with Fred, Candy, and David Dowd taking up the rest of the space around the table. It was a tight fit, but they'd made it work.

"Did Future-Hope say anything more?" asked Jenny.

He had told them everything he remembered from his trip to the future five years ago, minus Hope and Jim's relationship, and they were still trying to wrap their heads around it. So was he, for that matter.

"That's pretty much it," he said, nibbling a bite from the carrot he'd snagged from the tray of food in the middle of the table.

"And she really said Azazel could be an ally?" Katy asked. "That's just...so hard to believe."

"Any harder to believe than David Dowd sitting here with us?" asked Ben, glancing over at the 6'7" giant at the end of the table.

"He's got a point," said Dowd, and Ben had to laugh.

"Let's not explore the 'Azazel option' until we have to," Shawn said, and everyone around the table agreed.

"What I don't get is that if Future-Hope knew our Hope was going to be kidnapped, why didn't she set up a different key phrase, so you'd remember everything sooner and stop the kidnapping before it happened?" asked Fred.

"I've been thinking about that," Ben said, "and the only thing that makes sense is that she needed to be kidnapped for something else to happen, something we don't know yet."

"Maybe so she or Emily could get the nickel, so they'd have it when we rescued them," said Katy.

She had told them about her most recent conversation with Azazel, and about him hypothesizing that, because she was Ben's daughter, Hope may be able to access the power of the fused nickel.

Ben hoped like hell that wasn't the case, but it did make sense. If Azazel were to be believed, all the power contained in the combined nickel could remake the world. In comparison, it would make the energy of the five combined talismans look like peanuts.

"I hate this," said Jenny. "I feel so helpless."

"I think we all do," Shawn said, as he opened a bottle of water.

"I'm going to try to contact Emily tonight," said Katy, and Ben squeezed her hand under the table. "She has to sleep sometime, and if she sleeps, I'm hoping I can dreamwalk to her and maybe find out where she and Hope are."

"You can use the three talismans I have again if you think it will help," Dowd said.

"Thanks," said Katy, "I appreciate that."

Ben glanced at David Dowd. He still couldn't get used to him having two eyes again, let alone sitting at their dining room table. He was glad Katy had apparently found forgiveness for the man. They all needed to go into whatever was next with clear heads and hearts if they were going to have any chance of success.

"We're pretty much in a holding pattern until we know their location," said Fred.

"There is one more thing we can do," Shawn said. "Claire Locke. She helped us once, she might be able to help us again. I'll give her a call as soon as we're done here."

"It's worth a try," Ben said.

*** 

Shawn sat in the little downstairs library, cellphone in hand, preparing to call Claire. He'd talked to the others and decided they needed as much help as they could get. They owed Claire so much already for her part in getting Ben back. He hoped she'd be willing to help one more time.

"Claire, this is Shawn Spencer," he said into the phone, after she answered. "I'm so sorry to bother you, but we need your help again."

"Hey Shawn. What's going on?"

"They kidnapped Hope."

"The demons? Jesus. Why?"

"Yes, the demons. Actually, they're called the Vīrya, and I don't know why they kidnapped her. She doesn't even have any abilities, at least none we're aware of."

"I can be to Tulsa in two hours," she said. "Have Emily meet me behind Trader Joe's, like last time."

"That's the thing," said Shawn, "they also have Emily. They…enchanted her and used her to teleport them to a park in Keokuk, a little town in Iowa about 20 minutes from here. We don't know where they went from there."

"Well, shit. You'd better tell me the whole story."

Shawn told her all about Katy's discussions with Azazel, about Azazel's "father" Elohim wanting to remake the world, and about the lists of addresses and talisman keepers Ben had found. He told her about Dowd and the three talismans he'd collected, and about Ben getting his powers back. Finally, he told her about Emily being controlled by Ben's twin brother Colin, who was apparently behind everything.

"Wow, that's a lot to digest. The Vīrya, huh? Okay, give me 10 minutes. I think I may know someone who can help us."

"Kingfisher and Quarry?" asked Shawn.

"Someone else, but that's not a bad idea. Kingfisher and Quarry are notoriously difficult to get in touch with, but I'll reach out to them as well. Talk to you soon."

Shawn paced the length of the library, waiting for Claire to call him back. They had all these people with powerful abilities and talismans at their disposal but had no idea where Colin had taken Hope and Emily. He was trying to keep it together, but truth be told he was absolutely terrified over what the demons—the Vīrya, he corrected himself—might do to his daughter and granddaughter.

Shawn's phone buzzed. It was Claire.

"Kingfisher and Quarry aren't answering," she said, "but my friend agreed to help. His name is Gavin Young, and he has abilities similar to Emily's. He can get me to your house. Do you know where they're holding Hope and Emily?"

"Not yet," Shawn said, "but we're working on it."

"Okay, great. Gavin just got here. Is there anyone in the downstairs bathroom right now?"

*The downstairs bathroom?* "Um, no," he said, "I don't think so. Why?"

"Can you take a quick picture of the bathroom with the door open, please?" she said, ignoring his question.

"Sure, I guess," he said, walking to the bathroom.

"Thanks."

He snapped a quick shot of the bathroom with his phone and sent it to Claire. "Will that work?"

"Perfect."

"Why do you need a photo of my bathroom, Claire?"

"Because that's," she said, and then they lost connection.

"Claire? Hello?"

"Where we'll be coming from," said Claire's voice from behind him, finishing her sentence. "Hi, Shawn."

Shawn spun on his heels. Claire stood before him, along with a man dressed in blue jeans and a green hoodie. He was maybe 5'10" with brown hair and green eyes. "How?"

"I told you," Claire said, with a smile, "he can do things like Emily can do."

"Pleased to meet you," said the man, holding out his hand. "My name's Gavin Young, and any friend of Claire is a friend of mine."

Shawn shook the man's hand. "But…Emily has to have physically been to a place or at least able to see the place before she can teleport to it, and you've never been here. Oh, and pleased to meet you, too."

"I can open a bathroom door in, say, Claire's house, and then show up in a bathroom somewhere else. It helps to know where I'm going, hence the photo, but even if I don't, I can usually hit my mark."

"That's amazing," said Shawn.

"No more so amazing than your family, from what Claire has told me," said Gavin. "Speaking of family, I'm so sorry to hear about your granddaughter. I'll do whatever I can to help you get her back."

"Claire!" said Jenny, walking into the hallway.

"Hey, Jenny," she said, giving her a quick hug.

Claire introduced Gavin to Jenny, as Shawn got her up to speed on the conversation and Gavin's abilities.

"If we can figure out where they're keeping Hope and Emily," Shawn said, "hopefully you can teleport us somewhere near there."

"If there's a Starbucks, a Walmart, a Target…anything like that near wherever they are, I can get you there, assuming we can get to one here."

"There's a Walmart in Keokuk. So how would that work?" asked Shawn.

"We'd go inside, find a door—probably the bathroom—and I'd open it. You'd go through and I'd follow. We'd appear inside the bathroom in the other Walmart."

"What if someone's in that bathroom?"

"From their perspective, they'd see us walk through the door as if we'd been in their Walmart. If they looked through the door, they might notice something off, but most of the time people don't pay attention."

"How about we all go into the dining room so Gavin can meet the rest of our crew?" Jenny said.

They all followed Jenny into the dining room. After the introductions were made, Claire said, "I think we've got a pretty solid team here. Now all we have to do is find out where they're holding Emily and Hope."

"I have an idea about how we can figure that out," said Katy, and they listened as she told them her plan.

# Chapter 67

The knight stood in a vast hallway that seemed to stretch on for miles, though he knew that probably wasn't the case. Perspective, after all, is everything. His hand on the hilt of his sword, he crept quietly across the marbled tile floor, trying to figure out his location.

Even if he didn't yet know where he was, at least he finally remembered who he was. He remembered everything, though he understood almost none of it.

He remembered the monster known as the fetch drowning him in Carthage Lake. He remembered waking up inside his own coffin, in abject terror, inhabiting the body of the 8" Mego Galahad knight action figure his sister had buried with him. He remembered Shawn freeing him from the coffin, and he remembered sacrificing his life, such as it was, to distract Ahpuc long enough for Fred Ruskin to throw the jar of pennies to Shawn and for Shawn to switch a normal nickel for the magical talisman before "surrendering" it to the priest.

His name was Tanner McGee. He'd been Paul and Abby's son, Jenny's big brother, and Shawn's best friend. He was barely sixteen years old when he'd died the first time.

All of that happened so very long ago, and he'd missed out on so much of what life had to offer. He'd never graduated high school, never went on a date, never kissed a girl, never owned a car, never went to college, never lived on his own, never held a job, never got married, and never had a child. But it was what it was.

He'd woken up again six months ago, in the body of another 8" Mego Galahad action figure, alongside a toy tiger he now knew to be inhabited by the soul of Shawn's cat Samson. Samson had also been murdered by the fetch, not long after the fetch had murdered Tanner.

The tiger had been his constant companion as together they kept watch over his grandniece from the confines of her dollhouse and all the wonders within. They had thought their mission was to keep Hope safe, but in the end that had proven impossible. What they had done instead, however, was to sneak into their charge's backpack when Michael kidnapped her.

The tiger was still in the backpack, in fact, ready to do what he could to protect Hope, while Tanner explored this massive labyrinth in which he found himself. He'd jumped out of Hope's backpack at the last second as they were bringing her and Emily into their new quarters, hiding behind one of many large potted snake plants that filled one side of the hallway.

Tanner almost felt naked without his helmet. When Hope had thrown down the backpack in the park, he had taken the opportunity to roll the helmet out into the grass, in hopes that Shawn or Jenny might find it and at least figure out that he was looking out for their granddaughter. It was a longshot, at best, but it was something. Perhaps when all of this were over, if he were still alive, they'd be able to return the helmet or at least find a replacement.

He thought they were on the second floor of a very large, very fancy house or maybe a swanky hotel, but he wasn't sure. It was hard to take stock of your surroundings when you were hiding inside a backpack. He hoped he could find something to tell him where they were, though how he'd get that information to Shawn he had absolutely no idea.

Hope and Emily were being held at the end of a long hallway filled with doors. He had no idea where the doors went because he couldn't reach the doorknobs. He hoped to find something, anything, that might give him a clue as to their location.

There were windows spaced periodically down the hallway, opposite the plants. There was no way to climb up to a window, but he might be able to scale the third plant from the end and get a peek out of the window that stood directly opposite.

"…always end up doing the grunt work," said a man's voice down the hall, getting closer.

They were coming! Tanner threw himself behind one of the plants, trying to stand as still and be as quiet as possible.

"It'll all be worth it in the end," said another voice, this one female. "Eventually, it'll be the humans doing all the grunt work."

"They should be serving us *now*."

"Patience, Usiel," the woman said. "You know father doesn't allow the unclaimed into his home. Well, other than the guards and these two."

He dared a peek around the plant. The man was dressed in slacks and a blue, button-up shirt, while the woman wore a red dress. She was carrying a tray of food.

Tanner watched as they reached Hope and Emily's room. The man withdrew a key and unlocked the door.

"Dinner time," said the woman, as she entered the room.

The man closed the door behind her, then stood guarding the room. About a minute later, the door opened. The women joined the man outside the room, and then watched as he locked the door.

"Cute little girl," said the woman, "but I'm not a damned babysitter."

"Thankfully, we won't have to worry about either one of them much longer," said the man, as they walked down the hallway, turned the corner, and disappeared from sight.

Shit. Whatever they had planned for Hope must be happening soon. He had to find out where they were and somehow get that information to Shawn and Jenny before it was too late.

The pots that held each plant were tall, probably at least a foot tall, 4" taller than his current 8" of height. He wedged himself between one of the pots and the wall, using the wall to steady himself as he slowly ascended the pot.

After what seemed like forever, he finally reached the top. He tumbled into the soil, safe for the moment. The plant didn't seem to have a stalk, but rather about 20 long, thick leaves shooting up from the soil. Choosing two of the sturdiest of the leaves near the middle of the plant, he slowly shimmied up until he could see out one of the windows on the other side of the hallway.

His plastic heart fell. A huge Douglas-fir tree filled most of his vision. Douglas-fir trees grew pretty much anywhere, as far as he knew, narrowing down the possibilities of their location not even remotely.

How did he know that? He wasn't sure he'd even known what a Douglas-fir was when he was alive. The afterlife, however, seemed to provide him all sorts of information about the world around him, but seemingly never the right kind. It was frustrating.

Tanner loosened his hold on the leaves, sliding down to land in the soil. He took a running leap and jumped from the pot, bounced against the wall, and landed on the floor below.

There was no way around it. He was going to have to risk exploring the rest of the house. Darting from one plant to the other, he slowly and methodically made his way down the hallway to a huge staircase leading downward.

Taking a deep breath, he began to descend.

# Chapter 68

Katy had tried countless times to enter Ben's dreams while he'd been controlled by Azazel, but it had never worked. Ben, however, had been possessed by the demon, while that didn't seem to be the case with Emily. At least she hoped it wasn't the case. If it was, she may never see her daughter again.

*Focus, Katy,* she told herself, holding back tears.

She lay in the bed in her dream cabin, inside the spirit room, staring at the ceiling. She could usually access people's dreams without being asleep, simply by using her connection to the spirit room. She'd tried connecting with Emily that way but couldn't make the connection. Her dream abilities always worked better if she were actually asleep, however, so they decided to try it this way.

Ben sat beside her, holding her hand. In her other hand, she held not only the jaguar's tooth but also the three other talismans Dowd had managed to collect.

Dowd. Was the man who'd been behind burying her alive in 1977 really on their side? She had a hard time believing it, even though he'd saved her parent's lives and used the talismans to heal her father's broken kneecap. He'd even loaned her the three talismans again, leaving himself defenseless if she decided to keep them and not honor their agreement.

Perhaps she needed to learn a little forgiveness.

"It might help you sleep if you actually closed your eyes," Ben whispered.

"What might really help me sleep is having my daughter back," she said, snapping back at him.

"How can I help?"

Katy sighed. "Sorry. I'm just scared. Hold me, okay? Snuggle with me. I think that might help."

Ben got under the covers, circling his arms around his wife. Katy pushed closer, resting her head on his shoulder. It felt good to be lying in the arms of the man she loved. She shifted the geode and the twig to her other hand, holding two talismans in each. *Balance*, she thought, as she closed her eyes.

Katy opened her eyes, still in bed, but something had changed. The air around her was almost static with electricity, and the world seemed crisp and bright. She was dreaming.

"Hey, Beautiful," said Ben, sitting up in bed, looking down at her.

She sat up, startled. "How are you here?"

Ben shrugged. "I have no idea. I guess I fell asleep, too, and you brought me with you."

"I didn't know I could do that."

"Me either."

"These talismans…" she said, but then realized she no longer held them. "Where did they go?"

"They're probably still in your hands, back in the real world."

"This feels amazing. The power, it's so incredibly addictive."

"Let's just hope it's enough to get through to Emily."

They assumed that, wherever Colin had taken Emily, she'd have to eventually sleep. With any luck, she'd be asleep and dreaming now. Assuming she was still alive. It was just after three in the morning. They first tried at midnight, then at 1:30, and finally at three, but this was the first time Ben had been able to come with her. Maybe the third time was the charm.

Katy rolled out of bed, walked into the living room, and sat down on the couch in front of the huge widescreen television that served as her portal into other people's dreams.

"Do you think I'll be able to come?" Ben asked, sitting beside her.

She reached out to grasp his hand. "We won't know until we try."

Katy pressed the remote control, bringing the television to life. She imagined a button on the remote that would sync to Emily's dreams, and it appeared. She pressed it and watched as images coalesced on the screen.

Emily was sitting in a darkened corner of an empty room, hugging herself and softly crying. There was nothing else in the room with her, and no one else was there. Just Emily, weeping silently in the corner.

Katy felt like her heart might break, and then she remembered Emily teleporting her daughter away from her. She knew it wasn't Emily's fault, that the girl was being controlled by Colin, but she still couldn't help but feel angry at her new sister-in-law.

Why had she let herself be tricked by the Vīrya?

"Probably the same way I did," said Ben when she put voice to those thoughts. "There'll be time for recriminations later. For now, let's just concentrate on getting our daughter back."

Katy knew he was right.

"Are you ready?" she asked, squeezing his hand.

"As ready as I'm going to be," he answered, returning the squeeze. "Let's do this."

Katy and Ben stood before Emily in the dark room of her dreams. Katy cleared her throat and Emily jumped, startled. She stared at them, uncomprehending for a second, and then her eyes grew wide.

"Am I dreaming?" she asked, her voice trembling.

"You are," said Katy, "and we're really here, in your dreams. Where are you?"

Emily jumped to her feet, throwing herself into their arms. They held her for a moment, not speaking, waiting for her tears to subside. Eventually she stopped crying and pulled away from them.

"I'm so happy you're alive. Colin said he was going to kill everyone I love. Are Mom and Dad okay? Uncle Fred and Aunt Candy? Hercules?"

"Everyone is okay," said Katy. "We were attacked, but we're all fine and they're all dead."

"I'm so, so sorry, about all of this," Emily said. "I didn't want to do it. They made me. They made me kidnap Hope, and I'm so sorry."

"It's okay," said Ben. "We know you'd never intentionally do anything to harm Hope. We need to find out where you are, so we can come get you and our little girl."

"I can't tell you where I am," Emily said, "even if I knew, which I don't. They put a hood over my head on the plane."

"How long was the flight, and where did you leave from?"

Emily tried to speak but couldn't. "It…it won't let me tell you anything. I made an agreement, even though I didn't mean to, and it won't let me. It won't fucking let me!"

"It's okay," said Katy. "We're still going to find you, and we're going to bring you home."

She hadn't expected Emily to be able to tell them anything, but she thought she had a workaround. With Ben's luck and the four talismans, it just might work.

She concentrated, imagining all three of them being in Emily's apartment in Carthage. For an instant they were there, but then they were back in the dark, depressing room. What the hell?

Focusing on the talismans she knew to be in her hands in the spirit room, reaching out to take Ben's hand, she whispered to Ben, "take her other hand and my hand and think about Emily's apartment in Huffman Heights."

Ben took Emily's hand, and, with all three of them connected like that, Katy once again concentrated on Emily's room. In an instant they were there, and this time they stayed.

"Oh!" said Emily, a slow smile creeping over her face. "It feels so good to finally be out of that awful place."

They were in Emily's bedroom, surrounded by all her things, including the paintings she'd taken from the lodge in the Yukon.

"Are they controlling your dreams?" asked Katy.

"Kind of. They made me wear a weird metal necklace before letting me sleep. They said it would prevent you from contacting me, in the event you survived the attack, but apparently they were wrong."

"I don't think they counted on Katy having four of the talismans, or me getting my abilities back. For once, they don't know everything," Ben said.

"You have your abilities back?" Emily asked, raising an eyebrow. "How?"

"Long story. I'll tell you when we rescue you."

Emily looked at Katy. "And how do you have four of the talismans?"

"It's just temporary. Like Ben said, we'll explain everything once we get you and Hope home. Suffice it to say, we got help from a very unexpected source," Katy said. "For now, I want to try something. Lie down in your bed, okay? Get under the covers and pretend it's bedtime."

Emily climbed into bed. "Now what?"

"Now we see if you can dream within a dream. Ben, turn the lights off, please?"

Ben walked over to the wall and switched off the lights.

"Emily, I want you to think about whatever you think Colin doesn't want us to know. Picture yourself where you first fell under their control and allow yourself to fall asleep and dream."

"I'm not sure I can sleep with you two just hovering there," Emily said, "but I'll give it a try."

Katy concentrated on the combined power of the four talismans she knew were still in her hands, willing Emily to sleep, and seconds later she was snoring. A few minutes later, with Ben watching over them, Katy joined Emily in her dream within a dream.


Katy was in a hotel room, in Chicago, having followed Emily from O'Hare airport where she'd been picked up by a familiar-looking blonde girl in a rented car. She was invisible and flew above the vehicle as the blonde drove Emily to the Peninsula, a beautiful 4-star hotel in the heart of Chicago.

She followed them as they entered the hotel, got on the elevator, and got off on the 20th floor. She ghosted behind them as they walked their way to room 2037 and let themselves inside.

The moment they were inside the room, they began kissing, and less than 5 minutes later they were in bed. This must be the girl from Las Vegas Emily had mentioned.

She felt pervy watching them make out but didn't avert her eyes. She needed to know everything. And why did this woman look so damned familiar?

The scene changed and there was light coming through the window. It must be the next morning. Emily was still in bed, while the blonde stood before her, wearing only a towel.

She let the towel drop to the floor and climbed into bed, whispering to Emily, "I have a confession to make. I think I'm falling in love with you."

Even the woman's voice sounded familiar, but Katy had no idea from where or when she might have encountered her before.

"I'm so in love with you, Cassie," Emily whispered back, "I've just been afraid to say it. You're all I can think about. I think I fell for you the first moment I saw you."

So, this was indeed the Cassie who Colin had mentioned on the video in Rand Park. That was good to know. She had to assume it was also the Cassie Emily had met in Las Vegas.

The two kissed, and Cassie whispered, "God, Emily, that feels so good. I love your kisses."

It was in that instant that Katy remembered where she knew the woman from, and if this wasn't a dream, she would have pulled her out of the bed and beaten her senseless.

"And I love to kiss you," Emily murmured.

"I'd do anything for you, you know."

"I'd do anything for you, too, anything, until the day I die," said Emily.

"That feels really good to hear," said Cassie, "though you really didn't have to add the dying part. I'd love to hear it again, though."

"You can hear it as many times as you want. I'd do anything for you until the day I die. Oh! That is so perfect."

"Say it again," said Cassie, "it makes me so fucking hot."

"Mmm. Say what again? This feels amazing."

"That you'd do anything for me until the day you die, anything at all, just like I'd do for you. Please say it."

"Cassie…oh my lord. This feels amazing, don't stop."

"Say it, then. Tell me you'll do anything for me."

"I'd do anything for you, Cassie, anything at all, until the day I die," she moaned. "Now fuck me with your tongue."

Katy shuddered. She did not need to hear the girl she thought of as her little sister say such things. She wanted to bleach out her brain, but nevertheless continued to listen to them. She thought she knew where this was going.

"Your turn," Emily said, "I want to make you feel just as good as you made me feel."

Cassie didn't say anything, just sat there looking sad.

"What's wrong? Are you okay?" asked Emily.

"I'm sorry," Cassie said.

"For what?"

"For this. Emily, slap yourself in the face," said Cassie, and Emily slapped her own cheek.

"What?" Emily asked, looking confused and afraid.

"Sorry, I just had to make sure it worked."

"Make sure what worked?" Emily looked confused and more than a little scared.

"The binding," said Cassie. "You're mine now, Emily Spencer, for always and forever, until your death do us part."

There we go. Cassie was a demon and had tricked Emily into binding herself to her. But there was one little caveat. "Until the day I die." The demon clearly hadn't wanted Emily to say that, but once she had Cassie just rolled with it.

Now Emily was in the bedroom of her apartment in the Huffman Heights building, tears streaming down her face. She watched as the teenager tried to swallow a bottle of Tylenol, and then to slit her wrists, both times her binding to Cassie preventing her from killing herself.

It was just an hour or so later when Colin walked into her apartment and found her hugging herself on the couch.

"Go into Hope's room at exactly 1:00 this afternoon," said Colin, "and I'll follow you in a few minutes. I'll pick her up and then you'll teleport us to Rand Park in Keokuk."

"Why are you doing this?" Emily asked, her eyes puffy from crying.

"Because it's what I was born to do. Now remember, 1:00 p.m. exactly."

Now they were in Rand Park in Keokuk. Colin, Emily, and Hope were surrounded by an ever-increasing crowd concerned for Emily and Hope's safety.

Seeing Hope crying, screaming for people to help her made Katy feel like her heart was being ripped from her chest. She held back her tears, though, because she may never get another chance to mine Emily's memories and needed to concentrate.

This was the scene Aubrey Daniels had recorded, but up close and personal.

"Miss…are you okay?" a dark-haired man in jogging shorts asked Emily. "Are you here against your will?"

"Emily," Colin said, grabbing Emily's arm, "teleport us to Cassiel's room in Chicago. Now."

"Who's Cassiel?" Emily asked.

"You're not taking her anywhere," said the dark-haired man.

"Emily!" shouted colin. "Teleport us to Cassie's room in Chicago and do it now."

Cassie's real name was Cassiel? If she were remembering correctly, the comparative religion class she'd taken in college listed Cassiel as one of the Archangels, along with Michael, Gabriel, Raphael, and several others. She was an angel, not a demon. Not that there seemed to be much difference as far as the Vīrya were concerned.

Now they were in Cassiel's hotel room, in Chicago. Hope looked lost and alone, and Emily was trying to comfort her while at the same time looking like she wanted to strangle someone. The man who'd tried to help Emily and Hope in the park lay dead on the floor, his neck twisted at an unnatural angle.

Katy watched as Emily and Colin went back and forth about who he really was. When Emily mentioned him murdering Natsumi Hashimoto, he turned wild-eyed and slapped her across the face.

"Michael..." said Cassie, after the slap, "take a breath and calm down."

Colin was Michael? It made sense, in a confusing sort of way. Azazel had disguised himself as Michael to visit her and Ben before their trip to 1977, because Michael, if their plans went correctly, would be hiding inside Colin once the necessary changes were made to the timeline. Hijacked *in utero*, as Azazel had said.

Now they were at a private airport, in Keokuk, getting ready to board a small plane. Emily was holding a sleeping Hope, while Colin and Cassie talked to the pilot.

"...three, maybe three and a half hours," said the pilot, in such a low voice that Emily and thus Katy could barely hear. "It always depends on the weather, to be honest, but the radar looks pretty clear."

"The faster, the better," Colin said, to which Cassie nodded agreement.

Hope mumbled something in her sleep, which caused Emily to look down at her, missing the rest of the conversation. After they had climbed aboard the plane and were situated, Cassie slipped a hood over Emily's face.

"Just in case," she whispered, kissing Emily's masked lips.

"I hate you," Emily said.

"I know, and I wish you didn't, but what Daddy wants, Daddy gets. This was all put into place literally eons before you were even born."

"You're responsible for your own actions," Emily said. "No one made you do this to me, and no one made Colin kidnap Hope."

"Emily, you're special to me, but this is bigger than the both of us. I wish you could understand."

"I understand that you're a monster, just like...just like Michael is."

"Oh, shut up and take a nap," Cassie said, and the next thing Emily knew she was waking up in a room somewhere.

She lay in a large bed and Hope sat beside her, playing with her toy tiger. Katy looked around the room, hoping for some hint of where they might be, but there were no clues. It was a nice room, extravagant even, with a plush green rug covering a beautiful wooden floor, and a stately oak dresser against one wall of the room.

Emily stood up and looked out a large pane glass window to the right of the bed. A huge sycamore tree took up most of the view, and beyond were more trees and what looked like a huge mansion in the distance.

"Don't worry, tiger, Mommy and Daddy will save us," Hope said to the tiger, and Katy felt tears welling up in her eyes again.

"They will," said Emily, turning to look at Hope. "Your Mommy and Daddy love you very much, and so do I. So do your grandparents. We all love you, sweetie, and I promise we're going to get out of here."

"Mommy will help us. Isn't that right, Mommy?" she said, staring right at Katy.

A shiver ran down Katy's spine. Hope could see her?

"What do you mean?" asked Emily, staring at the little girl.

"Mommy's right there, standing beside the bed."

Oh my God, Hope could see her! But this didn't make any sense. It was a dream in Emily's past. How could Hope have known she was there? Or, perhaps, Hope was also dreaming, and had entered the dream with them.

"Can you see me, sweetie?" asked Katy, walking over, brushing a phantom hand through her daughter's cheek.

"I can see you, Mommy," said Hope, smiling. "Look, Auntie Em, she's right there."

"I don't see anyone, sweetie, but I believe you. Katy, please help us. I have no idea where we are, and I couldn't tell you if I did, but you've got to find us."

"Hope, this is important. Do you know where you are?"

"I don't know, Mommy. Please find us. I miss you so much."

"We'll find you," Katy said, eyes welling with tears, "I promise. Your daddy and I both miss you so very much. Hope, I love you. Tell Emily I love her, too, and that we're coming."

"I love you, too, Mommy. Auntie Em, Mommy says she loves you and she's coming to save us."


Katy woke up with a start, heart pounding hard against her ribs. She was lying in Emily's bed in Carthage, beside Emily, inside Emily's dreams. Ben paced back and forth, his eyes growing wide when he saw her sit up.

"Did it work?" he asked.

"It worked, all right. Remember the blonde in your dream?"

"Don't remind me."

"Well, her name is Cassiel."

"That's right," Ben said, "I remember now. But what does she have to do with this?"

"She seduced Emily the night we got married in Las Vegas. Emily told me about her, and said her name was Cassie. Emily teleported to Chicago to see her yesterday, and she tricked Em into binding herself to her."

"Pretty much, yeah," said Emily, awake now. "I feel like an absolute idiot."

"Don't," Ben said. "They trick people, and they're very good at it. It's not your fault."

"Thanks, big brother, but I just feel so stupid and useless. If not for me, Hope would be home and safe with you right now."

"Remember, I'm the one who was possessed by a demon for five years. You're not stupid and you're not useless, and we're going to rescue you."

"Emily, have they done anything to you or Hope?" asked Katy.

"That's one question I can actually answer. We've been alone in that room the entire time. They brought us food, but that's it. Whatever plans they might have for us, they haven't actually done anything yet."

"Good. I think I have an idea about how we might break Cassiel's binding," said Katy, "and if we do that, you can grab Hope and teleport the hell out of there."

"You do? That's amazing. How?"

"We're going to kill you."

Ben stared at her. "Kill my sister? You're joking, right?"

"I don't think she's joking," said Emily, a smile forming on her lips. "I've thought about that, too."

"What are you two talking about?"

"When Cassiel tricked Emily into binding herself, Emily added the phrase, 'until the day I die.' Cassiel didn't seem very happy about that," Katy said, "but she let it pass. Emily repeated the same phrase two more times, and the binding was complete. She'll do anything Cassiel tells her to do—until she dies, that is."

"You saw all that?" asked Emily. "Oh boy. If I could blush in a dream, I'm sure I'd be red as a beet right now."

"This isn't like with me," Ben said. "There's no one there who'll revive her."

"You died?" asked Emily.

"I did, not long after Azazel possessed me. I didn't remember it until recently. They revived me, and after that my abilities didn't work. But the point is, no one is there to revive you."

"This is different," said Katy.

"How?"

Katy stared at her hand and a silver dagger appeared. "Because we're going to kill her inside a dream. Death is death. Because the binding didn't specify physical death, I think this'll work."

Emily smiled. "Do it. I mean, what have I got to lose?"

Ben and Katy sat together in the bedroom of their apartment, going through the address book they'd found at the Yukon lodge. There were about three dozen addresses and phone numbers in the book, and about a third of them were located in the United States.

Some were easy to eliminate. Pearl City, Hawaii, for instance, according to Google, took a lot longer to fly to than 3 hours, while the address they found in Atlanta, Georgia was too close. They were able to disqualify several other destinations based on how long it would take to fly there, including addresses in Oregon, Maryland, and Arkansas.

In the end, it came down to three cities: Bangor, Maine; Sacramento, California; or Seattle, Washington. He remembered being in California when Azazel had his body, when they'd tried to use him to go back in time. He was pretty sure that's where Elohim lived, so Sacramento seemed to be their best bet.

"Azazel said he never stays in any one place for long," countered Katy, "so we can't know for sure."

"We have to start somewhere," Ben said.

"We're only going to have one shot at this. If we pick the wrong house, whoever is there will alert Elohim and we'll never see our daughter again."

"Then we have to make sure we pick the right house."

"I really thought killing Emily inside her dream would work. Damn it, Ben, I'm terrified."

It'd been an hour since they'd dreamwalked with Emily, and she still hadn't teleported home. Katy had been sure she'd found a loophole, but apparently not. She felt like screaming.

Ben reached out to take her hand. "We'll get them back. I promise."

"You can't promise that."

"We'll get them back or die trying. How's that? But for now, let's try to get at least a little bit of real sleep. We're not going to be any good to anyone if we're asleep on our feet."

Katy knew he was right. There was nothing they could do now other than wait. If she could make contact with Emily again tomorrow, she might have figured where they were.

They turned the lights out, held each other, and went to sleep.

# Chapter 69

Emily awoke with a start, clutching her chest. She almost expected to see the hilt of a dagger sticking out from between her breasts, but of course nothing was there. The pain, though, that was real. It had really hurt, and still hurt, though it was fading fast.

She sat up from bed, careful not to disturb Hope, who'd fallen asleep beside her. The little girl shifted and rolled over on her side, clutching her tiny toy tiger in her hand. Emily slipped out from under the covers and rolled out of bed.

It was still dark outside. She looked at the antique silver clock that sat atop the bedside table. It was a little past two in the morning. All told, she'd slept maybe three hours.

Had she really died in the dream? It certainly felt that way. The pain had been awful, and she'd felt herself leave her body, and then…nothingness, for an instant, right before she awoke.

Had Katy's plan worked? There was only one way to find out. She walked around the other side of the bed and picked up Hope's backpack, reached out to touch Hope, then imagined them home, in Hope's bedroom. Nothing happened.

She dropped the backpack to the floor, defeated. She was so sure it would work. Unless their family could rescue them, she and Hope were never going to get out of here. All they could do now was wait for whatever Michael and Cassiel had planned for them and pray Ben and Katy found them first.

Emily heard a key rattling in the door. Startled, she ran around to the other side of the bed, dove under the covers, and feigned sleep. The door opened and she heard footsteps, and then someone was shaking her awake.

"What?" she said, rolling over to look into Cassiel's eyes.

"Did you try to teleport?"

Her pulse quickened. "Teleport? How? I was asleep."

"Your necklace said you tried to teleport."

"What are you talking about?"

Cassiel sighed. "Your necklace does a number of things, one of them being that it prevents you from using your ability. If you try, however, it alerts me through this," she said, touching a metal bracelet on her left wrist.

Thinking quickly, Emily said, "You told me not to use my powers, how could I teleport? I sometimes teleport in my sleep, though. Maybe that's what happened?"

"I didn't know you could do that," Cassiel said.

*I can't*, Emily thought, but said nothing. It worked. It really worked. When Katy killed her in the dream, it broke her binding to Cassiel. It was only that stupid necklace they'd locked around her throat that prevented their escape.

"I've done it since I first got my powers," said Emily, building on the lie. "It scared the hell out of me, at first."

Cassiel smiled. "I bet. Okay, Emily, you are no longer permitted to teleport without Michael's or my permission, even in your sleep. There, that should do it."

"Gee, thanks. Can I go back to sleep now?"

"After you kiss me."

Emily stared at the woman, wanting nothing more than to rip her heart out. She couldn't do that, though, at least not yet. Instead, she said, "I'll never kiss you again."

After all, it hadn't been an order.

"You know that's not true," whispered Cassiel. "Kiss me, Emily, like you did that first night in Las Vegas."

She didn't hesitate, not for a second, for doing so would have given away the fact that she was no longer bound to the demon. Instead, she closed her eyes and kissed Cassiel with passion, getting into it, almost letting herself enjoy it.

"Okay," Cassiel said, sighing as she finally pulled away. "Go to sleep."

Emily let herself fall back on the bed, eyes closed, and pretended to be asleep. She listened as Cassiel walked across to the bedroom, opened the door, went through the doorway, and locked the door from the other side.

She waited a full ten minutes, counting from one to 60 ten times in her head, before opening her eyes. She finally had the advantage, and she didn't want to blow it by making a stupid mistake. Good, Cassiel was really gone.

In addition to guarding her dreams against Katy's visits, the necklace apparently also prevented her from teleporting. She wondered what else it might do, and how to remove it. It clearly wasn't perfect, as it hadn't been able to stop Katy from dreamwalking, not once she'd had the four talismans and Ben's abilities to back her up.

Emily slid her fingers around the necklace feeling for a clasp, but it wasn't there. Instead she found a tiny hole. Was it a keyhole? Without being able to actually look at it, she had no clue.

She'd get it off, though, one way or the other. And once she did, she and Hope would teleport home.

For now, though, all she could do was try to sleep.

"Wake up, Auntie Em," whispered Hope, into Emily's ear.

Emily opened her eyes and looked at the clock. It was morning. She'd tossed and turned for what seemed like hours, but in the end, she'd finally managed to fall back asleep.

"Hey, sweetie," she said to Hope. "How're you doing?"

"I want to go home."

"Yeah, me too. And we will. Soon. I promise."

"I talked to Mommy in your dream."

"That was real, in the dream? You saw your mother?"

Hope nodded.

"How?"

"I don't know," Hope said. "I just did."

She was about to press her for more when they heard noise coming from the door, and the sound of a key turning the antique lock. It was the same woman who had brought them dinner last night, carrying a large tray for breakfast.

"When are they going to let us out of here?" asked Emily.

The woman, tall with long, dark hair, said nothing, and instead walked over to them and deposited the tray containing their breakfast on the bed, but only after closing the door behind her. They were taking no chances.

The tray contained paper plates with eggs, bacon, and waffles, a small box of Captain Crunch cereal, two plastic bowls, plastic pitchers of milk, orange juice, and water, four plastic cups, and plastic utensils. At least they were feeding them.

"It's polite to answer someone when they ask you a question," said Hope, looking at the woman.

The woman laughed. "I suppose you're right. Okay, you'll both be going downstairs in just a few hours, for some…experiments."

"What sort of experiments?" Emily felt the bottom drop out of her stomach.

"I honestly have no idea."

As soon as the woman exited the room, Emily poured herself and Hope a bowl of cereal. It wasn't the most nutritious cereal, but at least it was sweet. They picked at the rest of the meal in silence, Emily dreading what the day might bring.

# Chapter 70

Emily stood in what looked like a recreation room in the basement level of the house, wishing she could teleport Hope and herself home. The necklace, however, was still around her neck, and try as she might she hadn't figured out a way to remove the damned thing.

About five minutes ago, the woman who'd brought them breakfast and a man they'd never seen before showed up to escort them down two flights of stairs to this room, where Cassiel and Colin waited.

Emily looked around the room. A huge widescreen television stood against one wall, opposite a long leather couch. A bar stood off to the side, along with three barstools. Various chairs, bookshelves, and cabinets filled out the room.

Hope squeezed Emily's hand, and she squeezed back. She'd do whatever she had to do to protect her niece. The problem was, at least currently, there wasn't much she could do.

A few minutes later, a red-haired man in a black suit joined them. Their escorts said something to the man and then left, leaving Emily and Hope alone with Colin, Cassiel, and the man in the black suit.

He wasn't a large man; he stood maybe 5'8" at the most. He had piercing blue eyes, a neatly trimmed goatee, and a bit of a pot belly. Emily got the sense that he was the one in charge, however, because of how everyone seemed to defer to him.

"Ah, Miss Spencer," he said, "it's so lovely to finally meet you. You too, Hope."

He reached out a hand to Emily and she took it, because Cassiel had ordered her to be "polite and cooperative" as soon as they'd entered the room. She couldn't wait until she could punch Cassiel in the mouth, politeness be damned.

"Likewise, I'm sure," she said.

"You can call me Elohim," the man said. "This shouldn't take more than a few minutes, and then we'll have you back to your room again."

"What are you going to do to Hope?" she asked.

"Emily, that wasn't very polit—" Cassiel said, but was cut off by a wag of the man's finger.

"That's a perfectly fine question. We're just going to perform a quick test. She's in no danger, I promise you. Now please sit down over there," he said, gesturing to the couch at the back of the room, "and wait."

"Sit on the couch and be quiet, and don't get up until I say you can," Cassiel said, and Emily did as she was told, her heart racing as she left Hope alone with Elohim.

"Now, sweetheart," Elohim said, crouching down next to Hope, "I know you want to go home, and we'll try to make that happen as soon as possible. For now, though, I need to see what you can do. Okay?"

"Okay," Hope said.

Elohim pulled something out of his pocket. Emily was ten feet away so couldn't tell for sure, but it looked like a coin. Was it the nickel that had been stolen from Ben five years ago, the one her father had been tasked with keeping safe?

"You know about your mother and father's…abilities, correct?"

"Yes, I do," Hope said.

"Can you do anything like they can do?"

The little girl shrugged. "I don't think so, at least not yet. Maybe when I get older."

"Well, I think you can now," said Elohim, "because you're special. And I have something that just might help a special little girl like you access your abilities."

It was all Emily could do not to race across the room, grab Hope, and run up the stairs. She knew she wouldn't have a chance of getting away, however, so she stayed seated, doing her best to stop trembling.

"Michael," he said, looking at Colin. "Can you set up the demonstration, please?"

"Certainly, Father," Colin said, retrieving some red plastic cups from one of the cabinets.

He walked over to the bar and picked up a barstool, brought it over next to Hope, and set up the cups in a triangle on top.

"Now, honey," Elohim said, "I'm going to give you a very special coin, but first your uncle Colin is going to give you a pretty necklace just like your aunt Emily is wearing. Is that okay?"

Without waiting for the little girl's response, Colin walked over to them, pulled a necklace out of his pocket, and fastened it around Hope's neck. The necklace briefly flared with a blue light as he fastened together the ends.

"There we go, you're all ready," he said, handing the nickel to Hope. "How does the coin make you feel?"

"Not like anything," said Hope, looking at Emily.

"That's okay. What I want you to do is hold the nickel very tight and, without using your hands, knock over those cups your Uncle Colin put on top of the barstool. Can you do that for me?"

"But how, if I can't touch them?"

"Use your mind, Hope. Hold the nickel and look at the cups. Imagine them falling over. Will you give it a try?"

"I'll try," said the little girl, staring at the cups.

They all watched as absolutely nothing happened.

"Are you really trying, Hope?"

"Yes, I'm trying."

"I don't believe you, dear."

"I'm trying!" yelled Hope.

Tears trailed down Emily's cheeks. She pulled at the necklace with all her strength, willing it to snap in half, but nothing happened.

"Try harder!" Elohim yelled back at her.

Hope swung her hand at the cups, knocking them from the barstool. "There!"

Elohim looked like he might hit her, but instead took a deep breath, and said, "That's cheating, dear, and we can't have that. Cassiel? It's time for the second test."

"Yes, Father," she said, pulling out a small pistol.

Colin went over to the couch and stood beside Emily.

"What…what are you doing?" whispered Emily, ready to bolt.

Cassiel aimed the gun at Emily.

"Please don't hurt my Auntie Em," screamed Hope, eyes wet with tears.

"We don't want to hurt anyone," Elohim said. "But you cheated, Hope, and cheating has consequences. Now, you have two choices. You can watch Cassiel shoot your Auntie Em, or you can stop her. Which is it going to be?"

Emily started to rise from the couch, but Colin stopped her with a hand on her shoulder.

"Don't shoot her," said Hope.

"I'm going to count backwards from ten," Cassiel said, winking at Emily. "When I get to one, I'm going to shoot Auntie Em. I don't want to shoot her, Hope, but it's your choice. I'll have to shoot Emily if you don't stop me. Ten."

Emily pulled against Colin, but his grip was strong. Her heart beat staccato in her chest. If she died, Hope would be all alone.

"Nine."

"I don't really like you, Hope," said Colin. "I don't think you can stop Cassiel. How about you prove me wrong?"

"Eight. Any last words, Emily? You can talk now."

"Why are you doing this?" screamed Emily. "Why?"

"Seven," said Cassiel, ignoring her pleas.

"Hope, concentrate," Elohim said. "Feel the power of the fused talisman and use it. Use it!"

"Six."

"I can't," sobbed Hope. "Please don't."

"Five."

"Cassie, stop," said Emily. "You don't have to do this. I still love you. We could go away somewhere together, just the two of us. Just help Hope get home."

"Now you're lying," said Cassiel. "Don't lie to me. Four."

"I'm not lying," she said, realizing it was at least a little true.

"Three."

"We could go away and—"

"Emily, please be quiet. Two."

"Stop her, Hope," said Elohim. "She's going to shoot Auntie Em. You have the power to stop her. What's it going to be?"

"One," Cassiel said, her eyes filling with tears. "I'm sorry, Emily."

She pulled the trigger.

Cassiel's arm flew straight up into the air, and she shot the ceiling.

The sound of the gunshot vibrated in the room, hurting Emily's ears, but at least she wasn't dead. Why wasn't she dead? Had Cassiel changed her mind at the last second? But, no, she seemed just as surprised as Emily.

She looked at Hope. The little girl was floating about a foot off the floor, and her eyes were glowing a deep azure. She looked pissed.

"I knew it," said Elohim, a huge smile on his face. "You, Hope Spencer...you will be our salvation."

# Chapter 71

Emily couldn't stop shaking. Cassiel tried to shoot her, would have shot her, if not for Hope. Cassiel clearly didn't *want* to shoot Emily, but the fact that she would have done it anyway spoke volumes.

"You did it, Hope!" said Elohim, crouched down on the ground next to Hope. "You're a very brave, very smart little girl, and you and I are going to do glorious things together."

"You're a very bad man," said Hope, still hovering in the air, pointing her finger at Elohim.

"Some might argue that I'm a very bad man indeed," he said, laughing. "Hope, I do what I do for the good of the world. Humanity has all but destroyed this planet. Tell me, why should I allow that to continue?"

Hope scrunched up her face and glared at the man.

"Now you're trying to use the talisman on me, aren't you? That isn't very nice. Fortunately for me, your necklace prevents you from doing just that. Now give me the coin and you and Emily can go back to your room."

Hope slowly floated to the floor, her glowing azure eyes fading back to their normal green. "Fine."

Emily rushed over to Hope, sweeping her into her arms as the little girl began to cry. "It's all going to be okay, sweetie. I promise."

"Your Aunt Emily is a wise woman," Elohim said, holding his hand out for the coin. "Because you did so good today, Hope, I'm going to send up ice cream for you after lunch."

Hope's lower lip trembled as she handed the nickel back to Elohim. Pocketing the coin, he left the room, leaving Emily and Hope alone with Colin and Cassiel.

"I don't like you," said Hope, staring at Cassiel.

"That's a shame, sweetheart, because I really like you. Who knows, maybe I'll grow on you."

"Can you take us back to our room now?" asked Emily, taking Hope's hand.

Cassiel looked at Colin, who nodded.

"I'll do it," said Cassiel.

"But father said—"

"I know what father said, always two of us, but I want a little play-time with my girl," Cassiel said, winking at Emily. "At least as much as I can get with a four-year-old in tow…"

"I suppose I can watch my precious little niece for 30 minutes or so," Colin said. "Just hurry, okay?"

Emily's heart raced. "I will not leave Hope alone with you."

"Be quiet," Cassiel said, looking into Emily's eyes. "And do what I say."

Emily stared defiantly at Cassiel. She wanted to grab Hope and run, but she knew they wouldn't get far. She had to keep up the pretense of being under Cassiel's control, at least for now. She hung her head, defeated.

"It's okay, Auntie Em," said Hope, walking over to stand beside Colin.

"30 minutes and not a moment longer," said Colin, as Emily followed Cassiel out the door and up the stairs.

# Chapter 72

Tanner watched from the shadows as Hope used the power of the combined nickels to stop Cassiel from shooting Emily. *C'mon, Hope*, he thought, seconds before Cassiel fired the gun into the air.

Thank goodness. Of course, that meant they now knew that Hope could use the nickel. But at least Emily wasn't dead. This definitely went into the "win" column.

He watched as Elohim, who appeared to be the one in charge of everything, left the room. A few minutes later, Cassiel and Emily also left the room, presumably heading upstairs and to the room where Hope and Emily were being held captive.

"What games do you like to play?" asked Colin, sitting on the couch beside Hope.

"I don't want to play games with you," the little girl said.

"You might as well get used to being here, kid, you're not going home anytime soon. Here, let's try checkers."

Colin walked over to the cabinet underneath which Tanner was hiding, opened a drawer, and pulled out a box. He closed the drawer and took the checker set over to the couch.

"Tell you what," he said, as he set up the board, "beat me and I'll make sure you get double the ice cream. Choose a hand."

She glared at him before finally choosing his left hand. It was the black checker, which meant she got to go first.

Tanner wished he could do something to help Hope, but he and his tiny sword would have no chance against Colin. For now, all he could do was keep watch and wait.

He had spent all last night carefully exploring the parts of the house he could access and had finally found an old telephone bill behind the wet bar in this very room. It was dated last year and addressed to Harold Butters in Seattle, Washington. Did that mean the address on the bill was this address? He had no idea, but it was the only piece of evidence he'd found so far identifying where the house might be located.

He also had no idea who "Harold Butters" was, other than perhaps the real name of the host body occupied by Elohim or one of the other demons who seemed to call this place home. Really, it could be anyone.

In addition to Elohim, Colin, and Cassiel, Tanner had spied seven other people while sneaking around, not including the two who brought Emily and Hope their meals. All told, there were at least 12 people currently in the house. The house had eight bedrooms and all sorts of extra rooms, including an exercise room, a wine room, and three dens, so there might be even more.

Now that he thought he knew where they were, he had to somehow get the information to Shawn and Jenny. Tanner thought about trying to find a telephone but realized he didn't know anyone's telephone numbers. No one had real telephones anymore anyway, just those strange portable computer things they carried around with them. He wasn't sure he liked the future, but there was no going back to 1975, so hopefully he'd get used to it. Besides, he wasn't sure he was at all likely to survive the upcoming battle anyway.

He knew Katy had dreamwalked with Emily last night, so hopefully, if he could get the information to Emily, she'd be able to relay it to Katy tonight. He'd have to reveal himself and explain who he was, but that couldn't be avoided.

"Good try, you almost beat me," said Colin, and Tanner peeked out from under the cabinet.

"Can we play again?" asked Hope.

"Maybe another time. It's about time to get you back upstairs."

Tanner heard footsteps leading out of the room, and then silence. He waited a good 5 minutes before crawling out from under the cabinet. He didn't see or hear anyone, and so he scuttled toward the stairs. As soon as he reached them, he pressed himself flat against the wall, waiting to make sure he didn't hear anyone coming. The coast seemed clear, so he proceeded upwards.

# Chapter 73

Emily followed Cassiel up two flights of stairs to her and Hope's room, anger coursing through her veins. She couldn't believe she'd gotten them into this mess. Had she really been so desperate for love and affection that she'd blindly bound herself to a so-called angel?

The day that Ben had married Katy, she'd been so jealous. Ben had Katy, Sabrina had Ferris, Colin had Sumi, her parents had each other, and she had no one. Her petty, childish jealousy had all but destroyed her family. She deserved to be alone.

Once they entered the room, Cassiel locked the door.

"Stand on your head," Cassiel said.

What the hell? Emily had been involved in gymnastics when she was younger, so she knew how to stand on her head, but why did Cassiel want her to do this?

She knelt down to the floor, placed her head and her hands against the rug, and raised her legs into the air, pointing her toes at the ceiling. She hadn't done this in a very long time and felt the blood rush to her head. How long was Cassiel going to make her stay like this?

"Okay, that's enough. You can stop."

Emily dropped to her knees and then climbed to her feet.

"You can talk now."

"Why did you make me do that?"

"Kiss me," she said.

Walking over to Cassiel, she kissed her on the cheek.

"On the lips, silly," said Cassiel.

She kissed Cassiel on the lips, but only a quick peck.

"Kiss me like you did in Las Vegas," she said, and Emily did as she was instructed.

The kiss was long and lingering, and it made Emily wish for probably the thousandth time that Cassiel was Cassie again, and that she hadn't turned out to be one of the Vīrya. It was a stupid wish, and she knew that boat had sailed, but her heart wasn't quite there yet.

"Now what?" asked Emily, when the kiss was finished.

"Now nothing," Cassiel said. "I just wanted to see how far you'd go. I'll really miss your kisses, though."

Emily glared at the woman. "What are you talking about?"

"Cut the crap, Emily. I don't know how you did it, but I know you're no longer under my control."

Shit. "Then why did I just stand on my head? Why did I kiss you?" she said, recovering.

"In the rec room, you said you loved me."

"I do. I don't want to, but I do. I couldn't lie. I'm still under your control."

"No, you don't, and no, you're not. I never said you could get up from the couch when we were in the rec room, but you did anyway. Before that, you talked when I said you couldn't. That's when I knew for sure."

"Well, fuck," Emily said.

She stared as Cassiel, getting ready to rush her. If she could somehow knock her unconscious, maybe she'd be able to get the drop on Colin when he brought Hope back and they'd at least have a chance of escaping.

"Don't worry, I'm not going to tell them. As far as Michael and Father are concerned, you're still bound to me."

"You're not going to tell them?" asked Emily. "Why?"

"Because I love you," Cassiel said, "and because I almost killed you. I didn't want to, I swear it, Emily, but when Father tells you to do something...you do it, no questions asked. But once that gun went off, it was like an alarm clock, jarring me out of a nightmare. I can't do this anymore. If you're weren't already unbound, I would have broken the binding myself anyway."

Emily's heart began to race. Was this a joke? Some sort of trap? Or was Cassiel being sincere? She wanted to believe her—wanted to with all her heart—but Cassiel's betrayal still hung heavy in her heart.

"Take my necklace off," Emily said. "If you're not lying to me, take this damned necklace off my neck."

"I can't, I—"

"I knew it! This is all some sort of sick game to you. I was almost starting to believe you. I'm so stupid."

"You're not stupid," Cassiel said, "and I'm being honest with you. I can't remove your necklace not because I don't want to, but because I literally can't. Michael crafted your necklace as well as Hope's, and he has the keys. If I tried to cut it off, it wouldn't work out well for either of us."

She remembered Hope's necklace glowing with a blue energy as Elohim put it around her neck. "*Can* it be cut off?"

"Not without killing you, I don't think. Let me do some research, though."

"How do I know you're telling the truth? That this isn't just playacting?"

"When I called you my plaything, when I said humans are expendable, the things I said and did after I bound you in Chicago, all of that garbage...that was playacting. I was being who I'm supposed to be, who Father wants me to be. I love you, Emily. I wasn't supposed to fall in love with you, and Father would have my head if he ever found out, but…I love you, and you don't deserve this, and neither does Hope. No one does."

"You know we can never be together, right? Not after all this."

Cassiel hung her head. "I know, and that's…well, I understand. But it's not about us, it's about finally doing the right thing. Plus, I don't exactly want to kill off humanity."

"You want me to believe you?" asked Emily.

"More than anything."

She thought back to a conversation she had with Katy last year about the true names of angels and demons. "Tell me your real name."

"You already know my name. Cassie was just a shortened version of Cassiel."

"No, I mean your…your Vīrya name."

Cassiel arched an eyebrow. "You know a lot more than you've let on."

Emily said nothing, just stared at her.

"Okay. Well, it's Casiatenh. Not that far off from Cassiel, actually."

"Casiatenh, I bind you to me, as my servant. Casiatenh, I bind you to me, as my servant. Casiatenh, I bind you to me, as my servant."

"And now I'm bound to you."

"Slap yourself in the face."

Cassiel slapped herself in the face. "Ouch."

"Kiss me like you did in Vegas," Emily said.

Cassiel kissed her deeply, passionately, taking her breath away.

"That was nice, but I would have done it anyway. Are you going to make me do a handstand now?"

Emily smiled. "Do a handstand."

Cassiel did a handstand.

"Okay, you can stop."

"Anything else, my queen?" Cassiel asked, grinning.

"No, that'll do it, I think. Casiatenh, I free—"

Cassiel stopped her with a finger to her lips. "Please don't do that. At least not yet."

"You *want* to be bound to me?"

"Well, yes, I very much do. Don't you know that by now?"

Emily could feel herself blush. "Yeah, I guess I do know that."

"It's just…if I'm bound to you by the rule of three, I think I can resist father's orders. After all, one can't truly serve two masters, can they?"

"I suppose not."

"This morning, you really did try to teleport, didn't you?"

Emily nodded and was about to say something when she heard a knock on the door. "Whatever you're doing, finish." It was Colin's voice.

"Be right there," Cassiel called out.

Emily ran to the bed and slipped under the covers. She gave Cassiel a thumbs up. Cassiel unlocked the door and let Colin and Hope inside.

"Thank you," Cassiel said. "I got what I wanted. Let's go."

Hope ran over to Emily as Cassiel and Colin left, locking the door behind them. Emily took her niece into her arms and gave her a long hug.

"Are you okay? Did he hurt you?"

"I'm okay," the little girl said. "He didn't hurt me. We just played checkers."

Thank goodness for small miracles.

"That…thing you did, with the nickel. Floating in the air and all that. Have you ever done anything like that before?"

"Not yet," she said cryptically.

Not yet? She was about to ask her what she meant when the sound of the door being unlocked again interrupted them. It was the same woman who had brought them breakfast this morning and supper last night, and now she was bringing them lunch.

*With any luck*, thought Emily, *we won't be here for many more meals.* It was time to formulate an escape plan. With Cassiel's help, if she could indeed be trusted, she just might be able to make good on her promise to get Hope home.

# Chapter 74

Emily picked at the roast chicken, mashed potatoes, and carrots she'd been given for lunch. She wasn't hungry, but knew she had to eat so she'd have energy for whatever came next. Hope didn't seem to have that problem, having already wolfed down her peanut butter and jelly sandwich and potato chips.

Another knock on the door, and Mary, the woman who always brought their food, was back with their promised dessert. Two hot fudge sundaes. As the woman was leaving, she paused to bend over and pick something up from the floor.

"You shouldn't leave your toys lying around," Mary said to Hope, Hope's Galahad action figure in her fist. "I almost stepped on it."

"I'm sorry," Hope said, taking the figure from her outstretched hand.

"Apology accepted. Enjoy your ice cream," Mary said.

They both watched as she left the room and locked the door behind her.

"That's weird," Emily said, "I didn't even know you brought that with you, and I certainly don't remember you playing with it, just your tiger."

Hope stared at the figure for a moment before answering. "Auntie Em, this is my friend Tanner," she said, as she sat the doll on the bed.

Tanner? Why would she name her doll Tanner? Tanner McGee was Emily's uncle, who'd been murdered in 1975 by a monster named the fetch when he was just a teenager. Hope didn't even know about that, as far as Emily knew.

"Well, Hello Tanner," she finally said.

"Hello to you, too, Emily," said the action figure.

Emily jumped back, nearly dropping her ice cream sundae. "What the fuck?" She covered her mouth with one hand. "Sorry, Hope! But…what the actual fuck?"

Hope laughed. "That was funny."

"I've been Hope's 'imaginary friend' for about six months now. Well, me and Samson," said the action figure. "Speaking of which…here, kitty, kitty, kitty."

Hope's toy tiger crawled out of her backpack, ran up to Tanner, and licked him on the face. Tanner tousled the cat's fur, and Samson began to purr.

"Okay, this is freaking me out. Did you do this, Hope? Did you somehow bring them to life?"

"Nope, wasn't Hope," Tanner said. "But don't ask me how I'm here, because I don't have any idea. Same as before, but Samson is along for the ride this time."

"And your name really is Tanner? As in, Mom's brother Tanner? My uncle Tanner?"

"In the plastic," he said.

"Holy shit. And Samson…my Dad's old cat, from when he was a kid?"

"Yep."

Emily stared at the knight and the tiger. "If you've been…in these bodies for six months, why didn't you say anything?"

"Well, I did. To Hope. And now I'm talking to you. I didn't remember my name until you and Hope got kidnapped. All I knew was that I was supposed to protect Hope."

"Can you help us escape?"

"That's why I'm here. I think I know where we are. I found an old telephone bill downstairs."

"Okay, where are we?"

"The bill is for Harold Butters in Seattle, Washington. The address is 12 Silphium Way. If you can dreamwalk with Katy again—"

"Wait a minute," she said, interrupting him. "How do you know about that?"

The little knight shrugged. "That's the $10,000 question. Sometimes, I just know things, and other times I have to spend hours and hours looking for a stupid address in a house the size of Texas."

Hope giggled at that, while Emily just shook her head.

"Washington is on Pacific time, I think," said Emily, "while Illinois is in the Central time zone. Right now, it's 1:37 here, so it'd be 3:37 there."

She was trying to decide when she should try sleeping in order to best contact Katy. Emily wished she'd thought to suggest a schedule when talking with her last night, but they'd both been so sure she'd be able to teleport after Katy killed her in the dream that it hadn't even occurred to them.

"I'm not sure we have time for that," said Tanner.

"What do you mean?"

"Before Hope's 'test,' I heard Elohim and Michael talking. They have more tests planned, and if they're all successful…they think they can use Hope to carry out whatever their plan is tomorrow."

Emily felt her stomach go sour. There was no way in hell she was going to allow anyone to use Hope for anything. "If I could get this damned necklace off, I could teleport us all out of here right now."

"I don't know anything about the necklaces," Tanner said.

"Cassie said she was going to try to find out more about them. Hopefully, she can."

"Cassiel?" asked Tanner.

Shit. She was back to thinking about her as Cassie again. She really needed to get her head straight when it came to the Vīrya. It didn't matter if she thought of her as Cassiel, Casiatenh, or Cassie, she had betrayed Emily. She seduced her, made her fall in love with her, and helped kidnap her and Hope. Was she just supposed to forget about all of that because Cassie had apparently had a change of heart?

"Sorry. Yeah, Cassiel. She…well, she said she's on our side now. She knows I'm not under her control anymore. In fact, she told me her true name, and I've bound her as my servant."

"Why would she do that?"

"So I'd trust her."

"Do you?"

"I think so. I mean, she's bound to me, right?"

"But how do you know she really gave you her true name?"

That stopped Emily cold. Tanner was right. For all she knew, this might be another one of Cassie's games. Sure, she'd done everything Emily told her to do after she'd been bound, but so had Emily, and she was no longer bound, either.

"I don't know," she admitted. "She knows I regained my ability to teleport, so I can only hope she's telling the truth."

"I think she is," said Hope, smiling up at Emily, that beautiful little smile that always made her heart melt.

"I hope you're right, sweetie," said Emily, pulling her niece in for a big hug.

"So do I," said Tanner, "because otherwise we might all be royally screwed."

Her heart told her that Cassie was telling the truth. Then again, it was her heart that had gotten her in trouble in the first place. Cassie was a master at manipulation, having had many long centuries to perfect her craft. Still, she believed her. God help them all if she were wrong.

# Chapter 75

The waiting was killing him. Ben had gotten to spend exactly one week with his daughter, and now she had been taken from him. He couldn't help but think that, if they hadn't rescued him from the Yukon, Hope and Emily would both be safe.

Of course, he knew from his visit with future-Hope that wasn't true. They would have come for her sooner or later, because she had been their goal all along. Knowing this, however, didn't really help much with the guilt.

He sat alone in his and Katy's apartment, trying to come up with a solution. Between Katy and David Dowd, they had four of the five talismans. They also had Claire's abilities and Gavin Young's travel power at their disposal, not to mention Katy's dreamwalking and his own ability to influence causality. None of this mattered, however, if they couldn't figure out where Colin and Cassiel had taken Hope and Emily.

He'd briefly thought he had a workaround. He wrote "Maine," "California," and "Washington" on three different slips of paper, put them in a hat, and drew one out, trusting in his ability to find the right one. The first time he'd drawn Maine. But then he'd done it again and drawn Washington, and after that Maine again, and then California. He did the trick again and again and drew each roughly the same amount of time.

Gavin had a similar ability. If he held or wore symbols of good luck, like a four-leaf clover or a horseshoe, he'd actually have honest-to-goodness real good luck. He drew from the hat as well, with the same results. The houses must have wards to prevent detection, Claire said. She'd tried to reach out to Mr. Kingfisher and Mr. Quarry, to get their advice, but they hadn't as of yet returned her call.

Their best bet at this point was for Katy to try dreamwalking with Emily again. Even now, Katy was in the spirit room, periodically checking to see if Emily were dreaming. If she took even a brief nap, Katy would know and could probably reach her. Realistically, however, they'd more than likely have to wait until nightfall. He wished he could time travel again, though even then he'd never been able to travel into the future and traveling into the past would probably mess things up more than they already were.

They would just have to be patient.

Patience wasn't exactly his strong suit.

Gavin and Claire had gone home but were on call. The moment they figured out where Hope and Emily were, Gavin would teleport to Claire and together they'd teleport here, and then they'd go to the Carthage Chamber of Commerce building and from there teleport *en masse* to the chamber of commerce in either Sacramento, Bangor, or Seattle, depending upon which address turned out to be the correct address.

Ben had Googled businesses near each potential address, as well as near each chamber of commerce. If Sacramento turned out to be the correct address, for example, there was a Starbucks near both the chamber of commerce and the address they had. They would teleport to the chamber and then walk three blocks to the Starbucks, and from there teleport to the Starbucks near the house where Hope and Emily were being kept.

It wasn't the best plan in the world, and there were plenty of areas where things might go awry, but it was the best plan they had. Once they approached the house, he, Katy, Claire, and Dowd would go in, metaphorical guns blazing, followed by Shawn, Fred, and Gavin.

Speaking of guns, they'd each carry a handgun and a taser, just in case. Both Fred and Claire had insisted on that. The Vīrya were magic personified, to be sure, but in the end, they inhabited human bodies, and human bodies could be hurt or even killed. If that happened, the Vīrya would leave their host's body until they could find another host, and at least that would give them some breathing room.

They didn't want to kill anyone, and the weapons would only be used as a last resort, because as Ben's mother had pointed out, there was no way of knowing which of the hosts belonged to the Society of the Great Exodus, and which were people who'd been tricked the same way Ben had been tricked. If it came down to it, though, he'd kill as many of them as he had to in order to bring his daughter and sister home.

# Chapter 76

A gentle wind blew through the tall pine trees that filled the boundary of the yard behind the huge house, raising goosebumps on Emily's skin. She wished she could pause to enjoy the nature around her, but she and Hope were prisoners here, and Elohim was about to perform another test on Hope.

She and Hope stood outside with Elohim, Colin, Cassie, and two men and a woman she'd never seen before. The yard was empty save for the trees and a huge potted Agave plant that stood in the middle of the yard.

Colin and Cassie fetched them from their room a few minutes ago, interrupting Emily's nap before she'd been able to dream. Hopefully, she'd get another chance later, and, with any luck, they'd be rescued before day's end.

"Okay, Hope, it's time for another test," said Elohim, crouching down beside the little girl.

"I don't want to," she said, pouting.

"How about if I promise you more ice cream?"

"No!"

"Well, then…you're not being a very cooperative little girl, are you?"

Hope said nothing, just crossed her arms and stared at Elohim.

"Michael?"

Without warning, Colin punched Emily hard in the stomach, causing her to double over in pain. She gasped, unable to catch her breath, while at the same time feeling like she was going to throw up. She sunk to her knees in the grass, as the edge of her vision darkened.

"No!" Hope screamed.

The little girl tried to run to Emily, but Elohim held her back with a hand on her shoulder. "Oh, yes, Hope. You don't have to do as I ask, but everything comes with a price. Do you want to see what happens to Auntie Em next?"

Hope was crying now, trembling, and Emily started to crawl towards her, but Colin stepped in front of her, preventing her from moving. Cassie looked both angry and scared, while the other three people remained stoic.

"Please don't hurt her," Hope begged.

"Do what I say, and your Auntie Em will be just fine," said Elohim.

"Okay," Hope whispered, looking down at her feet.

"Excellent. Now, take the coin again," he held the nickel out to her, "and we'll get started."

She took the coin from his outstretched hand, still staring at the ground.

"Hope, do you see that plant?" He pointed to the large potted plant in the middle of the yard. "That's an Agave plant. Do you see its many large leaves, and how it almost resembles an octopus?"

"I see it," she said, her voice still shaking.

Emily's stomach felt like it was on fire, but she could breathe again. She slowly stood up from the ground, glaring at Colin. If she could kill him this very instant, she would, no questions asked. He wasn't her brother and never really had been.

"Hope," Elohim said, "I want you to take a good, long look at the Agave plant, and then close your eyes. I want you to imagine the plant moving, gaining sentience, and actually becoming an octopus. Can you do that for me?"

"I don't know," she whispered.

"Will you at least try? If you can try—and I promise you, I'll know if you're not really trying—then your Auntie Em will remain safe. If you don't, however…"

"Okay!" the little girl yelled, scrunching up her eyes.

Everyone, including Emily, stared at the plant. Nothing happened at first, and then the plant slowly began to tremble. Its leaves grew little fleshy tendrils, and those tendrils waved around in the air, seemingly searching for something.

The tendrils grew larger, the leaves that held them bursting open and drying up, turning to dust. A green head shot out from the middle of the plant, its gaping mouth filled with broken and disjointed teeth. The plant opened its eyes, and Emily began to cry. This horrible, awful creation looked to be in pain, its newly formed head darting this way and that, as its tentacles grew larger.

"Stop," screamed Emily, and Colin was on her in a second, snaking one arm around her throat and clamping his hand over her mouth.

"Be quiet, Emily," said Cassie, but the damage was already done.

Hope opened her eyes and the creature instantly shriveled up, its grotesque head slumping into the pot. It shook once and then fell still.

"If you ever do that again," Elohim said, marching over to Emily, "you'll be her next experiment. Do you understand me? I need you in order to control her, but your stay here needn't be pleasant."

Colin released his hold on her, and she repeatedly nodded. Tears filled her eyes, clouding her vision. She hadn't meant to scream and hoped she hadn't just signed their death warrant.

"Cassiel, tell her to speak."

"You can speak now, Emily," Cassiel said.

"I'm so sorry," Emily said. "I didn't mean to. It just…it scared me."

"Do you understand what will happen if you interfere again?" Elohim repeated.

"Yes," she said, nodding. "I understand."

"Good."

Hope ran over to Emily, throwing her arms around her waist. She wrapped her arms around the little girl, never wanting to let go.

"Cassiel, you should have silenced her before bringing her down. I'm disappointed in you. Make sure it doesn't happen again."

"Yes, father," she said, hanging her head.

"Luckily, I think we saw enough," Elohim said, then turned to the three strangers in the yard. "Wouldn't you agree?"

The two men nodded, and the woman said, "Absolutely, Father. I think we can safely proceed to the next test."

Elohim nodded. "All right. Michael, Cassiel, please take our guests back to their room. We'll reconvene later today for the final test."

"Yes, Father," Michael and Cassie said, in unison, leading Hope and Emily back inside.

"I'm scared," said Hope, taking Emily's hand.

"There's nothing to be scared of," Colin said, "as long as you listen to us and do exactly as we say."

They walked up the stairs in silence, Cassiel finally speaking when they reached Emily and Hope's door. "Give me a few minutes alone with Emily?"

"Why?" asked Colin.

"She embarrassed me down there. I want to ensure that never happens again."

"Do what you want, but I'm not a babysitter," Colin said. "Besides, it might actually be a good idea if the brat watches. She needs to be more cooperative with Father."

"You always have the best ideas, Michael," said Cassie, smiling, as she led Emily and Hope into their room and closed the door behind her.

The lunch and dessert dishes from earlier had been removed, and their bed was made. Emily wondered where Tanner and Samson were, but didn't say anything.

"Don't you ever embarrass me like that again," Cassie said loudly, then whispered in Emily's ear, "I'm so sorry. I'm going to slap you now."

Emily nodded, steeling herself for the blow. Cassie slapped Emily hard across the face. She stumbled back against the bed, her cheek on fire. Cassie certainly hadn't pulled the slap.

"Hope," Cassie whispered to the little girl, "yell at me."

"Leave Auntie Em alone!" the little girl screamed. "I'll be good. I promise."

"Shut up, Hope," yelled Cassie.

"You're a bad person," Hope yelled.

"Okay," said Cassie, her voice low again, "that's probably enough. We won't have much time."

"That was fun," said Hope, and both women had to stifle their laughter.

"Are you okay?" Cassie whispered, gently touching Emily's cheek.

"I'm okay. It hurts. Hopefully, it'll leave a red mark."

"I was wrong about you," said Hope. "I'm glad I was wrong."

"That just might be the sweetest thing anyone has ever said to me," Cassie said, squeezing Hope's shoulder. "Thank you."

"Hope is a pretty good judge of character," said Emily.

"And now…I need to say something to you, Emily. I never wanted to hurt you. I never wanted to hurt anyone. Something you said to me on the plane…you said I was responsible for my own actions, and you were absolutely right. I'm sorry for everything I did to hurt you and your family. I'm done doing what Father tells me to do. You don't have to forgive me now. Hell, you might never be able to forgive me, and if you don't, well, that's okay."

"But how can I know you're being honest? Did you really give me your true name? Look me in the eyes, Casiatenh, and tell me the truth."

Cassie looked Emily in the eyes and said, "I'm being honest. That really is my true name. I've been alive a very long time, Emily, longer than you could possibly imagine, and I've never really loved anyone, certainly not like I love you. I've never felt as alive as I do when I'm with you. You make me want to be...human."

Emily's heart fluttered. She wanted so much to believe Cassie, but what if she were lying? Cassie had already betrayed her, what if she hadn't really given her true name and this was just more of the same? Just because she said it was true didn't make it true. What if, what if, what if.

Oh, to hell with it.

She pulled Cassie into a long, lingering kiss, the world falling away around them. The kiss only lasted a few seconds, but it felt like forever. Finally, she pulled away.

Hope clapped her hands, and they both laughed.

"I don't know what the future holds for us," said Emily, holding Cassie's hand. "It will take a while for me to completely trust you again, if I ever do, but I do forgive you."

Cassie beamed. "Thank you. That's more than I have any right to ask for. I'll never betray your trust again, I promise, and I won't make you sorry."

"It would help things considerably if you could get this stupid necklace off me."

"Unfortunately, that's easier said than done. I've been asking questions, as many as I can without drawing suspicion, and the necklace is enchanted in such a way that cutting it off would probably kill you. Obviously, we don't want that to happen.

"As far as I know, Michael has the original keys for both of your necklaces, and Father...Elohim has a set of duplicates. I'm going to try to get Michael's set of keys. Also, there may be a way to 'de-enchant' the necklaces. I'm researching that as a backup plan in case I can't get both keys."

"Please, please, please be careful," Emily said. "Don't do anything that could get you caught."

Cassie grinned, a gorgeous smile that made Emily want to kiss her again. "Oh, I'll be careful. I promise."

"Do you know Michael's true name?"

"That would make things easier, would it not? Sadly, I don't. Neither do I know Elohim's. We Vīrya…we're very guarded when it comes to our true names, for obvious reasons."

"Something I've been wondering about…at your hotel room in Chicago, you said Colin wasn't supposed to bring me there. Where was he supposed to take me?"

"Straight to the plane. I was supposed to join you later."

"But I'd never been to that part of the airport before. There's no way I could have teleported there."

"Isn't there? Both Elohim and Colin think you're a lot more powerful than you think you are, and I think they're right. According to Colin, you said your passenger limit was one, but yet you brought him, Hope, and that poor jogger to the hotel in Chicago, and then teleported Colin, Hope, and me to the bathroom inside that little airport in Keokuk."

"Yeah, I've been wondering about that."

"I think you can do a lot more than you ever thought you could."

"Well, damn. Okay, one other thing I'm curious about. How many people are currently in the house?"

Cassie cocked her head to the side. "It depends. Right now, not including you and Hope, there are maybe 20 people here. There are ten human guards, and the rest are Vīrya. Why?"

"Cassie, tell Auntie Em to slap herself," interrupted Hope, a faraway look in her eyes.

Both women stared at her. Hope always seemed to know things before they happened, and she wasn't about to stop believing her now.

"Say it, and say it loud," whispered Emily. "Hurry!"

"Emily, slap yourself in the face."

Emily slapped herself across the face just as the door opened. She moved back from Cassie, her cheek on fire, as Colin walked in the door. She held her cheek and stared angrily at Cassie.

"That's enough," said Colin, laughing. "You don't want to permanently damage my poor sister. Besides, Father needs us to meet him in the dining room."

"Don't ever embarrass me like that again," said Cassie, as she slipped something into Emily's hand. "Now go stand in the corner for five minutes."

Emily walked to the far corner of the room, faced the wall, and remained silent. What had Cassie given her? It felt long and metallic, but she knew it wasn't the key to her necklace. She'd have to figure it out after they left.

"You're getting good at this," Colin said.

"Oh, you have no idea," said Cassie, as they both left the room.

# Chapter 77

Katy sat on the couch in her imaginary little cabin in the middle of the woods, staring at the huge television screen on the wall, hoping like hell that Emily would take a nap.

She held the jaguar's tooth in her hand as well as the stick, the geode, and the emerald, again borrowed from David Dowd. If Emily had managed to get a location for them, they could be to her inside of an hour.

The television remote in hand, she idly scanned through her pre-programmed dreamers. Ben was at the top of the list, followed by Mel, Emily, Jenny, her father, and Shawn.

Noticeably absent was Hope. She'd tried to dreamwalk with Hope more than once, but it had never worked. Did her little girl have some sort of ability that prevented Katy from sharing her dreams, or was she just too young?

A blip from the television sounded, interrupting her thoughts. Emily's name was blinking. She was asleep and dreaming. Katy leapt to her feet and ran for the frosted glass door that separated her from the dreams of others. She opened the door and stepped through.

Emily sat in the corner of that awful dark room again, singing softly to herself. "Oh, I'm so human, we're just human." She thought she recognized the song as one that Emily had played for her a few weeks ago, probably a Dodie tune, or perhaps Tessa Violet, Jax, or one of the other singers she liked.

"Hi Emily," she said, walking over to her.

Emily looked up. "Am I dreaming?"

"You are. I guess killing you in the dream didn't work, huh?"

Emily jumped to her feet and pulled Katy into a hug. "Actually, it did work. This stupid necklace Colin put on me, it prevents me from teleporting. If I even try to teleport, it alerts them."

"Well, shit. Can you get it off?"

"Not so far," she said. "Cassie is going to try to steal the key from Colin, and—"

"Cassie? The same Cassie who bound you?"

"Yeah, that's her. She never wanted to do it. She's on our side now and is trying to help us escape."

"Em—be careful. That's all I'll say."

"I will be. I have an address for you."

"Thank goodness! What is it?"

Emily rattled off an address in Seattle. "How quickly do you think you can get here? They have Hope performing these…tests. Using the nickel. She can use the nickel, Katy, and I'm afraid they're going to make her do something awful."

The bottom dropped out of Katy's stomach, and she felt like she was going to throw up. "Tests? What kind of tests?"

"Right now, they're just seeing what she can do with the nickel. A couple of hours ago, they took us outside and Elohim had her turn this Agave plant into this horrible octopus-like creature. It was awful."

"Oh my God. He's going to use her to remake the world."

Emily nodded. "Cassie thinks they're going to do it tomorrow, but it might be sooner. You need to hurry."

"We'll be there within the hour, hour and a half, tops."

"We'll be ready," said Emily.

"Do you know how many people are guarding the house?"

Emily began to fade. "Shit, I think I'm waking up. Tanner—"

Katy's sister-in-law vanished, leaving Katy alone in the darkened room. She'd never been inside a dream when someone woke up before. How was she still in this room?

For that matter, who was Tanner?

Katy willed herself back to the cabin, but nothing happened. What the fuck? She tried again, and again, with the same results. She spun in a circle, looking around the room. Darkness everywhere, and no doors.

She was trapped inside her own mind.

\*\*\*

Ben walked up the stairs, to the third floor of the house. Katy had promised to check in with him every hour, and it'd been almost an hour and a half since he'd last heard from her. He hoped that meant she'd contacted Emily and together they were working on a plan to get them out of wherever she and Hope were being held, but he was worried.

He slipped the pentagram necklace over his head and stepped on the marble pentagram in the center of the room and was instantly teleported to the matching pentagram in the hidden room behind the wall. Walking through the shimmering curtain of light, he was confused to enter utter and complete darkness on the other side.

"What the fuck?"

"She's over here," said Azazel's voice.

He jumped, startled by the demon. "What did you do to her?"

"Nothing, I swear. I was in my room, reading a book, and suddenly everything vanished, and I was surrounded by darkness."

"Dark is right. I can't see a thing."

"Follow my voice," Azazel said. "I can see her, but just barely. She's...well, she'd just standing here, staring off into the distance."

He followed Azazel's voice, a few seconds later bumping into something. It was Katy. He reached out and grabbed her arm, but it was like holding a statue. She didn't react, didn't even move. He wished he could see.

"What was she doing?" asked Ben.

"I don't know. I tried yelling at her, but she won't respond."

"Katy?" asked Ben, but no response.

"She has four of the talismans. I can sense them."

Ben moved his hand down her arm until he clutched her hand. Her fingers were closed into a fist. He held one hand under hers and slowly peeled back her fingers. Something dropped into his hand, and he felt an immense surge of energy pump through his body.

He could see now. It was still pitch black in the room, but somehow he could clearly see Katy. He looked down at his hand. He was holding the tooth and the geode. He gently opened her other fist, removing the emerald and the jaguar's tooth from her hand.

"Can you help her?" asked Azazel.

The power enveloping him felt incredible. His entire body was buzzing with electricity. Why hadn't she shared the power with him? For that matter, why had Dowd shared the geode, the stick, and the emerald with her? Were they sleeping together? Was David Dowd screwing his wife?

"Be careful, Ben," he heard a voice say.

Why should he be careful? He'd been imprisoned for five long years. He was through with being careful. He deserved this power. "Who are you to tell me to what to do?"

"The talismans…they can corrupt you if you're not careful, especially if you're not used to the power they hold."

"You ruined my life, held me prisoner for five years, and now you think you can tell me what to do? I should kill you."

"No, what you should do is help your wife, so you can rescue your daughter and your sister. Do you remember them, Ben Spencer? Katy, Hope, Emily…they need you."

Ben blinked. What had he been thinking? Azazel was right. Katy had said the power was seductive, but he had no idea how seductive it truly was. He wanted it, craved it. Needed it. He shook his head.

Concentrating on the talismans, feeling their energy flow through his body, he felt full to bursting.

"You're right," he finally said, as he reached out to touch Katy's cheek. "Wake up."

The room was flooded with light and then they were in Katy's imaginary little cabin in the woods again, just like that. Katy blinked her eyes, shaking her head.

"What happened?" She asked.

"I don't know, I was hoping you might tell us."

Katy closed her eyes and then opened them again. "Shit. I was dreamwalking with Emily and she woke up, and...I think I got trapped by this necklace they use to control her. Everything was dark and I couldn't see. I couldn't find any doors, and I couldn't wake up."

"When that happened, the darkness invaded the spirit room," said Azazel. "If Ben hadn't come looking for you, who knows how long this might've lasted?"

Ben stared at Azazel, the demon who'd stolen five years of his life. If it hadn't been for Azazel talking him down when the power of the talismans overtook him...he didn't even want to think about that. Perhaps future-Hope was right about trusting him, after all.

"Oh! I have the address. Harold Butters, 12 Silphium Way, Seattle, Washington," said Katy.

"Are you sure it's right? We're only going to get one shot at this."

"Emily seemed sure."

"That's good enough for me," said Ben. "Let's go downstairs and call Claire."

"Um, what time is it?"

Ben glanced at his watch. "6:42. Why?"

"Shit! Shit, shit, shit!"

"What's wrong?" Ben asked.

"It was just a little after 5:00 when I entered Emily's dream. I promised her we'd be there in about an hour."

"Then you'd better hurry," said Azazel.

They both turned to look at the demon. "Thank you," said Ben. "You didn't have to help me just now, and you did, so…thank you."

Azazel nodded. "You're welcome. I've been to that house many times. If you want, I can draw you a map of what I remember."

"If you were to come with us," said Katy, "is there anything, anything at all, you could do to help? Emily is wearing a necklace around her neck that prevents her from teleporting. Do you think you could remove it?"

The demon looked surprised. "How could I come with you, without a body?"

"Never mind that. Could you remove the necklace?"

"Who put the necklace on her?"

"Colin…Michael, whatever you want to call him."

Azazel frowned. "Then probably not, not unless we could get the key. I know the sort of necklace you're talking about. It can't be opened except with the key it was forged with, and Michael more than likely carries that key with him at all times. I'm sorry."

"The necklace was also supposed to prevent me from dreamwalking to her, but I was able to get around that by using the talismans."

"Then perhaps you could do the same with the necklace. Just be careful."

"Remember when you agreed to answer three more of my questions?" asked Katy.

"How could I forget?"

"Well, after I wasted the first one asking why you wanted to help, I asked you what you wanted most in the world."

"And I said to be human. But that doesn't look like it's going to happen."

Katy waved a hand, and Azazel's eyes grew big as a dark-haired man appeared. It was one of the men who'd attacked them yesterday, the one Katy had killed. He wasn't moving but didn't look exactly dead, either.

"I killed this man after he tried to kill us, so his body is mine to do with as I will. I've already healed him, so he can live again if he has a soul or a consciousness or whatever the hell you are."

"Didn't you and Dowd put the bodies in the cellar?" asked Ben.

"We did, all but this one. This one I healed and put in stasis. We need all the help we can get. We have to save Hope and Emily. Is this okay with you, Ben?" asked Katy, looking into his eyes.

How could he ever say no to her? Plus, she was right. They needed all the help they could get. "Go for it," he finally said. "But first…what was your second question?"

"I asked him if there was any part of him that regretted stealing your body."

"And I said yes," Azazel said. "Once your body was taken back from me, I realized what I'd stolen from you."

"Okay," Ben said, "let's get this done."

"Azazel, will you agree to help us?" asked Katy.

"I will."

"Say it three times and add that you'll never try to harm us in any way ever again."

"I agree to help you get Hope and Emily back and never to harm you or anyone in your family in any way ever again," said Azazel, repeating it two more times.

"Azazel, I give you—"

"Use my true name" Azazel said, interrupting her. "It's Syrentha-kim."

"Saren…what?"

"Syrenthakim." He sounded out the name for her until she got it right. "It would work with 'Azazel' but…it feels better this way, some-how."

"Syrenthakim, I give you this body, contingent on the vow you made earlier," Katy said, repeating it twice more. "Ready?

The demon looked like he might cry. "You won't regret this. I'm ready."

Katy reached out, grabbed Azazel, and shoved him into the body.

The body opened its eyes. "Thank you," said Azazel.

"Remember your promise," said Katy.

Azazel nodded. "This is so strange. This body has no memories. Maybe because he died? I'm just…me."

"All right," said Ben, heading towards the curtain of light, "let's con-tact Claire so she and Gavin can get us to Washington and we can kick Elohim's ass and get our family back."

# Chapter 78

Ben typed "Harold Butters" into Google on his laptop and was amazed that the man had his own Wikipedia page. He stared at the accompanying photo and recognized him immediately from five years ago, when Azazel had tried to use Ben's abilities to time travel.

Butters was the red-haired, middle-aged man Azazel and Cassiel had referred to as "father," and whom they now knew to be the most powerful of all the Vīrya: Elohim.

The Wikipedia page said he was the owner of several investment companies and had a net worth of $187.5 billion dollars. No wonder he could afford 37 houses all over the world.

Ben wondered how long Elohim had been Harold Butters. Had the man made his billions before or after the Vīrya had possessed him? The article said Butters made his first million at 23, investing in stocks. Perhaps he had made a sort of deal with the devil, and given up his body years later in return for wealth early on?

In the end, Butters' backstory didn't really matter. The man had his daughter and was forcing her to use the fused nickel for God only knew what. They had to stop him. Azazel claimed the Vīrya couldn't be killed, but that didn't necessarily mean he was right.

"This is incredible," said Azazel, who up until now had been sitting quietly on the couch in Ben and Katy's apartment.

Ben turned to look at him. "What's incredible?"

"This life. This body. The fact that it has no memories to deal with, to push down. All of it."

"Remember, it isn't free. You still have to help us rescue Hope and Emily."

Azazel nodded. "I know, and I will. And...I know it doesn't make up for it, all the time you lost, but I am sorry."

Ben was about to respond when Katy ran into the room. "Claire and Gavin just got here. We leave in five minutes."

"It's showtime," said Ben, as he got up off the couch.

He said a silent prayer to whoever or whatever might be listening that they were successful in rescuing Hope and Emily and once and for all stopping Elohim.


Ben, Katy, and Azazel stood in the downstairs living room, together with Ben's parents, Fred, Candy, Claire Locke, Gavin Young, and David Dowd. In just a few minutes, everyone except Candy would climb into Fred Ruskin's giant silver Suburban.

He'd tried to talk his parents into sitting this one out, but they insisted on going. If push came to shove, he was concerned that they might give Colin the benefit of the doubt. Colin had tricked them all and stolen Ben's child, not to mention his sister. He no longer deserved the benefit of anyone's doubt.

The drive to the Carthage Chamber of Commerce would take less than 5 minutes. From there, Gavin would take them to the chamber of commerce in Seattle, right next door to a Starbucks. The Starbucks would take them to another Starbucks next to an Enterprise Rent-a-Car, where Claire had a huge SUV waiting for them, which she'd rented under an alias. From there, it was less than ten miles to 12 Silphium Way. It was too many steps and adding the car into the equation only slowed things down, but it was the best they could do, given their destination was pretty much out in the middle of nowhere.

If everything went right, they should be there in under an hour.

According to Google Earth, 12 Silphium Way was a huge mansion on nearly 300 acres of land. Ben suspected they would have guards, much like Azazel's Yukon hideaway. Katy had tried to asked Em how many guards there were, but Emily had woken up before she could answer.

"From what I could find on Google Earth," Claire said, "there appears to be a large iron fence around the home, and a gate with guards on the road leading up to the front door. They probably have cameras as well. We don't have the time to do a full reconnaissance, obviously, but it appears the best point of entry would be straight through the gate."

Ben nodded. Just like in the Yukon, Claire would lead the raid. Unlike the Yukon, however, she hadn't had the time to fully prepare for the mission. The fact that she was willing to do this on such short notice despite that spoke volumes, and he couldn't think of anyone better suited for the job.

"All right, one more time before we go: everyone has a gun and a taser, right?"

Everyone nodded. Both Claire and Fred Ruskin had insisted on the weapons, which Claire and Gavin had retrieved from Claire's stockpile in Arkansas.

"Our goal is to get in, get Emily and Hope, and get out. There won't be time for much else." She glanced at Shawn and Jenny, who both gave her a curt nod.

They had mentioned wanting to grab Colin, bring him home, and try to "de-program" him, but had been voted down. Colin was there of his own volition, whereas Hope and Emily were his prisoners. They had to be the priority.

Ben offered once again to restore their memories from the previous timeline, the one where Colin had never existed, but they still refused. He guessed he couldn't blame them but, if push came to shove, he'd do it anyway, with or without their permission.

Fred, however, had taken him up on the offer. He'd touched Fred's hand, thought of how the timeline had been before his and Katy's time travel trip to 1977, and Fred had blinked and stared at him.

"No chain of Ruskin's Pizzeria, huh?" he had asked. "Also, no Colin, and I died years ago in a car crash. I'm glad that part changed, at least. You were right, Ben, and I'm sorry for doubting you."

"All right," Claire said, bringing him back to the present, "let's go. Hope and Emily are waiting, and we're not about to let them down."

***

Emily was terrified. Katy said they'd be here within an hour and a half, and it'd been almost three hours. She looked at the switchblade Cassie had pressed into her hand the last time she'd been in the room. At least now she had a weapon, but really, what could it do against someone like Elohim or Michael?

"The next time someone comes in here," said Tanner, sitting beside Samson on the bed, "you need to stab them and then we run like hell."

"There are twenty people here, Tanner, and Cassie said most of them are guards. How do we get past 20 people? We certainly can't stab them all."

"Keep your voice down," said Tanner, gesturing towards Hope, who was napping on the bed. "The poor girl needs all the sleep she can get."

"Sorry. I still can't believe I'm talking to a doll."

"Action figure," he corrected her, smiling. "And, yeah, I know we can't stab everyone. It'd be nice, though, wouldn't it? Hopefully, Katy will be here soon."

"I don't think she's coming. Something must have happened."

"Oh, ye of little faith," said Tanner. "They'll be here, it's just taking them a bit longer than she thought."

"I hope you're right."

They both turned to stare at the door as they heard a key inserted into the lock. It was time for the third and final test.

"Remember what we talked about earlier," Tanner said, as he and Samson leapt for the floor and scrambled under the bed.

The door opened and in walked Mary. "It's time," the woman said.

"Hope, sweetie," said Emily, gently shaking the little girl. "It's time to get up."

"Is Mommy here?" Hope asked.

Mary laughed. "Sorry, Hope, but that's not going to happen. Now hurry, Father is waiting. It's a beautiful day, and we've got a lot of work to do."

Hope got out of bed and together they walked to the door, where the man who always accompanied Mary to their room was waiting. Emily tripped and banged her shoulder against the door frame. "Shit!"

"Watch where you're going," said the man, grabbing her by the wrist.

"Get off me!" she yelled, pushing him away.

"Okay, calm down," said Mary, pushing herself between the man and Emily. "Are you all right?"

Emily rubbed her shoulder. "Yeah, I'm all right, as long as that asshole doesn't touch me again."

"My apologies. Let's go, then," said the man, and Mary, Hope, and Emily followed him out of the room and down the stairs.


Where were Ben and Katy? Something must have gone horribly wrong, despite Tanner's assertions to the contrary. Emily and Hope once again stood in the backyard of the huge mansion, with Cassie, Elohim, Colin, and two of the three nameless people from last time. It was quickly approaching dusk.

Someone else was there, too, an old, gray haired woman who was dressed in a pair of ripped and soiled jeans and a shirt three times her size. Her hands were tied behind her back and she had duct tape covering her mouth. She looked terrified.

"Hope," said Elohim, "this is your third and final test. Her name is Greta, a woman we found living in a tent on the edge of our property."

Emily stared at Greta. After what they made Hope do to the Agave plant, she could only imagine what might be in store for this poor home-less woman who just happened to be in the wrong place at the wrong time.

The moment they walked into the yard, Cassie had come up to her and instructed her to be quiet and do whatever Elohim told her to do. It was all for show, of course, but neither Elohim nor Colin knew that.

"Come here, Hope," said Elohim, and Hope walked over to him. "You see this woman? She looks like a nice woman, yes?"

Hope nodded.

"Michael?"

Without a word, Michael walked over behind the old woman and ripped off the duct tape from her mouth.

"Please, let me go," Greta pleaded. "I didn't mean to trespass, I'm so sorry—"

Colin grabbed her head and twisted, snapping her neck. He released her and she fell to the ground, dead.

Emily had to clamp her hand over her mouth to keep from scream-ing. How could Colin—the man she'd grown up with—do such a thing? She realized then that, in some small part of her mind, she'd held out hope that he would come back to them, that he really was possessed or controlled or something equally awful.

Colin looked into Emily's eyes and smiled, almost as if he had read her thoughts. He was a monster, and whatever had remained of her brother was long gone if it had ever been there in the first place.

Hope was screaming, tears running down her little cheeks. Elohim grabbed her wrist as she tried to run from him. With his other hand, he pressed the nickel into her palm.

"Use the nickel, Hope. Bring her back to life. She doesn't have to die! You and you alone have the power to resurrect her."

"I can't," sobbed Hope, squinching up her eyes.

"Yes, you can!"

"I can't!"

"Yes, you can, but you'd better hurry. Her spirit has already left her body. If you take too long, her brain will be damaged from lack of oxygen and..."

Hope clutched the nickel in her tiny fist, staring at the dead woman. The woman's body glowed an ethereal shade of blue as it floated two feet off the ground.

"I'm trying, but I can't," she whispered.

"Michael," said Elohim, "you know what to do."

Before Emily knew what was happening, Michael was behind her, wrapping her arms around her neck, squeezing. She struggled against his grasp, to no avail.

"Hope, I'm so sorry," Elohim said, "but if you refuse to bring poor Greta back to life, then Michael will have to kill Auntie Em."

"No!" the little girl screamed, turning to stare at the leader of the Vīrya.

Greta's body flew through the air to slam into Elohim, sending him tumbling backwards, the dead woman landing on his chest. The body rose into the air, then zoomed down to slam into Elohim again, and again, and again.

Colin loosened his grip on Emily's throat, and that's when she pulled the switchblade from the pocket of her jeans. She stabbed him hard in the thigh. He screamed and let go, and then she was on him, shoving the knife deep into his throat, twisting it, pulling it out again.

He grabbed his throat, eyes wide, tried to say something, and then fell face first into the grass, not moving. Cassie was there, reaching into Colin's pocket, pulling out a pair of keys. She fumbled with them, almost dropping them, and then she was inserting one of the keys into Emily's necklace, turning it, and the necklace unlocked with a pop, falling from her neck.

"Cassiel, what are you doing?" screamed one of the nameless Vīrya, a woman.

"What I should have done a long time ago," Cassie said.

Emily looked down at the knife in her hand, blood trickling down its sharp edge to stain her fingers, and she felt like she was about to have a panic attack. No, she couldn't lose her shit now, not now. There would be time for that later, but not now. She let the knife fall to the ground.

She turned to look at Hope just in time to see the old woman's dead body explode, sending blood and bits of bones and gore everywhere. Elohim floated into the air, his eyes blazing with fire, staring down at them. Hope stood on the ground, covered in the woman's blood, glaring at Elohim.

"You dare?" he asked, pointing at Cassie. "Traitor!"

She grabbed her throat, coughing and gagging, and her knees buckled. Her eyes rolled back in her head, and she stumbled into Emily.

"I can't breathe," she managed to eke out.

Hope stared up at the floating Vīrya, her fists clenched. "Leave her alone!"

"Or what, Hope? I'll admit, you caught me off guard. Very clever. You couldn't attack me directly, so you threw poor, dead Greta at me. But that's not going to happen again."

Emily teleported beside Hope, shoved the other key into her necklace, and removed it. The necklace fell to the ground and Hope turned to her and smiled.

"Thanks, Auntie Em," she said.

They both turned to look at Elohim, and for the first time there was fear in his eyes. Cassie gasped from behind them, falling to her knees. She sucked in deep, greedy breaths of air, finally able to breathe again.

The two remaining Vīrya rushed at Emily and Hope, only to be thrown through the air and into the side of the house. They crumpled to the ground, unmoving, unconscious or worse.

"Hope, drop the nickel," said Elohim. "If you don't, I will kill Emily."

"That's not going to happen," said Emily. "Cassie, Hope, and I are going to leave here, and you're going to leave us the hell alone."

Elohim laughed, long and hard. "You still don't understand, do you? You humans had your chance and you squandered it. You all but ruined this planet. It's our turn now. You will serve us, as you should have been serving us all along."

"You don't care about any of that," said Cassie, joining Hope and Emily. "You just want power. As fewer and fewer humans believe in you, you're losing power, just like when you were Odin and all the times before that. You don't give a shit about the planet or about anyone but yourself."

Emily's fingers found Cassie's and squeezed them. Hope took Emily's other hand, and together they stood against perhaps the most powerful being on Earth.

"You know nothing, you insolent, ungrateful little girl," screamed Elohim. "What is wrong with you? Why do you align yourself with these...these humans?"

"Because we had our time," said Cassie. "We schemed and we plotted, and every time it fell apart. This isn't our world, it's theirs. It was always theirs.

"That, and I'm in love with Emily. A human. A beautiful, kind, funny, intelligent human, and I'd do anything for her."

A gunshot sounded in the house, and they all turned towards the noise. Colin, covered in blood and holding her switchblade, stood before them. He drove the blade into Cassie's stomach, jerking it upward, then watched as Cassie slid off the blade to the grass.

"No!" screamed Emily.

Hope flicked her wrist and Colin flew backwards, slamming into a tree. He stood up, dusted himself off, and smiled.

Emily dropped to her knees beside Cassie, tears clouding her vision. Cassie was still breathing, but the wound looked awful.

"Take Hope and get out of here," Cassie whispered, looking up into her eyes.

"I'm not leaving you," she said, holding Cassie's hand. She turned to look at Colin. "Why aren't you dead?"

"Remember when the mercenaries attacked us and you thought I got shot, but I didn't?" asked Colin. "Well, actually, I did get shot. They were careless, but no matter. That tattoo on my hand, the one you referred to as a 'squiggle,' heals this body. I'm impossible to kill. You lose. Again."

"Why are you doing this?" asked Emily.

"Because I want to," snarled Colin. "Because Father is right. You humans don't deserve this planet."

Something snapped over Emily's neck. It was that damned necklace, placed there by Elohim's telekinesis. She shot into the air, floating ten feet in a second. She couldn't move. Her body spun around, and Elohim floated before her. She tried to teleport away but couldn't, the necklace once again blocking her ability.

"Hope, dear," said Elohim, staring down at the little girl. "Auntie Em is going to die. I can destroy her before you can stop me. There's only one way out of this."

Emily tried to scream, tried to tell Hope to run, but the words wouldn't come out of her mouth. She floated helplessly beside Elohim, not even able to blink.

"Leave her alone!" screamed Hope.

"I promise not to kill her, Hope, but you have to do one thing for me. I need to inhabit your body, just for a little while."

"No!"

"Yes."

"You can't have my body!"

"Oh, don't worry, I don't need it forever. In fact, one short hour should probably suffice. Say, 'I give Elohim my body for one hour' three times, please. You'll get your body back when I'm finished, Emily lives, and you get to go home."

"You're a liar!"

"Hope, Hope, Hope…" Elohim said, then gestured in the air toward Emily.

Emily's left arm snapped, bending at an unnatural angle. She tried to scream but nothing would come out. She felt like her arm was on fire. *Run, Hope*, she yelled in her mind. *Run.*

"Stop it, stop it, stop it," yelled Hope, "please!"

"Just an hour, Hope. Say it. 'I give Elohim my body for one hour.' That's all you have to do, and then I'll release Auntie Em. I didn't want to have to do it this way, but you and your family have left me little choice."

"Father never lies," said Colin, moving to stand behind Hope. "Do as Father asks, and Auntie Em gets to live."

Hope looked back and forth between Colin and Elohim. "I give Elohim my body for one hour," Hope said, her voice trembling.

"Hope, no," whispered Cassie, struggling to sit up.

"Again," said Elohim.

"I give Elohim my body for one hour."

"I promise you, Hope, I'll let Emily go the moment you give me your body."

"You promise?" asked Hope.

"I promise."

"Hope, run—" Cassie said, but Colin interrupted her with a kick to the face.

"Stop hurting her!" yelled Hope.

"Don't hurt Cassiel again, Michael."

"Yes, Father," Colin said.

"Hope, Cassiel will come to no further harm. Now say it," said Elohim.

*Please, Hope, please don't say it*, thought Emily, looking down at her niece. *Just run.*

"I give Elohim my body for one hour," said Hope.

Emily fell ten feet to the ground, landing on her left leg, snapping her femur. She screamed in pain as the world dimmed around her, and she struggled to stay conscious.

"You lied!" yelled Hope.

"I never lied," said Elohim, floating down to stand beside Hope. "I said I'd let her go, and I did. And now…"

He reached out to grab Hope's shoulder, then immediately collapsed to the ground.

"…the real fun begins," said Elohim, from Hope's mouth.

The world spinning around her, her arm and leg on fire, Emily tried to speak, failed, and then felt her eyes close as everything faded to black.

# Chapter 79

Their rented Chevy Tahoe approached 12 Silphium Way at just a little past 6:00 Pacific time. It was still light out, which was both good and bad. They would be able to see where they were going, but they'd also be spotted more easily by the guards.

The road went straight up to the gate. Apparently, theirs was the only house on the road. The gate looked to be about a quarter mile from the house itself. Plenty of room to get shot.

Claire drove, and Katy rode in front, beside her. The rest of them were crouched down behind the seats. Claire's reasoning for this was that the guards would take two women as less of a threat. Katy hoped she was right.

She had the jaguar's tooth and one of Dowd's talismans, the emerald, clutched in her fist as they pulled up to the gate. Claire held a map of Washington state in her hand as she rolled down the window, watching as one of the two guards stationed at the gate approached their vehicle.

"This is private property, ma'am," said the guard, a dark-haired man in his early thirties. "You need to turn around and leave."

"I'm sorry," said Claire, fumbling with the map. "We're lost. Do you know where 12 Sylvan Lane is?"

The guard stared at her. "I said you need to leave."

Claire started to cry. "I'm so, so sorry. I just don't know where we are, and we're almost out of gas."

The other guard, a blond, walked over to the window. "Is there a problem here?"

This is what they were waiting for. They had to take both guards out at once to prevent one from calling for reinforcements. Katy squeezed the talismans, feeling their chaotic magic course through her body.

She reached out with her mind, grabbing both guard's heads and smashing them together. They crumpled to the ground, unconscious.

Claire was out of the SUV in a second, securing their hands and feet with zip ties and putting duct tape over their mouths. Dowd clambered out of the car and dragged the two unconscious men into the little guard-house. Claire followed him, and a few seconds later the gate opened.

They climbed back into the vehicle and then sped down the winding cobblestone road that took them through the sprawling estate of Harold Butters. There were stately oak trees and massive sculptures everywhere, and a meticulously maintained flower garden that took up a third of the front yard. The home itself, a two-story mansion with a third story underground, was made of white brick.

Two more guards stood by the front door, rifles slung over their backs. One of them pulled out a radio, but Katy used the power of the talismans to rip it out of his hand and fling it into the flower bed.

The other guard raised his rifle and pointed it at the car. Katy concentrated and yanked the rifle from the man's hands, taking a finger with it. She hadn't intended for that to happen, but didn't feel particularly bad about it, either.

A near-transparent orb appeared around each guard's head, cutting off oxygen, courtesy of David Dowd. They clawed and scratched at the orbs, to no avail. Moments later, they both collapsed to the ground, unconscious.

"Neat trick," said Katy.

"I learned it from a good man," Dowd said.

"Okay, that was the easy part," said Claire, tying the guard's hands behind their backs with zip ties. "You know the plan. Let's go."

The plan was for Claire, Katy, Ben, Azazel, and Dowd to advance into the house, looking for Hope and Emily. Azazel had been here before and drew them a map of everything he remembered about the layout. The house had three floors, one beneath the ground. The majority of the bedrooms were on the top floor, so that's where Azazel thought they were probably keeping Emily and Hope.

Gavin, Shawn, Jenny, and Fred would enter the house immediately after they did. Gavin would locate a bathroom, closet, or something else equally accessible with a door, and that would be their doorway to escape, while Fred, Shawn, and Jenny would work with Gavin to secure the doorway and keep it safe. Neither of Ben's parents were happy about that arrangement, as they wanted to participate in the search for Emily and Hope, but Claire insisted, and Fred and Ben backed her up on her stance.

Gavin had loaded himself down with good luck symbols, while Dowd loaned Shawn one of the talismans, just in case they came up against trouble that Gavin's luck, handguns, or tasers couldn't handle. Having a means of escape was essential to rescuing Hope and Emily.

Katy stared at the front door and, using the magical energy provided by the tooth and the emerald, *pushed*. The door exploded inward, wood and metal going everywhere. Claire went through first, followed by Dowd and then everyone else.

"There," said Gavin, pointing at a bathroom just to the left of the entrance. "That's where we'll meet."

Claire nodded. "Sounds good."

Gavin, Shawn, Jenny, and Fred disappeared into the bathroom, securing their point of escape.

Katy took stock of the house. It was huge. An entryway into the dining room lay before them, and a living room was off to their left. Off to the right was a hallway as well as a set of stairs leading upward.

A man came running around the corner, holding a handgun. He aimed at Ben, but Dowd sent him flying backwards with a nod. Two more men rounded the corner, the first aiming a gun at Dowd, the second at Katy. Ben stepped in front of Katy and the man's gun misfired, exploding in his hand. Screaming, he stumbled against the wall, staring down at his ruined hand.

"Show off," Katy muttered under her breath, and Ben flashed her a smile.

Claire kicked the gun out of the other man's hand, sending it skittering through the door and into the dining room. Katy tasered him into near unconsciousness, then kicked him in the face, completing the job.

The first man, the one Dowd had knocked down, scrambled back to his feet, gun clutched in his hand. Dowd was on him in a second, grabbing his head and driving his knee into the man's face. A sick crunch reverberated through the entryway, and the man collapsed to the floor.

The guard whose gun had exploded stared at them, white hot fury on his face. "You can't rescue them, you know."

"We can," said Katy, kicking him hard between the legs, "and we will."

A spinning round kick to the jaw sent the man reeling into the wall, out before his body hit the floor. Dowd secured all the guards with zip ties and duct tape, while Claire took point, ready to ascend the stairs.

They reached the top floor, walking into a huge hallway that stretched in both directions. The top floor seemed vacant of guards, but there was no way to be sure.

"They probably would have put them in the far bedroom," said Azazel, "though I can't guarantee that."

"We'll start there," said Claire. "Lead the way."

They passed five bedrooms and a second set of stairs before reaching the bedroom Azazel had targeted. Claire pushed herself in front of Azazel, her finger to her lips, as she slowly opened the door to the bedroom.

It was empty, save for Hope's backpack. Katy grabbed the backpack and slung it over her shoulder. She thought she was keeping it together pretty well, but the moment she saw the backpack she lost it. She just couldn't stop crying.

"We'll find them," said Ben, reaching out to squeeze her hand.

"Let's check out the other bedrooms," said Azazel. "If they're not there, they might be down in the recreation room or one of the bedrooms down there."

"Or outside," Katy said, flashing back to her dream conversation with Emily earlier. "Azazel, where outside would they take Hope to…test her?"

"Probably the back yard. It's fully enclosed, so they'd have privacy."

"It's your call," said Claire.

Katy looked at Ben, and he nodded. "The backyard," Katy said, "but let's check the other bedrooms as we go, just in case."

They checked each bedroom, but they were all empty. As they entered the last bedroom, they heard a loud crash from outside. Katy ran to the window and looked down, gasping as she watched her daughter rise into the air, laughing maniacally. The pit dropped out of her stomach. This wasn't good. This wasn't good at all.

Emily lay on the ground, her leg buckled beneath her. Colin was there as well, holding a bloody knife, and a young, blonde woman lay bleeding from a stomach wound at his feet. Below Hope was a short, red-haired man, lying on the ground.

"They're out there," Katy said, her voice shaking. "Oh God, what've they done to Hope?"

They all joined her at the window. Azazel's face fell as he looked through the glass.

"Father has possessed her," he said, looking back and forth between the scene unfolding below and Katy. "There's nothing we can do now."

"Bullshit," said Claire. "There's always something we can do."

"I'm not going to let that monster take our daughter," Ben said.

"He has the fused nickel," said Azazel. "He's…unstoppable. Invincible. I'm sorry, but he's won."

"We'll see about that," Claire said, turning from the window. "Come on, we're going out there."

They all followed Claire out of the room and down the stairs, where three more guards awaited them. Dowd took a bullet in the thigh before they were able to take all three guards down, but Claire quickly healed him.

A woman appeared out of nowhere, carrying a butcher knife. Claire caught her wrist and the woman aged 50 years in a second. The now-old woman screamed and then collapsed to the ground, unmoving.

Ben pulled the back door open, and Katy immediately felt like sick to her stomach. Something was happening outside, something bad, and if they didn't stop it, she and Ben were going to lose their daughter forever.

Hope floated about 15 or 20 feet in the air, while Harold Butters, sitting in the grass, stared up at her from below. Colin stood beside Butters, and Emily lay about ten feet from him. Two other people lay unconscious against one of the house walls, and the bleeding blonde woman lay just a few yards from Emily.

Katy looked back and forth between Hope and Emily, wanting to scream. She felt like her heart was being ripped apart. Elohim had possessed her daughter. It had taken them five years to get Ben back, and now the father of the Virya had stolen Hope. What chance did they have of ever rescuing her?

Claire rushed to Emily, dropping to her knees. Emily opened her eyes, trying to talk, her voice eking out, "Help Cassie."

"Shh," Claire said, "let me heal you."

"Cassie," she whispered, pointing toward the dead blonde woman, "heal her first. I think she's dying."

Katy looked at Cassie. She wasn't dead, after all, just painfully close to death. Her breathing was very shallow, and her face pale.

"Katy, can you heal Emily?" Claire asked, but Katy didn't answer, instead staring at the scene taking place around her, frozen in place. "Katy?"

Her heart was racing. She tried to answer, to say something, anything, but the words just wouldn't come out.

"I can heal Emily," said Dowd, running over to Emily.

"Thank you," said Claire, as she turned her attention towards Cassie.

Though both she and Dowd could use the talismans to heal, Claire was the embodiment of the gateway between life and death. She could heal faster and better than they could, and Cassie certainly seemed to be in far worse shape.

Colin turned to them. "You're too late. You might heal them, but it doesn't matter. We'll just kill them later, and you along with them. All of you. We've already won."

"Like hell you have," said Ben, pulling his gun out from its holster and shooting his twin in the chest.

Colin took two steps backwards, then smiled. Ben watched as Colin's ruined chest healed before his eyes, spitting out the bullet to land in the grass below.

"I'll kill you with my bare hands if I have to," Ben screamed, launching himself at his brother, tackling him around the waist.

Ben was on top of Colin, punching him over and over, but the demon just kept laughing. Katy looked from Ben to Hope to Emily, unable to move. She was having a panic attack.

Harold Butters backed away from the fighting brothers, looking confused and disoriented. Was he a willing participant in all this, or had he been tricked by the Vīrya like so many others had been tricked or coerced?

"Come to me, sons and daughters, brothers, sister, brethren one and all," Elohim, in Hope's body, screamed at the top of her lungs. "Now is our time to remake this ruined, desecrated world in our image. Come to me."

It had all seemed so simple. Go to Seattle, get her daughter back, rescue Emily, and live happily ever after. If she hadn't gotten trapped in her own mind, or Emily's necklace, or whatever the hell had happened to her, they would have been here earlier and maybe Hope wouldn't be possessed.

Fuck that. There would be time to beat herself up later. She took a deep breath, and then another, clutching the jaguar's tooth and the emerald tight in her hand. No fear. There was no time for fear, only action.

"Give me my daughter back," screamed Katy.

Hope looked down at her, and the sneer on her little girl's face broke her heart. "You can have her back when I'm through with her."

Katy once again connected with the talismans she held, preparing to somehow fling herself into the air, and could suddenly see the sky was filled with Vīrya. There were a multitude of angels and demons, a woman with four arms, a giant spider, a man with a jackal's head, another man with a skull for a face wearing a top hat, and more, all surrounding her daughter. This wasn't good.

"Azazel," yelled Elohim, "join us. Leave that wretched human body and take your rightful place among your brothers and sisters."

"No," said Azazel, staring up at Hope.

"What do you mean, 'no?'"

"I mean, no. I like being human, and I won't let you take it away from me or anyone else. Now let Hope go."

"You disappoint me, Azazel."

Hope pointed a finger at Azazel, who began to rise into the air. "Stop!" screamed Azazel, but he kept rising.

"Leave him alone," yelled Katy, as she concentrated on the tooth and the emerald, willing Azazel back down again.

It did nothing. Compared to the power Elohim now wielded, her talismans were almost inconsequential. Azazel continued to rise into the air, all the while screaming at Hope.

"He only has Hope for an hour," Emily said, standing beside Dowd. "It's been maybe ten minutes already. If we can distract him long enough…"

"He's wanted this forever," said Cassie, looking weak and covered in blood but made whole again. "He won't allow himself to get distracted."

"Oh my God, you're okay," said Emily, throwing her arms around Cassie.

"Thanks to your friend," she said, gesturing at Claire, "I am."

"I love you so much."

"I love you, too," said Cassie, "and I'm so sorry about all of this."

"So what can we do to stop him?" asked Claire.

"We can't. He's calling the Vīrya, and as soon as enough of us are here, he'll perform the ceremony. You can't see them, but there are already about 500 of us here."

Katy glanced up at the sky. "I can see them. I have two of the talismans, I think that lets me see them."

"I also see them," Claire said. "They're more spirit than I realized."

"I can see them, too," said Dowd. "What ceremony?"

"I don't know, exactly," Cassie said, reaching out to take Emily's hand, "but he wants to enslave all of humanity, essentially taking away your sentience. That way, you'll just be bodies for us to inhabit."

"Em, she doesn't exactly sound like she's on our side," said Katy, looking at Emily. "She keeps saying 'us.'"

"I am on your side," Cassie said. "It's just...the call. It's so hard to resist. Father's...Elohim's damned call."

"Cassie, you can't hear Elohim's call," Emily said.

Cassie blinked. "Wow, that actually worked. Thank you, my love."

"How did you do that?" asked Katy.

"Cassie bound herself to me. Of her own free will, I might add."

"So how many Vīrya does he need to do this ritual?" asked Claire.

"I'm not sure," Cassie said, "but I think about half of us, so...5,000?"

Harold Butters ran up to them. "What is happening?"

"What do you mean, 'what is happening?'" Katy asked him. "You don't know?"

"I was 11 years old when Momma told me to let him in," Butters said. "I don't remember much after that. Where's Mama?"

Emily gasped. "Eleven years old? My God..."

Cassie stared at him. "Are you...what year was that?"

"What do you mean?" asked Butters.

"Harold, what year did your mama tell you to let him in?"

"Harold? Who's Harold? My name is Archibald James Baker, but Mama calls me Archie."

Katy looked at the red-haired man. Archie? Apparently the entire 'Harold Butters' persona was a lie.

"Okay, Archie," Cassie said, "what year did your mama tell you to let him in?"

"It was 1864. Papa died in the war, and Mama needed money, she said. She didn't want to lose the house."

The war? He must mean the civil war. Elohim had possessed his body all this time. It was almost unfathomable.

Archie looked down at his body, shaking his head. "How did I get so tall? And my hands are so big. I don't understand."

"We'll figure all this out later, Archie," said Claire, putting a hand on his shoulder. "For now, I need you to be quiet and stay out of the way, so you don't get hurt. Will you do that for me?"

Archie nodded his head. "What's your name, ma'am?"

"I'm Claire. This is Katy, Cassie, Emily, and David."

"Okay, Miss Claire," he said.

Katy turned just in time to see Shawn burst out the back door, running for Ben and Colin. Her heart seemed to skip a beat. Had the Vīrya found their hiding place?

*** 

The bathroom was large, to be sure, bigger, in fact, than any bathroom Shawn had ever seen, but it just wasn't made to occupy four people. Jenny sat on the closed toilet, Gavin sat on the edge of the bathtub, and Fred stood next to the door. Shawn, however, couldn't stop pacing.

"There has to be something we can do other than just sit here," Jenny said, echoing his own feelings.

"This is important," said Fred, gun drawn, standing beside the door. "This is our doorway out of here."

"Claire is a smart woman," Gavin said. "We're where we need to be."

"My family is out there. My granddaughter, my daughter, and my two sons. Along with Jenny, they're my world. I can't just stand by when their lives are in danger."

"You're worried about Colin," Fred said. It wasn't a question.

"You're damned right I'm worried about Colin. If Ben has the chance, I think he'll kill him."

"I wish you'd let Ben give you back the memories of the original timeline."

"I don't want to forget my son!" yelled Shawn, instantly regretting it. "Sorry, Fred. None of this is your fault."

Fred put his hand on Shawn's shoulder. "I still remember Colin. It's like…I have two sets of memories now. Both timelines. There are a lot of things the same, but a lot of differences, too."

"Maybe we should have let him give us back those memories," Jenny said, "as long as we can keep the ones we already have."

"But what if we—" started Shawn, a loud scream coming from somewhere outside the bathroom interrupting him.

"Holy hell, what was that?" asked Fred.

"Okay, that's it. I'm going out there."

Fred moved to block the door. "Shawn, think about it for a second. Ben, Katy, Claire, David Dowd…they all have powers. They can take care of themselves. You don't have powers."

"Dowd gave me this," he said, holding up the twig talisman, "and I have these," he said, holding up his handgun and taser, "Now, move."

"From the sounds of it, Elohim has more than a stick, a gun, and a taser. And Michael—because I believe Katy when she says Colin was Michael all along—who knows what he can do?"

"Maybe he's right," said Jenny.

Shawn hung his head and turned from the door. Fred relaxed, and that's when he made his move. Maneuvering around the former sheriff, Shawn ran to the door and flung it open.

"I'm sorry," he said, just before he shut the door again.

He knew he was probably making a mistake, but he was long past caring. He walked away from the door, past the fallen guards, past the dining room, and straight for the back door. He could already see Katy through the window, staring up into the sky.

Shawn opened the door and stepped out into chaos. David Dowd was helping Emily to her feet, while Claire kneeled beside a blonde woman lying in the grass. Hope floated in the air, and Azazel was flying as well, moving toward his granddaughter.

"Nothing you do matters, Ben," said a voice. It was Colin!

Shawn turned to see Ben on top of his brother, raining down fist after fist, bloodying Colin's nose, his mouth, blackening his eyes. Ben's fists were bloodied, too, but that didn't stop him. He just kept punching.

He didn't even think. He was on Ben in a second, pulling him off. "Dad," screamed Ben, "what's wrong with you?"

"Yeah, 'Dad,'" said Colin, laughing, "What's wrong with you?"

Shawn watched in amazement as Colin's injuries healed before his eyes. How was this possible?

"Colin?"

"He's Michael, Dad," said Ben. "You know this. Colin never really existed."

Ignoring Ben, Shawn turned to Colin. "Are you Michael?"

"Yes, dimwit, I'm Michael," he said, pushing himself up from the ground. "What gave it away?"

"There's no part of Colin left in you?"

Colin laughed, long and hard. "You *still* don't get it. I was never Colin! Sure, I thought I was, but that all burned away when you rescued this asshole." He gestured at Ben. "It was painful, and I hate you for making me go through it, for making me murder Sumi."

"No one made you murder Sumi," Ben said.

Colin spit in his face. "Oh yes, they did. They couldn't leave well enough alone. If they'd left you where you were, I wouldn't have had to experience that pain. But in the end, it's probably for the best. You humans are less than nothing, while we are everything."

It was like a punch to the gut, hearing those words from the man he'd called his son for the last 24 years. "Colin, I—"

"Want to know something really funny?" he asked, interrupting Shawn. "I was never even supposed to be Colin! I was supposed to take his body," he said, pointing at Ben, "along with his gifts. Colin wasn't supposed to exist."

Colin wasn't supposed to exist? None of this made any sense. "But when we met you in 1975, when you were Michael, you were so…kind, and good."

"I was playing a role! Jesus Christ almighty, when are you going to get that through your thick head? My job was to get you to this point, and it worked. What else do you need to hear?"

"Nothing, I guess," said Shawn, feeling like he was about to throw up. "Can I at least hug you one last time?"

"Bring it on home, Pops," said Colin, going in for a hug.

Shawn brought the Taser up into Colin's ribs, shocking him. Colin spasmed and fell to the ground, and then Shawn was on him, tasering him over and over. Tears rolling down his cheeks, he finally let the taser fall from his fingers.

"Dad…" Ben began.

"That thing you did with Fred," Shawn said, interrupting him, "can you do it to me now?"

"I'm so sorry, Dad," said Ben, pulling him into his arms. "I'm just…I'm so sorry."

As Ben folded his arms around him, Shawn's world changed. He now had two sets of diverging memories.


He was in the delivery room, and Jenny was giving birth to Benjamin. They were supposed to be having twins, but Ben's twin had died months earlier in the womb.

They'd lost him just before the start of the second trimester. It was called Vanishing Twin Syndrome, the doctor had told them, which meant the surviving twin, the mother, or sometimes the placenta itself had absorbed the missing twin. Knowing what happened helped them make sense of the loss, but it didn't make the loss any easier to take.

Shawn had many sleepless nights after learning one of the twins was gone, remembering the loss of his little sister Sarah from Sudden Infant Death Syndrome when he was just seven years old. That in turn brought back memories of both his childhood best friend (and Jenny's brother) Tanner and his cat Samson being murdered by the Fetch. Just another loss in a long chain of losses, and they all added up.

Jenny had been hurting too, of course, but together they got past the pain and enjoyed the birth of Benjamin Tanner, their beautiful, perfect baby boy. Two days later, he drove Jenny and Benjamin home, feeling elated. Five-and-a-half years after that, they gave Ben a little sister: Emily Margaret. Their family was complete, and Shawn and Jenny would love and cherish each other as well as Benjamin and Emily. It was a good life.

He was in the delivery room, and Jenny was giving birth to Ben and Colin. The delivery went perfectly. Ben was born first and then, just a few minutes later, Colin. Two sweet, beautiful baby boys.

Three days later, Shawn drove Jenny, Ben, and Colin home from the hospital. That night, as they lay sleeping in their cribs, Shawn and Jenny couldn't help but spend the night in the nursery. They were in love with their new family. It was perfect.

Five-and-a-half years later, their daughter Emily Margaret was born. She was a surprise, albeit an incredibly happy surprise. They hadn't intended on having more children but loved little Emily just as much as they loved their boys. Their family was complete, and Shawn and Jenny would love and cherish each other as well as their three children. It was a good life.

Benjamin's first birthday

The twins' first birthday.

Benjamin's first day of school

The twins' first day of school.

Ben getting straight A's in school.

Colin jealous of Ben's grades.

Ben discovering his magical ability.

Colin hating Ben because he had an ability while Colin did not.

Ben graduating high school.

Ben and Colin graduating high school, standing far apart.

Ben dating a girl named Burgundy.

Colin leaving home because he was jealous of Ben's girlfriend.


Shawn pulled away from Ben, to look into his eyes. "I'm sorry I didn't believe you."

"It's okay, Dad," Ben said. "If I were you, I probably wouldn't have believed me, either."

"We were supposed to have twins, you know. In the correct timeline, your twin died before the second trimester. I'm sorry we never told you. I guess I just got too good at keeping secrets."

"It's okay, Dad," said Ben, reaching out to squeeze his father's hand.

"These memories…it's so strange. It's like I lived two different lives."

"I hope it helps to make sense of all this, at least a little."

"It does," said Shawn, "a little."

"Now come on," Ben said, "let's get Hope back and get the hell out of here."

"Wait a second," Shawn said, before pressing the talisman that looked like a stick into Ben's hands, "Right now, I trust you with this more than I do myself."

After being wrong about Colin, Shawn wasn't sure he would fully trust his own judgment ever again.

He shook his head, trying to clear the confusion and grief. What was important now was rescuing Hope and Emily, and he'd be damned if he were going to let anyone stand in their way.

# Chapter 80

Emily stared into the sky, watching as Elohim, in Hope's body, rallied troops she couldn't even see. She reached out to touch Katy's hand, the hand that held the jaguar's tooth, gasping as the Vīrya in the sky came into focus. There were probably 1,000 of them now, and they formed a huge circle around Hope, holding hands. Shit. There weren't 5,000, not nearly, but maybe Cassie was wrong about the number. And even if she wasn't, what could they do against 1,000 wannabe gods, let alone 5,000?

"Hey," said Cassie, bending down to grab something from the grass, "I just found the keys. let's get that stupid necklace off of you."

She flashed Cassie a half-smile as Cassie unlocked the necklace, removed it, and snapped it in half before dropping it to the ground. Good. She hated that necklace and never wanted to see it again.

"You son of a bitch!" Yelled Ben, running up to Archie Baker, Shawn behind him.

"No, Ben," said Katy, stepping between them. "He's in the same boat you were, only he's been possessed a lot longer."

"Boat?" asked Baker, looking between Katy and Ben. "I'm not in a boat, am I? I wish I was in a boat. Mama always said she'd take me down the Mississippi River in a boat, but she never did."

Emily felt so sad for him. Archie Baker was over 150 years old, but still had the mind of a child. She thought he might also be mentally disabled. His possession hadn't been like Ben's, not exactly. Elohim had apparently shoved Archie's soul or spirit or psyche or whatever into a little box, keeping him locked inside, completely unaware of what was happening in the outside world.

"I'm…sorry," said Ben, "I didn't know."

"That's okay," said the man, reaching out to give Ben an awkward hug. "Mama always said forgiveness is free."

A chill ran down her spine. She wondered who had originally inhabited the body Cassie wore, and what she'd done to get that body. She shook her head. They'd have to have that conversation later, but right now there just wasn't time.

"I'm glad you're okay," said Shawn, pulling her into an embrace. "I love you so much."

"I love you, too, Dad," she said, hugging him fiercely. "Thank you for coming for us."

"My brethren, our time is now," yelled Elohim. "Hear me, brothers and sisters, sons and daughters, abandon your frail human bodies and come to me. Come to me, so that we may take this world as our own."

The man Katy had referred to as Azazel floated in front of Hope, looking terrified. She didn't even think. She teleported to him, grabbed his hand, and teleported back to Cassie.

"Thank you," whispered Azazel, and she could see tears running down his cheeks.

"Oh, Emily," said Elohim, laughing, "you really shouldn't have done that."

"Are you okay?" asked Emily.

Azazel tried to say something but stopped in midsentence as Hope gestured at him. He shook back and forth for a few seconds before splitting in half, blood, bones, and organs going everywhere. The Vīrya inside screamed, a blood curdling howl that hurt Emily's ears, before rising into the air, translucent arms flailing and legs kicking.

"Oh my God," screamed Emily, covered in Azazel's blood.

"Why?" screamed Azazel, as he continued to float upwards.

"Because you betrayed me," Elohim said, in Hope's voice, as Azazel continued to float upward.

"Oh, shit," whispered Cassie, "I bet there's 2 or 3 thousand of them up there now. If we're going to do something, we'd better do it quick."

"Give me back my daughter," yelled Ben, into the sky.

"Ben Spencer, what a disappointment you were," Elohim said. "We had such grand plans for you, only to have you lose your abilities. You're less than useless now. Yesterday's hero."

"Wanna bet?"

Colin tackled Ben from behind, knocking him to the ground. Emily didn't even think, she teleported behind Dowd, sliding his sword out of the sheath tied to his back, then teleported to Ben and Colin, driving the sword deep into Colin's chest.

"Emily, no," screamed Shawn, but Colin was laughing.

"When will you humans learn?" he asked, bleeding all over Ben, whom he still straddled.

"How about now?" asked Emily, as she swung the sword again, slicing through Colin's right wrist.

He stared at his hand, the one with the tattoo, as it fell to the ground.

"Well, shit," he whispered, as he tumbled off Ben and into the grass.

"His tattoo," Emily said, in response to Ben throwing her a quizzical look. "It healed him. But it can't heal him if it's no longer attached to his body."

Emily stared down at Colin, feeling sick to her stomach. She'd killed her brother, her own flesh and blood, but it was the only way. He was her brother only in the purely physical sense, however. His skin had housed something much more sinister.

"Join me, my son," shouted Elohim.

Emily reached out to help Ben to his feet, at the same time connecting with the talisman he held. They both watched as Colin's spirit—no,

Michael's, she reminded herself—left his ruined body and rose into the sky to join the other Vīrya.

He looked back at them, anger in his eyes, an empty anger of a truly soulless being. Colin had never been real, and not realizing that before now might just cost everyone their lives.

# Chapter 81

Tanner knew he wasn't likely to survive the night. The thought made him sadder than he expected. He'd come back from the dead twice now but was pretty sure it wasn't going to happen a third time. He wasn't scared of death, but he would have loved to have had the chance to speak to his mother, Jenny, and Shawn one last time. At least he'd been able to talk to his niece Emily and his grand-niece Hope.

His father, Paul McGee, had died last year. He would give anything to have been able to see his old man one last time, but it just wasn't in the cards. His mother, Abby, was still alive, though she was out of reach for him as well.

Tanner and Samson had rushed out the door when Emily pretended to trip and bang her shoulder against the door frame. From there, they'd hidden behind a potted plant until the coast was clear, and then made their way to a window.

It'd taken them way too long to pry the window open, and even longer to scale the side of the house to the roof, but they'd done it. If they could buy their family even a few seconds reprieve, it would all be worth it.

Tanner gazed out into the sky. There were so many Vīrya that they nearly blotted out the sun. If he looked above them, however, the view was just about perfect. The sun hung low in the sky, about an hour from setting, and the sky was as blue as the ocean.

It was the last sunset he'd ever see. He did his best to memorize it, imprinting it upon his soul, hoping that wherever he went when this was all over, he'd be able to hold on to that image.

"You've been the best companion any action figure could ask for," Tanner said, ruffling the fur of the tiger that stood beside him.

The tiger licked his hand, letting him know the feeling was mutual.

Together, they walked over to the edge, looking down. Elohim, inhabiting his grand-niece Hope's body, floated almost perpendicular to the roof, looking down at Ben, Katy, Emily, and the others.

Elohim began to chant the spell that would remake the world.

It was almost time.

# Chapter 82

Ben stared up at Elohim, wearing his daughter's body. There was no way in hell he was going to let this monster destroy the world. He couldn't attack him directly, not while he wore Hope's skin, but there were other things he could do.

He clutched the talisman disguised as a stick in his hand, reaching out with his mind, seeing all the gossamer threads of reality. There were so many, thousands, some thick as a shoelace and others as thin as a hair. They were constantly changing, weaving in and out of each other, disappearing, reappearing, merging, then splitting apart again.

Some were so tenuous that they'd dissolve if he stopped to examine them for even a second, but others were stronger, and he concentrated on those threads, seeing where they led.

Each thread represented a different potential reality. Most of the threads ended in Elohim's victory. He saw the timelines Future-Hope told him about, and so many more, a seemingly infinite number of threads stretching out as far as the eye could see. All but a tiny percentage of humanity turned into mindless drones, worshipping the Vīrya, giving up their bodies to the "gods" upon request.

In every single one of them, he died, and so did most of his family and friends. He had accepted death 5 years ago; the moment Azazel stole his body. Hell, during the worst of it, he'd even craved oblivion. If he had to die, so be it, but he was damned if anyone else was going to join him, especially not Katy or Hope.

"I know what you're trying to do, Ben," said Elohim, through Hope, "and it's not going to work. We've considered all the possibilities, planned for ever contingency. Finally, this world is ours."

"As it should have been all along," said Michael, his insubstantial form floating in the air beside Elohim.

"It's not yours yet," said Ben, though he feared Elohim's words would prove to be prophecy.

He chanced a look up at Hope and fear shot through his body like adrenaline. If there weren't 5,000 Vīrya here already, the count was perilously close. They circled the sky like locusts, all holding hands, grouped around Hope.

"*Nāṅkaḷ inta ulakattai urimai kōrukirōm, atai eṅkaḷ contamākkukirōm,*" chanted Elohim, over and over, as the Vīrya wove around him.

Ben had no idea what Elohim was saying, but he knew it couldn't be good. The ritual had started, and soon the world would belong to the Vīrya.

Archie Baker trembled and gasped, then collapsed to the ground. Shawn and Claire followed suit almost immediately. Fred, Jenny, and Gavin stood at the back door, staring up at the sky, until they, too, began to pass out. First Gavin, then Jenny, and finally Fred. One by one, they all slumped to the ground, unconscious or worse.

Katy stood at the other end of the yard, holding hands with Emily. Dowd and Cassie stood beside them, both still conscious. Cassie made sense; she was, after all, Vīrya. But why were the others still awake? For that matter, why hadn't Ben himself passed out?

He looked down at the stick in his hand. The talisman. Katy had the tooth and the emerald, Emily had connected to them by holding Katy's hand, and Dowd had the geode.

"It's the talismans," Dowd yelled, apparently coming to the same conclusion he had.

"Here," said Katy, holding out the emerald to Emily, "take this."

Emily snatched the emerald from Katy's outstretched hand, just as Elohim began to chant again. "*Manitarkaḷ iṭattil uṟaintu pōvatāl, nām vāryā atikārattil uyarkiṟōm.*"

Ben felt his muscles tense and become rock hard. He couldn't move, could barely blink his eyes or even breathe.

"He said, 'We the Vīrya rise in power, as the humans are frozen in place,'" whispered Cassie, "that's why you can't move."

"We're fucked," said Ben, just as he heard a voice from above them scream, 'Geronimo!'"

Ben's eyes grew large as he watched Hope's Galahad action figure fling itself from the roof of the mansion, landing on Hope's shoulder, driving his little sword into her arm. What the hell was going on?

Elohim screamed and grabbed the action figure, eyes blazing with anger. "You dare?" he asked, through Hope's mouth, as Galahad begin to melt in her hands.

"Tanner!" screamed Emily.

"Tell Jenny and Shawn and Mom I love them," yelled the figure, looking at Ben. "You, too, Dad."

Ben stared at the figure in Hope's hand. How could it talk, and why had it called Ben "Dad"? He forced himself to put that puzzle out of his mind for now as he realized he could move again.

He tried to see the threads but couldn't. He concentrated, willing them to appear, and they flickered into existence. They all ended in the same outcome, with Elohim remaking the world.

Something else flung itself off the roof at Hope, and this time it was her toy tiger. It smashed into Galahad, knocking him loose from Hope's hand, and time seemed to slow as they tumbled toward the ground. Right before they hit, they both burst into flame, melting in an instant.

"No," Emily yelled, starting toward the ruined figures, but Katy held her back.

"There's nothing you can do," she whispered.

"There's nothing I can do, either," Ben said. "The threads...they all lead to Elohim's victory. I can't find a path. I'm just not strong enough."

Dowd stared at him, then turned to Katy and Emily. "Give him your talismans. I'll give him mine, too."

"What? No. You'll pass out," said Ben, "just like Dad and Claire and everyone else."

In the sky, Elohim began to chant again. He felt the hairs on the back of his neck stand up, and a shiver ran down his spine.

"David's right," said Katy, holding out the tooth.

Ben remembered how he felt in the spirit room, when he'd held all four of the talismans. Thank God Azazel had been there to talk him down. But this time...what if he succumbed to the power? What good was saving the world only to introduce it to a hell of his own making? Because if he lost control, that's exactly what might happen.

*You won't*, said a voice in his head.

Ben spun a quick circle, looking for the source of the voice. "Who said that?"

"Who said what?" asked Katy.

*You know who I am*, said the voice.

*Grandpa Paul?*

*I've been with you since the cemetery,* whispered his grandfather.

*I think somewhere in my mind, I knew that,* Ben whispered back, remembering how much stronger and more self-assured he'd felt after visiting his grandfather's grave.

*So let's kick this son of a bitch's ass and get your daughter back.*

"Ben are you okay?" asked Katy.

"Give me the talismans," he said. "It'll work. It has to."

She pressed the tooth into his hand. "I love you," she said, as she let go and tumbled to the grass.

"I love you, too," he said to her unconscious form.

Next was Emily, and finally Dowd. It was just him and Cassie now. Everyone else lay unconscious at his feet.

"*Maṉita uṭalkaḷ nam'muṭaiyavai, nām virumpiyapaṭi ceyya,*" chanted Elohim, and now he could hear other voices as well, joining in the chant.

"'The human bodies are ours,'" Cassie translated, "'to do with as we will.'"

"Cassie, watch over Katy and Emily and the rest," Ben said, "and keep them safe as best you can. My sister trusts you, so I'm going to trust you, too. Don't let us down."

Cassie nodded. "Do what you need to do. I've got your back."

He held all four talismans in his fist, his body vibrating with chaotic energy. He felt his grandfather's presence, helping him master the emotions that came with this much power. He closed his eyes, took a breath, and opened them again.

The threads were everywhere, so many, in all the colors of the rainbow. Gossamer strings stretching out into the heavens, pulsing, flashing, some vanishing and some growing brighter, stronger, thicker.

He scanned through the threads, looking for the one that would solve everything, that would save the world and his family and destroy Elohim forever.

That thread didn't exist, or if it did, he couldn't find it. Time had slowed to a crawl for him, and he had already examined a million different threads, perhaps more, but none of them led to the perfect outcome.

He was running out of time, so he would have to make do.

Ben pulled a red thread, melded it into a light blue one, then cut off a snippet of a sea foam green thread and wove it into the mix. He caught an errant, nearly translucent purple thread that was about to disappear and twisted it around the red part of the thread he was creating, melding them together, then adding the barest sliver of a yellow thread to the blue.

When he was done, he tested the thread, giving it a little tug. It didn't break. This wasn't the perfect solution, not by a longshot, but he thought it just might work, if he could only find a few more snippets to bind it all together.

*"Itu eṅkaḷ viruppam, ākavē irukka vēṇṭum,"* chanted the Vīrya, in unison.

"Do something, Ben," Cassie screamed. "'This is our will, so mote it be.' That's the final part of the ritual."

Shit. He needed more time, but he was out. He looked at the thread before him and willed it to stay where it was, hovering in the air, waiting for him. Time for plan B. Using the magic of the four ancient talismans, Ben launched himself into the sky, aiming for Hope.

He zipped past a startled Azazel, still hovering helplessly in the air, as he snatched his daughter from the sky, propelling both of them into the future.

# Chapter 83

Holding the four talismans had opened up something within Ben, helping him remember how to time travel. He'd never before travelled to the future, however, wasn't even sure it was possible, but nevertheless here they were, exactly one day later.

"Hi, Daddy," said Hope, as they landed in the grass.

The yard was deserted.

"Hi sweetie. Are you okay?" Ben asked his daughter.

"I'm okay," she said, "but I don't think the world is."

As if on cue, Katy walked out the back door. "Right on time," she said, smiling.

Ben stared at her. Something wasn't right. The way she held herself, her stance. That eerie smile. "You're not Katy, are you?"

"No, Daddy," said Hope, still in his arms, "that's not Mommy."

"Elohim?" asked Ben.

"Got it in one, dude," said the Vīrya who had stolen his wife's body.

"But…why? How?"

"Because you can't stop me. No one can. Before too long, Hope snaps back to me, the me who inhabited her body just 24 hours ago, and I complete the ritual. You die, your father dies, your mother dies, your sister dies, but I keep Katy around, just for this moment. It's over, Ben Spencer. You lost, and the world is mine."

This couldn't be happening. "Hope, give me the nickel."

The little girl looked at her empty hands. "It's gone, Daddy."

Elohim held up the fused nickel. "Looking for this?"

"How?"

"Never mind that, Ben. You can't win."

This didn't make sense. Hope had the nickel when Ben grabbed her, didn't she? If not, where did it go?

Gavin Young walked out from the backdoor, leading Cassie and Fred, both gagged and in chains.

"Hey, bro," said Gavin, winking at Ben. "Emily may have destroyed my body, but you were kind enough to bring me this one, which is even better." It was Michael!

"That's not Grandpa Fred," whispered Hope.

"That's right, Hope," said Elohim, "it's not Grandpa Fred. It's the other traitor, Azazel."

Ben glanced to his right. The thread he had begun creating was still there, though he didn't think anyone else could see it. The thread represented a potential reality. It wasn't quite finished but he wasn't sure what else to add.

"What should I do with the traitors, Ben?" asked Elohim, with Katy's voice.

"Let them go."

Elohim laughed. "That's not going to happen, unless...You know what, Ben? I think I may have a solution. I'm tired of all this fighting. I've already won, and it won't hurt me to be a little magnanimous.

"You can have your daughter, and your wife. Your little family. Like this house? You can have it, too. We no longer need it. We'll leave you alone, to live as you wish."

"And what do you want in return?"

"Just for you to give up. Go back where you came from, let this play out, and finally be done with it. It'll happen regardless, of course. Hope will start feeling the pain of breaking the terms of her binding any second now."

Almost as if on cue, Hope began to scream. "It hurts, Daddy!"

"What hurts, Hope?" he asked her, his heart racing.

"My tummy. My head. Everything."

"And it'll keep hurting until you let her go back to yesterday, Ben," said Elohim. "She has to keep her promise."

"But it's a whole other day. That hour was over 23 hours ago."

"Not for her."

Hope held her stomach, squirming in his arms.

"Take my deal, Ben. You, Hope, Katy…you get to live, to have a life, this house, whatever you want. And we'll leave you alone. I promise, we'll leave you alone."

Ben stared at Elohim. Why was the Vīrya so eager to make a deal when he'd already won? It just didn't make sense, especially considering Elohim had been nothing but viscous and calculating just 23 hours ago. Unless…

"Can I have Cassie and Azazel as well? If I agree, will you let them go?"

Elohim paused as if to consider. "As loathe as I am to give mercy to traitors…yes, I can do that."

Cassie gave a slight turn of her head, an almost-imperceptible sign for him not to take the deal. She needn't have worried. There was no way in hell he was going to let Elohim win.

"Daddy," said Hope, "it's getting worse."

"Better hurry, Ben Spencer," Elohim said, through Katy's mouth.

"Let me tell you what I think," said Ben, stroking his daughter's hair. "I think you're very scared right now. Sure, in your timeline, we came back, you took possession of Hope, you completed your little ritual, and you enslaved humanity. You won.

"But we both know it doesn't have to go down that way. My twin brother is evidence of that. Time isn't immutable, and neither is reality. You can affect things in the past, as you did when you sent that damned necklace to 1977 and let your pet demon Leonard possess Brody Huffman, but you're stuck in the here and now. Unlike me."

"You think you know everything, Ben Spencer, but you do not."

"You're right, I don't know everything, but I know this much. You have the nickel, which must mean you dropped it right as I tackled Hope and brought her here. Or maybe you tossed it into the air. Who knows? Regardless, the fact that we don't have it means that, at least for a few seconds, you didn't either."

"You can't win," said Elohim. "Merely holding the fused talisman will corrupt you, especially now that you have all the other charms. You'd die almost immediately."

"He just wants to be the hero, Father," said Michael, "no matter the consequences, even if one of those consequences is his own death."

Ben shrugged. "Better mine that my wife's, or my daughter's, or the entire freaking world," he said, pausing to cover Hope's ears, "you fucking psychopath."

He now knew what he had to do, but he also knew it would kill him. The thought didn't make him happy, but it also didn't make him sad. It was what it was.

Elohim started to say something, but he'd never know what, for at that moment Hope started to scream, and he sent her back in time, something he hadn't even known he could do before he did it. A nanosecond later, he followed, but to a slightly different destination.

He prayed to whoever might be out there listening that his gambit would work.

# Chapter 84

Ben watched from the roof of the house as the disaster unfolded. He watched as his daughter's toy knight and tiger sacrificed themselves just so they could interrupt Elohim's ritual long enough for Ben to see the threads. He watched as past Ben accepted the talismans from Katy, Emily, and David Dowd, enabling him to stand against the Vīrya's magic and seize the threads of reality.

He watched as past Ben hurtled through the sky, snatched Hope, and vanished. He watched as, just before they disappeared, Elohim flipped the fused nickel into the air, watched as Elohim, now a phantom without a body to possess, stared helplessly at the coin as its momentum reversed and it arced towards the ground.

A fraction of a second later Hope appeared, and Elohim's non-corporeal form was immediately sucked into her body. Elohim snatched the coin from the air, a triumphant smile on Hope's lips.

Ben didn't hang around to see what might happen next. Instead he stepped back in time, mere seconds earlier, and launched himself off the roof. The coin was falling, and Elohim, a phantom again, was reaching for the nickel, and then Hope was appearing, Elohim once again possessing her body, reaching...

...only to grasp air. Hope's eyes grew big as she stared at Ben, hovering before her, holding the coin.

"How?" Elohim asked.

Even as he was dying, Ben had never felt so alive. Pure, raw energy coursed through his body, crackling from his fingertips, as his skin slowly turned a translucent blue.

The world was his, to remake however he wanted.

But he didn't want to remake the world, just change it enough so that the Vīrya were no longer a threat. He held onto that thought, trying to ignore the part of him that wanted to impose his will on the planet.

It was so hard.

If he ruled the world, there would be no more poverty, no more poisoning of the oceans, no political parties, no prejudice, no hate. Everyone would get a fair shake, cancer would be a thing of the past, and no one would starve. Nuclear weapons would vanish, for there would be no need for them. The world would unite under his rule, and if some people didn't like that, well, they would be punished, and…

He shook his head.

If the world were ever to improve, it would have to be because its people decided it needed improving and worked together to make it happen. Forcing his will upon the world would be no better than Elohim remaking the Earth in his own image.

"Give me the coin," said Elohim, staring at him through Hope's eyes. "You can't control it, and I'll just take it from your lifeless corpse anyway."

"Get out of my daughter," Ben said, and Elohim shot out of Hope's body, hurled ten feet away.

"How? My hour isn't up and I—"

Ben silenced him with a wave of one hand, while catching his falling daughter with the other.

"Daddy? You're…glowing."

He looked at his arm. He was indeed glowing. Well, how about that? "Honey," he said, floating to the ground, "I want you to always know how much I love you and Mommy. You mean everything to me."

He gently sat her on the ground.

"I love you, too, Daddy," she said, looking up into his eyes.

He gently caressed her cheek, willing her to sleep. She crumpled to the grass.

She didn't need to see her father die.

"Ben?" said a voice. It was Cassie. "What's happening?"

He looked at her, then at the sky. The Vīrya, all 4,592 of them, stared down at him, venom in their gaze. There was no venom from Cassie, only confusion and concern.

"Cassie," asked Ben, "do you love my sister?"

"With all my heart."

"I remember…when Azazel controlled me, having sex with you, more than once."

She blushed. "That's not me anymore."

He pulled her into a hug. She stiffened for a moment before hugging him back. "I believe you. Just…please, don't hurt Emily. That's all I ask of you."

She pulled away. "I promise I won't, but you're sounding like you won't be around to make sure. Please don't sacrifice yourself. There has to be another way."

"There isn't," Ben said, and he turned around and walked to the thread he'd been creating either moments or a lifetime earlier.

Cassie started to come to him, but he stopped her with a shake of his head. He created an invisible, soundproof wall around himself and the threads. It wouldn't do to be disturbed right now.

He imagined Azazel's host body whole again, and then it was. He pointed up at Azazel, floating helplessly in the air, and pointed to the body, shoving the Vīrya inside. He got his body, after all, and there wasn't a damned thing Elohim could do about it.

Across the yard, he saw Katy and Emily climbing to their feet. Cassie rushed to Emily, taking her into her arms. His parents were awake now, too, along with Claire, Fred, Gavin Young, David Dowd, and Archie Baker. They were all staring at him.

Ben waved a hand in their direction, giving his mother and Emily back their memories of the original timeline without Colin. After that, he ignored them, instead concentrating on the threads.

There were billions of them now, trillions, a seemingly infinite amount. He looked at the thread he'd woven earlier and dismissed it with a wave. In that reality, the one he'd been trying to create, the Vīrya would all become trapped in the spirit room. It was the only solution he could find at the time, but now he saw that, in 126 years, they would escape and start this mess all over again.

Only one reality seemed to permanently put a stop to the threat. It wasn't perfect and could potentially cause other problems down the line, but he didn't have forever. There was no way his body could contain this much chaotic energy for more than a few more minutes.

Now all he had to do was build it.

An incredible pain shot through his body. He stumbled, almost dropping the emerald.

*Fuse them all together*, said his grandfather, in his mind. *That'll help contain the energy a little and will buy us a few more minutes.*

Ben nodded, and then put the stick, emerald, geode, jaguar's tooth, and the fused nickel into his left hand, closed his fist, and opened it again. He was holding a beautiful, glowing blue orb. It glowed so bright, it hurt his eyes.

Katy was at the translucent wall he'd created, banging her fists against it, eyes filled with tears. He held out a trembling hand, touching the wall, and she did the same, their fingers separated only by the glass. This was as close as they'd ever again get. It wasn't at all what he wanted, but it was better than nothing.

She was shouting something, and he almost allowed sound in, but stopped himself. If he could hear her, he might not have the courage to do what needed to be done.

He mouthed the words, *I love you*, and then turned away from her.

With his right hand, he began to once again snatch threads from all the possible realities. There was a thread that pulsed blue, then red, then green, then silver, and then back to blue again. He'd never seen a thread like that before. He touched it, seeing the reality it represented. He smiled. Combining this one with a few others would make the thread he needed.

He grabbed another thread, and then another, and finally a third. He wove them together and the new thread shined a bright blue, matching the talisman in his other hand and his own body.

It was time.

Elohim would finally have what he wanted, though definitely not in the way he'd imagined. Be careful what you wish for...

Thinking of Katy, of Hope, of his parents, grandparents, of Fred and Candy, Ben pulled the thread and—

# Chapter 85

Katy watched through the glass wall Ben had created as he vanished. He was there one moment, his body nearly translucent and glowing blue, pulsing with energy, and then he was gone, just like that. She screamed at him to come back, screamed until her throat was raw, but he didn't reappear. He was just...gone.

She punched at the invisible wall, but it was also gone, almost as if it had never been. She stumbled, tumbling to the grass, landing beside all that was left of Ben: his cybernetic right hand, now reverted to its original shade of obsidian, and the five talismans.

Katy began to sob uncontrollably, and then Jenny was beside her, holding her, and together they wept. Her father dropped to his knees beside them, pulling them both into his arms as they cried into his shoulders.

"My wonderful, beautiful little boy," mumbled Shawn, staring at the mechanical hand Katy now held, "is gone?"

Katy dropped the obsidian hand and reached out for Shawn. He took her hand and he, too, dropped to his knees beside them, a howl of anguish escaping his lips.

"The Vīrya," said Cassie, her voice low, "they're also gone. I could feel them, they were so angry, such rage, and then...then they just vanished. Ben did it. He saved the world."

"But where are they?" asked Emily, her voice breaking. "Where are the Vīrya?"

"I think he made us—made *them*—into what we always pretended to be," said Azazel, somehow whole again, standing beside Cassie and Emily. "Angels and demons and other assorted gods and goddesses. They won't remember what they used to be, only what they are now."

"How do you know this," asked Katy, climbing to her feet, "and why are you still here? Why are you here while Ben is gone?"

"He…he saved me," Azazel said. "He didn't have to, he could have sent me off with…with them, but he didn't. He resurrected my body and he saved me, and he told me what was happening, somehow, even though we didn't speak. After all I did to him, he gave me this gift. He saved me."

"He was a good man," Katy said, barely holding back tears. "He saved us all."

"They're really gone," said Claire, holding Hope, walking up to them with Gavin, David Dowd, and Archie Baker trailing behind her. "I can't see them, can't even sense them. They're gone."

Katy took Hope from Claire, hugging her tight.

"They are gone," Cassie agreed, reaching out to take Emily's hand, "and I'm…human. Fully, 100% human."

"What's this?" asked Shawn, picking up a clump of melted plastic from the yard.

"That was Tanner and Samson," said Emily, folding herself into her father's arms. "I don't know how, but your childhood best friend and your cat came back to life, to save us."

"I knew Tanner would come back," whispered Shawn, his voice trembling, "somehow, someway, but I had no idea he'd bring Samson with him."

Jenny walked over to them and hugged them both, and then all three were crying again.

"Ben gave me back my memories before he…" Emily said, between sobs. "Why didn't we believe him about Colin? If we had, if I had, maybe he'd…maybe he'd…"

"Oh honey," said Shawn, kissing her forehead, "none of this is your fault."

"But…but…"

"Shawn's right," said Katy, setting Hope down and pulling Emily into long hug, "none of this is your fault. It's not anyone's fault but Elohim's. We were all manipulated by the Vīrya, pitted against each other."

"He gave me back my memories as well," said Jenny. "I wish I'd been brave enough to let him do it earlier."

"It's okay, Grandma Jenny," said Hope, "We'll see Daddy again."

Katy picked up Hope again, hugging her close. "Yeah, we will, sweetie. Someday. For now, though, I think it's time to go home."

# Chapter 86

Ben was in a corn field, giant cornstalks stretching out as far as the eye could see. He blinked, shaking his head. Where was he, how had he gotten here, and why wasn't he dead?

He looked up into a bright, beautiful blue sky, cloudless, with the sun straight above him. He couldn't stop staring at the sun, almost like it was drawing him to its light. He shook his head again, forcing himself to look away.

The last thing he remembered was bringing the thread of reality he'd created to life, and then…and then the raw magic of the fused nickel, two identical items that never should have existed together bound as one, and the four other talismans…had ripped him apart, destroying him, obliterating his body.

He was dead, after all.

But had it worked?

"It worked," said a voice, a few feet away, through the corn.

"Grandpa Paul!" he yelled, as the old man appeared through the stalks.

He threw his arms around his grandfather, hugging him tight. They stayed that way for a good minute or so, just holding each other.

"You did it," said Paul, "The Vīrya have all been transformed into what they pretended to be for so long. Angels, demons, gods, demi-gods, whatever their last form was. To them, that's what they always were, will always be."

"And Elohim?" asked Ben. "He played the role of both God and Satan. What is he now?"

"Well, he's certainly not God," said Paul, smiling.

"Hey guys," said a voice, and Ben turned around to see a chubby teenage boy with brown hair and freckles holding an orange and white cat pushing his way through the corn.

"Tanner?"

"Yep, it's me," said the boy, "and Samson, of course."

Paul dropped to his knees, taking the boy into his arms as Samson leapt to the ground. "God, Tanner...I never thought I'd see you again. I love you so much."

"I love you, too, Dad," he said, tears rolling down his cheeks.

Ben let them stay like that for a while, hugging and enjoying their reunion, before saying, "I don't understand any of this."

"Don't understand what?" Tanner asked.

"I know Dad said you came back to life inside the Galahad action figure that was buried with you in 1975. He thought it had to do with the nickel he put into your casket, and his blood. But this time, there was no talisman, no blood, and it wasn't even the same Galahad figure."

Tanner shrugged. "There's something else out there, Ben, something bright and good. It's been trapped for a very long time, locked away by the Vīrya, but it's still been able to help from time to time. I think it's what brought me and Samson back."

A shiver trailed up Ben's spine, or whatever served as a spine in this incarnation of his body. Was there a God, a creator of the universe and everything it held, out there somewhere? Or maybe another being or beings like the Vīrya, but who had decided to use their vast power for good instead of using it selfishly.

Then again, it didn't necessarily have to be just one or the other. It could be both. They weren't, after all, mutually exclusive. Whatever the force or forces were, they had chosen to help, not hinder. That would have to be enough.

"How do you resist that light?" Ben asked, shielding his eyes.

"You get used to it," Paul answered.

A wind rustled through the corn, and he looked up just in time to see a flock of crows flying by overhead, heading towards the sun.

This world, this universe, was vast and mysterious. Were these crows perhaps vessels for other souls, newly dead, rushing off to wherever souls go after their bodies pass on, or were they simply crows who'd been enjoying the corn? For that matter, was the afterlife really a cornfield? He shook his head. In the end, it didn't matter.

"So, what now?" Ben asked, looking between his grandfather and Tanner. "What's next?"

Samson rubbed at his ankles, purring. He reached down to stroke the tabby's fur. What a gorgeous cat. He could see now why it had been so hard for his father to have another pet after losing this beautiful boy.

"Now it's time to go back," said Tanner, "at least for you."

Ben stared at the boy. "Go…back? I don't understand."

"You're not dead, Ben, though you're not exactly alive, either. You're more like…what's that cat in a box, both alive and dead at the same time?"

"Schrödinger's cat," said Ben. "The cat is in a box, along with poison that may or may not have been activated by a radioactive isotope, and you won't know if the cat's dead or alive until you open the box."

"Okay, yeah, Schrödinger's cat. You're Schrödinger's Ben."

"But…how?" Ben asked.

"Energy doesn't disappear, it just changes."

"It's true," said Paul. "Look at your hands, Ben."

He looked down at his left hand. He was still holding the glowing blue orb he'd created from the talismans. He could feel the energy pulsing, but it wasn't corrupting his body, because there was no longer anything to corrupt. His right hand, he also noticed, was no longer the mechanical hand he'd worn for the last 5 years.

"Can...can I bring all of you back with me?"

"I wish," said Tanner, "but I don't think that's possible."

They both turned to look at Paul, who shrugged.

"So I can?"

"I don't know, Ben. Let's ask Margaret."

"The lady from the cemetery?"

"My sister, your great aunt Margaret," he said, nodding, and a few seconds later she appeared.

"All this corn," she said, "is enough to make a girl hungry."

She wore blue jeans and a white blouse; different than the first time he'd seen her a week ago at Moss Ridge cemetery. Her bright red hair was cut short in a bob, whereas it had been long.

"It'd be boring to be stuck in the same clothing and the same hair-style for an eternity," she said, as if reading his mind, "don't you think?"

He shook his head. "So, can I bring them back? Can I bring *you* back?"

She shook her head. "Not me, no, because I don't want to go back. I'm happy where I am, with Jacob. And I still have work to do. The others...possibly, though it'll take almost all of the magic in that orb to do it."

"I don't want to go back, either," said Paul. "For better or worse, I lived my life. I got to see my son, my lost little boy, one more time. I'm happy. And..." he glanced at Tanner, almost as if unsure how much he should say, "Abby will be joining me soon."

"Aw, no. Mom?"

Paul reached out to touch Tanner's shoulder. "She's got at least a few more years left, don't worry. Maybe longer. Time is different here, so 'soon' is relative."

"So how do I do it?" asked Ben. "How do I bring myself, Tanner, and Samson back to life? Assuming you want to, Tanner."

"You bet your sweet ass I want to," said Tanner, and everyone laughed.

"Become one with the magic, with the energy," Margaret said, "and imagine yourself going through a doorway, to your beautiful wife, to your little girl, to your parents.

"There is, however, a price. The fused nickel will be cleaved in half, becoming the talisman it was before it was merged with its alternate reality counterpart. And your magic, Ben, the magic that's part of your soul, the magic that lets you time travel and win at Monopoly… I think you could lose that, or at the least it might change a little."

"There's always a price," said Ben, knowing what he had to do.

# Chapter 87

They'd won, but at what cost? Shawn couldn't help but ponder that question as he followed Gavin Young through the bathroom door in the mansion and reappeared in his own house, nearly 2,000 miles away. They were all there now, everyone except for Archie Baker, Azazel, and David Dowd, the latter two of which had chosen to stay behind to free the captive guards and help Archie deal with his new life, the life Elohim had created as Harold Butters.

He held four of the five talismans in his pocket, but they no longer seemed to contain magic. Now they were simply what they appeared to be: a stick, a geode, a jaguar's tooth, and a Buffalo head nickel. Dowd kept the emerald, saying he wanted to return it to Agatha Muir, even if it was now just a simple gem. Whatever mystical, chaotic energy the talismans had once possessed seemed to vanish along with Ben.

Gavin shook his hand, once again expressing his condolences about Ben before vanishing back through the door, back to his wife Rose in Colorado. It was just Shawn, Jenny, Emily, Katy, Hope, Fred, Claire, and Cassie now, joined by Candy and of course Hercules, his beautiful, good boy who he hoped could help soothe even a fraction of his broken heart.

He'd lost two sons today. Though he now knew that Colin was never supposed to exist, hadn't existed in their original reality, it still hurt. And Ben...he didn't think he'd ever feel whole again. But he'd be strong, for Jenny, for Emily, for Katy, and for Hope. He had to be. They deserved all of him, and nothing less would do.

**Five Days Later**

Katy sat with Jenny and Claire on the couch, playing with Hope. Shawn's granddaughter seemed like her old self again: a funny, smart as a whip 4-year-old little girl. She'd reported that Future-Hope no longer communicated with her, which was probably for the best.

Emily and Cassie sat in the corner, holding hands and talking softly. One of Ben's last acts had been to make Cassie fully human, it seemed. The girl seemed thrilled with her new mortality, and Shawn believed she really did love Emily. He would be keeping an eye on her, however.

David Dowd and Gavin Young would be here in an hour or so, along with Abby, Shawn's parents, and a few other people. He didn't think Azazel was coming, though, which was probably for the best. Though Ben seemed to have forgiven him at the end, the rest of them just weren't there yet.

They knew Azazel had been just another pawn in Elohim's grand plan, but that didn't change the fact that he'd stolen five years of Ben's life. Forgiveness would be difficult for Shawn, especially now that Ben was gone.

Fred was in the kitchen with Candy, getting trays of food ready for Ben's memorial. Shawn felt too numb to eat, but he was sure he would eat something, just to keep going. He was about to join them and offer his help, when Hercules barked, startling him.

The dog turned to stare at an empty corner of the house, barking again. It made the hairs on Shawn's arms stand on end. He looked around the room and noticed both Claire and Hope staring at the same spot.

The air in that part of the room began to shimmer, and his heart caught in his throat. What was happening? A burst of light pulsed through the shimmer, then seemed to stabilize as a circular doorway of sorts appeared in the hazy yellow glow. Beyond, inexplicably, he thought he saw stalks of corn.

A hand burst through the doorway, and Hercules barked, running toward the shimmering light.

"Hercules, no," called Shawn, but it was too late.

The hand met Hercules' head, ruffling his fur. Hercules licked the hand. An arm appeared, along with a leg, and then Ben was stepping through the doorway, Ben, somehow alive, crouching down beside Hercules, hugging him, the dog licking his face.

Ben still had one arm in the shimmering void. He pulled, and a short, chubby boy carrying an orange and white cat followed him through the doorway, and then the doorway was gone, vanished as if it had never been.

He opened his right hand and let five impossible objects fall to the floor: the stick, the geode, the jaguar's tooth, the emerald, and the Buffalo head nickel that had started this whole thing so very long ago. They vanished the moment Ben dropped them, and Shawn could feel power once again coursing through four of the identical items he held in his pocket.

Ignoring the talismans, Shawn stared at his son and the teenager he'd brought with him, slowly walking towards them, as if in a dream.

"Ben!" screamed Katy, launching herself from the couch and into her husband's arms. "Oh my God, Ben, you're alive. You're alive!"

"Ben?" asked Emily, standing up now, staring at him. "Is that really you?"

"It's really me, and I'm really alive," he said, hugging Katy tight, "and I've brought company."

"Tanner?" asked Jenny, staring at the boy.

"Yay, Daddy brought Tanner!" Hope yelled, running up to hug Ben.

And then Emily was there, crying tears of joy, hugging her big brother and her niece.

Tanner? Could it really be Tanner, after all these years? Shawn looked at the boy, a teenager. He closed his eyes, shook his head, and opened his eyes again. Ben and Tanner were still there, and that cat Tanner was holding…Samson? He would recognize that orange and white tabby anywhere. It was Samson!

Jenny ran to them, hugging Ben and Tanner. Samson jumped from Tanner's arms, landing beside Hercules. The two animals circled each other, sniffed, and then the cat licked Hercules' nose and the dog nuzzled Samson's head.

"Hey, now," said Tanner, a voice Shawn would recognize anywhere, even after all these years, "enough of that mushy stuff already."

Jenny laughed, then hugged him even harder, and laughed again as he returned the embrace. Shawn felt hot tears streaming down his cheeks. A stultifying weight seemed to lift from his shoulders, a weight he hadn't even realized was there, and then he ran to them, hugging his son and his best friend, his wife, his daughter, his daughter-in-law, and his granddaughter, crying happy tears, laughing, full of joy and happiness.

# Chapter 88

Ben and Katy sat with Claire, Emily, and Cassie, in the dining room. Lunch—tiny sandwiches, hors d'oeuvres, and iced tea—had never tasted so good. Fred and Candy had gone home, but not before Ben told Fred that Margaret sent her love. He seemed rattled by that, a little, but happy. Ben had worried that Candy might somehow be jealous, but she seemed happy as well.

Why had it taken him five days to get home? Grandpa Paul had said time worked differently in the afterlife. That was as good an explanation as any. In the end, though, it didn't matter. He was home, free to live out the rest of his life with the woman he loved and the beautiful little girl he'd helped bring into this crazy, wonderful world.

His parents had immediately canceled his memorial, and then taken Tanner to see his mother. They brought Hope along, because the little girl absolutely loved her great uncle Tanner and didn't seem to want to let him out of her sight. Ben was a little sad at missing that reunion, but he needed to ask Claire something.

"You knew, didn't you?"

"That Paul was with you?" she asked, a smile tugging at the corners of her mouth. "I did. I didn't tell you because it wasn't my secret to tell. I figured he'd let you know when the time was right."

"He did," he said, squeezing Katy's hand. "He sure did."

Hercules and Samson wandered into the room. The dog and cat had been almost inseparable since they'd first met two hours ago, and already seemed to be the best of friends. Samson jumped into Ben's lap, while Hercules licked his hand. He could get used to this.

"So your hand is real now?" asked Emily. "Not just a flesh-colored android hand, or whatever it was?"

"As real as the rest of me," Ben said. "When I was able to remake myself, Tanner, and Samson using the energy housed in the fused nickel, I figured why not go for the upgrade?"

"Speaking of changes," asked Katy, looking at Cassie, "does it feel weird knowing that you're going to grow old and eventually die, just like the rest of us?"

"It does, a little, but it also feels…right," the former angel said. "I know we've still got some work to do, but I'm hoping if I play my cards right, I just might get to grow old with your beautiful sister-in-law."

"I think maybe that can be arranged," said Emily, "but I have to ask you one thing…where did you get your body?"

"From a little girl just a little older than Hope is now," she said, "who died from a fever in the early 13th century. I never liked possessing people, partly because I didn't like having to deal with their memories, I must admit, but also…it just felt wrong.

"Anyway, that was in Ireland, and her name was Áine. She was dying and for whatever reason, her parents prayed to me…well, to the angel Cassiel. I couldn't heal her from the outside, not without her permission, which she couldn't give me because she was unconscious.

"But what I could do was take her body the moment she died and heal her from the inside, so that's what I did. I stayed with them, pretending to be their daughter, until they died in a storm 15 years later.

"Emily, I hope you don't think that was wrong?"

"Wrong?" asked Emily, blinking back tears. "No, it wasn't wrong, it was beautiful. You gave those parents their daughter back, in every way that you could."

Ben had to agree and said as much. Cassie had done bad things in her impossibly long life, to be certain, but she'd also done good. She was, in other words, human. Both figuratively, and now, literally. He was glad he'd made the decision to turn her human. It suited her.

"I tried to bring Colin back," Ben said slowly, "the Colin my parents knew, the Colin you knew, Em…but Michael was telling the truth when he said the part of him that was Colin had burned away. There just wasn't anything left."

The room grew silent, and this time it was Katy who squeezed his hand. "You did what you could. You came back, and you brought Tanner and Samson with you. You gave such a gift to your parents and to Abby…and you, you're my gift, the love of my life come back to me and our wonderful little girl."

Katy pulled him in for a long kiss, and Claire, Em, and Cassie clapped. When they came up for air, he knew he was probably blushing.

"Well, I think that's my cue," said Claire, as she stood up from her chair. "Actually, I really want to get home to Leesie and Jimmy. It's been one hell of a week day."

Everyone laughed, and then Claire was hugging Ben and Katy.

"We literally could not have done this without you," Katy said. "Thank you so much. Hope and I will forever be in your debt."

"I'll second that," said Ben.

He hadn't told anyone about Hope and Jimmy being together in the future, because it wasn't his story to tell. If they were to someday get together in this timeline, that would be great, but the last thing either of these precious children needed was to feel pressured to try to live up to some sort of prophecy.

"Let me call Gavin and see if I can hitch a ride," Claire said, but Emily closed her hand around Claire's phone.

"Actually, let me give it a try. My ability is a lot stronger than I thought it was. Do you have a pic of your house? Inside and out?"

"Absolutely," Claire said, flipping through her phone. "Will this do?"

"That'll do just fine," she said. "Ready?"

"I am ready, but I have an idea. Do you two want to come over for a while and hang out? Give your brother and his beautiful bride a little alone time?"

Emily looked at Cassie, who smiled and nodded. "Sure! Be back later, guys."

She hugged Ben and Katy, then took Claire's hand in her left hand and Cassie's in her right, winked, and vanished.

"Wow," said Ben, "she's never been able to do that before."

"What about your abilities, Ben?" Katy asked. "You said Margaret told you they might change or vanish altogether."

He shrugged, then asked, "Do you have a quarter?"

Katy reached into her purse and pulled out a quarter. "For you? Always."

He laughed, then said, "Heads," as he flipped it into the air, caught it, and slapped it on the back of his other hand.

It was heads. He flipped it again, and it was heads again. 23 more times, it was heads. Well, he could still bend causality, it seemed. He could no longer see the threads, however, and he didn't seem to be able to time travel, either. And that was okay. After all, he'd still kick ass at Monopoly.

"So…what're we gonna do with these?" asked Katy, indicating the 4 talismans Shawn had given them spread out on the dining room table. "Did Margaret give you any clue?"

"Not really. Just to keep them safe. I figure the tooth is safest with you." He slid the charm across the table to her. "The stick and the geode, I guess that's up to Dowd."

"When we thought you were…gone, he said he wanted to return the emerald to Agatha Muir but didn't want any of the others. That they'd served their purpose and were never really his."

"We'll find new guardians for the stick and the geode, then. I don't think any one person should have that much power."

"What about the nickel?"

"That's up to Dad, I think," said Ben, gently moving Samson from his lap as he stood up from the chair. "For now, though, let's take them all up to the spirit room, where they'll be safe."

Katy stood up, smiling. "And maybe spend a little time up there before everyone gets back? Umm, celebrating, I mean."

He returned her smile, took her hand, and said, "Well…we do have a lot to celebrate, don't you think?"

Ben and Katy walked hand in hand up the stairs and into the spirit room.